MW01468865

# DEAD CITY

## Dead World Book One

SEAN PLATT

JOHNNY B. TRUANT

STERLING & STONE

Copyright © 2016 by Sterling & Stone

All rights reserved.

No part of this book may be reproduced in any form or by any electronic or mechanical means, including information storage and retrieval systems, without written permission from the author, except for the use of brief quotations in a book review.

The authors greatly appreciate you taking the time to read our work. Please consider leaving a review wherever you bought the book, or telling your friends about it, to help us spread the word.

Thank you for supporting our work.

*To YOU, the reader.*
*Thank you for taking a chance on us.*
*Thank you for your support.*
*Thank you for the emails.*
*Thank you for the reviews.*
*Thank you for reading and joining us on this road.*

# DEAD CITY

# Chapter One

## HELL ON EARTH

THE HELICOPTER RIDE WAS BUMPY enough to make Alice spill her coffee, but not her lunch. The way the pilot was acting, this particular ride was no big deal, and if she threw up now, Alice could forget about keeping anyone's respect. She was already a woman heading into what had (of course) become a male-dominated sector of the government, society, and even the specific geographic area. If she tossed her cookies on the chopper floor, no one would take her seriously — not the pilot, not the on-site leadership at Yosemite, not Bobby Baltimore, who'd met her before. Even the undead might laugh and point, such as they were still able.

"This your first time to Hell on Earth?" the pilot asked, projecting his voice above the thumping rotor. The helicopter's side door was open, maybe for breeze, and the idea of plummeting to her death made Alice uneasy. She couldn't help glancing at the 'copter's gaping mouth before turning back to the pilot.

"Officially, I'm supposed to pretend you didn't say that." Then, when the pilot seemed unwilling to fix his politically incorrect *faux pas,* she answered his question. "I've talked to Bobby in Aberdeen Valley. But this is my first time to Yosemite."

"Pfft. Then you're in for a treat. How many ferals they run across out there in Dead City?"

"It happens in the sticks, not in the city. But I've never seen one in person."

"The idea of being here freak you out?"

"I visited some scary places before the borders were closed. It takes a lot to freak me out."

"You've been abroad?" The pilot seemed impressed. Alice, for her part, was amazed that he could fly without looking forward all that often, even though his inattention made her nervous. Yosemite's wide expanse yawned ahead — all granite and trees. She'd asked for a flyover of the park section before entering the contained zone but now felt too ill for proper appreciation. The duty sergeant's response had been acceptable but not conciliatory. Her request had been granted, but Alice had the distinct impression it was only because what the military said went around here, and she'd happened to request the same approach route air traffic always entered the restricted northern section — reporters' preferences notwithstanding.

"When I was younger," she said.

The pilot turned fully in his seat, one arm slung conversationally over the back. He was chewing gum and wearing a flight helmet. He looked maybe twenty years old. Nearly young enough to be her kid, if Alice ever had any.

"You don't say? Tell the truth, Ms. Frank. What was worse? Baghdad in the middle of the conflicts, or this?"

Alice watched the park crawl beneath the 'copter, the first bits of Yosemite vanishing at the windshield's bottom from her vantage in back. Soon, if she scooted toward the open door, she'd be able to see the open park below. If she fell after that, a parachute wasn't likely to save her. The hunters did fine in Yosemite, but an unarmed woman plunked among the nation's oldest ferals wouldn't last long. She might as well be wearing meat-flavored perfume.

"Are you my pilot on the way back?"

The pilot pretended to tip a cap, touching his helmet with a glove. "Yes, ma'am. Fresno to Hell on Earth, at your service."

This time, Alice didn't bother to correct the pilot. Everyone knew the name that even the highest officials used for Northern Yosemite, non-politically correct or not. If she was going to break any big secrets today, that wouldn't be one.

"Then I'll have to tell you after my tour," Alice said, trying on a companionable smile.

The pilot turned back to the windshield.

"Don't get bitten, and it's a date," he said.

# Chapter Two

## CALAIS

THE OFFICER WHO GREETED ALICE was tall and broad, with an action hero's square jaw. His face looked midfifties but seemed to have maintained his body like a trophy. He shook her hand before Alice felt comfortable standing fully upright, so their greeting, from the outside, might have looked like a penitent bowing to meet the pope. Alice had disembarked from many choppers while covering stories abroad, before she was official, back when unofficial, paired with the name Alice Frank, meant less than nothing. But it had been a long time since she'd needed to fly like this, and her silly fears were back with their old stripes: that she'd grown several feet overnight, and if she stood fully near the whirring blades, she'd find herself halved.

"Col. Thomas Calais," he said. "C-A-L-A-I-S. It's French. Officially, I'm 'Colonel Calais'; unofficially, my superiors call me The Frog, and I pretend not to hear them." He smiled. To Alice, his square jaw seemed stuffed with too many teeth.

"Thanks for meeting me."

"You're welcome, but you can thank Mr. Haydock's producers for setting it up. I just work here."

"Mr. Haydock?" Alice asked. They were both still speaking overly loud, the helicopter's rotors winding down behind them. The engine was off, but the sound of metal cutting the rare Sierra Nevada air was like the whoosh of a circling broadsword.

"I'm sorry. I meant Mr. Baltimore. Please tell me I didn't blow his cover."

"Everyone knows Bobby's real name, Colonel. It's no worry."

The big man nodded and continued to smile his excessively toothy smile.

Alice's experiences with the military had been mixed in the past, but Calais seemed friendly enough. Everyone here was at least nominally Department of Clarification and Containment, and the DCC was as adjunct to the CDC as it was within the purview of Panacea, or under its wing, or funded by it, or some other complicated government contrivance. Alice doubted that anyone other than the on-site bosses knew how the agencies were related or how the army fit into its command structure. It didn't matter. The outbreaks hadn't *clarified* government itself. The fact that nobody seemed concerned that the DCC beside the CDC might be confusing was but one obvious example of how much America still had its head up its own ass, plague containment aside. And hence the reason the country only talked about Panacea. It was easier that way.

"For the record, if my name was Rupert Haydock, I'd change it too." The colonel nodded toward a low-slung, utilitarian-looking building across a tarmac from the helipad. "Right this way, Ms. Frank."

# Chapter Three

## BLOWBACK

"WHAT'S YOUR BRA SIZE?"

ALICE looked at the kid dressed in green fatigues, barely old enough to drive.

"Excuse me?"

"Apologies, ma'am. I thought you'd been briefed by the colonel. All visitors to the park's contained section are required to wear a long-sleeved viscose shirt and gloves, but we all wear specialty fit body armor, front and back, as well. They're specialty fit, ma'am. Because you'll be wearing it for so long."

Alice shook her head.

"Specialty fit. You know." He gestured across his chest.

"Someone finally started putting boob indents in body armor."

"Um. Yes, ma'am. Our female colleagues say they're much more comfortable for long-term wear."

"Fine. I'm usually a 42C. Unless you use Victoria's Secret sizing."

"Ma'am?"

"Never mind."

Alice looked around the supply room. It was nothing but gear. She'd watched Bobby Baltimore's several shows many times and met him on a handful of occasions. He'd dominated YouTube since before landing his first network deals, and she'd seen a lot of those, too. She'd never once seen Bobby wear a helmet. There were helmets in the room now — some with visors and some without — but nobody on TV ever wore them. Maybe they never came for the head. Or maybe they made it harder to aim and fire.

"And for your viscose shirt, ma'am?"

"How old are you, Private?"

"Eighteen, ma'am."

"Let me tell you something about women. The first is that you should never ask a girl her size. The second is that you should never, under any circumstances, call a woman ma'am."

"I'm sorry."

"Call me Alice."

"If you wish, ma' … of course, Alice."

"I guess I'll take a medium, if they're small, medium, and large."

"Of course." Now the kid seemed flustered. He began to search, and Alice decided conversation was warranted, to de-embarrass him over the ma'am, size, and tits remarks.

"Why are they called viscose shirts?" she asked as he rummaged through shirts. "Are the shirts particularly slow-running, like molasses?"

"Not *viscous*, ma'am. 'Viscose.' It's a semi-synthetic blend sometimes known as rayon."

"Fashionable."

"It's what attack dog training shirts are made of."

Humor drained from Alice like a plug had been pulled. "Oh."

He handed her a long-sleeved gray shirt and a pair of thick gloves. "You want a helmet?"

"Do I need one?"

"It's optional. You're not likely to encounter a horde our spotters don't see coming, but it's possible you'll get blowback."

"'Blowback'?"

"Blood or tissue. From a close-quarters kill."

"Oh. No." Alice forced a laugh, even though the idea was equal parts revolting and terrifying. She'd covered Sherman Pope and Hemisphere almost exclusively for years now and knew the realities, but being this close to the disease's rotting face made her heart beat harder than she cared to admit. "I guess I'll turn my head if guts start flying. And hey, if I get infected, I can always go on Necrophage, right?"

She said it as a joke, but the kid was nodding, probably ready to tell her about their on-site clinic. *Ma'am.*

"This will do," she said, stopping him before he could speak.

"Did you bring boots, ma'am?"

"They're in my bag. Do I need *leg viscose*?"

"Denim should be sufficient," he said, gesturing toward Alice's jeans. "Once the inhabitants reach the rage phase and start to rot, it doesn't take long before their teeth become unstable in their gums. The state of living death allows them to experience tooth decay in a way a normal corpse can't, until it's fully arrested. But even subjects who've managed to lose all their teeth — and those are few and far between — often bite rocks and other objects to force bone back through the gums. Still, you'd be hard pressed to find one that could bite through jeans quickly enough that your escorts wouldn't be able to intervene."

Alice supposed that was supposed to be comforting. It was the opposite.

"What about weapons?"

"Only licensed hunters are allowed weapons inside the park. Would you like to apply?"

Alice shook her head.

"Just as well. We don't supply anything, so you'd need to have brought your own guns and blades." He nodded. "Right this way. You can change in that room there, ma'am."

# Chapter Four

## HUMAN CONTAINMENT

CALAIS STOOD AT THE FRONT of a small room, gesturing at a projection on the wall. He'd dimmed the lights as if for an old-fashioned slide show even though the display was electronic, but Calais was older than Alice. He might remember slides. He might even miss their blunt honesty, before the razzmatazz of digital had swallowed everything.

"Yosemite Containment Reserve spans approximately a quarter million acres at the north end of Yosemite National Park," the colonel was saying. "The reserve is about one-third the size of Rhode Island and composed of everything north of the Tuolumne River and Hetch Hetchy Reservoir. At the east end, its border follows Tioga Road. There are approximately — "

"I'm sorry. Colonel?" Alice said.

"Yes?"

"I mean no offense, but I already know pretty much everything about the reserve. And about Sherman Pope's phases, for that matter."

"My apologies, Ms. Frank, but this is required briefing

for all park visitors." He smiled a little to show he knew how stupid it all was then added, "Panacea regulations."

"Okay. Then let me ask: Why Yosemite?"

"You mean for containment?"

Alice nodded.

"I think it was the simplest resolution to a complex problem that needed an immediate solution, and minimal red tape. The national parks are government land, and converting use was surely a lot easier than co-opting anything privately owned. We needed a place for those past their inflection points and hence selected against to graze before turning in the interest of humane containment."

"Humane containment," Alice repeated. "You mean before they're allowed to be hunted."

The colonel could have been defensive, but Alice was getting the distinct feeling that she and he were copacetic, on the same wavelength despite his uniform and her reputation as a pot stirrer. He answered with the most straightforward possible answer.

"Hunters are only allowed to take down ferals — those who have already entered the rage phase. But if those who are hopelessly and inevitably infected with Sherman Pope are simply allowed to develop-out at home with their families … " He shrugged.

"I understand the necessity," Alice said, to let him partly off the hook. She was a blogger and reporter first but wasn't unrealistic. There were many, even today, who were diagnosed as incurable. The current system was questionable, but probably the least of evils — certainly a better option than letting fatally infected patients wait to turn in the presence of friends and neighbors. Even the hunting might feel like necessary population control (they were already dead and clearly dangerous; might as well end it quickly) if not for the world's Bobby Baltimores.

Alice liked Bobby. She was maybe even a bit attracted to Bobby. But there was no question that making entertainment out of shooting things that were once people's friends and family was morally wonky.

"There are some, in all quarters of the DCC, Panacea, and even the army, who see the Yosemite Reserve as the best we can do. It's a beautiful spot, and a quarter million acres is plenty of room to move around. They get to live out their last cogent days in nature, and despite what you may have heard, the vast majority of coherent necrotics survive without ever getting attacked by ferals."

"I know better," Alice interjected. In truth, infected *never* attacked infected. It was the ultimate double-jeopardy scenario — the single benefit of having the disease.

Calais nodded. "They seem to know who's on their way to join the club and leave 'em alone. I agree it's all very ugly. But the impact, all things considered, is minimal. The park's chief attractions, from El Capitan to Half Dome and all the major trailheads, are still accessible outside the reserve itself. Honestly, given the relative proximity to Bakersfield, it's ideal."

"What do you think about the Bakersfield solution?"

"Regrettable. But if you're asking if I agree with the people who say infected should go there instead of Yosemite because it's already lost, then no, I don't agree. The city is quarantined and will eventually die off. Adding new residents will only delay a time when we can go in, clear the streets, and take the city back as we were able to in San Diego, LA, and San Francisco."

Something occurred to Alice — the kind of aggressive reporter question she should ask to put her interviewee off balance, but she hesitated because she liked Calais. He turned back toward the screen, and Alice found herself asking anyway.

"Do you have anyone working here who's Sherman Pope positive?"

"I'm sorry to be stubborn," the colonel said, looking at a time display in the corner of a park map projection on the wall, "but the clock is ticking, and we'll get you to your appointment faster if I can just press on and get you through this briefing ASAP."

# Chapter Five

## MPS

CALAIS HANDED ALICE OFF TO a sequential chain of three different people in uniforms — all men, as Alice had figured, even in the modern army — before she ended up in the custody of two MPs (one blessedly a woman, though she was the most stone-faced and least friendly of the five). The MPs asked Alice for her reserve guest permit and, when she said she didn't have one, sent her back two people up the chain to an annoyed-looking man with thinning hair who seemed to have thought he was done with her. The man acted like the mistake was her fault, asked Alice to sign her name on a tablet after pretending to read something far too long and legalese to actually be read, then stamped something onto her hand.

This all seemed to be a terrible inconvenience. At first, Alice thought she'd received a hand stamp like kids got for reentry to a fair, but it turned out to be an implanted GPS chip. "You're hotter than the rest of them, so we'd find you regardless," the annoyed-looking man said.

Alice figured he was hitting on her until she saw him enter something into a computer and realized "hotter" referred to body temperature and "we" referred, at least in part, to satellite tracking. This finished, he waved a small device, like a cell phone, over her hand, and its screen flashed green. Alice, unimpressed with the stamp-as-permit, asked sarcastically why he didn't just give her a bright plastic wristband like they do at water parks. The man didn't realize it was a joke. He said, "We used to, but it just gave them something more to grab onto."

Once her pass was apparently in place and her duty was duly logged, the man sent Alice back to the MPs. They must have been waiting specifically for her because they seemed annoyed by the delay as well.

Alice looked from the female MP to the man. The woman was larger, stronger looking, and generally more impressive. Both wore two weapons, one on each hip. On the right for both was some sort of handgun. On the other side, where she was used to seeing other utility-belt peripherals on civilian cops (handcuffs, pepper spray, maybe something to summon the Batmobile or hold screwdrivers and pliers), was an apparatus that resembled a length of pipe. If pipes had triggers.

Before Alice could ask (she was the reporter here, after all), the female MP, who had the surname *Hayes* stitched on her breast, gestured through a door and nudged Alice to follow the other MP, seemingly named Burrows. In the room beyond, they found a large depot space filled with vehicles. Most were ordinary army Jeeps, but a few were specially reinforced carriers Alice had never seen despite her extensive coverage of disease and cure.

"We'll be in this Jeep here, Ms. Frank," Hayes said, opening the rear door. "Watch your head."

Alice looked up. She was watching her head so she didn't hit the roll bar, not the door frame. But there was barely a half door, and almost no top.

"The vehicles are open?"

"Safari practice, ma'am. We'll be traveling mostly empty land and sat recon shows it mostly free of deadheads. There may be some in the bushes, but that's likely the worst of it."

"And for those in the bushes?"

"Easier to shoot without encumbrances, ma'am. Don't worry."

"I'm not worried. I'm — "

"Did Colonel Calais tell you roller coaster rules?"

"I'm not sure."

"Keep your hands and legs and head inside the vehicle at all times," Burrows recited, "lest you get them bitten off."

Hayes reached across to buckle Alice into the seat like an infant. Her long-sleeved undershirt shifted, and Alice found herself staring at an old wound on the woman's neck. There were suture lines around the wound as if the thing had been stitched, but the whole area had the look of something deflated, like rotted fruit. The skin was still gray and soft looking despite the wound clearly being years old.

"I apologize if I'm being overly personal," Alice asked, "but do you mind if I ask you a question?"

The woman saw where Alice was looking, shifted her shirt to re-cover the wound, and straightened to full height before closing the door with Alice inside.

"It's not a problem, ma'am."

# Chapter Six

## BIVOUAC

BY THE TIME THE JEEP pulled up outside what looked like a massive, heavily armed survivalist's tree house with a fence thirty or forty yards circling its base — a place she'd seen Bobby call Bivouac — Alice felt an intense moment of relief. She could see Bobby Baltimore's tall, quickly moving form stalking the area, pointing at a camera crew and shouting orders. She'd only met Bobby a few times, but right now he seemed like her port in the storm. She'd been up since 4:30, caught a one-stop flight — Aberdeen-Atlanta-San Francisco — before taking a military shuttle plane to Fresno Air Force Base for a helicopter ride so she could get ping-ponged all over the Yosemite incoming center, fitted, tested, chipped, and briefed. It was barely afternoon Pacific time. She hadn't reached her purpose, yet the trip had her wiped and ready for bed already.

Adrenaline — both from nerves and the kind that stemmed from excitement — had been bolstering her like a boost of strong caffeine, but now she was running low. She'd seen a few accommodating faces but none that weren't in a rush to get her on to the next thing. Ironically, this fortified station in the middle of the country's prime undead reserve couldn't help but feel to Alice like an oasis, a place to finally rest her weary feet.

The gate dragged open then closed. Only once it was seated did a second, inner gate roll back on wheels. The MPs handed Alice off like a package being delivered, nodded their good luck, and left. The incoming building complex where Alice first arrived by helicopter had been on the reserve's edge behind an enormous fence-and-guards infrastructure. This outpost was surrounded by hostile territory. The MPs looked brave but clearly didn't like being out here any more than Alice's guts told her to be.

The trip's final leg lasted only about fifty feet. The woman who'd accepted her from the MPs (Sydney or Cindy; Alice hadn't heard which) seemed to be one of Bobby's assistants or possibly show producers and practically dragged her over to Bobby — who, blessedly, seemed just as delighted to see Alice as Alice was to stop moving for ten seconds.

"Alice Frank! Imagine my shock in seeing you here!" Bobby extended a hand and gave her the smile that charmed a nation. His blue eyes actually sparkled. It was impossible to not be a little in lust with the man if you were compatibly inclined, which Alice was.

She held out her hand. Bobby shook it.

"Nice trip?"

"Horrible."

"Really? Which part?"

"The part where some asshole booked me an interview in the middle of zombie central." Then she smiled because they'd already had this discussion on the phone. Nobody booked for Alice but Alice. She hadn't had help when she'd been a nobody blogger and didn't have any now that she'd become the go-to source on Sherman Pope or the company that had rescued the world from its menace. She'd told Bobby that it was hard to consider yourself well known or wealthy when your job was essentially gumshoe reporting, even though Alice, these days, was technically both.

"We don't like that word around here. You know that, Ms. Frank." Bobby made a *shame-shame* gesture, wagging a finger.

"Interview?"

Bobby smiled. There was a rusty chair nearby on the decaying grass, so he slouched into it and, again, flashed his famous smile. "Oh, no. I only hire people who are total whores, so that's a word we like plenty."

Bobby gestured to a second chair. Alice took it just as something, somewhere out in the trees past the fence, started to scream. Alice ignored it. This situation called for airplane turbulence rules: if the stewardesses (Bobby and his crew) didn't react as if something was unusual or wrong, she'd better pretend it didn't scare her shitless even if it did.

"Not yet, though," Alice said. "I'm honestly not in the right state of mind for an interview." Meaning: She needed rest. Just a few minutes of meaningless chat to put the odd world around her into some sort of order. Sleep would be best, but even a beer would do.

A large vehicle pulled around from the back of the massive, multi-platform, high-rise observation fort behind them. Unlike the Jeep, this one was covered, armored, and serious business.

"Not yet," Bobby agreed, standing. "First, we hunt. Then we talk."

# Chapter Seven

## HULKA

THE RESERVE-SCOUTING VEHICLE WAS a cross between a troop carrier and a party RV. They loaded through the back and sat in racks with harnesses. Alice kept irrationally expecting the back to open at any moment to shouts of, *DISEMBARK! DISEMBARK!* while some military cliché (Alice imagined Sergeant Hulka from *Stripes*, an old comedy her grandfather once showed her on his antique DVD player) waved his arms for them to fall out and kick some ass. But instead of loading with armed troops, Bobby Baltimore's carrier filled with a few hunters who'd booked passage … but mostly mild-looking camera operators, sound men, production assistants, and a woman in a severe gray suit that might be an executive on the network's worst assignment. Instead of Sergeant Hulka shouting to disembark, it was Bobby who, once they were clear of the fence, motioned for anyone who wanted to climb a ladder and ride. Bobby was alone in his desire, but he grabbed Alice by the sleeve and forced her to go topside as well.

The day was warm. They were seated like tourists atop

a bus with the interior hatch closed (maybe locked; that made her nervous in a new and horrible way). Bobby gave Alice a tip of his head and another winning smile. They weren't moving terribly fast. It was slow enough, she thought, that anyone who wanted to jump onto the thing and start climbing after the hors d'oeuvres up top could do so. But the engine was loud — surely diesel and manually steered because it needed the torque and computers still weren't smart enough to navigate through reanimated bodies wanting to eat the passengers. Bobby shouted to be heard over the roaring engine and howling wind.

"Did Calais give you the incoming speech about the park, about the people who are sent here, blah blah?"

"Yes. It was very 101."

"That's government for you," Bobby said.

Alice reached into her pocket. If she were a pro, she'd travel with a team, as Bobby did to make his shows, but at her core she was still a hack working solo behind a computer. Besides, humility made for superior journalistic integrity. These days, you didn't need professional sound and video to make it as an investigator. Gonzo journalism almost demanded shaky work and sub-par quality. No need for a team when a camera app would do.

"Are we on the record?" he said, still projecting his voice.

"Probably should have been on the record from the beginning. It's okay. I've got it here." She tapped her head. "Do you mind?" Her finger hovered over the big red record graphic on her screen, waiting for permission.

"It's why you're here."

Alice started recording. She had a small prehensile tripod in her trip bag, so she scanned the landscape then attached the camera to the railing, focused on Bobby.

"Did you ask why the reserve is in Yosemite?"

"I did. You know me so well." And he seemed to. Bobby got along with everyone, a friend to all. It's why his shows were so successful. They'd only met a handful of times, but deep down, Alice had to admit he seemed like an old best friend. It was dangerous to trust, but trust was definitely something that Bobby Baltimore routinely inspired. Just as Alice, for most of the nation, inspired trust.

"Part of it's the official answer. But part of it's climate. There's a fair amount of sun and warmth here, but not always. Some people argued for Bakersfield since it had to be walled off anyway. Why not just toss people in there if they're too far gone? But the problem is that SoCal weather's too perfect. There's a lot of outrage from leftists about what people like me do — not as a quasi-celebrity, but as a hunter — but the truth is we're a drop in the bucket. There are still thousands of newly infected brought here every month, all selected against and deemed incurable. Hunters can't kill that many. But the cold does it fine."

"Cold kills them?"

"Not always. But did you ever freeze a steak?"

Alice nodded. "Cooks up fine after you thaw it."

"Sure. If you wrap it up right. But once these things rage, they don't know how to wrap themselves up anymore for the winter. And then guess what happens?"

The vehicle came to a sudden stop. They were in an area like all the others they'd passed, but this time the back gate lowered and the hunters in their company began to casually unload, as if preparing for a Sunday picnic.

Bobby must not have realized they were going to stop. He looked surprised then rapped on the hatch. It was opened from below by a bland-faced PA.

"Wait," Alice said. "What happens to the rage-stage

deadheads when winter comes and they're not 'wrapped' well?"

Bobby was halfway down the ladder. Someone was pushing a giant weapon into his hands. One that Alice, who'd watched a lot of Bobby's hunting shows like everyone else, recognized as "the BFG" — short for "Big Fucking Gun."

"They get freezer burn," Bobby said then extended a hand to Alice. "Come on down. This is where things get fun."

# Chapter Eight

## BIG FUCKING GUN

SEEING BOBBY HUNT IN PERSON was little like seeing it on TV. The BFG, while large and multi-barreled, was smaller than it looked onscreen. Bobby's calm (which Alice had always thought must be put on considering the tense situations he was always in) now appeared genuine, even as they strode into the brush with all its granite outcroppings and excellent hiding spots. There was nothing nervous about him. Alice, on the other hand, was plenty tense. She knew this song and dance in theory — considering all the reporting she'd done on Hemisphere BioTech, Archibald Burgess, and the sticky ethical issues that came with overprotective government agencies and a blended, perhaps aggressively mainstreamed society — but being in the hot zone was so much more nerve-racking than sitting behind a computer.

"There," Bobby said, pointing. "You see?"

Alice did. There was one man shambling along what seemed to be an old hiking trail, climbing over boulders, intermittently stumbling, moving with an unsteady gait.

Alice had a neighbor who moved just like him, but Kelly Pulombo didn't share this man's vacant, bloodthirsty stare.

Alice looked at Bobby. She knew his shows were best-of reels by definition (Bobby said it took forty hours of hunting to get enough good footage for twenty-two minutes' worth of show), but she still hadn't been prepared for how much missed nuance was in front of her now. The devil might be in the details, but apparently it wasn't in the aired show, the outtakes, or the bonus footage.

"Why is nobody taking aim?" She looked at the other hunters — those who were part of Bobby's team and those who'd booked paid charter on his bus. None were raising weapons to sight on the deadhead across the rock scree. There were hunters scattered across the reserve, but those who chose to ride with Bobby Baltimore were supposed to be the richest — and, supposedly, the best at bagging game.

"Because he's not raging yet."

"How can you tell?"

"Years of hunting."

"But if you got closer, maybe he'd—"

"He wouldn't, and he's not. Trust me. That one's still grazing. I'll bet if we went over there, we could even have a simple conversation."

That gave Alice the chills. It had often occurred to her that Panacea clarifiers had the worst jobs in the world, choosing who was curable and who was bound for Yosemite. Or rather, they had the worst jobs in the world *if they were psychologically healthy* … which, now that Alice considered it, wasn't a condition that clarifiers were likely to maintain if they stayed on the job long. And if they were sadistic bastards, then clarifying was a dream job. *Who lives? Who dies? I get to decide!* Because if they got one wrong, who would know?

Alice's neighbor Kelly seemed safe, but with her shambling gait, forgetfulness, and penchant for the rarest beef, she had to have been in the ballpark of her inflection point when initially clarified. But even the newly infected would eventually turn if left untreated, and then ultimately vanish in the Yosemite wilds.

"How long does it take for the greenest of them to turn?" Alice asked.

Bobby looked at her with amusement. Alice returned the look, feeling jealousy at his easy calm. The smug bastard wasn't even breathing heavy. He certainly wasn't watching every tree and boulder as if a group of deadheads was about to spring out and rush forward. But Alice couldn't help it.

"I thought you were an expert."

"I'm just asking for an on-the-ground account," Alice replied, her tone more defensive than she'd intended. "I've heard rumors that the disease is evolving, with shortened incubation times. Plus, the chatter I'm getting from every Tom, Dick, and Harry who visits my blog. Some are legit and plenty are wackos, ranging from conscientious objectors to tinfoil theorists, but most are saying that clarifiers are erring on the side of selecting-against *way* too often for new infections. I figured that since you spend *so much* time in the wild, you might have some insight into aspects of SP-terminal behavior that we, who *aren't* in the trenches, couldn't possibly have enough perspective to —"

*"Look out!"*

Bobby shot a hand toward Alice mid-rant, the heel of his palm striking her chest hard enough to knock her backward. His weapon came up in one fluid motion, like a reflex. Alice heard a guttural roar, like an animal's, and suddenly saw three half-decayed things coming toward them too fast, seemingly having sprung from nowhere like macabre jack-in-the-boxes. There was a loud, booming report, flat and hollow like a cannon fired into an enormous pillow.

The sound echoed five times in rapid succession as flashes and activity strobed from the right. A great glut of something exploded from where Alice had been standing, and by the time she'd drawn another two breaths, she found herself looking down at her shirt, now covered in semi-congealed blood and clots of gore.

She looked up at Bobby, who was entirely covered in red. He lowered his weapon, as did the two hunters to his right who'd unloaded into the sneak attackers. All three guns were smoking at the ends, but the deadheads were now invisible: carcasses on the ground ahead, maybe, or burst like water balloons.

"Three weeks," Bobby said.

Alice was still on her back, her heart pounding out of her chest, panting like a dog.

*"What?"*

Her eyes were everywhere at once, unable to focus. How many tens or hundreds of thousands of deadheads had Calais said were wandering the park? And of those tens or hundreds of thousands, how many were in the rockfall ahead of them now, waiting to tear Alice in half?

Bobby pulled a handkerchief from his pocket and casually wiped his face. "You asked me a question. The answer is that it takes three weeks for those dropped here, closest to their inflection points, to rage."

# Chapter Nine

## PURGATORY VALLEY

CALAIS AND THE OTHERS (NOT to mention Bobby Baltimore's producers, before she'd left home) had promised that although the act of hunting ferals in Yosemite was a high-risk experience by nature, Alice would be perfectly safe as long as she stuck with the crew. During the pop-up horror show that had just occurred, the camera operators had never flinched even when Alice realized she may have been screaming. They'd merely hung a few paces back, waiting. Apparently, spring-ups like that happened all the time — and, in fact, were highly coveted action sequences that viewers loved. While Alice had been on her back, mentally making her will, much of the crew had been silently cheering.

The trick was to stay back from the frontline hunters. Yosemite had a lot of terrific hiding spots. It was even a selling point for the family and friends of those who needed to be briefed: during the grazing period, their loved ones, who'd still have some of their right minds, would have plenty of places to stay low and out of sight. Nothing would get those people before their time, and hunters were only allowed to shoot what came at them. And when they turned and lost most of their interest in hiding? Well … at that point, they weren't really people anymore, no matter what they looked like.

So Alice hung with the unarmed civilians. From back here, things were tolerable, though only barely. Maybe the crew had grown used to being in the hot zone, but to Alice it was as if the air itself was soaked in adrenaline. Deadheads might not try to hide, but there were enough obstacles that they did it accidentally all the time. As the group moved around, hunters in a wide outer perimeter and unarmed citizens in the center, surprises kept happening. Most were macabre discoveries: forgotten corpses from previous hunters who hadn't cleaned their messes, deadheads who'd been devoured by animals, detached limbs and occasionally heads that refused to stop moving. But a few were targets, and the cameras grabbed more for their precious broadcast minutes.

Mostly, though, the hunt was tense but uneventful. Despite Alice's early start, the time change meant she'd barely reached Yosemite by lunchtime, and Bobby's group seemed to have saved what promised to be the more interesting hours for Alice to witness, record, and report. On the surface, she tried to be a pro: taking photos, taking video that could later be supplemented by his crew's video, scribbling notes, asking questions when the mood didn't seem to call for quiet. But deep down, Alice never unclenched. Every moment was life or death — or, depending on how you saw Yosemite's residents, perhaps *somewhat dead or more dead*.

When they were high up with land sprawling below, Bobby identified vast herds of ferals roaming like wolf packs below them. They occasionally stopped, but never appeared to rest. There were three reasons for their breaks:

They got bored by a zombie's definition of ennui or forgot where they were going, they found something to tear apart, or they simply got stuck. That's what had happened with the three who'd attacked earlier. They were in a small dip in the land with slippery sides to the rear, and had only found their way out when the approaching humans had called their attention to the dip's other side, where egress was easy.

"The trick," Bobby told Alice as they walked in the open, "is to outsmart them."

"Okay." That sounded somewhere between a platitude and a ridiculously obvious truism.

"It's not hard. They're only feral once they have virtually no brain left. You know that kids game, where you stick out your thumb and pretend you've grabbed the kid's nose?"

Alice nodded.

"That would work on a deadhead. Except with one difference."

"What's that?"

"They don't care if it's their own nose; they'd want to eat it anyway. Come on. I want to show you something."

They crossed a rise. Once upon a time, Alice supposed much of what they were traversing must have been spectacular hiking ground. Now it was a fenced-in reserve for mad dogs needing to go madder. There was debate — particularly within higher-functioning levels of the SP-positive (or "necrotic") community — whether euthanasia would be more humane than the Yosemite solution. For necrotics, it wasn't an entirely hyperbolic discussion; before Necrophage, they'd have been shipped to Yosemite as well. But the problem with euthanasia always came down to the same sticky issue: Clarifiers (or perhaps doctors) would need to look still-coherent human beings in the eye and tell them it was time to die. They'd need to inform friends and family that Cousin Joe, who everyone had figured was curable and could still play backgammon, needed to be put down like a dog. There would be footage, if things went that way, of SP-terminal patients who disagreed with their clarification and had to be dragged, screaming, to their executions.

As places to go slowly insane before dying went, Yosemite wasn't bad. And to think: after you died, you got to keep on going … until you rotted in the sun, freezer-burned in the cold, or a hunter ended you for good.

"Jesus," Alice said when they reached the lip of a rise.

Below, in a shallow valley, was a collection of rudimentary lean-tos cobbled from fallen limbs and covered with pine branches. Some of the structures were elaborate, as if they'd taken months to construct and perfect. Milling between the makeshift shelters were twenty or thirty people who looked like they had palsy. All were slow and shambling but otherwise mobile, passing one another with acknowledgements and greetings. Even from high up, Alice could see intelligence on their faces through her binoculars.

"We call this Purgatory Valley," Bobby said. "There's a large, flat, clear space over there where they drop off new arrivals, and a kind of delta in the land funnels them in this direction. For some reason, there aren't many ferals around here, and they leave the new arrivals alone anyway, though you'd never know it from the way newbies spend all their time looking around, trying to build barriers to defend against nothing."

Alice scanned the group with the binoculars, feeling sad.

"It's like a little village," she said. "The *houses* are so … elaborate?"

Bobby nodded. "The shelters have been here almost from the beginning. Each new wave takes them over and makes them a little bit better. This is where they hide at first, a lot of them, hoping for something to save them."

"Three weeks," Alice said mostly to herself, remembering Bobby's earlier words.

"They'll stay one week at most," Bobby said. "After that, the highest logic seems to leave, and they stop thinking of society and start thinking only of a more primitive form of self-preservation."

"What's that?"

"Going somewhere else. Then they turn. And then they die."

Alice watched the small group of ramshackle structures. One of them seemed to be significantly taller than the others, as if it were the village's center.

"Is that Town Hall there in the middle?"

"That's Golem's house," Bobby said with something like wonder in his voice. He sat up straighter and, as if cued by Alice's question, scanned the horizon. Behind him, the crew started to mumble as if anticipating what was coming and not liking it even a little.

"We don't have time today, Bobby," said the severe-looking woman in the gray suit. She still looked ready to attend a board meeting, and here was Alice, covered in crusting blood and guts.

"What's Golem?" Alice asked as Bobby sighed, disappointed.

The woman answered, her voice thick with eye-rolling indulgence. "Golem is Bobby's white whale."

# Chapter Ten

## THE MAN WHO SAVED THE WORLD

MORE SHOOTING. MORE KILLS.

ONE of the non-team hunters tried sneaking up on one of the deadheads he'd ended to cut something off as a trophy, but Bobby yelled at him. Maybe it was for Alice's benefit as a reporting journalist, but she didn't think so. Bobby was a curious fellow, famous for killing undead things that were once US citizens, but strangely respectful. The official line on Yosemite hunting was that it was about population control, like deer hunting, but most of the people who contacted Alice through her blog argued that it was sadistic, macho bullshit: killing made legal so psychopaths could finally come out and play. But she didn't think that was true of Bobby, even as sensational and famous as Sherman Pope had made him. He played the game with respect. And for that, Alice found her already entrenched regard for Bobby deepening.

By the time they piled back into the troop carrier recreational vehicle, the sun was setting. Bobby reclaimed his position on the roof for the ride back to the outpost, and Alice joined him. He seemed almost wistful, his deep-blue eyes watching the passing scenery like a sailor staring out at the sea.

She waited for him to speak first, not wanting to break the mood. In the between time, her mind moved to the vehicle below, and the landscape around them. Colonel Calais and the PFC who'd equipped her had said there were all sorts of control systems and safeguards observing the reserve: cameras everywhere linked by a rudimentary, experimental AI hub to follow and predict movements, tags like the one in her hand meant to keep watch on the movement of inmates both dead and alive, satellites in the sky watching for rogues here like the satellite network kept an eye on the nation's cities and farmland.

But despite all of that — despite assurances that even if Alice somehow became separated from Bobby's crew, there were armed rangers always at the ready who'd storm in to save her — Alice couldn't help thinking of the vehicle, its rubber tires, its gas tank with a finite capacity, its engine that was as susceptible to breakdown as her own temperamental Prius X. They were perhaps a half hour from twilight, an hour from full dark. And no matter what safeguards existed, this wasn't a place Alice wanted to be when light fled the sky.

"So," said Bobby. "Did you get what you needed?"

Alice blinked, her thoughts slow to return from the horrors of a monster-filled darkness.

"For this part, yes. But we still have the interview."

"How will it be different from the other interviews we've done?" Bobby wasn't annoyed. His charming smile was back, his expression bright in the waning light. Despite being covered in guts, he remained camera friendly. He had two days' stubble on his face and wavy brown hair that was too long for Alice's taste but still worked well on the handsome Bobby Baltimore.

"Now I've been hunting with you."

"And how was it?"

"Gruesome."

"So then," said Bobby. "What kinds of questions do you have for our interview?"

A parade of inquiries marched through her mind. She was as eager to ask as he was to know:

*Do you ever wonder if people tune in and watch you blow away their family members? If so, does it bother you?*

*Have you ever interacted with a deadhead who hadn't yet raged, who might still seem harmless, like a slow human?*

*How interested is Hemisphere in what they do here? Is it a testing ground, or something else?*

*Who is Golem, and what does he mean to you?*

And perhaps most niggling of all: *Does it strike you as conflicted that some of the staff here at Yosemite Reserve, where deadheads are hunted, are themselves Sherman Pope positive?*

"I can't tell you that," Alice said. "It will give you time to prepare. I need a genuine reaction, when I ask my questions on the record."

"Shock reporting? Cornering the interview subject? I thought you were better than that, Ms. Frank," he said with a winning smile to blanch the sting. Another lighthearted jibe, as expected from a guy like Bobby, who could get away with anything.

"Nothing so sinister. But if you answer me now and I'm not recording, the little details will all be lost, and you may not give them again later, when they matter."

"Fine. Spoilsport." He looked into the distance, where moaning noises seemed to come from the rocks themselves. Alice had heard that: In areas with large feral populations (and these days, there were really only two left: Yosemite and Bakersfield), undead groans were as much a part of the aural landscape as chirping crickets or hooting owls.

"Then tell me this: Will Archibald Burgess like the report you'll give about this little trip, or will he hate it?"

*The man who saved the world? The hero who came to the rescue when all seemed lost?* That was the official line on Burgess, but Alice had a few rather unpopular opinions to the contrary. There was no question Hemisphere was all too aware of her thoughts, and Alice Frank's fly in their ointment.

"Archibald Burgess," Alice said, finally feeling less uneasy and more herself as the well-lit tree house outpost loomed ahead. "Yes, Bobby. Let's talk about *him.*"

# Chapter Eleven

## DEAD CITY

"I'M JUST SAYING," TED DOYLE said from across the table, "I'd still do her."

Ian laughed. He wasn't supposed to think that was funny, but hell if it wasn't. The official Hemisphere stance on SP-positive individuals — casually termed "necrotics" but more unfortunately known as "twitchers" — was to act like nobody knew who had the disease and who didn't. More realistically, the polite stance was to treat affliction like any other handicap or condition — hopefully with respect and understanding, albeit with some resistance. But in practice, most people were like Ted … and, Ian thought, like himself if he'd laughed. Nobody afflicted wanted the disease, and they surely weren't to blame, but that didn't change the fact that only four years ago, anyone infected for long enough would eventually try to eat you.

Gennifer gave Ian a glance. He was the executive vice president; he was senior to everyone at the table to the tune of a quadrupled salary; he, if anyone here, should be reinforcing proper company behavior. But Gennifer had always been this group's den mother, and that made her the human embodiment of Burgess's evolutionary theory: When something provided artificial assistance, natural mechanisms relaxed and stopped trying so hard. Gennifer was like antibiotics for the unruly crew. The more she tried to control Ted, the less he stopped trying to control himself — and the less Ian found himself needing to intervene.

"Knock it off, Ted," Ian said.

The table suffered a lull. Kate, as usual, seemed thoughtfully uncomfortable. Gary wore his usual expression of polite concern — he didn't approve but would roll with the punches. Ian sat amused by it all, and Gennifer kept staring, urging Ian to follow up. Maybe he should chastise Ted for being a bigot. Issue a formal reprimand.

Instead, Ian laughed again, unable to contain himself after his oddly stressful morning.

*"Ted!"* Gennifer barked. Then, when Ted finally quieted: "Holy shit, Ian. You're an awful example."

"You could ride the spasms, is all I'm saying," Ted added.

Ian wanted to snicker again, imagining Sarah the temp succumbing to Ted's wiles, unable to control her reflexes. In reality, the scene would be uglier than Ted was joking it would be. Sarah wasn't just limping and jerking; she was also sloughing. It wasn't uncommon to find blood all over the coffee station after she'd visited. You'd point it out, and Sarah would realize she'd lost most of the skin from a finger again.

"She's right, Ted. Knock it off."

Ian tried to straighten his face. It wasn't hard now that Gennifer had tossed cold water on the irreverence. But once Ian's mood had dampened, his mind turned to the other thing and began to wander. To the oddly disquieting happenings on his computer. To guilt over nothing at all.

To his morning spent reacting to someone's meddling, his gut twisting into a knot.

"Fine," Ted pouted, breaking Ian's spell. "I was just trying to be *UN*prejudiced, despite what you bigots seem to be implying." He gathered his tray and stood then dropped his garbage in the black trashcan after almost depositing it in the biohazard barrel.

The others stood to follow. But lunch *couldn't* be over; Ian had done nothing more than eat and make small talk. Somehow, this group of scientists was supposed to miraculously shed light on the mystery that had been poking Ian all morning. The mystery that Ian somehow felt he needed to hide, even though he'd done nothing wrong.

Ian stood to follow. When the group reached the cafeteria's edge, Ian grabbed Gennifer's shoulder before she could wave her card over the scanner.

"Gennifer. You got a minute?"

"Sure." She looked at the others then apparently decided Ted, Gary, and Kate could be trusted to go on without her. For five minutes, at least.

"I'll catch up with you," she told the group. Then to Ian: "What's up?"

"This might sound kind of strange, coming from me," Ian began.

"Damn. Don't tell me you already had dibs on Sarah, and now I have to intervene."

"I'm being serious."

Gennifer practically snapped to attention. She could joke, but adherence to protocol was closer to her style.

"I'm sorry. You've seemed distracted all through lunch. I actually meant to ask about it, but … well … *Ted* happened."

Ian inhaled, then slowly exhaled, trying to decide where to start. He hadn't been kidding; the questions he wanted to ask, given their stations, weren't typical. But he had to start somewhere, so he decided on the issue's far side — not delving into the meat of the matter, but into the way it had surfaced.

"Have you assigned me any tasks in the system lately?"

"That's not that strange a question. And no, I haven't. You asked me not to assign you tasks. I think your exact words were, 'I'm the boss, so stop fucking micromanaging me, Gennifer.'"

Ian wanted to laugh as she'd no doubt intended, but he couldn't. The need to get this out and be done with it had him rushing on.

"Who else might give me tasks?"

"Just look at the assignee, Ian. That'll tell you who gave them to you."

She was looking at him with a quizzical expression. His heart was beating too hard, and his palms were sweating. This wasn't normal behavior when discussing to-do's, and her eyebrows were already rising.

But the truth was, he'd already looked at the assignee, of course. And according to the company software, the person who'd assigned all those odd, sticking-his-nose-where-it-doesn't-belong tasks to Ian was Ian himself.

As if he was being framed for something. Something he'd had nothing to do with.

*It's just a glitch,* he told himself.

But he'd repeated that refrain over and over in his office before coming down to lunch, and it hadn't helped. It sure hadn't *felt* like a glitch. The strange to-do's had come at him like unrelenting pillbox fire, each task burdened with accompanying attachments.

The material he was being sent, so far as Ian could tell, was all public data — nothing wrong with having or reading any of it. Except that *everything* was wrong with it.

They were the kinds of questions a troublemaker like Alice Frank might ask because she had an agenda against the company … which, of course, Alice Frank always had. If anyone saw the list Ian had apparently given himself for the day, they'd have had plenty of questions, about loyalty and suitability for his current job.

*Why so curious all of a sudden, Ian? What are you trying to prove that has no basis in reality except for insinuations made by muckraking journalists, Ian?*

"I'll do that. I'll just check the assignee." He turned.

"Wait." This time, Gennifer grabbed Ian's shoulder. "That's not weird enough."

"What?"

"That's not really what you wanted to ask me. What is it, Ian? You look like you saw a ghost."

"I was just curious."

"About what?"

"Virology." He had to spit the word out to get it past his lips.

Gennifer laughed. Then she said, "Seriously?"

"Never mind."

"Wait. Is this for the designer formulation tweaks Burgess wants? For Nice and Pretty?"

"Yeah," Ian said. In reality, he had no idea what made any of the designer versions of Necrophage (Nice, Pretty, or any others) different from the plain old base Phage that anyone could get for free. That was something for scientists, not executives. But if it opened the conversational door with Gennifer in a way that didn't make him look guilty, all the better.

"What *about* virology?"

But that was exactly the problem. Ian had no idea. All of those to-do's had been vague, and he didn't so much as know what to ask.

*Research virology.*

*Research cell receptors.*

*Research vascular decay as a mechanism for crossing the blood/brain barrier.*

None of which Ian understood. All of which Ian knew practically nothing about. He understood business, not biology. None of those things or the others that kept coming up were any of his concern … and yet, taken as a whole, they sure looked like Ian had big doubts about the company — the kind of doubts a mole or anonymous source for certain troublemakers might have, for instance.

"Never mind, Gennifer. Seriously. It's nothing."

"You're sure?"

Ian almost laughed. Before, she'd been trying to pry information out of him. Now, having heard Ian ask (rather nervously) about a word he could barely pronounce, she seemed perfectly willing to let it go. That, more than anything, proved that his concerns had been judged and found unworthy.

"I'm sure."

"You seem overworked."

"I'm always overworked."

Gennifer bit her lip, put her hand on Ian's arm, and watched him for a long second. Then she said, "All right. Well, tell Bridget hello for me, okay? And we'll see her at the Family Picnic, right?"

"Sure thing."

"Gary's bringing his wife. I wouldn't bring your daughter, though."

Ian wanted to roll his eyes. It was like she thought he was retarded. The Hemisphere Family Picnic was the biggest PR event of the year, and he'd been to two of them in the past. He knew the drill just fine. Why would anyone bring kids? It was a picnic, yes, but it was a photo op for the necrotic cause more than anything else.

"I won't," he said instead.

Gennifer smiled, turned, and headed through the door. Ian followed. And as his shoes echoed down the corridor, he grew increasingly certain that no matter what he'd just learned or failed to learn, something was wrong — or, perhaps more accurately, that anyone who glanced at Ian's computer would think *Ian Keys believed* something was wrong.

With the Sherman Pope virus, now kept in check save the occasional outbreak in the sticks.

With Hemisphere, the company that rescued the nation from a plague when things had seemed hopeless.

And, maybe, with the drug that saved the world.

# Chapter Twelve

## TO BE READ

IAN TOOK THE LONG WAY to reach his office in Alpha Building. It required him to take the sprawling hallway past the accounting department on the first floor then take the elevator up on the far side. Usually, he rode the first elevator, just past the security doors, but that route required him to walk through the cubicle farm. For some reason, he didn't want to do that today. It wasn't elitism, about not wanting to mingle with the rank and file. It was something deeper, tinged with nerves, unease, and perhaps even guilt.

Why had all those new to-do's shot to the top of Ian's list, assigned by a ghost? And he hadn't even told Gennifer the rest — about the to-read information that had risen to the top of his list. Why would the EVP care about virology and epidemiology? It had to be a simple mistake on par with someone clicking the wrong box — *Oh, sorry, Mr. Keys. I was supposed to assign those tasks to Paul in R&D* — and that was likely all there was to it. But Ian couldn't shake the feeling that he was sticking his nose where it didn't belong even if he wasn't sticking it anywhere.

Ian arrived in his spacious office and found that his queue had been stocked with several Alice Frank articles bookmarked in his to be read list.

Ian felt his pulse rise. Frank's articles weren't any more damning or restricted than the research the system had suggested to Ian earlier, but seeing someone read her stuff, listen to her occasional podcast episodes, receive her email newsletters, or especially watch her upcoming Bobby Baltimore interview inside Hemisphere's walls was a bit like seeing someone reading communist propaganda in the 1950s. It wasn't against the rules, but it felt like sleeping with the enemy. Ian, who was nowhere near the PR department or media relations, still knew the legends of how often Alice Frank had tried to land an interview with Archibald Burgess and how stalwartly he kept refusing. Some people thought Archibald didn't know what to expect from the often-rogue, deeply skeptical reporter. But others said he refused because he knew *exactly* what to expect.

Working quickly, his eyes darting side to side even though his screen wouldn't be visible from the door and across the large office, Ian removed the bookmarks and deleted the tasks directing him to them. If it all turned out to be a big mistake (if, say, the boss had decided to talk to Frank after all and wanted Ian to bone up), it would be simple enough to find the articles again. But safe seemed so much better than sorry.

This done, he sat behind his desk and stared at the screen as if it had done something to offend him. So far, the only things that had struck Ian as amiss (research that someone at executive veep level would never care about and bookmarks from Wrench-In-the-Works Number One) hadn't breached even the most rinky-dink level of security. Nobody had broken into Ian's office; nobody had remotely accessed his computer; nobody had rummaged through his stuff. A few tasks had been misassigned, that was all.

Still, Ian couldn't flee his creeping unease.

That prickling, back-of-the-neck sensation.

Ian hadn't assigned himself these particular bits of research, but they painted a questionable picture for anyone who came across them and thought he had.

*Why is Ian Keys reading up on the history of Sherman Pope? What's this about viral genetic shift? And why all these articles from Alice Frank, who seems to disbelieve everything Hemisphere and Mr. Burgess says, even though the rest of the country accepts it with nary a question? What exactly is Ian doubting? Does he think something's amiss, and is he planning to … gasp! … blow a whistle?*

*Certainly not. Not the loyal Ian Keys.*

*After all, Ian knows what a great company this is, and how noble its aims. He's deeply loyal. The company has been generous to Ian, and he's not the kind of person who'd betray his own kind.*

*Ian would never distrust years of research — aspects of the disease that are so accepted now that no one ever bothers to investigate. He'd never think there was something about the disease agent's structure that needed more attention — say, the specific sequence of nucleotides in … in …*

Ian stood up. This was stupid.

It was simply entered wrong. No one was trying to direct Ian's attention or send him a message. Half the company was SP-positive; it was Hemisphere's way of literally taking its own medicine. When Necrophage was still new, Hemisphere had been the first company to hire infected people in whom the disease's progress had been safely arrested. Hiring necrotics of all functional levels remained excellent PR juju, so Hemisphere had committed to the practice. With so many necrotics on staff, a simple clerical error like this wasn't a shock.

*Because let's face it, it's not like they all do great work.*

Most necrotics didn't improve by the day. Most stayed exactly the same. And given that someone entering data and assigning non-sensitive tasks and information at Hemisphere might have an incubation period of a week or more, mistakes were bound to happen. Necrotic workers had modified keyboards to account for their spastic movements, but there was nothing to be done about their lack of focus or easily distracted dispositions.

Or for their drooling. Or groaning.

Ian looked at the screen. Stupid necrotic bastard, assigning the EVP information meant for a research assistant or clerical worker.

There was a knock at Ian's door. The visitor didn't wait before entering because the blinds over the glass panels flanking the door were open anyway, but the turning knob made Ian jump up fast enough to bang his thighs against the desk's heavy polished-wood edge.

Raymond Smyth entered his office — one of the men between Ian and Archibald Burgess, and the one man who would surely fire him if he had reason to doubt his loyalty.

## Chapter Thirteen

REALITIES OF THE DISEASE

"IAN?"

IAN SWALLOWED. HE WASN'T doing anything wrong. Why the hell did it feel so much like he was naked and playing with fire? Some damned twitcher had fumbled their task assignments. Ian wasn't sitting here in his big, high-powered office sowing doubts about the company. He wasn't reading Alice Frank's articles, thinking that she might have a few valid points that an insider's investigations might easily shed some light on, one way or the other.

"Hey, Raymond."

Raymond hovered in the threshold, assessing. Ian didn't think he was sweating, but his entire physiology was wrong. It probably looked like Raymond had walked in and caught him masturbating.

"How was lunch?" Raymond didn't care, and was clearly assessing. He was a large man in his fifties with reddish-blond hair and a permanent haze of barely-there stubble. He had a curious, almost sideways way of speaking that seemed to use too much palate. It made him seem almost innocent, maybe naive, but in the years Ian had worked under Raymond, he'd learned that underestimating the man was always a mistake.

Right now, he was giving Ian a look that was almost playful. As if he knew something.

Like, maybe, that Ian had been snooping.

Which Ian definitely hadn't. Someone had made a rather ordinary, uninteresting mistake. And that error had nothing to do with him.

"It was fine."

"You feeling all right, Ian? I just saw Gennifer. She said I should check up on you."

Ian tried on a smile. *"Gennifer."* He laughed. "She's a good girl, but she sure doesn't know when enough is enough. She thinks I'm sick or something."

"But you're not."

"No."

"Because I have to say, you don't look well."

"I —"

"Never mind." The strange standoff ended as Raymond took a few steps into Ian's office, not bothering to close the door behind him. "I think you know better than Gennifer how you feel. It's not why I came. I needed to talk to you anyway."

Raymond sat with one butt cheek on the corner of Ian's desk, dangerously close to a view of the non-incriminating no-big-deal stuff filling Ian's screen.

Ian picked up some pens, pretending to fuss over his otherwise meticulous desk. Of course the screen got an adjustment as part of the refurb. It seemed so much more *organized* after it was angled farther away from Raymond's potentially wandering eyes.

"What about?" Ian asked.

"Did you see Alice Frank's interview with Bobby Baltimore?"

"No. Of course not."

Raymond's blond brow furrowed. Even his eyebrows were so light they seemed to barely be there.

"Why 'of course'?"

*Right.* That would be protesting too much. "I just didn't have a chance."

"She raised some interesting points. Overall, an excellent report on the Yosemite Reserve that had nothing specifically to do with us, but I *swear* her tone was still vaguely anti-Hemisphere."

"What else is new?"

"Well, exactly. And there will always be detractors. It's fine. I suppose it's good that there are people out there asking the questions others are thinking, even if they won't voice them because they think it's un-American to do so. Don't get me started. I have a whole political rant to go with this."

"So … " There was a point here, of course, and he'd prefer that Raymond find it. His boss never came to chew the fat. Unless maybe Gennifer just told him that Ian was asking strange questions that required immediate attention.

"I kind of like the dings in our stellar reputation. It makes us look real. Nobody believes anything that's universally adored. And that's especially true for the foreign markets, who are only hearing about us over the satellites and through the Internet. Which might be a good thing, really. When we used to travel, everyone hated Americans. Now they feel sorry for us. I guess I can accept pity. It's better for the bottom line."

"Nobody's buying Phage because they pity America, Raymond."

"No, no, of course not. But there will always be the doomsday people, and Archibald thinks a large portion of at least Western Europe might be looking to institute widespread preparedness campaigns. Just in case, you know."

He stopped then glanced at Ian's screen, perhaps wondering why it was cocked clear the hell around to point into the corner. Ian watched Raymond's eyes on his monitor. Then he looked up again, his face wearing the same expression of could-be-friendly, could-be-up-to-something as always.

"You look up anything about Alice Frank lately?" Raymond nodded toward Ian's computer.

"No," Ian said too quickly. Then, more steadily: "Why would I?"

"I try to ignore her too. But that's Archie's point: We're all turning away and pretending she doesn't exist. But it's not a good idea. She made herself relevant a long time ago, and today we're the only ones who act dumb and say 'Who?' when someone mentions her. The media's big boys seem to have permanent love hangovers for us — cure a plague once and everyone remembers — but you and I both know that independent media and the Internet's pulse are far more influential and have been for decades. Ms. Frank is a big voice there, and this interview was huge. *Huge*, Ian, and still spreading. Everyone loves Bobby, and everyone respects Alice. Now they're on the same screen discussing everyone's favorite topic. Ignoring her is no longer an option."

"So … what … is Archibald going to accept one of her interview requests?"

"No. But everyone on the executive team needs to watch the Baltimore video. In the right light, it's actually pretty flattering. One of the MPs who took her to Baltimore once she arrived at Yosemite was necrotic. A three-day incubation period, I think. High-functioning, minor necrosis and atrophy, a few verbal tics. But trusted to handle a weapon. And this woman, one of her jobs is clearing fences for incoming."

"What's that?"

"Sometimes at Yosemite, when they need to bring a vehicle through the gates, there are deadheads in the way that might escape if the gates are opened. They have to clear the fences when that happens." Raymond made a pistol with his thumb and forefinger and mimed a few shots.

"Oh."

"Frank talked to the MP. It's a great piece of reporting. This woman is infected, and her job is to kill people — well, what used to be people — who are also infected. Without Necrophage, the same MP would have been one of them. Comes off as an endorsement on one hand and a huge vote of trust on the other. The MP trusts us, and Panacea — hence the US government as a whole — trusts the MP."

"Sounds like a good thing," Ian said.

"That part is. She's fair, I'll give her that. But then there are other parts. Like footage of grazers who've formed a little village. The population there recycles, with the old members going increasingly feral and wandering off while incoming take the huts over as if they'll bunker down and stay forever. She's showing this footage as B-roll while talking to Baltimore about whether he ever feels bad about hunting."

"That's on Baltimore. And on Yosemite. And, hell, on the fucking disease. How is that Hemisphere's problem?"

"It's hard to put a finger on, Ian. But when you watch it, you'll see. Somehow, Hemisphere is still the bad guy to Alice Frank."

Ian wanted to protest as if it were Raymond, not the reporter, being unfair. Every hero had haters, but it had always seemed so wrong to Ian in Hemisphere's case. Burgess had been the first to seek a solution (rather than fueling panic) when Sherman Pope had shown its face as a world-threatening epidemic.

Burgess had opened all of Hemisphere's research to the Internet and rallied the world's best minds to crack the case. Even then, it had been Burgess and Hemisphere — not the world's complainers — providing the cure. Some hated Hemisphere just because the company had become the wealthiest in the world. But it had done ethically, in Ian's opinion. The designer versions of Necrophage cost a fortune, but the base formulation was as cheap as generic antibiotics. Those who truly couldn't afford it were provided their supplies free of charge. In Ian's mind, those people should be thankful. A ruthless capitalist who didn't care would let the poor go feral without their cure then ship them to Yosemite so they could … well, so they could be part of Alice Frank's documentary decrying the company that had so generously provided the solution.

Raymond had been staring at Ian's cocked monitor. Without warning, he reached for it and straightened it, as if its lack of square had been bothering him the entire time and he'd finally reached his breaking point. Ian winced as his boss leaned in to glance at the screen, but instead of commenting, Raymond stood as if to leave.

Ian chanced a look at the screen for himself. The bookmarks he'd yet to clear and the odd research had been tidied up — either organized out of sight or cleared from Ian's queue. Maybe the drooling, groaning, half-undead clerk who'd set Ian on edge all day over nothing had finally realized his mistake.

Ian thought he should feel better, but the near-miss had set his heart to a trip hammer.

"Anyway," Raymond said, now nearing the door, "something to think about as you watch the interview. Try to come up with some ways we can twist negative — or at least skeptical — into positive. Anything she raises that needs addressing, we'll want to do it. That'll score us some brownie points. But anything that comes up that we could honestly improve, maybe we should look into upgrading what we're doing. This company tries hard, but nobody's perfect."

Ian nodded after Raymond as he vanished. Once he was gone, Ian sat in his chair and breathed, willing his overreacting body to calm the hell down, because whatever had been wrong was over — or even more poignantly, it had never actually begun.

There was movement on Ian's screen as a new task notification appeared on the desktop.

*Copy this, read it, and then delete.*

# Chapter Fourteen

## DELETED SCENES

ALICE WAS SCRUBBING THROUGH HER Yosemite footage, wondering if it was best to archive and be done with it, or if there was more to mine for immediate use. Alice knew herself well enough to believe it was only the part of her craving disorder that insisted on not dumping the footage onto a drive straightaway, but still — there was so much she hadn't been able to use. So much stuff that had been trimmed for time and attention constraints, snippets of which, even out of formal context, might make for great website content.

As just one of many examples, Alice had all of her ancillary interviews. She'd used a few bits from the MP in the hour-long special, but it was aired on the network and that meant that *hour-long* actually broke down to forty-six minutes to account for commercials, so non-Bobby time (given that it was supposed to be a Frank/Bobby feature) was limited. She could make longer versions for herself and YouTube, of course, but who had the time? It had taken forever to log all she had, plus the editing, and Alice didn't know any editors she trusted enough to do it for her.

But if she could get her head around it, she had many additional voices: Calais, more from the necrotic MP, even the kid who'd given her the bite shirt and body armor. And plenty more with Bobby Baltimore, of course.

There were hours and hours of footage of the next day's hunt, which had unnerved her far less than the first day's, now that the worst of the shock was over.

There were casual moments back at the Bivouac. She'd used a pan from its top platform (a zillion stairs' worth of climbing) as B-roll in the opening sequence, but she had plenty with Bobby and his crew as well as the other hunters along for the ride. *Those* were interesting folks. The vast majority of Yosemite's hunters came in on day passes, riding around in open Jeeps, and shooting anything that moved in their direction. But the hunters who paid to stay at the Bivouac in the reserve's middle were those with money to burn or a psychosis to feed. They seemed to stay an average of four days, but one man had admitted off the record (while drunk) that he'd been around for more than two weeks because he was looking for one deadhead in particular: his son-of-a-bitch father, who'd been bitten, denied it for three weeks as his symptoms worsened, and finally was heard by a neighbor and sent here by clarifiers. Ironically, that man's exodus to Yosemite had saved him. The hunter had tried beating him to death with a shovel before clarifiers had pulled him away so they could do their formal testing.

Bobby was a talker, and their interview — not including all the casual chats over the next two days — had lasted three hours. Alice had full-length tangents that she hadn't been able to include. A proper producer could see about getting those segments pulled as yet more Alice Frank exclusive content. She could sell that stuff, and the ad revenue would pay for another plane ticket, even if she posted it for free. But Alice had plenty of money already, wasn't greedy, was an admitted control freak about her work, and quite honestly didn't give enough of a shit to sit through all the minutiae to assemble the pieces.

But she could watch it all. Seeing her footage — all shot guerrilla style on her slightly-better-than-average cell phone camera for the touch of reality — was simple. She attached the wireless dongle to the phone and pressed play. Now she could kick back, have a glass of wine on the couch, and order a pizza. Wine and pizza didn't always go together. The trick was in not caring, or being tired enough not to bother with anything else.

It was all fodder for articles and blog posts she wanted to write anyway. It all sank in — endless hours of Bobby Baltimore. Hours of reanimated corpses ambling toward her then being raked back as if by invisible hooks while hunters fired. Target practice back at the Bivouac, where the only targets were large cantaloupes placed mostly at eye level.

She'd caught a single bite incident on camera — a segment that Alice had opted to keep from the final cut with some amount of journalistic regret. She wanted to portray reality, and it had been plenty real when the deadhead had come from behind a rock to bite a hunter named Dave between glove and shirt, but it was also an atypical kind of reality. Most people didn't head into a park filled with tens of thousands of dead looking for something to kill again, so the Dave-gets-bitten footage would only have been inflammatory.

Alice queued the latest unused clip, pressed play, and kicked her feet up on her coffee table. Bobby Baltimore's blue eyes and bright smile filled the right side of her screen.

Off to one side, Alice heard herself say, "Tell me about your white whale."

A giant smile from Bobby. The kind that seemed to pull the corners of his mouth on fishhooks, exposing his white teeth all the way back. A few crowd-pleasing dimples formed, and his eyes sparkled playfully.

"What do you mean?"

"That's what Cindy called him. The one who built the big shack in Purgatory Valley."

On the couch, Alice crossed one foot over the other atop her coffee table. She'd mostly forgotten about this section of the interview, but it was a good one. She'd very much wanted to include this thread for personal interest (the hunter captivated by his prey), but it didn't exactly lift right out. She'd have lost five minutes or more to setup, exposition, and decent resolution for the arc. And doing so might weaken the emotional impact of the Purgatory Valley segment.

"Ah yes. *Golem.*"

"Is that his name?"

"Not unless his parents were cruel. Believe me, I've tried to find his name, but Yosemite doesn't keep personal records. Only designations."

Alice's voice said, "Isn't that a bit twisted, trying to find the name of a man — a former man — you mean to kill?"

"That's the impression I got when I asked, yes. I got the most horrible look from the clerks. And that's why they don't keep personal records. Biologically speaking, the people who come here are still alive until the native machinery gives up the ghost and the reanimators fully take over, but legally they're declared dead on entry. I even hear that most families hold funerals at that point, likely while the subjects are still breathing."

"That's morbid."

"That's *the disease,*" Bobby countered, still with his winning smile. Alice hated to admit it, but if a less-attractive, less-charming man did the same things that Bobby did, she'd probably judge him far more harshly.

"So why do you call him Golem?"

"It's a word from Jewish mythology: a being animated from inanimate matter. They're characterized as big, tall, strong … like monsters."

"Are you Jewish?"

"Just a goy with a decent education."

"So he's big, your white whale. Appropriately."

Bobby nodded. "Oh yes. I'd guess he's six-eight or more. Not truly broad, but broad enough. I'm sure he bloated when he died like all the rest, but by the time I started, he was already dead. I've only known him as thin. A lean kind of muscular. He's kept his hair, like a lot of them do as the disease props them up. He's blond. Scandinavian, maybe. With severe, hawklike features. Some necrosis, but not as much as you'd expect. Definitely seems to have reached equilibrium."

"And you still haven't found him? The way you talk, it sounds like he stands out."

"I haven't. I see him here and there, so I know he's still around. But always from a distance. And when I get close, it's like he somehow knows it. Others, I can catch up to. But not him."

"How long have you been chasing this … Golem?"

"Two years."

Watching, Alice remembered her surprise when he'd said that. She felt it anew, a hundred questions again percolating to the surface that she was sorry she hadn't asked.

"You said they don't survive the winters," asked Alice offscreen.

"Some do; some don't. Luck of the draw, maybe. In the absence of stimulus, they might stay in holes and caves. It doesn't get incredibly cold here — lows that barely dip below freezing in the dead of winter. And Golem seems tough."

A pause from Alice on the recording. A bit tentatively, she said, "You seem to have built up quite the picture of this particular deadhead."

"Now you sound like Cindy," said Bobby, laughing.

"Well, haven't you?"

"Are you worried about my sanity? My psychological well-being?"

"I think it's worth asking."

"Maybe it's my way of coping. Tell me, Alice. Who did you lose in the epidemic?"

On the video, Alice said nothing.

"We all had to adjust. Sherman Pope didn't just wipe out — what? A *third* at the time? — of our friends and family. It turned them into something else. They kept existing, and we all, before Necrophage, had to turn against them in some way. My mother got it. Just like anyone left untreated today, it took about six weeks for her to fully turn. I remember how horrible the wait felt, because we all knew what it was — everyone, everywhere knew — but what were we supposed to do? Kill her out of hand and be done with it? Walk away? No. Our only choice was to wait. And at the end, it was just like something out of a movie. We tied her down, and every day we wondered if it would happen, or if we'd have to keep waiting."

Bobby shifted in his chair, leaning forward.

"Tell you a secret, Alice?"

"Would you like this to be off the record?"

Bobby looked directly into Alice's mounted camera. Then, back to Alice: "No. Because maybe this is something people want to hear. Or *need* to hear."

A creeping dread crawled up Alice's spine as she sat on the couch, remembering what was coming. Part of her wanted to kill the video, but her journalist's fascination kept her rooted.

"Starting about two weeks after Mom was bitten — or maybe it was three, so right near the so-called inflection point where a clarifier today would declare her too far gone — I started to want her to be dead just so it'd be over. Those first weeks of knowing what was coming and being unable to stop it were hell, and I couldn't take another three, not when she'd barely be my mother anymore. So I got my father's gun. And every day, I'd load it. I'd stand outside her door with the thing in my hand, bullet in the chamber, safety off. And I'd try to make myself go in and do it. But I couldn't. And so every day, I'd unload and put it away. It wasn't until the very end when my uncle did it to save all of us from needing to."

Alice — both on the video, she remembered, and now on the couch — swallowed.

"Maybe that's why I do this. There needs to be something out there for me to punish; so as long as it's legal, I'll take what I can."

At the time of the live interview, Alice had had no idea what to say. If she hadn't been rolling (not to mention sitting right there asking questions), she would have walked away.

Bobby looked at the camera. There were no bottoms to his suddenly empty eyes.

When the doorbell rang, Alice actually jumped in place. Then she switched the TV off and went to the door.

It was the pizza man, of course, but he had more than a box in his hands.

On top of the pizza was a plain manila envelope, fat with documents and God knew what else.

"Someone left this on your porch," the kid said with a helpful smile.

*Alice Frank* was written on the envelope in thick black marker.

There was no stamp, no return address.

# Chapter Fifteen

## DANNY

IAN WAS HALFWAY ACROSS THE parking lot, clutching the small device in his pocket as if to keep it from jumping out and announcing its traitorous presence, when someone approached from behind.

"Hey."

Ian turned too quickly, sure he'd been caught — again for something he hadn't asked for and wanted nothing to do with. And it's not like he'd done anything wrong … until, that was, he'd copied a folder full of unknown and possibly confidential documents onto a thumb drive and walked out of the building with the contraband in his pocket. The files could be nothing, but they could also be something. And although permissions shouldn't have allowed him to copy the files, the settings on this particular folder had all been made green across the board: *Take and share, friends*.

But the person behind him was only Danny Almond.

"Oh. Hey, Danny."

"You heading out for drinks?"

"No, I've gotta get home."

"Oh, come on, Ian. Everyone's going."

Ian wasn't trying to outrun Danny, but he wasn't slowing down. His body language was the same as someone who barely removes an earbud to stop listening to their music long enough to hear an inquirer. He didn't particularly want to slow down, or have a chat. He definitely didn't want to go out for drinks — something that would be dubious at best and inappropriate fraternizing at worst, given that Ian was a few dozen rungs higher in the company and the outing was sure to be filled with drug reps like Danny. And yet Danny wasn't taking any hints.

"Bridget likes to have dinner right at six," Ian said.

"Really? That's nice. I'd like stability like that."

"Yes." Still walking. "It's great."

"Hey, Ian. How come everyone else burns the midnight oil around here, and you manage to get home for a 6 p.m. dinner?" Then Danny held up his hands to indicate he wasn't questioning Ian's work ethic. The rate at which Ian had risen through Hemisphere's ranks couldn't have happened by accident. Ian knew it was due to the rather clichéd notion of working smarter, not harder, and shockingly, his coworkers seemed to honestly know it, too. "I'm not saying that — "

"I understand what you mean. It's just about setting boundaries." Ian gave Danny a smile, turned his head forward, and kept walking. His hand was still buried in his pocket, clutching the drive. He felt like he was running from a bank robbery, fending off good-natured hellos from cops on the local beat.

"That's great. What do you mean, 'boundaries'?" Danny was taller than Ian by maybe four inches, and all of the difference seemed to be in his legs. Ian felt like he was speed walking, but Danny's cadence was easy. He was wearing a light-blue shirt and a barely matching tie, now flapping in the breeze. His ordinary-looking brown hair was in a mess the girls seemed to find adorable.

"Just ... you can't let work consume you. Do your time, do it well, then set appointments with the people that matter to you, like family. And keep those appointments."

"Yeah, that makes total sense. Ask you a question, Ian? There's this girl I'm kind of seeing, and — "

Ian turned, cutting Danny off mid-sentence. The kid was moving so quickly to keep up that when Ian stopped, Danny stuttered forward two steps and ended up between Ian and his car, now just a dozen feet away.

"Danny, I don't mean to be rude, but — "

This time, Danny cut Ian off. Ian genuinely liked Danny and didn't want to offend him. But now wasn't the time. *Today* wasn't the time, for a hundred reasons.

"Oh. Sure. No, it's fine. I'm blabbing on and keeping you from dinner. Don't let me keep you." Danny gave Ian his winning salesman's smile, pivoted, and gestured toward the car like a game show host.

But now that he'd stopped, Ian felt the need to say more. The strange things that had happened today — the message to meddle he felt increasingly sure he'd received before lunch, Gennifer, Raymond Smyth, the temptation and his nefarious file transfer at day's end — it all had to do with him, not Danny. Danny was a good kid. He was in his midtwenties, ambitious, and good to his clients. Now he had this girl that Ian, in all of his selfish impatience, hadn't bothered to hear more about. He shouldn't go out for drinks with the whole rep team, but maybe he was due to have a beer with Danny. The plague had rearranged the world's priorities (well, those inside America, at least), and in its own boring, small, inconsequential way, good people finding ways to make time for what mattered most was important. Vital, even.

"Did you end up getting that bonus you were gunning for?" Ian forced a pleasant expression.

"What? Oh, that. Yeah, I did. Thanks for asking."

"That's great!"

"It is. Thanks. And thanks for helping me out with it."

Ian shrugged, now wondering if maybe he should go for drinks after all. Was anyone looking for the information he'd taken? Was it honestly something he shouldn't have? Probably not; only Burgess and Smyth had more access than Ian. Someone was probably messing with him, and he'd find out once he had a chance to see what he'd pilfered. Surely, it was nothing — all a big goof. And really, was someone going to grab and frisk him? He could get a beer. He *deserved* a beer.

"No problem."

Danny leaned in, keeping his voice comically low. "Anyone ask about it?"

"No. I told you. First of all, you filled that bonus quota six full months ago, so who'd ask me about you using my card now? And second, it's not a big deal. You've come with me into Alpha Building as a guest before. And it's not like you weren't entirely within your right to … gee … I don't know. Go to the auto-dispensary and requisition *what you're supposed to sell anyway.*"

"Well, thanks in any case. I couldn't have filled that order if I'd needed to wait for supply. I appreciate the help, man."

"No problem. Of course."

Ian waited to see which direction the conversation would turn, both of them smiling like fools, two heads bobbing slowly. Whatever insult Ian may have implied with his rush, it seemed to be healed. One man helps the other; bonuses are achieved; thanks are given. Friends mattered as much as family, Ian kept realizing. Now more than ever.

"Well, anyway," Danny said, his hands on his narrow hips, the salesman's smile still on his face — more genuine on Danny, Ian thought, than on the other reps. "I'll let you get home. Tell the fam hi for me, okay?"

"Sure," Ian said. It was a pointless platitude. Bridget and Ana had no idea who Danny Almond was, but the thought was nice.

Danny gave a final wave and walked back toward the building while Ian climbed into his car, unknown secrets in his pocket, waiting to be popped open.

# Chapter Sixteen

## JORDACHE

MAYBE THIS WAS A BLESSING in disguise, Danny thought.

He and Ian were buddies, and if the day ever came that Ian's code stopped working on the doors and the dispensary, Danny already had his in. There was no urgency now at all. And hey, if Ian was going home, there was no reason for Danny to go out with the other reps, either. Which meant he could do what he wanted instead. What he'd been *aching* to do, really.

Danny fished the phone from his pocket then ducked into an alcove between buildings and sat on a sun-bleached park bench. There was a necrotic worker picking up garbage in one far corner of the alcove, but it was otherwise deserted. Danny doubted the guy would understand his half of the conversation if he overheard. The man had to be right above his inflection point. It was prejudiced to not merely accept the worker's presence (or assume he was too dull to understand conversational nuance), but Danny still kept an eye on him. Supposedly, the clarifiers knew what they were doing when they selected for people like this guy, and Danny was supposed to know better than anyone that Necrophage kept even the most dire cases from degrading.

But still. Danny had been in Oakland when Sherman Pope peaked, and in the thick of it the dead had swarmed into the bay from San Francisco. Boaters were still finding them in the water today — mostly rotted, often just heads and torsos with working jaws, still plenty contagious.

Danny ran his thumb across the phone's surface, still watching the worker prowl the perimeter. He was bleeding on the grass, fluids seeping from wounds that wouldn't heal. In grounds workers, that kind of thing was permissible. Blood dried fast, and the grass got mowed every week anyway.

Danny brought up his contacts. Rolling through them, looking for Jordache, he saw that about a third of the entries had red backgrounds behind them. Somehow, this made him feel better about watching the twitcher in the courtyard more than he'd watch an uninfected worker. *Who* was prejudiced? The *DCC national database*, not Danny Almond. Maybe if Panacea had been in charge in the early 1800s, they'd have put red backgrounds behind the phone-book entries of all black people, just so everyone would understand whom they were choosing to fraternize with.

His conscience assuaged, Danny found Jordache's entry. Before he tapped to call, he took a moment to look at her photo. Her dirty-blonde hair looked immaculate but casually styled, and he could see large earrings beneath her pretty locks. She was wearing lipstick that was deep, deep red, like smoke-stained bricks, and had on a fair amount of eye makeup. The look was sexy as hell, but Danny wondered why he'd never, despite it all, seen her not so made up. It was like she didn't trust her natural look.

Which was absurd, in Danny's opinion. She was beautiful. In time, maybe he'd be able to help her see that.

He tapped Jordache's entry. The screen went red to match her background while the call tried to connect. Danny fought a strange desire to hold the phone up to show the lurching, groaning worker whom he was calling and how unfair the profiling was. Maybe he could hold up a fist in solidarity. *Right on, brother*.

"Hello?"

"Jordache? It's Danny."

"I know who it is, silly." The "I" came out like "Aah."

"What are you doing tonight?"

"Cleaning."

"Now, what kind of a thing is that to do on Friday night?"

Jordache's slightly accented voice took on a hectoring feel. "The kind of thing that needs doing," she said.

Danny could picture her right now, sure that she'd just put a hand on her slim hip. There was nothing Jordache did that Danny didn't think was cute — except the things she did that were downright hot. She sat on the chairs in her lawn cute. She crossed her legs cute. She walked cute, and on the few occasions Danny had been at one end of the trailer and watched her make her way down the middle to the other, the view from behind (all short-shorts and long, tan legs) had teased him with an inappropriate boner. Back then, he'd been an acquaintance, walking the line between friendly man and pusher. Their boundaries hadn't been drawn yet, and there was always the possibility she'd turn him in. Looking back now, that seemed ridiculous. She'd asked about the designer Phages, and he'd told her what they did. The notion that she'd rat on him for offering free samples seemed absurd in retrospect.

"Do you want to do something, maybe?"

"You mean go on a date? Tell me so I can do my face."

Danny fought a nervous swallow. Jordache was always blunt and allowed no subtlety. She'd told him more than once, unasked, "You can't fuck me yet." That had been simultaneously disappointing and scintillating. He'd spent the rest of those nights trying not to look at her tits, or at the spot between her legs that he was apparently denied access to … for now.

Danny considered making a joke about how instead of doing her own face, maybe she could do his. He could get away with saying it; Jordache's sense of humor was crude, and people told Danny he had a boyish, innocent charm. The fact that it felt too honest for a joke stopped him.

"Yeah."

"You don't have to take me out, Danny."

"Maybe I *want* to take you out."

There was the slightest pause on the other end of the line. Danny, who knew that being a high-performing salesman entailed being a decent psychologist, knew precisely what the pause meant. Jordache's last boyfriend had been a fucker, and it was no loss that he'd gone off the deep end before getting shipped to Yosemite. Her boyfriend before that had apparently been a fucker as well. And the one before that? He'd been, seemingly, a fucker. Jordache seemed to have decided she had one and only one thing to offer men. The fact that Danny kept coming around despite never receiving payment seemed to puzzle as much as flatter her.

"Honey," she said, her voice robbed of its earlier edge, "why are you so good to me?"

"Because I like you."

She didn't ask why. The fact that she wondered was implied.

"Can I come over?"

"Danny, I don't want to — "

"To pick you up," Danny interrupted, not wanting to hear again what she didn't want to do with him. Yet.

Another pause. Jordache had a car and was fully licensed to drive. "Pick you up" wasn't the standard between them. It wasn't even accurate to say they were dating. They were more like good friends who each knew what the other was thinking, but resisted for some arbitrary reason.

"You don't have to pick me up."

Danny's eyes flicked around the courtyard. Even the necrotic cleanup guy was gone.

"I have something I need to give you."

Jordache made a pleased little noise. "One of these days, Danny, your guy — "

"Don't say his name."

"He's gonna change things on you and you won't be able to get it anymore."

That last was Danny's fault. He'd been getting PhageX off of Ian's requisition account for six months now, and there was no reason for that to change, but he wanted her to appreciate what he got. So there was always the looming threat of a cut-off supply … but then that was all just made up by Danny, for theatrical effect. There was no drama without peril, and he doubted he'd be as much a hero to Jordache if she knew the simplicity of it all.

As things turned out, he didn't only have access, as Ian, to the designer formulations that he didn't have as Danny; he could also order in greater quantities. As long as he didn't get greedy enough that people wondered why Mr. Keys was requisitioning so much Phage, there was no reason this couldn't continued forever.

"I managed to get more." With an ominous tone, Danny added, "*This time.*"

"So … I *don't* have to go back on base Necrophage?"

Danny was glad she couldn't see him because he was doing a horrible job of keeping a straight face. He was grinning widely enough into the phone to hurt his cheeks.

"Nothing but the best for my girl."

Jordache actually squealed. He wished he'd done this in person because she'd have wrapped him in a hug — probably one of those low-rent but incredibly appealing full-body hugs where she used her legs as well. Maybe, if she'd done that, he'd have fallen over and they'd have been horizontal together. And maybe if she'd been grateful enough to kiss him down on the floor or bed, things could have progressed from there. Based on Jordache's stories, she'd made some very poor spur-of-the-moment decisions in the past — her indecent exposure charge with her old, now-deadhead boyfriend, Weasel, behind the Panera being the juiciest. Was it amoral for Danny to want her to make another poor decision with him? He didn't think so. He wasn't an asshole, so in the end things would be as they should be.

"So," Danny said, smiling wide enough to fit a coat hanger in his mouth, "can I come over tomorrow?"

"Bring your boots," she said, giving Danny one of her odder countryisms, "and you and me'll kick up some dust."

# Chapter Seventeen

## SECRETS

BRIDGET KEYS PULLED HER THYROID pills from the medicine cabinet and shook one out into her palm — triangular and purple, with a *Z* embossed into its hard-shell front. It looked nothing like a thyroid pill, and not for the first time, Bridget wondered if anyone would ever be nosy enough to figure that out. Her old thyroid pills, before she'd finally gone in and had the damned issue perma-fixed, used to be tiny, pale pastel things with a line bisecting the center. These things even *looked* fancier — probably stuffed with fillers and lacquered at the factory to make them appear worthy of the hefty price tag.

Her husband was executive vice president of the largest drug company in the world (arguably the largest *anything* company in the world); he'd never know that what was in her little orange RX bottle in the upstairs medicine cabinet wasn't levothyroxine. He was a businessman, not a doctor. So unless he thought to violate her privacy before consulting the Physician's Desk Reference, he'd never know.

Not that he'd care. If mother needed a little helper to get through her day sometimes, it was nobody's business but Bridget's. Ian married a fun, spontaneous girl. It shouldn't surprise him that after fourteen years of needing to plan every tiny thing, some of her spontaneity had finally returned.

Except that Zen didn't make you spontaneous.

Zen brought the kind of calm that only money could buy.

Bridget swallowed the pill then returned the Zen-in-thyroid-bottle to the cabinet. It bothered her that she was keeping this a secret, and that nobody other than Gabriella knew. The secrecy suggested to Bridget that it was probably something to be ashamed of. But the quiet of being a housewife was its own kind of mania; if she wasn't managing Analise's activities and homework, she was dealing with worries about Ana: whether she had enough friends or the proper sorts of friends, if Bridget was doing right by her as a mother, if Ana was well adjusted and up to grade standards. She'd hired help long ago to keep the place clean and sometimes make their dinners, but the freedom afforded by maid services and those high-end vacuuming robot thingies was anything but … well … *Zen*. The house was too quiet with no one around. Bridget had figured she'd use the time to pursue her old interests, but more often than not she'd filled those hours with worry. And with Gabriella, who definitely wasn't someone Bridget aspired to be.

She sighed then went downstairs. Ana was drawing something on her tablet. Bridget watched her for a while from behind. The girl tapped something, and the drawing came to life, shambling through several other frames of motion Ana must have already stored. It was a nice bit of animation. Something to pass Ana's time in a way that was both recreational and educational. Definitely better than popping pills.

*Stop it,* Bridget told herself. *You don't have a habit.* Gabs *has a habit.* She'd even looked it up. Zen didn't form physical addictions. And psychological addictions? Well, reliance depended on the user.

*You don't need them. They're just nice for quieting worries.*

But then again, that's what all addicts thought.

Ana seemed to unsettle, as if sensing something amiss. She turned and half jumped, finding her mother just a few feet back.

"Mom!"

"Oh, I'm sorry, Honey. I was just watching you work. That's really cool." She pointed at the tablet.

Ana's hand went to her chest. It was flat for now, but in another two or three years, Bridget supposed she'd start to grow boobs. Great. Something else to worry about.

"You scared me."

"I didn't mean to. I guess I'm just quiet like a mouse."

Ana half rolled her eyes at the expression. For now, she was mostly willing to keep humoring her parents, but Bridget had likely given her mother and father several quiet heart attacks in her teens. That was something else that would change soon: her daughter growing distant, thinking her odd if not downright uncool. Her primary companion during summer and afternoons, inevitably lost to better adventures and friends than her boring old mother.

"When's dinner, Mom?"

"When Dad gets home."

"Are you cooking, or is Greg?"

"I am," Bridget said. "It's already in. I made that lemon chicken."

Ana made a face. She was polite, but still a kid. It

wasn't always easy to pretend you liked something you didn't, or that your mother's cooking was a tenth as good as their sometimes private chef.

"Oh," Ana said.

There was a low rumbling from the other end of the house. Ana jumped to her feet and ran off fast enough that she practically shattered her tablet on the ground. She was gone, eagerly yelling for Ian, faster than you could say, "Daddy is more fun than Mommy."

But when Ian entered the room with Ana on his arm, Bridget had pushed down all of her annoying self-doubts. She wasn't a whiner. She also wasn't a pill popper. She was a woman who'd settled perhaps too deeply into a routine, and who needed to find her way again. She had all the freedom in the world, and Aberdeen Valley afforded plenty of options, especially given Ian's salary. She just needed to get out. With Ana in school again these past few days, there was no better time than now.

There was a moment of shame — a sense that she should feel more grateful and alive than she actually was — but then it was gone, and she was back to being plain old Bridget.

Good mother. Adoring wife. Luckiest woman in the world.

Ian didn't merely peck her on the cheek. He set his bag down and wrapped both arms around her at the waist. Hands lingered and interlocked as he leaned in to kiss her. Bridget rubber-stamped the welcome kiss for the first two seconds, but then Ian's right hand moved up under her hair and his other hand pulled her chest into his. Then the kiss became real, and Bridget felt herself responding. All of her fears and doubts from minutes ago felt suddenly foolish. Even after fourteen years of marriage, Ian didn't just love her — he was *attracted* to her, *infatuated* with her, *adoring* of her. Bridget had something inside her marriage that Gabriella went outside her marriage to get: a man who'd never stopped taking her for granted.

With the thought came more guilt. Guilt over where her thoughts sometimes strayed during the endless dull afternoons; guilt over the secrets kept, and the lies Ian had always believed that she could no longer take back.

The kiss ended. Ian pulled away, gave her a tight little smile, and turned to his daughter.

As if he didn't want to talk to her.

Which was absurd. He'd just given her a kiss from the cover of a romance novel. Seeing that fifteen-second display — about which, she now noticed, Ana was making gross faces to her father — anyone would know this was a marriage worthy of envy. Gabriella may like having affairs, but Bridget didn't need one. Maybe the touch of another man put the zip back in Gabriella's bedroom even when she was with Jim, but Bridget's bedroom had plenty already. At their last house, before Hemisphere had become the juggernaut it was today, the adults' bedroom had shared a wall with Analise's. Today, it was clear across the building. They could rattle the headboard all they wanted, and did at least three times a week.

But still, Bridget couldn't shake the feeling that something was strange with Ian. There had been an odd look in his eyes when he'd pulled away, as if the kiss had been a requirement but he couldn't make his words, which were harder, follow suit. Even now he kept looking up at her, asking quiet questions.

*What do you do around here all day, Bridget? Sometimes, I wonder how you fill your time.*

*Why aren't you as cheery or fun as you used to be, Bridget?*

*Have you ever considered taking a little "help"? Nothing habit forming, of course. Just something that forms a dependence you follow more days than not.*

*Have YOU ever considered having an affair, Bridget?*

But no, no, no. None of that. She had the one little thing she kept shamefully under wraps. If she'd considered having an affair, it was only because Gabriella made it sound so delightfully reasonable, like a spa treatment that a good woman should luxuriate in when she deserved it. She'd never act on it, and even the thoughts (which she couldn't control; nobody could control their thoughts and shouldn't be blamed for them) made her feel guilty enough to hide.

Although sometimes she wondered if Ian had the same thoughts.

Surely not, because he'd always adored her so much, right from their earliest days. But weren't sex and love two different things for men, more so than with women? Of course they were. And if he *did* ever think about having an affair with all that time he spent working, it would be nothing personal. They would be thoughts, like hers. Innocent, harmless *thoughts*.

To shake the creeping feeling away, Bridget waited for Ian to finish squatting and talking with Ana then caught his eye, put on a bright smile, and asked how his day was.

"Oh, it was fine."

"Any new Ted stories?"

Instead of answering, Ian gave her a little thin-lipped smile and turned to grab his bag. As if he figured she was being rhetorical.

"I can't live without my Ted stories," Bridget said, trying again, now behind him.

"What?" He turned, and his eyes cleared. "Oh, I'm

sorry, Bridge. Feeling a little scrambled. What did you say?"

But the fun was gone. She was hoping for lighthearted banter, but if she had to drag the fun, lighthearted stories out of her husband, it defeated the point.

"Nothing."

"Did you have a good day around here?"

"Um, sure. Same old thing, really." That almost sounded loaded, so she said, "I planted mums."

"Mums? Really? Aren't you supposed to plant in the spring?"

"I think the rules are different here in North Carolina," she said, feeling dumb. She really had planted mums today. Why not? She'd been meaning to since … well, since the time of year that planting made sense.

"But we got snow last year."

"Well, then maybe they'll die. What am I supposed to say?"

Again, too impulsive. When he turned around, she put the placid smile back on her lips. She didn't seem to need the apology because Ian wasn't paying attention. He'd set his bag on the table and was searching through it, hunting at the bottom.

"I was thinking, do you want to go for ice cream after dinner? Laura's son just got a job at Mr. Frost, and I think Ana likes him."

"He's sixteen," Ian said, not pulling his attention from the bag.

"Yes, well, I had a crush on a student teacher in his midtwenties when I was in middle school."

"I don't know that I want her into someone like that," Ian said.

"She's eleven. I'm not looking to arrange a marriage,

Ian. I just thought ice cream would be fun, and Ana was asking."

Ian didn't answer. He now had the bag pulled wide open and was pulling items out and setting them on the table, seeming somehow frustrated.

"Besides," Bridget said. "What do you mean, 'someone like that'?"

More rummaging. She might have been imagining it, but he looked furtive, maybe nervous.

"Ian."

He looked up, one hand deep in the bag like a kid caught raiding the cookie jar.

"Sorry. What?"

"'Someone like that,'" Bridget repeated.

"Well, he's infected."

"That's a bit bigoted, don't you think? Half my friends are infected."

"I just … who knows what could happen?" He'd resumed rummaging. Now he *definitely* looked nervous, as if he couldn't find something he desperately needed. His eyes flicked to the floor. Like maybe what he was searching for had fallen and been kicked under the table.

"What do you mean, 'What could happen'?"

"I don't … *shit!*" His bag tipped sideways at the mercy of his searching hands and spilled dozens of small items, mostly mechanical pencils. Why did he have so many pencils? It didn't even make sense. "Look, I don't know, okay? There's just too much we don't know."

"Like what?"

Ian squatted and began looking under the table.

"What are you looking for?"

"Nothing. Never mind. I'm sorry. It's been a strange day."

"Strange how?" But now her thoughts had turned to this idea of Ian's reservations. The official Hemisphere position on Sherman Pope — the position of Aberdeen Valley as a whole, as home of the cure — stated that the plague was mostly an unfortunate outbreak that rapid intervention and luck had managed to solve. Fewer and fewer people today were oblivious enough to let new bites go until the inflection point was passed, and reports of ferals in populated areas were increasingly rare — though it still happened plenty in the wild. But Ian expressing prejudice like this was so unlike him. It made Bridget wonder what he wasn't telling her, what might have changed since their last conversation.

He stopped, seeming to realize how this must look and seem. Calm crept over his features — reluctantly but surely. Only his eyes still betrayed something amiss.

"I'm sure it's nothing. Someone shuffled the file tree at work and … well, never mind. It's all stupid. But I don't know; I've been uneasy. Ignore me. Okay? I just need to get out of *work mode* and into *home mode*."

"Okay."

"And yes, ice cream sounds great."

She wanted to ask more about why a teenager with a one-day incubation period might somehow have become an undesirable — especially considering that Laura was a helicopter parent who'd never let the kid slip even an hour from his Necrophage dose. Why there should be any unknowns at all after years under Panacea's integrated system, Bridget couldn't imagine. But Ian didn't keep secrets from her (she had to admit it, even though it made her feel guiltier about her own), so if he had something to tell her, she'd know it in time.

"Sure."

Ian's hand went with sudden inspiration to the side of his thigh. He slapped the fabric above his pocket then his face visibly relaxed. The hand stole into the pocket and grabbed something. His relief clicked another notch forward. He palmed whatever he'd found, slipped it into the bag, then shoved the bag away and turned to Bridget.

"What's for dinner?"

"Lemon chicken." Her eyes flicked to the bag, to the unknown but very important thing.

"Sounds good."

"I *hope* it's good."

"I'm sure it will be."

"I do try."

"And then ice cream afterward." His hands went to Bridget's waist. She could still see something wrong on his face — some concern from the day's strangeness that hadn't been totally assuaged — but his earlier panic was gone.

He still hadn't mentioned whatever was bugging him, or acknowledged the vital missing thing that, until thirty seconds ago, had Ian about to upend the house in search. Did he think she hadn't noticed? Were they really going to pretend that hadn't happened?

"Are you okay?" Again, she looked at the bag. Asking him to explain. To tell her about the thing she wouldn't care about, just so she wouldn't stay curious.

"Yes. Of course. I'm fine." He pulled her closer. "I'm home."

In Ian's other pocket, his phone began to vibrate. She wanted to laugh. It was a private joke between them: he was on Hemisphere's time so much, all work stopped hard at the front door. There were no emails other than those that couldn't wait. No books, no computers on laps in front of the couch. And certainly no phone calls. Whoever that was, they'd have to wait.

He was *home*. Until morning, he was *hers*.

Ian slipped the phone from his pocket and looked at the screen.

Then a new look crossed his face, and he excused himself to take the call.

# Chapter Eighteen

## A KNOCK AT THE DOOR

ALICE TRIED THE CALL AGAIN. As before, Keys hung up. The first time he'd hung up on her, she'd thought it was annoying. The second time it struck her as odd, and this third time, it was flat-out amusing. Alice had been hung up on before, but Ian Keys did it in grand dramatic fashion. It was possible that the Keys family had a landline that rang into the house, but Alice seriously doubted it was more than a service extension. She was calling his mobile. So after the first time he hung up, he should have declined future calls and sent them right to voicemail, where she'd at least be able to explain herself. But instead, Keys was answering each call, letting her get out a few words before killing the connection. It was like a kid tempting fate by peeking repeatedly into the dark closet to make sure the boogeyman was still there.

To Alice, he sounded guilty.

She'd tried to get Archibald Burgess on the phone dozens of times and had been rejected by his army of gatekeepers, but the one time she'd used some underground connections to sniff out a personal line, he'd done as she'd expected: given her a few annoyed words then declined and eventually blocked all calls to follow. Ian Keys didn't sound like Burgess or the other Hemisphere reps she'd contacted. Usually, they were terse and annoyed — something Alice supposed she understood, given her reputation of giving the company a hard time even though everyone else treated it like the nation's darling. But Keys? He sounded jittery. Unseated. As if her call was almost expected in the most unwanted way.

The fourth time she tried his number, Keys didn't answer and did, mercifully, finally let the call go to voicemail. She left a message with her name and credentials (entirely unnecessary) and the skeleton of her query (vague and undefined). Bothered more than she expected, and in the most unsettling way, Alice settled back with what remained of her pizza, not bothering to stop at one slice too many.

There was a knock at the door, followed by another. Finally, there was a sort of banging preceding the sound of a sack of grain being dropped.

Alice opened the door to find her neighbor, Kelly, slumped on the stoop. She was mostly on the ground, reaching for Alice's doorbell. Not because she wanted in, but because it was a little bright light that might be fascinating to Kelly's addled mind.

"Hi, Kelly," Alice said, looking down. She considered extending a hand to help her neighbor up, but she'd spent too long at Yosemite with Bobby to be fully reintegrated into the normal world just yet. Of course Kelly wouldn't attack her, but between Yosemite's hunt, the package she'd just received, and the fact that it was already dark outside, her skin was crawling.

There was a shuffling from across the yard. Alice looked up to see Kelly's sister, Nicole, rushing over, a mostly open sweater flapping as she beckoned impatiently for the slouched form at her door with both arms.

"Kelly!" she barked.

Kelly looked back and moaned.

"I'm sorry, Alice," Nicole said, still waving her arms for the woman on the stoop. "I left the back gate open."

"It's no problem. Really."

"She just likes you, is all. She saw your interview with Bobby Baltimore."

"Bobby," said Kelly.

"Kelly. Get up, Honey." Nicole extended the hand that Alice hadn't. She pulled her sister upright. Kelly stood easily on her own but continued to sway as if in a breeze, looking at Alice with a happy but vacant expression.

"I'm really sorry," Nicole repeated. Then: "Oh, and now there's crap all over your door."

Alice looked down at the mess on her door's front. Part of it was blood, but part of it was just the offal that further-along necrotics shed as the Necrophage in their systems fought to restore the cells that Sherman Pope kept killing off. The result was a bit like full-body pus. Supposedly, a human body refreshed itself every seven years, but for necrotics the process was much faster. They were more like snakes, constantly rotting on the outside while new cells tried to keep pace on the inside.

"Please. The same thing happened with a UPS delivery guy the other day." Nicole seemed exasperated enough that Alice decided to chance something that might be over the line, but they'd had this discussion before. With Kelly distracted by the bush near the bay window, Alice whispered, *"He left the skin of an entire hand under my packages, like a glove."*

Nicole sighed. "Tell me about it. You should see her sheets."

Something pricked at Alice's reporter instincts as she looked from one woman to the other — the uninfected now turning to herd the infected back home. Something from the package. On the surface, there'd been nothing incriminating in the paperwork, but the meta of it all — the organization behind the papers rather than the papers themselves — clearly pointed to someone trying to pop the top on a Hemisphere secret but not quite willing to go all out. Whoever had sent the thing wouldn't serve Alice the answers on a platter. She'd have to work for whatever story might be there.

"Nicole."

Nicole turned, one hand on her sister's shoulder. Kelly was already shambling off, head twitching like a bird's, jaw slack.

"If you don't mind me asking, is Kelly on standard Necrophage?"

Nicole watched as Kelly crossed the lawn. She was halfway there when she staggered and almost fell. She might've broken a bone or snapped a ligament. It had happened before, and having a necrotic as far down the chain as Kelly in a cast wasn't fun. Some doctors wouldn't even fix necrotic bones past a certain decay point. Apparently, it was like trying to reinforce papier-mâché.

She turned back to Alice, presumably confident that Kelly knew her way home.

"The free kind. Yeah."

"Did you consider the other formulations?"

Nicole laughed but stopped when she realized Alice was serious.

"For, like, two seconds."

"Why didn't you go with them?"

"You know why, Alice."

Across the small lawn between the big houses, Kelly

reached the door and opened it. Nicole had outfitted her door with a swing knob when she'd taken Kelly in, so the staggering woman was able to easily open the door. She left minimal mess behind. Then the door closed behind her. Based on what Alice had seen, Kelly looked worse than she was. She could hold rudimentary conversations and more or less take care of herself. She could safely make food in Nicole's modified microwave and entertain herself for hours with the mind-numbing, necrotic-centric programming on the Funtime Channel. She mostly just needed someone to keep an eye on her, but still Alice felt awful for Nicole. Things could have turned out differently. A week earlier, and Kelly might be a less problematic houseguest. A week later, and she'd have gone to Yosemite. Nicole would never admit it, but either option would probably be an improvement.

"You mean because she's … " Alice prompted.

"Mostly. We might be able to afford the one they call Truth or Beauty, but why? Let's be honest. Kelly's *truthful* and beautiful days are behind her."

Alice wanted to prod further, but it seemed rude. "Would you like to come in for a drink?"

Nicole looked back at the house. Then she pulled out her phone, opened her security app, and pressed something that made about half of the lights in her home click on. If Alice understood the app, it also locked the doors, shutting her sister in for the night.

"Sure," she said, re-pocketing the phone. "Thanks."





# Chapter Nineteen

## TRUTH AND BEAUTY

NICOLE FOLLOWED ALICE INTO HER messy living room. The pizza box was front and center on the coffee table, open, the piece she'd been eating when Kelly had knocked looking like the most delicious slice of a pie chart. The envelope she'd received earlier probably looked like it had exploded; the game of 52 pickup she'd played before deciding Ian Keys was her logical starting point had been merciless and untidy. Once Keys had hung up the first and second times, Alice had begun sifting anew. Given that nothing here was confidential, reading between the lines was hard. Alice had compensated by spreading her mess wider, hoping a pattern emerged.

"Sorry about the way the place looks," Alice said.

"You working on a story?"

"Sort of, yes."

"I saw your Bobby Baltimore interview," Nicole said.

That stopped Alice. Of course Kelly had seen it; Kelly had a crush on Bobby Baltimore like half the female population, both infected and uninfected. But pieces like that always made Alice socially nervous. Lower-functioning necrotics like Kelly would miss the subtext, but those tasked with caring for them, like Nicole, probably wouldn't.

Alice decided to play casual. "Oh?"

"It was fair."

"Thanks."

She looked around. "What's the story?"

"The usual. Hemisphere. Sherman Pope."

Nicole was still surveying the apartment. She looked at Alice. "Don't take this the wrong way, but … well, what's left to talk about?"

"I just want to know the truth, the whole truth, and nothing but the truth."

"You don't think someone is telling the truth?"

Alice pursed her lips. The simple answer was no, she didn't think someone was telling the truth. Hemisphere's *discovery* of Sherman Pope's cure had struck her as overly convenient from the start. The scientists she'd spoken to all agreed that the company's solution to regenerative necrosis, as they called it, was perfectly logical once they'd seen it. But on the flip side, who would think of it? Emma Sherman had contracted and begun slowly spreading the rabies-like infection commonly called Rip Daddy three months before it had mutated in Miles Pope and gone bad, and it was only six months after *that* — long enough to lose Bakersfield and large chunks of New York and Eastern Pennsylvania — when Necrophage had come to the rescue. Of course Panacea's predecessor had rushed past the FDA to emergency-approve it in no time, but how had a literal d*eath-stopping drug* been created from nothing in nine months? Everybody knew all about movie zombies, but the move from silver screen to front page had been a big surprise, so it's not like research into stopping them had been anybody's major initiative.

Nobody denied that Necrophage's arrival was a miracle, but few people questioned how that was possible.

"I just want to understand, is all," Alice said.

"You were asking about Kelly's Necrophage. Was it because of this?"

"Sort of." *Entirely* was more accurate, but Alice didn't want to say so. She pulled a bottle of Zinfandel from the rack on the counter. "Wine?"

Nicole smiled thanks and took a seat. She had to move some pamphlets to make room. Each was official Hemisphere material, with the company's tagline on the front: *Upgrading Nature*. Alice had asked Hemisphere's reps about that a few times, seeing as the tagline didn't fit as well now that Necrophage and its helper products constituted the vast majority of the company's business — and, of course, most of its profits. The drug's basic form, like large sectors of Hemisphere's proprietary research both before and after the plague, was free to all who needed it, but the designer versions weren't. And although nobody official would confirm it, Alice knew that even base Necrophage was purchased (not accepted free) by most of the world outside the US. Sherman Pope had been fully contained by the time the borders were closed, but the world seemed eager to prepare, just in case.

The answer to the tagline question was simple, according to company rhetoric. Even though Hemisphere's primary business today was *Halting Plagues*, it stuck with *Upgrading Nature* because that had never stopped being Burgess's vision. Even Necrophage's roots were in the original life-extension mission. That, supposedly, was the incomplete answer to Alice's niggling questions about the drug's oh-so-convenient development.

"Do you know what I've never done an article or blog post on?" Alice asked. "What it's like to care for someone with arrested Sherman Pope."

"You've talked a lot about that," Nicole said, crossing her legs.

"I've talked about the spread, about families who've had people clarified in the wrong direction and sent to a camp or Yosemite. I've done pieces on the Skin District ghettos. And sure, I've interviewed people here and there who've had family and friends turn, or at least get infected. But never in the way I'm thinking now."

"Which way is that?"

Alice took a sip of her wine. "Do you mind?"

Nicole shook her head. "Not at all. What do you want to know?"

"You've gotten used to … how your sister is … right?" The question was rude and uncomfortable, but Alice didn't know how else to ask it. She'd talked to Nicole plenty before, though, and she liked Kelly. Kelly enjoyed playing sports, and while she couldn't play normal games, she loved the adapted ones. And Alice, who liked her research immersive, had learned a few herself and played on the same teams. Nicole would know she meant no offense.

"Of course."

"How long has it been?"

"She was after the big plague. Three years?" She shook her head. "Hell, has it been that long?"

"How did she get infected if it was after containment?"

"Oh, you remember how things were back then. Panacea hadn't contained the worst-hit neighborhoods yet, so there was still infection spreading under the radar. Clarification wasn't fine tuned, so sometimes they'd select for someone, dose them with Necrophage, and they'd turn anyway. We were from rural Montana and came to Raleigh after Mom got bitten. She had to be put down, unfortunately, God rest her soul."

Alice said nothing while Nicole crossed herself.

"But after Mom, we didn't really want to move back. We didn't come here until after it was already a mecca for the infected, but we did decide to stay in Raleigh. We weren't used to how things were in the cities. With the Internet still mostly shot and TV still half-reactionary, we were afraid all the time, with no idea what to do. Panacea wasn't in businesses yet, or in schools, or widely distributed enough to even hang fliers where we were. We went on a mission trip. We were way the hell out in the middle of nowhere, and Kelly was bitten by a rabid dog."

Alice sat up. She hadn't heard this part of the story.

"A rabid dog?"

"Well, not literally rabid. The *new rabid*. It must have eaten parts off of an infected body because it had that mad disease. Rip … "

"Rip Daddy."

"Right. But we didn't know animals could get it, or that it made them bite. The thinking at the time was that if they couldn't get full-blown Sherman Pope, what did it matter? So we treated the wound and got on with it."

"How fast did she turn?"

"We knew she was sick right away, like, the next day, but again we figured it was something less severe. Maybe three days later, we got back and the doctor told us what she had. She was clarified on the spot and given her first bolus."

*"Three days?"*

Nicole nodded. "They should have a different scale for different types of infection. I'm told it translates to a normal incubation of around eighteen days. They said that if we'd taken one more day to get her in for her first Necrophage bolus, she'd have been past the inflection point — even as conservative as they were estimating inflection points back then."

Alice almost whistled, her face hopefully conveying the surprised sympathy she felt for Nicole. She'd thought Kelly had been bitten by a feral. That still happened plenty, even today. Not in cities and never inside a place like Aberdeen Valley, but there would always be people who refused government help or felt Panacea was evil no matter how necessary its powers seemed for containment. There would always be hippies too good for medicine and hillbillies ignorant of it. But for Kelly's condition to have come down to being bitten by a vector animal? It was an aspect of spread that even Alice often forgot existed.

"And how has she been since Necrophage?"

"You see how she is."

"I mean, has she changed since she's been on it?"

"Changed how?"

"It's supposed to halt her progress. Has it?"

"Sure."

"But it affects the brain. So does she still learn?"

"She learned how to work the swing lock on the door. She learned how to use that monstrous new keyboard on her computer."

"Do you think she's improving?"

Nicole shrugged. "I think she's not getting worse. That's enough. It's not supposed to *improve* her, is it?"

"Supposedly, the advanced formulations might."

Nicole sat up straight then set her wine on the table. "I hadn't heard that. Are you sure?"

Alice wasn't sure at all. Part of this was a hunch, but part of it was a lot of still-not-classified information contained in the packet left at her door. The packet was a big, obnoxious tease. It felt like someone who wanted to say something but wouldn't speak, like a friend who wants you to guess what's different about them without any hints. And there was a lot in there about Ian Keys and how upstanding and moral he is — part of Hemisphere PR that might matter to someone looking for a potential whistleblower. And there was a lot about August Maughan, Archibald Burgess's erstwhile protégé. The man who used to push Burgess's work that final, optimized 1 percent and who was rumored to be using Hemisphere drugs in his own exclusive life-extension practice … wherever he'd disappeared to.

But she wanted a reaction from an everyday user, and now she had one. The response was predictable: desperate hope, requiring no basis in reality to be worth pursuing.

"I didn't mean it like that. It's just something I've heard."

"Are you saying Kelly could come back to how she was?"

"No. No, I'm not. I'm sorry if I implied otherwise." Alice held up a hand, and Nicole slowly sat back. "What I meant was that the advanced Necrophage versions might restore *parts* of the body. Temporarily. Like a trick, even — not all that different in concept from applying makeup to hide bad skin."

"We got some to sample once. Some of Beautiful, I think. But the pharmacist told us it would be wasted on Kelly because most of her facial muscles have decayed beyond saving. He said the advanced formulations only work on young necrotics. Ones with short incubations, I mean."

"But you got it anyway?"

Nicole nodded. "The pharmacist was right. Cost a fortune and did nothing. It was a two-week course. At the end, I asked Kelly if she liked it, and she nodded. Then I asked her why, and she had nothing to say. I poked around the edges. Asked if it made her feel beautiful, like the promise in the name. I ran through the other supposed benefits. I don't remember them all, but one was supposed to make her hair shine. But hell, you know Kelly. Her hair just sloughs off because her scalp is falling apart. It grows like fuzz on normal Necrophage, and all Beautiful did was to make it grow faster and look a bit better, but what help is that when it just pulls right out, same as before?"

"Did Kelly notice her hair being nicer?"

"Sure did. She combed it, even. But it just came out, like I said. I was willing to keep buying it if there was a point, but there wasn't. We have the money — not money for the super-high-end formulations like Stardom, of course, but for the *good-good*, not *amazing-good* ones. I asked Kelly again and again. She said, 'Pretty,' but she just wasn't, and you know I love my sister no matter how messed up she is. Whenever I tried to explain it or ask Kelly for details about what it felt like — 'improvements,' if there were any, like you said — she always got angry."

"Angry?"

Nicole flapped a hand. "Oh, you know how they rage. They're like babies."

Alice hoped Nicole didn't use that word often: *rage*. It was the word Yosemite officials used to describe the point at which a doomed necrotic stopped "grazing" and became truly feral. It was the point at which, in a televised segment of her Bobby Baltimore interview, Bobby had told the world that his hunters knew they were legally allowed to shoot to kill.

Nicole finished her wine and fished her phone from her pocket. Something she saw on her app made her stand, preparing to leave.

"Is everything okay?"

"She just wants me to change the channel. *Are You Smarter Than a Zombie?* is on, and she can't find the remote. It's like having a kid, I'm telling you."

Alice blinked. "She likes that show?"

"Bless her dead heart, she doesn't understand the many levels on which she should rightly be insulted. Unfortunately, I do. But I've learned to pick my battles." Nicole gave Alice a little smile. "Thanks for the wine. And thanks for your interest in Kelly. I think people like to pretend there aren't people as advanced as her still out there and still being treated every day, but there are, and they're American citizens, same as you and me."

Alice smiled back, feeling melancholy.

"So, hey — if you find out that there's a Necrophage out there that actually turns back the clock," Nicole said, "you let me know. Is it a deal?"

Alice nodded, but it was suddenly hard to concentrate. Several innocuous ideas were colliding in her mind, turning into something new.

Hemisphere was the only company that had come close to solving the problem of the Sherman Pope plague, and they'd solved it entirely, and without any help.

The company didn't make money on its base drug, though it did receive subsidies. Still, the real money was in the designer formulations with pretty names and in preventative sales to foreign markets. Both were lines of business that relied on emotion more than results: the emotions of hope and fear, respectively.

And lastly, her envelope leaver had given her a lot of publicly available information on August Maughan, who might know more about how the drugs worked than Archibald Burgess himself.

Maybe her questionably helpful tipster hadn't been pointing her toward Ian Keys after all.

Maybe she should have started where Burgess did: with chemist-turned-healer, August Maughan, secret weapon of the ultra-wealthy.

If she could find him.

# Chapter Twenty

## PRESTIGE

WHEN CYRUS WAS GONE, HOLLY clicked off the TV, silencing the yammering of *The Yo Yo Boys* — four idiots in brightly colored shirts who'd done nothing to advance the tomfoolery invented by the Three Stooges. She felt dirty. Watching necrotic TV always made her feel like she'd just gone to a shitty diner because it was cheap and she couldn't afford better.

There was something debasing about not just pretending to like *The Yo Yo Boys*, but also providing a tiny bit of the ratings that kept them on the air and employed. If Holly had her way, all four Yos would find themselves off the air and destitute. Maybe they'd have to move out of whatever expensive mansions they surely lived in and into one of the slums — and then, with luck, someone forgotten or negligent would turn, and they'd get bitten. It would be poetic irony: those fools learning to appreciate the entertainment they'd foisted upon the infected nation.

There was a knock on the door. She checked the ID on the security panel and saw it was August.

*Come in*, she heard herself say inside her head.

"C'mon," she said out loud. Then she remembered that she'd set the doors to auto-lock (her farce would fall apart if Cyrus or her other handlers came back in to see her reading or otherwise not acting like an idiot) and crossed to the door.

With concentration, Holly could walk without a limp. It wasn't always easy. When she'd crossed the Oscars stage last year, she'd barely been able to accept her award because she'd been so focused on not tripping in her elegant gown. The whole way across in front of the cameras, she'd been thinking back to the red carpet interviews and how they might turn on her if she fell.

*Who are you wearing?*

*Chantal Melange*, coming through Holly's lips as *Shampal Melaahj*.

*And where will you be falling on your zombie face tonight?*

Of course, Cyrus had told her, when she'd relayed her fear, that she was being ridiculous. She'd maintained her popularity because people saw her as the face of and spokeswoman for a besieged section of the population — one that, though treated, didn't seem to be decreasing. With nearly a quarter of the nation infected, Holly was a kind of avatar. Of course nobody would call her a zombie in public lest they be run out of LA, and contrary to how it felt on her dignity, falling atop her sluggish legs would endear Holly more to her people, not alienate them from her.

But that was easy for Cyrus to say. He'd started managing an underground star with more cred than income, and Holly's first big paychecks (and, consequently, Cyrus's) had only started coming around the time the big outbreak hit. Cyrus hadn't been bitten. He hadn't even been in LA at the time. But when he came to her in the hospital and she lay there crying, he just kept saying, *It'll be okay, Holly. We can parlay this,* while patting her gaping wound like a kiss.

Holly had known there would be a lag period between the disease's progress and her first Necrophage bolus kicking in to stop it, and she'd sweated out two harrowing nights while waiting to see how bad things might get. Los Angeles had taken a serious hit, and the National Guard hadn't been able to cut her group a path until ten days after she'd been bitten. By then, the thing had become more infected than any rational wound had business being, and her memory had begun to go. She'd had trouble concentrating — and, in the hospital, even after the bolus, her symptoms had worsened before finally grinding to a halt in the place her doctors swore she'd be forever. The waiting had made her feel even more helpless than she'd been in that LA basement, waiting for the fires to burn off and the swarms to pass. Her situation could only degrade until the Necrophage's regeneration reached equilibrium with Sherman Pope's decay. And so those nights, watching her mind fail more and more, she'd cried plenty.

She slapped at the *Open Door* button on the touch screen, missed it, then focused to try again. *Goddamn this disease.*

She used to be a dancer. She used to be desired by every man she passed, rather than just the star-dazzled fetishists who boned up over Holly Gaynor today. She used to fuck like a bull rider. Today, she could barely control herself. Half the time, she peed a little in her underwear no matter how much better her mind seemed underneath it all.

August clasped Holly's hand between both of his when the door opened, making a hand sandwich. She hoped she didn't feel too cold. Her body was, according to estimates based on the most typical three-week incubation period, around one-third dead. Extremities were the first to lose circulation, but at least her heart kept beating. She knew further-gone necrotics who weren't as lucky. How could they have relationships? If someone laid their head on your chest and heard nothing, how did they not run away screaming?

At least most of her body still worked. At least her face, hair, and boobs — her moneymakers — were still smooth, pristine, and expressive. Her girls were still perky and plump; her lips, though sluggish with words, could still give that flawless winning smile. Even her teeth had stayed in her gums and remained white. And at least when she found a man who interested her, she was still warm where it mattered.

"Honey. How are you feeling?"

"Ofay."

August's head cocked. "You don't have palsy, Holly. That's a learned speech pattern, not an inevitable one."

*"Okay,"* she managed to say.

"Better."

"Hard to talk."

August flopped into one of Holly's overstuffed chairs. It had cost somewhere around the average person's annual salary, or the amount Holly paid August monthly for her treatments.

"Bullshit," he said.

Holly tried to make herself look vampily disapproving. It took some effort, but she thought she managed. One hand went to a hip. The other hung limp, but not twitcher-limp. She was in loose pants and a tee, but her hair was done and up, her makeup still on from earlier. Maybe if he were interested in necrotics, she could come off as sexy — just to show him she could still do it when the cameras weren't on.

Insultingly, August pulled an apple from a bowl on Holly's coffee table and began to eat it. He had small round glasses, a goatee, shoulder-length brown hair, and a boyish manner that was easily twenty years younger than his chronological age. But that made sense, didn't it? If August was really an expert in life extension, he *should* seem young. Immature, even.

"It's *not* bullshit," Holly said.

August made a quick little motion, reaching behind himself and into his back pocket. When the hand came back out, it was holding a phone, pointed at Holly.

"I'm sorry?"

"I said, it's *not* bullshit," Holly repeated.

August's cheeks were full of apple. He chewed, looking like a squirrel. He turned the phone in his hand, touched something on the screen, and Holly heard her own voice played back, indicating her opinion on bullshit and lack thereof.

"You see? You can speak properly if you want to. Like when you're bitching about something. Now: tell me that your eggs Benedict aren't poached to your satisfaction."

"Up yours, August," Holly said.

"Very good. Now would you like to start with speech therapy?"

Holly shook her head. What August was telling her now, he'd told her plenty of times before. The Sherman Pope virus did two things: It caused damage, and it *got in the way* in and of itself. Necrophage got the virus *out of the way* but couldn't reverse the damage it had done. By then, though, most necrotics had experienced rapid atrophy of the facial muscles, including those needed to speak. Some of the smaller muscles could be retrained (in Holly, anyway, thanks to the formulation August had her on). It was a long road, though, August said, and the body was lazy.

If only she could retrain her legs. Or her sloppy hands. But at least it was something.

"Well. Then what *am* I here for?"

Holly felt annoyed. She knew what he was doing. He was trying to force her to speak. She was self-conscious about her palsy voice and usually pantomimed her way through their encounters, speaking only when necessary. If she was doomed to slur her words forever, what August was doing would be cruel and mocking. But because it was due to her own failure to practice, he was relentless. She felt like Eliza Doolittle in *My Fair Lady*, constantly harassed to make declarations about the rain in Spain.

"Tuh tell me about my testh."

"Come on, Holly. You gave an Academy Awards speech."

She'd given it in a whisper, into a microphone. That didn't count.

"To tell me about my … *tests.*"

August sat up. He'd plopped a leather bag onto the floor beside himself, and now he rummaged through it, finally emerging with a small tablet.

"Now, as you know, Stardom is supposed to have all sorts of aesthetic augmentations," he said, beginning the inevitable monologue before getting to the point about her blood test and brain scan results. "Follicle conditioners — not like in shampoo, but ones that actually condition the follicles. Same for stimulations of mostly decimated keratin and melatonin producers. For extra star power, of course, it increases moisture in the lips and, optionally, increases their pigmentation level as well."

"I read the bwoshur."

August tossed her a look then continued without reprimand.

"Yes, yes. That's the base formulation for Stardom, but really, without customization it's not much more than something like Beauty or Pride. What you also know from the *bwoshur* is that Stardom works in concert with the stem cells we've been injecting."

Holly knew that, too. But not from the brochure because everyone knew stem cell treatments were illegal outside of designated clinical applications, none of which applied here. What wasn't illegal was the *supposition* that one day stem cell treatments might augment a specialty formulation like Stardom. Any stem cell injections given by certain practitioners while authorities turned their heads would, of course, be purely coincidental.

"It helps. Sure," said August. "But let's be honest. If they're fetal stem cells, they're not your DNA. If they're your own stem cells and hence your DNA, they've got a ton of epigenetic errors, and that's not even accounting for the weird shit that Sherman Pope does to your system."

"Okay," said Holly, wishing he'd just get to the damned results already.

"But you're not on Stardom, are you, Holly?"

"I'm not?"

"You're on my *customized version* of Stardom."

"Great." She knew that, too. August was a tweaker. If he'd stayed at Hemisphere before having his highly publicized falling-out and subsequent hermit period, he'd probably still be tweaking drugs. He was supposedly making Stardom better fit Holly — but Holly, who'd been in the business long enough to smell crap when it was put in front of her, had her doubts. Like aromatherapy and reflexology, maybe a *tweaked formula* would work wonders on the suggestible, but Holly didn't think she was one of them.

Which, interestingly, was something that seemed to be changing lately — about since she'd begun taking August's tweaked version of the drug, come to think of it.

And maybe she really did believe she was somehow improving, even if she didn't allow herself to hope. Because hadn't she just waited until Cyrus had left the room to turn off *The Yo Yo Boys?* Didn't she still pretend not to understand the nuances of contracts she understood plenty? Didn't she exaggerate her limp when her handlers were around because it's what they expected?

"Wait," Holly said. "What'f different?"

"Maybe I have access to hospital birth records," August said.

"So?"

"Including the complete genetic sequence of anyone who had sequencing done."

Holly shook her head.

"Not a lot of people know it, Holly. I don't blame you for not. But all certified hospitals footprint new babies and take a heel-stick to obtain a blood sample. The footprints are an antiquated process meant mainly to give the parents a keepsake. But sequencing is so cheap these days … "

"What are you saying?"

"This is all beta. And don't get your hopes up, okay? Because Sherman Pope never leaves your system even if the drugs can get you nearer to nil, and nobody is close to figuring out how to permanently get rid of it. So no matter what we put into you, the disease will always fight it back. But — "

"Spit it out."

"I've taken some of your harvested stem cells, which are replete with a lifetime of insertions, deletions … damage you caused by sitting too long in the sun, receiving radiation from all over the place, and just plain getting older so your cells have to replicate over and over in an endless game of telephone. Let's just say those stem cells have a ton of mistakes. But part of Hemisphere's life extension research was focused on fixing those mistakes, using an original, at-birth copy of a patient's code. The world's largest proofreading job, basically."

"So you can … what?"

"*Not* fix the parts of your body Sherman Pope killed off. Let's be clear about that much, okay?"

"Okay."

"But in concert with a drug like Stardom, highly customized, we end up with something very special indeed."

"Which is?"

August pointed at Holly's canister of designer Necrophage — the cartridges bearing the Hemisphere split-brain logo and the trade name *Stardom*. Holly followed his finger, somewhat confused. She'd been injecting them in her Gadget for weeks now, and as far as August had told her, it was the Stardom formulation of Necrophage, slightly modified by her absurdly expensive longevity consultant.

"Stardom," Holly repeated, finding no difficulty in saying the word cleanly.

"*Stardom* is crap compared to what I've been able to do for you, using your code-corrected stem cells and those beautiful little vials over there. *Stardom* will pump you up and make you look better while the disease keeps its hooks in you. But *this*—" Again, he pointed at the bottle. "This, my dear, might just fix some of the damage clogging that brain of yours."

Holly looked to August.

"So what is it?"

August smiled. "I call it *Prestige.*"

# Chapter Twenty-One

## THE LATE SHOW

IAN COULDN'T CONCENTRATE.

HIS PHONE had stopped ringing, but there was still the question of how the hell Alice Frank — *Alice Motherfucking Frank*, of all people — had found his number in the first place. It wasn't listed anywhere. Ian did have an official Hemisphere number that forwarded to his cell, and it automatically routed to voicemail after 5 p.m. and on weekends. That number could also be selectively sifted; Hemisphere's reception program did a decent job of sending calls to the appropriate parties even if the caller asked for someone different. Alice was tops of the undesirable list and would be sent to public relations, the mail room, or worse thanks to her frequent attempts to reach Burgess, but that only worked if she called Ian's official number, which she very much hadn't.

She'd called his direct number. The good one. The personal one. The one that ran straight past the gatekeepers.

How had she known that number? Ian tried to think of who even had it, outside of Bridget. Burgess, of course, and Smyth. Ted, Gennifer, and the others had it, but even Danny Almond called on the official line. Outside of work, it was friends only. The thought made him shiver. Seeing as everyone at Hemisphere knew of Alice's rather large grinding-axe against the company, the most logical leak *was* from someone Ian knew personally. That meant that someone in his circle was an inconsiderate, possibly backstabbing asshole. It also meant, given that everyone in the world knew that Frank was Hemisphere's biggest critic, that the person who had blabbed wasn't just stupid. He or she was probably being deliberately malicious.

Ian glanced from the TV to the phone again. It was as if he expected it to not only ring, but possibly bite him.

Well, there was no point worrying about it. Facts were facts. Somehow, Alice Frank had Ian's number, but he couldn't start glaring at every acquaintance with an evil eye. And it's not like he had to answer the call again, or talk to the reporter. He hadn't before, so why would she even think he was interested in talking now?

And why had she *stopped* calling? That was troubling in itself. When Analise had been little, they'd prayed for her to be quiet. But when she'd been out of sight and suddenly *too* quiet, that was actually more cause for alarm than noise. And everyone knew children and reporters were so much alike.

Maybe she was finding another way to get at him, persistent to the end.

And if so, maybe it was because she somehow knew what he'd been up to today. What information he may or may not have copied from the company computer and brought home — files that he hadn't had the courage to open. Doing so would crack a seal and force him to decide one way or the other. So far, he'd only had a creeping sense of unease, but what if the files he'd been instructed to *copy*, *read, and delete* held confidential, high-access information? What if it was, not entirely coincidentally, the nefarious kind of company secrets that Alice Frank might be calling to hear all about?

"Stop being an idiot," Ian said aloud to his empty study.

He clicked the paused video back to life and resumed watching. There she was all over again: Alice Frank, on his study wall with the much-beloved Bobby Baltimore. Seeming to mock him now from two separate directions.

The video about the Yosemite Reserve, streaming from Frank's website as a replay, wasn't even a full hour long. And yet Ian couldn't get through it. He felt like he wasn't absorbing all Smyth had asked him to absorb because he felt guilty about *something he hadn't done.* It wasn't fair. But Frank's phone calls had interrupted him twice after he'd started, and once before dinner.

Bridget had let him go to the study without protest, but she clearly didn't like it. Ian didn't work after six and definitely didn't rush off to take secretive calls in private. He didn't close himself in the study after rushing through dinner then sit alone while his wife and daughter entertained themselves without him.

Onscreen, the camera (probably worn by Frank herself, run through stabilization software) showed the backs of several men as the Yosemite group marched through rocks and brush. The mic picked up heavy, adrenaline-filled breathing — likely Alice's, electronically magnified in post-production to make the segment more gripping. Ian had already watched this part a few times, rewinding over and over with renewed attempts each time to clear his mind and pay attention. He knew what was coming, and when Bobby spoke to one of the hunters beside him, Ian felt his own spike of adrenaline.

"Relax. They're not smart enough to form ambushes," Bobby's voice said from Ian's speakers.

Then there's commotion up ahead. The camera ducks away as if something is thrown, or shot, or coming hard. The rustle of garments. Someone yells, and the hunters part. For a horrifying two-beat moment, Alice Frank's camera is at the formation's point as the men with guns stream to the left and right, raising weapons the camera can only see as flashes of black. She's unarmed. That's been established, also for dramatic effect. But there are four (and yes, Ian already paused to count them on an earlier loop) deadheads coming straight for her.

Heavily decayed. Flesh sloughing from their skulls to reveal dull ivory white.

Mouths open. Teeth at odd angles. Hands up to grab.

Coming as fast as biology allows — which, it turns out, can vary quite a bit, depending on which parts of the body Sherman Pope preferentially props up.

On the video, the ferals coming for Alice are faster than anyone expects. If not for the offscreen rat-a-tat of automatic weapons, she'd have been taken down for sure.

Ian paused the video and made a note for his later conversation with Raymond Smyth about the fast ferals. Not many people knew how varied the disease's effects could be, and Alice might have considered the matter when compiling this footage. It was the sort of question she might pick up the phone and dial Ian's personal number to ask. Or maybe the sort of thing that might be corroborated by evidence on certain stolen drives:

*Copy this, read it, and then delete.*

But no. He'd copied it, but Ian wouldn't read it. Not unless he had to.

Ian pulled the drive from his desk and slipped it into a port in his study computer. Rushing felt necessary. Slowing to think might cost him his nerve. And there was no reason to lose his nerve because he was only reading. That in itself wasn't criminal or duplicitous or disloyal. No matter what he read, he didn't have to act on it. *Acting* would be crossing a line. But *reading* harmed no one, and was sensible, in the interest of staying informed about all he wasn't doing wrong.

When Ian dragged his laptop from the desk to his comfortable chair, his hand brushed the touch screen remote. The video resumed, and the room again filled with the sounds of screaming and staccato gunfire.

Blood spatters the camera's lens — partially congealed, like a wad of red snot. Because it's more lump than liquid, it sort of rolls away, and the view quickly returns.

The camera is up, its vista as much sky and cliffs as eye-level action. Feral deadheads can still be heard to one side or another — growls like animals, thumps when they're struck by bullets. Deadheads, it turns out, don't grunt when struck. Grunting is part exhalation, and reanimated corpses don't breathe.

Then the worst part of this segment. Alice must sit up as the furor dies down because the camera tilts more earthward and the screen shows a tree-and-rock horizon. The camera catches a sigh in the middle of her still-panicked breaths, but it's short-lived. Because at the screen's bottom, there's something that's just a head, a shoulder, part of a torso, and an arm. And it's grabbing Alice's leg.

A scream, very near the camera.

A loud gunshot.

Faster breaths, like a panting dog.

And then the camera is pulled away and held as Alice the hunted recovers and becomes Alice the reporter again.

Bobby Baltimore, smiling. Saying, "Well, that was close."

Ian paused the video again then realized divided attention was his enemy and went to turn it off. But between raising the remote and mashing his finger on the power button, he noticed something behind Bobby's head: a rock formation in the distance with one very large, very tall figure standing on a path around its edge, as if observing the action below.

The room went dark as the screen flicked off. There was a space of three heartbeats, and then Ian jumped when someone knocked on the door.

"Come in."

Bridget poked her head in. He must look odd in here: closed door, lights down to watch the video, now off. The footage had creeped him out the first time; now it was creeping him out even more. Only a small desk lamp and his laptop's bottled blue glow illuminated the darkness. But he didn't want to turn that screen back on. Nothing in Frank's special with Bobby Baltimore could be spun in one direction or the other. People died, were shipped to Yosemite, and were then killed again. The public could see that however they wanted, but Sherman Pope disease was to blame, not Hemisphere.

Bridget's red hair swung beside her face. White hallway light streamed around her, giving her a halo.

"You're just sitting in here?" she asked.

"Just doing some work."

"I thought you didn't work in the evenings?"

*I'm not doing anything wrong here.*

Ian sat up and said, "Raymond asked me to watch some special interview show Alice Frank did with Bobby Baltimore."

"The guy from the hunting shows?"

"You know a lot of Bobby Baltimores?"

Bridget's lips pinched. "I'm just asking."

Ian sighed, glanced at his computer, then covertly pulled the drive and pocketed it again. He closed the laptop and stood from his chair. Leather groaned beneath him.

Arms around Bridget, Ian said, "I'm sorry. It's just that Raymond wants me to watch this so we can come up with ways to spin it in our favor. But the video itself is … unnerving." He exhaled. "I don't know. It was just such a weird day."

"So you said. Anything you want to talk about?"

"No."

A pleased expression was starting to form on Bridget's face. It fell. "Oh. Okay."

"Not like that. I just mean I've thought about it enough. I'd rather stop thinking about it."

"You make it sound so dire."

Ian watched her green eyes. He knew exactly what she was thinking: He *was* making this nothingness sound dire, and *dire at work* would sound to Bridget like a threat to his job. They had all they did thanks to Ian's rapid climb, and they were only able to afford a house in this part of Aberdeen Valley — let alone in the Lion's Gate development — because of his hefty salary. Bridget wasn't truly materialistic, but security and stability were her highest values. Status didn't matter, but the threat of loss bothered her plenty.

"It's nothing." He kissed her. "Promise."

Bridget's eyes flicked sideways, down the hallway.

"Ana is asleep," she said.

Ian's arms slipped around Bridget's waist. "You don't say."

"I do say."

"Then maybe I should be done with all of this, and Raymond's errand be damned."

"That's not bedtime watching anyway," Bridget said.

"Give me two minutes."

Bridget gave him a little smile and walked away while Ian watched her from behind.

When she was gone, he pulled the small thumb drive from his pocket and slipped it into a hollow behind some books on his study bookshelf. He didn't need to read what was on it because he wasn't a fink or a traitor. Whatever Alice Frank thought about his company and Archibald Burgess, it wasn't true. Whoever was pushing Ian's buttons was only trying to start problems.

Ian didn't have doubts. His faith was rock solid, and he'd never do anything to sway the boat beneath his daughter and the love of his life.

He turned off the lamp and left the study. Approaching his bedroom, he saw the ghost of an image.

A rocky cliff.

A lone figure on an outcropping, tall and still.

Watching.

Waiting.

# Chapter Twenty-Two

## HANDLERS

HOLLY SNEAKED A LOOK AT the ornate clock mounted in her room's corner. It was nearly eleven here in Aberdeen Valley, which meant it was almost 8 p.m. back in what was left of Los Angeles. Too late for Cyrus to do any of the things he claimed to be doing, anyway, given that everyone he knew at the studios worked a strict nine-to-five.

Her eyes moved to August's brown leather bag. Somewhere in there — possibly on a drive, probably on the tablet August had hurriedly re-stowed when Cyrus had come knocking again — were her test results. Some of those tests Holly had known she was taking: the blood draws for sure; the ask-and-answer assessments August had put her through that had come off as practically insulting. But before Cyrus and his team interrupted, August had implied there were even more tests, conducted unseen. She had no idea what they'd be, but paid the man enough to trust him. Maybe he could help people live longer; his clients hadn't spent enough life under his care to know for sure. Holly would settle for living better, seeing as she was already half-dead.

Except that now she was on a designer drug a full step more advanced than most people ever saw and two steps higher than the free version that kept Panacea's New World Order from falling apart.

*Prestige.*

Holly was more curious about that simple word than she could ever remember being. Literally. She'd been infected with Sherman Pope for four years (though even that had only been a number on her ID card until recently, as she'd started to recall much of what she'd forgotten), and in those four years she seemed to have lost the trick of genuine inquiry. In retrospect, it seemed obvious that she'd accepted much that she should've been curious enough to question.

Like giving Cyrus a partial power of attorney.

Like letting Damon hire her accountant, lawyer, and foreign rights agents.

Like giving Carly carte blanche to make Holly's schedule without consulting her, the way Holly's brother used to make his son's schedule back when he'd been little.

And most troublingly, like giving Cyrus cosigning authority on her checking account and credit cards. Why had she done that? She felt like it made sense at the time; Holly seemed to recall having no idea how to subtract one hundred dollars from a thousand, and bringing on someone less damaged would make everything faster. But he could spend without her consent and got a weighty opinion on *how* she spent. Now that seemed dumb. If not for Panacea regulations to the contrary, Holly would have given Cyrus full control rather than simply enlisting him as an authorized party. Ironically, the much-maligned government had done something in her favor for a change.

"We have some contracts to discuss," Cyrus was telling August, who hadn't budged from the couch.

"Sure," August replied.

"It would bore you."

"I'm very interested in show business." August smiled.

Cyrus's eyes went to Damon, who'd perched himself in a ridiculous-looking chair that Holly was sure she'd paid for but didn't remember agreeing to purchase.

"It's confidential stuff." Damon was big and black, like Holly's father. Sitting in the odd chair, he seemed likely to break it.

"Oh, well," said August. "Then if Holly would like me to go, I'll go."

"She wants you to go."

August looked at Holly.

"Sfay," Holly said, not bothering to enunciate in front of Cyrus or Damon.

August looked smugly at Damon.

"She doesn't know what she's saying," Cyrus said from August's other side.

"Sfay," Holly repeated. She reached for a glass on the table, but her sluggish hand knocked it to the floor, where it spilled water into the carpet's nap.

Cyrus rushed to dab the water with a paper towel then looked at August as if to say, *See?*

"Sounds to me like she knows just fine," August said, watching him.

But Cyrus's attention had gone to Holly. His expression was intensely patronizing. Holly seemed to remember thinking of Cyrus like a father figure (now that her own dad was dead) and thinking that Damon, who even looked the part, made an excellent backup. But now he looked stupid, with that dumb soul patch under his bottom lip and the gaudy gold chain around his neck.

"Holly, Honey," said Cyrus, "we have business to discuss. I know you like Mr. Maughan, but it's time for him to go. Private stuff."

"I dun wan him da go." Holly felt like she was walking a fine line. Her mouth seemed to have cottoned onto the trick of proper speech, but she didn't want to show the men she could do it. There was so much in her that she couldn't articulate, but that frustration shouldn't prompt her to try. She didn't even know why. Even before the outbreaks, Hollywood only *claimed* to like a brainy woman. Dumbing things down wasn't new.

Cyrus looked at Damon for help.

"It can't hurt to let him stay, if she wants it so much," Damon said.

"This is the Tristar thing."

Damon laughed. "You don't need to bother Holly with that."

"I need her signature."

Holly watched the two men go back and forth. Had they always talked as if she wasn't there? She wanted to laugh in their faces but kept herself neutral.

"You don't have to discuss it to get her signature."

August piped up. He'd begun eating peanuts from a crystal bowl, and his words came out between crunches. "This is just my non-Hollywood opinion, but if I'm going to be signing something, I'd like someone to give me the gist."

"Nobody asked your opinion," Cyrus said.

"In fact, it might even be illegal to ask someone to sign a contract they don't understand."

Cyrus looked at Damon as if to say, *This is why I want this asshole out of here.*

"This isn't any of your business."

"Just Holly's," August clarified.

"I'm her legal guardian," Cyrus said, "and that makes it my — "

"Bullshit!" Holly blurted.

All eyes turned to Holly. Slowly, Cyrus looked back at August.

"In matters of contracts, anyway," he said, tossing Holly a pacifying look. "I'm her manager. As long as I understand it, she's — "

Cyrus pulled a folded stack of papers from an interior pocket. Holly snatched it mid-sentence.

"Holly," he said.

Holly opened the packet and began reading. Her eyes had trouble focusing these days, but she was able to see the words enough to make sense.

"Holly, Honey," Cyrus said, pinching the papers in Holly's hands. She tried to snarl, turning to pull them away, but her body betrayed her and the snarl left as a low, necrotic growl.

Damon laughed. "Oh, just let her look, Cyrus."

"Yeah, Cyrus," said August, still eating. "Let her look."

But Cyrus grabbed the papers and pulled. He growled back at Holly, *"Give."* He yanked them away, nearly giving her a forest of paper cuts, then re-folded and re-pocketed the contract. He glared at August, who was still kicked back, practically laughing. Cyrus turned away, looking Holly right in the eye as if encouraging her to join in.

"In the morning." Cyrus looked at August. "You should go, too."

"Stay." Too late, Holly realized she shouldn't have forced the word's hard T. But nobody seemed to notice.

"She wants him to stay," Damon said.

"I don't want him here."

"Don't be shy, guys," August said. "Just pretend I'm not here."

Cyrus looked right at August. "I don't want you here *at all.* Ever."

"I guess it's good that it's not your decision then."

"It could be. If I forced it."

Holly wanted to jump in and explain exactly why she wanted August here. How he'd helped her before and how the tests might show (and her gut *already* showed) he was helping her right now. Holly's mind was forming solid, cogent arguments, but even if she'd wanted to stop playing dumb for her handlers, she doubted her mouth would let those arguments pass. Thinking seemed to be getting easier, but articulating still seemed daunting. Maybe that was on its way to changing, too.

Holly put a limp palm on Cyrus's arm and stared hard at him.

*"Sfay,"* she said.

After a moment, Cyrus rolled his eyes and sighed dramatically. Then he looked at Damon, and the two of them stood, Cyrus locking eyes with August.

"No fucking her," Cyrus said firmly then walked out the door with Damon beside him.

# Chapter Twenty-Three

## DROPPED CALL

ALICE'S EYES SNAPPED OPEN. SHE'D been having a dream she'd been playing chess with her neighbor. Kelly had chased her king into a corner, and the game had ended almost before it began. Then Nicole, who'd been beside Alice the entire time, had reached into a candy dish and pulled out a handful of extracted teeth with bloody roots. Nicole said, "Told you."

After a moment of waiting for reality's return, Alice sat up in the darkness. The dream had borne the stamp of veracity, and in her dark bedroom it didn't want to shake loose on its own. It had the feel of a memory. Or a documentary she'd seen too many times.

A slow sigh. A glance out the window, showing only darkness and moonlight.

The clock projected its time onto the ceiling in red numerals. It said it was 6:04 a.m., but Alice didn't believe it. This was a middle-of-the-night feel if ever she'd had one, with dream skin clinging to her cortex.

Alice went to the bathroom and splashed water on her face. She looked in the mirror for a few seconds, taking herself in as the tick of her vents dripped upward from the register near the floor. In the basement, there was a HEPA filter attached to the furnace, guaranteed to trap and kill the Sherman Pope virus. Which was a joke because SP had never gone airborne and seemed unlikely to. It's why the first outbreak, though bad, had been easy enough to contain. Blood-to-blood and saliva-to-blood transmission had remained the disease's only communicability factor, and they turned out to be shitty ways for a disease to propagate itself. Flu spread because it was airborne, and the bubonic plague had been able to live inside fleas. Sherman Pope's viability remained exclusive to mammals, and only humans could manifest it. Turned out *not getting bitten by someone* was easier than Hollywood made it look.

And still, people sold crap like HEPA filters.

There were face masks. Bite shirts for use in the open — even inside cities. All sorts of barricading products, including how-to videos and books. Head-hunting scatter guns that were highly illegal but ubiquitous anyway. Not to mention the rip-off info products on how to fight your way out of an undead horde.

*Fear.* Fear moved product, no question about it.

Alice made her coffee, turned on lights to shake away the dream's last tendrils, and sat on her couch with the unhelpful stack of publicly available Hemisphere information her anonymous tipster had left on her porch.

There were pamphlets on Hemisphere's life-extension products. Some, among the first in the lines, were questionable — little more than high-priced vitamins. They seemed to substantially improve right around the time Sherman Pope claimed the nation. Even outside of the disease market, Hemisphere still offered lines for the uninfected. There was something called telomere lengthening treatments that came with all sorts of testimonials from government doctors. Hemisphere had started its lines involving stem cells rather dubiously in Alice's opinion — one of the reasons she didn't entirely trust the company, even today, to steer clear of bent rules.

What had started as borderline illegal with operations based in Singapore had become suddenly legit when Panacea's predecessors began their work in the wake of the first Rip Daddy outbreaks. Once people were scared enough, passing a few *special circumstances, but only for us* laws permitting stem cell research became easy, so long as it meant giving Hemisphere the tools required to find a cure. They never *had* cured Rip Daddy; it had morphed into Sherman Pope, which quickly bloomed into a much bigger problem. As far as Alice understood, stem cells didn't have anything to do with Necrophage or its development, but the die had been cast. And the world's richest company had kept rolling on.

There were several sheets in the packet about Ian Keys, including pre-Hemisphere bio and contact info. Alice had read them already, but even though someone seemed to be elbowing her about Keys as if to say *hint-hint*, he'd thus far been uninterested in talking. She set them aside and found a printout on August Maughan below them. One she hadn't noticed before because it had been sticking to the underside of one of Ian's sheets. But even after reading it, Alice felt no further along. August Maughan, genius protégé to Archibald Burgess — some even said "private partner" — had been the media darling Burgess never was, doing much to humanize Hemisphere when the company needed PR most. But some time after the outbreak, Maughan had left in a falling-out of unknown origin.

There was some *hint-hint* in the paperwork about Maughan, too. Between the pages of dense scientific jargon (cell and nucleus receptor structure, lists of formulary active and inactive ingredients, virology texts, something called competitive inhibition), there was a story that Alice had yet to put her finger on. Maughan was central to that story, just like Keys. Except that Maughan had pulled off the country's most public vanishing act, becoming less scientist and more high-ticket voodoo-doctor/guru. Everyone knew he was still out there, and knew his face with its odd mix of quiet intellect and savvy. But as far as Alice had found, nobody had any idea of where to find him or how to get in touch. Not even her deepest sources had been able to turn up anything.

But *something* was stirring. An untold secret in this pile of public data was trying to tell Alice the truth. She just had to figure out what it was. Her mind was already working. She'd been scouring her Yosemite footage, not sure at all what she might be looking for. She'd left a message for Bobby Baltimore, but Cindy told Alice he was "on safari" and would be a few days. Alice had tried Keys innumerable times because the packet's creator seemed to be telling her that he, out of all possible sources inside Hemisphere, was the man to contact. She'd even worked up a profile of Keys. He was smart, handsome, highly ambitious, apparently honest and loyal to a fault. Well connected for sure, and just a few rungs from the top on Hemisphere's ladder. The kind of guy who'd never, ever talk to the press out of turn because he *was* so loyal. Or maybe the kind of guy who'd be most likely to talk if he found reason to doubt those he'd been loyal to, because he was so honest.

There were too many loose ends. Too many things she'd learned at Yosemite that might mean something. Same for her research online; same for her trial-balloon phone calls that had yielded nothing; same for personal ruminating like her discussion with Nicole. When she'd been younger, Alice might have leaped at any one of a thousand red herrings, but there wasn't substantive reason to truly believe any of them.

Something in Hemisphere's corporate story had bothered Alice from the start. Yet no one but her seemed alarmed. The nation treated Hemisphere like saviors, and Archibald Burgess like grandfather to all those still living, and the tens of millions who were, thanks to his drug, still productive members of society despite being mostly dead.

*Necrophage was free. So how could Hemisphere have any ulterior motives?* the world seemed to think. Sure, the designer versions cost out the ass. Sure, everyone wanted them. Sure, there were rumors like the one that had so lit Nicole up, about the benefits of the higher-up-the-chain drugs. But the company's biggest product cost users nothing and saved their lives. Hard to hate a company like that, no matter the size of its coffers.

Alice jumped when her phone rang. She looked down and saw an Aberdeen extension that looked familiar, though the caller wasn't in her contacts.

"Hello," said a voice.

"Who is this?"

"Who is *this?*" The caller sounded annoyed. "You called me."

Had she? The number seemed so familiar.

"Refresh my memory," Alice said.

"About what? Who the hell are you?"

"The message. What did my message say?" Alice asked, getting annoyed herself. The caller had decided to call her back, so why was he being such an asshole? If he didn't want to talk to her, whoever he was, he shouldn't have …

"Is this Ian Keys?"

"You don't even know who you called?" Pause. "Is this Alice Frank again? I told you — "

"Of course it's Alice Frank. You're the one who made the call."

"I didn't call you. You called me."

Alice felt her brows furrow. It sounded like something that might have happened in the days of phone operators and landlines: a crossed connection somehow calling two people as if they'd called each other. But that couldn't happen today, right? She was misunderstanding.

"I'm not sure what you—" Alice stopped when the phone vibrated in her hand, then she pulled the screen away in time to see a new text message roll across the top — from a private number.

*Ask him about BioFuse.*

*BioFuse?* It sounded like an adhesive. She was pawing across the couch for her laptop, hoping to quickly look it up before embarrassing herself by asking out of the blue, when she heard Ian's end of the line marred with noise. Not static or interference but the rustle of something against the mic, as if the man was in motion, shuffling while talking.

"I'm going to hang up now. I've received all of your calls, texts, and emails. I don't know how you're finding all these numbers and addresses, but my answer hasn't changed. You want to talk to someone at Hemisphere, you go through the main number. If you do that and are cleared by PR, I'll happily talk to you. I'd *love* to talk to you if you go through proper channels. But if you keep harassing me, I'll … oh, hey."

"Hey what?"

"Now? No, I've got a client meeting."

"Okay. Go to your meeting," Alice said, puzzled by the odd change in the call.

"Archibald? Sure, of course."

"What are you talking about?"

"No, I've never talked to anyone. But what about—"

Alice pressed the phone tighter to her ear. He wasn't talking to her. Ian was speaking to someone else. Someone who'd interrupted him, but that Alice, despite straining, couldn't hear.

"What the hell is that supposed to mean?" Ian asked his other party. Then, sounding annoyed: "Just let me check in. I'll call up after I've had a cup of coffee if it's so damn important."

"What's going on over there?" Alice asked.

A rustle of fabric. Then Ian's voice: "Hey. Let go of me."

There was a crack as someone dropped Ian's phone.

She heard shuffling then breathing.

Then the call was disconnected, and Alice heard nothing.

# Chapter Twenty-Four

## CHECK-IN

THERE WAS A KNOCK ON the trailer door, waking Jordache from her sound sleep with a loud groan. When she rolled upright, Jordache saw that the sun was already up and streaming around her thin but pretty curtains. But screw the sun. The sun didn't work late, like she did.

Jordache hoped for a moment that she'd imagined the knock, or that some kid had rapped the wall with a book bag on his way to the park's main bus stop just up the internal road. But no, there was a silhouette clearly visible on her stoop, patiently waiting.

The knock came again, light like a reminder.

So annoying.

Jordache looked in the living room mirror, fluffed her hair (kind of oily from the diner's atmosphere last night but still cute), and blinked. She wanted to wipe the shit from the corners of her eyes, but her eyeliner and shadow were still in place (though her pillow had probably taken the mascara). If she wiped now, she'd look like a horror show. Mostly, Jordache was presentable despite her sleep shirt and missing bra. Her lips had even retained their brick-red color and dark liner.

She opened the door to find a man in a suit. He flashed a badge.

"Good morning, ma'am. I'm Agent Joseph Trent, Panacea. Are you Margaret Kyle?"

"No," Jordache answered, rubbing her face and yawning.

The man craned back, looking at the front wall of her trailer. Probably searching for the house number, but it was on the other side, on the mailbox.

"I'm sorry. Is this 516?"

"This is 512."

"Do you know Ms. Kyle?"

Jordache laughed. She didn't know any Margarets, but the agent's saying "Ms. Kyle" made it all make sense.

"She goes by Peggy."

"My appointment says Margaret."

Jordache nodded. "Peggy is short for Margaret."

The man's brow stitched.

"I know. It doesn't make sense to me, either, but it's true."

Jordache looked to the left, toward Peggy's trailer. Poor girl. She'd been bitten by a rat. It was hideous because that rat had been carrying Sherman Pope, but it was even more hideous because it was just making trailer park clichés that much worse. Peggy had been smart enough to get tested (she couldn't catch the rat, of course, and now it might get someone else) and was dosed within a few hours of infection, so she'd be fine, but the white trash stereotypes would linger. It was so unfair. Rats didn't get all undead like people did, but they did get more aggressive. Before the outbreak, the rats had always been cool. Now, trailer park tornados? Those things were still assholes.

The agent was already stepping off her small porch.

"You a clarifier?" Jordache asked.

He turned and nodded. "Yes, ma'am."

"She only got bit half a day before they took her to the clinic."

"Ma'am?"

"She ain't even a little dangerous."

"I'm sure, ma'am," said the clarifier. "But it's a federal regulation. All new cases must be clarified." He tapped his head as if he were wearing a hat, which he wasn't. "Thanks for your help." He stopped. Something seemed to occur to him, and he pulled a small tablet, just larger than a phone, from his pocket.

"Since I have you ... "

Jordache sighed. "You can't even tell. I'm not slobbering all over myself without seein' it again, am I?" She tried to laugh, but this wasn't funny. Oh, to be a Jew, gay, or a black person these days. Necrotics were the new persecuted class, with everyone else on discrimination holiday.

"I'm sorry. Federal regulations, like I said."

Jordache's tongue went into the corner of her mouth. She cocked her slim hip and put one hand on it. With all her makeup still in place, she might be coming off like a hooker. But whatever; if the clarifier found her hot, maybe he wouldn't annoy her too much. Check-ins could be quick, or they could take forever. There was one poor kid, Rory, who lived with his mamma out by the main road. When that bastard had to submit on these sweeps, it came closer to a full-blown reclarification. Every time, Jordache half expected to hear that Rory had been shipped off after all, that the first clarifier who'd given him a pass had screwed up and let one through that was about to go feral.

"Your name?"

"Jordache Dale."

"Is that your real name?"

What the hell was that supposed to mean? Did he think it was her stripper name? That was ridiculous. Jordache had never stripped, and if she had, Jordache was plenty sexy enough.

"Course it is."

The agent tapped on his tablet.

"How long have you been infected?"

"Since the first big wave."

"But after Necrophage."

"Of course. Think I'd be here without it?" Her pride wanted to add that she wasn't even on plain old Phage, but was on the fancy stuff rich people used. But that might raise questions, seeing as Jordache didn't exactly appear to be rolling in dough.

"And what was your incubation period?"

"Twenty-six hours."

The man looked up. "Really?"

"It's there on your pad, ain't it?"

He looked down then looked back up. "It's just that I don't see many first-wave patients with such short incubation periods. Nowadays, with clinics and public awareness of the disease, sure. But back then, it was kind of chaotic."

"I got bit near a clinic. The doc stayed the whole time, even when it got bad."

The clarifier nodded, apparently satisfied. It wasn't the whole truth. In reality, she'd been with Weasel at the time, and they'd both been very, *very* drunk. She'd been drunk and high a lot back then, and Weasel's thinking was that if the world seemed to be ending, they might as well get as shitfaced as possible and fuck until the hordes ate them alive. On pharmaceutical-grade shit (the kind that became available when there was a goddamned apocalypse and the pharmacy was left unguarded), even being ripped apart might be a gas. But then she'd got her bite, and Weasel had beaten the thing's head in, and that had been it. No horde. As soon as they'd sobered up, they'd gone inside the pharmacy and taken vast quantities of everything anyway, even injecting most things that weren't insulin and seemed likely to boost some altered states. One of the vials had contained Necrophage. She'd lucked into a short incubation because she was an addict, but ironically getting treated had helped her get clean. The idea of taking all those drugs today — when she had to be beholden to one specific drug — made Jordache shiver.

"Mmm hmm. And how are things for you today?"

"Fine. I'm tired as shit, but fine."

"Your mental state, I mean."

"Fine. But don't ask me to do the multiplication tables. I was bad at those before I got infected."

"It's not an intelligence test, Ms. Dale." He tapped his tablet. "How would you rate your thought quality relative to last month or last year? About the same or getting worse?"

It was time for another half truth. Honestly, since she'd been taking what Danny brought her instead of Walmart Phage, something was decidedly *better*. Not only did she feel more energetic and focused; she'd also been a lot more interested in stuff that hadn't appealed at all in the past: reading, the way space seemed so deep and endless at night, movies without explosions. But as with bragging on Danny's supply, saying too much felt like a bad idea.

"Fine. Same." She looked back into her living room as if she had something pressing. She did, she suddenly remembered. Danny was coming over at nine. He had the morning off and was planning on taking her to breakfast. It was cute how Danny was. She wanted to fuck him. Problem was, guys left after you gave it up. Or they became bastards once they saw you as a toy. Danny was so nice now, and Jordache liked him plenty. It hurt to hold back and keep turning him down, but she had to try a bit longer. This honeymoon before he became a real guy was too nice to ruin.

"Not to be rude, but … " Jordache trailed off.

"Almost done. Just one thing left." He pulled a device about the size of a triple-thick box of matches from his pocket. There was an accordion of disposable pop-up lancets on top where you were supposed to put your finger, and the clarifier pulled the top one off to expose the sterile one below. He touched a button on the thing's side to pair it to his tablet and held it out.

"Just go ahead and — "

"I done this before, thanks." Jordache extended a finger and placed it on the device's top. There was a tiny jolt of pain. Almost instantly, the thing's light flickered, and the agent's tablet flashed green.

"Looks good," he said, pocketing both devices. "Sorry to bother you. Do you need a tissue for that?"

He nodded at Jordache's lightly bleeding finger, but she slipped it between her lips instead.

She shook her head. "So it's all blood tests now?"

"Just for check-ins. It just shows if you have enough Necrophage in your system."

"Like a drug test."

"Sort of, yes, ma'am." He stopped, not wanting to rush on and seem rude. But when Jordache put her finger in her mouth — maybe looking a bit sexier than he was comfortable with — he just tipped his head and wished her a nice day. Then he moved on to bother Peggy, as well as the other infected residents of Sunny Day.

A bit later, after she'd cleaned up and applied fresh makeup, Danny's shiny black car pulled into the spot out front. Jordache hurried, grabbing her purse. It was a real *Pretty Woman* thing, when he came in his nice ride, but she didn't want him coming in. His car, which was a total mess inside, proved he was grounded. But even though Danny knew where she lived and had seen how nicely she kept her small place, Jordache still didn't like reminding him of her station. He had money — more than he should, for sure. And although she wanted to be proud, it wasn't always easy.

"Where we goin'?" Jordache asked Danny, opening his passenger door and dodging an empty McDonald's Big Mac box that tumbled out from inside.

Danny's smile came slowly.

"First, we need to get some pancakes," he said. "After that, I have something to tell you."

# Chapter Twenty-Five

## PURGATORY

"THIS WAY," SAID THE MAN in the hat.

Bobby looked over, crouched behind a large boulder, shaking his head.

"What, you don't believe me?"

"You just don't know the land. Even if the trail does go that way, we can cut to the chase by heading up to the bluff."

"Why did you bother to bring me here if you don't trust my ability to track, Bobby?"

"Don't get offended, Cam. I'm just letting you know something you don't about this particular hunt. I believe you if you say he went that way. But that's toward Purgatory Valley."

"Where the new ones are dropped off?"

"Where they funnel into after they're dropped off, yes. Ferals never go there. Something they smell, if I had to guess. But there's a ridge in that direction, and there's only one way it can go other than Purgatory, and it's to a bluff farther east. If you want to follow the path, we'll waste hours. But if we go right to where he's headed anyway, maybe we can cut him off."

"How do you figure?" Cam seemed to realize he was speaking too loudly, so he squatted and lowered his voice. Bobby could see the trampled vegetation sneaking out onto the ridge past Cam. Deadheads weren't subtle, and picking up trails through brush wasn't hard. It was the details that could be tricky: things like recentness through an area, how many were traveling, their gait and/or health (if there was such a thing for deadheads), and speed. That's why Cam was here.

"It's a hard path. Narrow. Perilous. It'll take him a lot longer to reach the bluff than us, if we go around."

"Maybe he'll fall to his death."

Bobby shook his head. "Not Golem."

"You said he was two years dead."

"He is. But he's special."

Cam raised an eyebrow. He was Bobby's friend — a professional hunter and tracker, a flat-out mercenary, based on what the company was paying him. But he was also officially Panacea, and couldn't stop thinking about containment.

"Special?"

"They're not totally mindless, Cam. You should know that."

"I don't know that at all. I believe they are the very *definition* of mindless."

"They're like animals. Not intelligent in the ways we are, but intelligent in a few base, primal ways. They'll run right at guns, but they know what's meat and what's not."

"That's not smarts. That's survival. And shit, Bobby. They're not picky. They'll eat meat that's been dead for a year."

"And then they always find something fresh immediately after," Bobby countered. "They might not know that the old, winter-preserved meat isn't giving them what they need, but their bodies do. They need protein or something."

"So they get hungry," said Cam. "Color me impressed."

"All I'm saying is that if you walked that path and he walked it, I'm betting on him to survive it over you. Even slouching along like they do. Maybe it keeps them lower to the ground. Lets them use their arms to stabilize."

"Until their arms rot off," Cam grumbled.

Bobby rolled his eyes. They didn't all rot to the core, and Cam damn well knew it. Sherman Pope mattered because it strengthened a body that should know well enough to stay dead.

Cam moved forward, down the path. He peeked out then turned to Bobby.

"Your path. To the left?"

Bobby nodded.

"This goes straight."

"It'll hook back."

"I see your hook-back. I see your deadhead's footprints past it."

*"Footprints?"*

"Christ, Bobby, yes. Look for yourself."

Bobby followed Cam and peeked through the fork, where the ridge continued on to the left. Straight ahead, on the easier of the paths, was an obvious line of shuffling footprints. Headed toward Purgatory Valley.

"He went into the valley?" Bobby said, aghast.

"Why is that so crazy?"

"They never go into the valley."

"But why wouldn't they? They don't think. You act like they do. Shit, Bobby. I say this to you as a friend, but you've been out here too long. When's the last time you stayed out of the park for more than a week?"

"Last month."

Cam sighed. "You were still in the park."

"In the cleared section!"

"Come on. You climbed El Capitan so you could see into the reserve from above. First time anyone's ever done a climb like that for utilitarian reasons. I swear, your brain is getting infected in here. Like you're *breathing* the shit. They're fucking *zombies*, Bobby. This one you're after? This fool's errand you're on? It's become an obsession. For your own good, when I get back, I'm calling in favors. Get Calais to dispatch someone to take it out. And then you'll never be able to say I never assassinated anyone for you. You're welcome."

Bobby didn't give Cam the dignity of a response. He had a good one, though. The truth was that at some point, Golem's tracker had stopped relaying information. Officially, the brass who'd return Bobby's calls said that the early chips were flaky and that it'd probably been smashed against a rock in a deadhead fit or saturated with decayed body fluids. The most interesting hypothesis involved Golem losing his hand to rot or an animal attack and the hand subsequently dropping to the bottom of a lake. But regardless, the only official evidence that Golem was still out there came from Bobby's own eyes — and, sometimes, cameras. Good luck calling someone to take him out, if nobody knew where he was.

Not for the first time, hearing his own thoughts, Bobby wondered if Cam and the others were right. Maybe he *was* obsessed. Just because you could manage something wasn't reason enough to pull out all the stops of rationality to do it. The expression said that mountain climbers climbed "because it's there," but Bobby's obsession piggybacked on that one. He'd climbed not because El Capitan was there, but in order to better see the true object of his attention.

Bobby sighed. He pushed past Cam, knowing he was losing even the tracker's paid attention. Cam would do what he'd been hired to do, but little more. Being Bobby's friend didn't mean he'd stay on the job. Being his friend made him more likely to bail after today, for Bobby's own good.

They headed through the fork, down the hill's slow decline. As Cam had said, the loose, sandy surface was clearly marked with recent footprints. They were huge, like a professional basketball player's. If they weren't Golem's, they were the Incredible Hulk's.

"He's never come down here before," Bobby said. "Not since the beginning. None of them have."

"First time for everything. Maybe he was homesick."

Bobby gave Cam an annoyed glance, feeling patronized. That was one nice thing about spending time with Alice Frank: She was a veteran as far as deadheads and necrotics were concerned, but she'd been a Yosemite virgin. It was the perfect mix. New enough to be shocked and impressed, but knowledgeable enough to appreciate what was happening. She hadn't condescended to Bobby. She'd looked up to him, duly fascinated by his theories rather than feeling pity because he had them.

The slight thrumming that had been in the background for the past hour became slightly louder. Bobby looked up, annoyed. The sky here could be big if you were high enough and the area was clear enough, but Purgatory Valley — empty now, as there hadn't been a recent drop-off — was the opposite. The sky here was much smaller, and Bobby's rule was that he'd tolerate the helicopter's presence as long as he couldn't see it and it didn't scare away the deadheads. The latter was easy; deadheads didn't scare much. But he could see the damned blades, creating an arc of gray at the corner of the sky.

"Tell that fucking thing to give us some space," Bobby said.

Cam looked like he might protest, maybe pointing out that cover couldn't be blown when your prey didn't have more than a semblance of a brain. But instead he pulled out his walkie and spoke into it. The helicopter moved back just enough to comply.

"I've been hunting a long time, Cam. I don't need to be babysat."

Cam looked like he might disagree. The helicopter had been Cindy's idea. She'd blamed it on Cam's newness to hunting human prey and the uncertainties involved, but really it was an excuse. Bobby wasn't an idiot. He was ratings gold, but there had been whispers lately. He couldn't keep raking in the sponsorships if he got killed doing something stupid, like letting his wild goose chase get the best of him.

"Let's go," Bobby said.

After a moment, Cam moved to take the lead, studying the rather obvious trail before Bobby could ruin it. But he didn't need Cam for this; Golem, for reasons unknown, had rolled out the red carpet.

Soon, they found themselves on the Purgatory Valley floor, just north of the rudimentary huts that had seemed to make Alice so sad. The rescue 'copter was out of sight, but with their feet stilled its sound was as obnoxious to Bobby as an insect's buzzing.

"That way," Cam said, pointing.

Toward the huts.

They moved down. The valley wasn't narrow, but the land did roll upward on both sides. During periods of heavy rain, there was an impromptu river through the center of Purgatory Valley, and Bobby, with mixed emotions, had watched the doomed drink from it. He hated running into grazers and was thankful they hadn't seen any today. They tended to hole up, still possessing enough sense for self-preservation. But when they neared the rage point, most of them came out. That was when things got tricky. It was only legal to shoot deadheads that attacked, meaning that a good offense, inside the reserve, was definitely *not* the best defense. You couldn't precisely *hunt* as a Yosemite hunter; that's what he'd tried to explain to Alice. You had to stalk, startle, then shoot back before the prey managed to kill you first.

They reached the huts. Below was a narrower section of valley the sometimes-river had carved in the hills, and that was unfailingly the way the doomed went as their minds departed and they left their shelters. Above was the trailhead that circled out onto the ridge to the bluff.

Cam was studying the ground, frowning.

"What?" Bobby asked.

"He didn't continue on that way. He … "

Bobby's head perked up. He'd heard it too.

Then he heard something else, from the other side.

"He's here," Cam whispered.

But Bobby knew the park far better than Cam did. He knew the way sounds echoed. And even with the goddamned helicopter overhead providing auditory cover for the deadheads, Bobby knew full well that there were more around them than Golem.

Another thing Bobby knew, that Cam didn't, was that Purgatory Valley was one of the single most difficult spots to land a 'copter, or even approach with one.

The color had drained from Cam's face. He was holding the walkie, but it was merely crackling with news from above, broadcasting something that Bobby had already figured out.

Bobby lifted his gun from its strap and moved it up to his eye, willing his breath to slow down.

“They surrounded us,” Cam whispered.

“Put away that radio,” Bobby said, swinging the barrel as he waited for the hiding deadheads to show themselves, “and raise your fucking weapon.”

# Chapter Twenty-Six

## VIOLATIONS

*YOU'RE BEING RIDICULOUS.*

BRIDGET KNEW that, of course. Repeating it inside her mind changed nothing and was just the sort of *neener-neener* thing her brain never did as a spontaneous college kid, started doing when she'd become a mom, and now only ceased again with a little pharmaceutical help. *You're being ridiculous* — along with other goodies like *I'm sure it's nothing, It'll be fine*, and the simple *Relax* — were anti-affirmations in affirmations' clothing. Self-help murmurings that created the opposite feeling of what they were intended to.

*You're being ridiculous* was something Bridget only heard herself thinking when she was reasonably sure she wasn't being ridiculous at all.

And *It'll be fine* was something she only thought when she was almost positive that things were miles from *fine.*

But this time, she felt reasonably sure that, past experiences aside, she truly *was* being ridiculous.

Maybe it was the Zen.

Maybe she'd been taking too much. Gabriella sometimes took three of the little pills in a day, but she was hardly a proper girl's role model. Gabriella had affairs because she deserved them, because her husband was always away, and because they "strengthened her marriage." Seeing as the excuses didn't work as a coherent whole (was she more into strengthening her marriage or getting her due for *deserving it*?), Bridget, hearing them, smelled rationalization. Because Gabriella believed what served her best, and what she wanted to believe.

Bridget had always thought that Zen made those little lies easier to believe.

Forget about self-murmuring; drugs would make everything better.

Or so she thought, before Gabriella had finally convinced her to give one of the pills a shot. And it had been nice. For a while, there'd been no worry whatsoever. She'd felt perfectly balanced. She hadn't been zoned out and careless, nor had she been a bundle of nerves. No wonder Zen was so expensive, not technically available to people like Bridget except on the suburban black market — it performed exactly as promised, with zero side effects.

But now she was taking one a day. Because why not? It wasn't a bad drug. It was safe. Just something to take the edge off.

It dulled the edge so effectively, in fact, that Bridget didn't particularly want to go through days without her *mother's little helper*.

She wasn't addicted.

She enjoyed being calm.

Except that a few times lately, she'd had doubts — like right now. Looking at the house phone, repeating to herself that she was being ridiculous … which meant that a rather large part of Bridget was sure she wasn't being ridiculous at all.

Maybe Zen was making her too used to … well … *a state of Zen.* And maybe she had lost the ability to deal with something as simple as a woman calling for her husband.

Never mind that the phone was bundled into the home's base network package, accessible only via a long computer address because they'd never bothered to get a real number. They both had mobiles, and even Ana had been carrying a cell since her last birthday. There was no need to establish a number. The phone sat there, costing nothing extra, available as a failsafe to call out in an emergency.

*You're being ridiculous, Bridget. If Ian was trying to keep something from you, why would he give out the home telephone … well, it's not even a* number, *is it?*

If Ian didn't want Bridget to know about a female caller, he would use his cell.

Except that Bridget paid the bills and saw his call log. That's a tip Gabriella had given her when encouraging Bridget to experiment with an affair of her own — something she'd never considered, other than in the most distant, quickly dismissible *what if* sort of way. It seemed safe to have your lover call your cell, but all those calls appeared on the bill. And what if he called during dinner and you'd forgotten to turn off your phone?

Best to get a second mobile.

And pay for it separately.

Except that it was one more expense to track (an expense certain husbands might notice), so why not forward the home phone line to a new cell? It supposedly wasn't hard to do and was almost entirely invisible. Bridget hadn't looked into it much because she wasn't going to have any affairs. But maybe Ian had.

*And then he'd forgotten to forward the calls so it'd ring right here in the house? Don't be stupid, Bridget.*

That was logical thinking, sure. But then why had the woman hung up when Bridget had answered, shocked that the phone had rung at all?

Why had she hung up twice? The first time, she asked for Ian before breaking the connection — sounding decidedly nervous, eager to find him fast. But the second time, she'd just hung up. It *had* to be the same person.

The same *woman*.

Bridget picked up her cell and called Ian. No answer.

Because he was at work, of course. Where else would he be? Never mind that he could slip out at any time. Never mind that he'd been working late more often. Never mind that he broke his own rule and took a work call at home. Never mind that he'd clearly been keeping something from her earlier then had grown nervous about something (possibly something incriminating) he might have lost. Never mind that after dinner, he'd closed himself in his study. With the lights down, as if to set a mood.

*He's just working hard. That's all.*

Bridget walked the upstairs hallway, paused at their bedroom, and cast her gaze toward the corner where, if she entered, she'd find the master bathroom.

But no. She wouldn't surrender to Zen. She was being irrational, and you couldn't just erase. It was a bad idea to get used to abdicating your emotions. She was being dumb, and needed to re-learn the trick of getting past being stupid. She didn't used to be this way. She used to be fun. She used to be outrageous and spontaneous.

The next room was Ian's office.

Maybe she should check his computer.

She couldn't. She *wouldn't*. It would be a violation. Ian wasn't the paranoid type *(Like me, har-har,* Bridget thought), so his home, including his office, tended to be an open book. Somehow, snooping where she'd barely have to exert any effort was so much worse than snooping by digging deep and attempting to access hidden records.

Which she'd never do, of course.

The woman on the phone could have been anyone. A colleague with her wires crossed. Maybe someone from the Internet company, informing Ian that his bill was overdue or that he could get a new TV package for 30 percent off this month.

Except that the only way for anyone to ring that phone would be to have … well … Bridget actually had no idea how anyone would ring that phone, but she doubted it could happen by accident.

Had that woman sounded hot? Yes, Bridget thought she had. Her voice was urgent, authoritative in a way that wasn't off-putting, a little throaty, a little sexy.

Ian's computer monitor came on. Possibly because Bridget had pushed the power button. Then his search history appeared on the screen. Possibly because Bridget's finger had dragged across the screen, pulling it front and center.

*Stop it.*

She closed the window. Turned off the monitor. Mostly because Ian deserved his privacy and her trust, seeing as he'd never once — not even a tiny little bit — given her any reason to doubt him. Ian loved Bridget more than she sometimes thought she deserved. Their marriage was perfect. Ideal. They had sex three times a week, and sometimes more. Never mind that he was keeping secrets and getting calls from attractive women.

Besides, there'd been nothing interesting on that first page of history. Just work stuff. She'd seen a page about protein synthesis. An epidemiology website. A search for Rip Daddy and another for something called BioFuse.

See? He wasn't hiding anything. Not in here, anyway.

So really, there was no reason not to look through his file history, too.

Bridget had the screen back on a second later and was pushing her finger around the screen when her own phone, in her pocket, began to ring. The sudden noise startled her, and she almost poked Ian's monitor right off the desk. Her eyes flicked toward the open door to the hallway, sure that she'd see him standing there, holding up his phone, having rushed back after seeing her missed call. Because Bridget meant everything to Ian, whereas he apparently wasn't even worth her trust.

Heart racing for no reason, Bridget looked at her cell's screen. It was Gabriella.

"I want lunch," Gabriella said when Bridget answered, before Bridget could say hello. "Let's have lunch."

"Oh, Gabs, I don't know ..." Bridget said, half her attention still guiltily on Ian's screen.

"Then let's have cocktails." Gabriella gave her a rich young woman's carefree giggle. "Or at least *tell* a few of them."

Bridget swiped the history away, prepared to close the file history. What did it matter what he'd opened and modified lately? What was she expecting to find? Naked pictures?

But instead of swiping, her finger jabbed, and one of the files opened — or at least attempted to. A dialog box came up that read, *Volume not connected. Insert drive [x].*

"The club," Gabriella said. "We'll go together? Give me five minutes to finish getting beautiful, and I'll walk over. You're driving."

Bridget touched another file, barely hearing her neighbor's voice. And another file, and another. They all had cryptic names, but none were available, all on some sort of a removable drive that wasn't plugged in. Something Ian had been browsing through — and then had disconnected and hidden.

"I know you're just plodding around over there with nothing better to do," Gabriella said. "I can see you through my binoculars." Another well-bred giggle. "And *just wait* until I tell you what else I saw with these babies, over at Bella's staff house, when the pool boys were getting into uniform."

"Sure," Bridget said.

After Gabriella hung up, Bridget tried Ian again. She tried his office and got his assistant. Tried his cell and got voicemail. But he always gave her a rundown of his day, and hadn't mentioned a single scheduled meeting.

Bridget went into the bedroom and exchanged her pants and shirt for a simple blue dress — not because the country club expected it, but because if she didn't fem it up a bit, she'd feel like a redheaded boy beside Gabriella.

The master bath was right off the master bedroom.

She really needed to calm down, so that she could think straight.

One little pill couldn't possibly hurt.

## Chapter Twenty-Seven

### THIS IS WHERE WE LEAVE YOU

THE MEN WITH THE GUNS were very polite. Once they had Ian's attention and made it clear where he'd be going next (i.e., "with them"), they'd practically started offering him hot towels for the ride. One seemed to be named Paul. The other man must have gone by his last name, because the first called him Stonegate. They weren't cops, Ian didn't think — maybe private security.

They sat in the limo's cabin, near the partition. Ian was in back with the wet bar, where he could be shot easily if he tried anything dumb.

Not that anyone was going to shoot him, or had threatened to. But men who carried guns were probably willing to use them, and right now, as keyed up as he was over things these men might not even know, Ian couldn't get that thought out of his mind.

"Where are we going?" Ian asked.

"As we told you, Mr. Keys," said Paul. "We're going to Hemisphere."

Ian looked through the tinted glass. "This isn't the way to Hemisphere."

"To the Apex facility, sir."

"Why?"

Stonegate answered. His voice was like sandpaper that's learned to behave. "Would you like something to drink, sir?"

Rather than asking again, Ian simply watched the passing scenery. The less he said, the better — and that included requests to know more about their errand. The two big men in suits who'd grabbed him earlier ("escorted," they said) refused to say more. Asking would only make him seem weak, and possibly guilty. The men had called him sir, opened doors, asked if he was comfortable. But this wasn't the way most summonses happened, and Ian didn't particularly want to rock the boat and find out why things were unfolding as they were — or what he may have done to require it.

Other than steal company data, of course.

Which, really, wasn't confidential at all. It was ... *suggestive*. Pointing to a link between ... well, he didn't understand what the link was between either.

"Do you work for Hemisphere?" Ian asked the two big men.

"Yes, Mr. Keys," Paul said.

"It's a great company."

Neither of the big men said anything.

Ten minutes later, the limousine pulled up to a glass-and-aluminum structure that Ian had seen a number of times — on the news, on specials like Alice Frank's, in the photos of company gatherings. Hemisphere's business happened mostly in the five-building complex Ian called home, but *this*, as far as the media was concerned, was the heart of the world's best-known company. The sleek, five-story Apex building was where the magic happened. According to modern legend, Necrophage was formulated, tested, and declared to arrest the progress of Sherman Pope by the FDA here, in a landmark press conference.

It was a beautiful building, mostly utilitarian — labs and think tanks — with a final distinction well known by the media: because Archibald Burgess would always be a scientist at heart, he preferred to be near his research at all times, sitting atop it in his round-room office with its panoramic view of the valley beyond.

"Shit," said Paul.

"Shit," Stonegate echoed, looking out the windows.

Paul rapped the partition with his knuckles. It descended with a whir.

"Shit," said the driver, who'd apparently already noticed whatever it was.

"You can say that again," Paul muttered.

"It must be because of the Alice Frank special."

"What must be?" Ian asked.

"Just sit tight, Mr. Keys. We're going to take you around to the rear entrance." He made a circular motion in the air with his finger then traded glances with the black-capped driver to make sure he'd heard and understood.

Halfway across the Apex's expansive, manicured front lawn, the limo bore to the right on one of the sweeping concrete driveways. When it did, Ian found he could see what the others had been talking about: the building's front entrance was crawling with crowds of people. The building had always had an open-grounds policy and actively encouraged lab tours to dissuade watchdog suspicions, but right now it was backfiring. Of all the watchdogs who'd caused trouble for Hemisphere, Alice Frank was the most persistent. Her special had been fair, Ian thought, but it definitely broadcast the slant Raymond had mentioned earlier. Ian hadn't come to Apex in months, but judging by the reactions up front, it wasn't usually this besieged with press. The lawn, near the doors, was flooded with news vans.

The rear entrance was protected by a gate, and the limo made it through before the people at the building's front noticed and ran over. But the ease of their escape stopped there because the rear seemed to be meant for deliveries, not luxury cars. There was a sharp decline to a loading dock area filled with detached trailers. The concrete was bumpy enough to warble Stonegate's voice when he talked.

"Do you have your Hemisphere card, Mr. Keys?"

"Of course."

The man nodded then spoke into his lapel. Ian hadn't noticed, but they seemed to be wearing mics like the old Secret Service used to. Ian didn't hear what was said because the limo rumbled over a ventilation grate and into an empty loading dock slot when he was speaking. When the car came to a stop, Stonegate opened the door for Ian and pointed without leaving the vehicle, his door being held open by a more pedestrian security guard in blue.

"Give him your card," Stonegate said. "We were supposed to take you through the front, but … well, you saw. You'll need to pass through an intelligent elevator, so it's simplest to re-key you for the day rather than taking the long way."

Ian's eyes flicked back toward the building's front, now hidden by walls of concrete and glass.

"Is it always like this?"

"More lately than Mr. Burgess would like. But not like this."

"Mr. Burgess? Is that why I'm here? To see him?"

The notion made a curious knot in Ian's throat. Ordinarily, a chance to speak with Archibald Burgess should feel like a ticket to see the Wizard of Oz. The man was one of his idols, and Ian's mother's life-extension bestseller was, supposedly, largely inspired by Hemisphere's pre-Sherman Pope days. But today, he was still dragging guilt like an iron chain, made worse by the strange way he'd been called here and that fact that he, too, had just watched Alice Frank's skeptical documentary. Fear had mingled with his usual awe. Now, visiting the company's head brought trepidation, as well.

"Straight ahead there, sir," said Paul. "Give him your card."

Ian exited. The limo doors closed and then, while he stood like a statue, pulled away.

And then it was just Ian and the guard, who was half-stooped, his face looking somewhat vacant and hungry, patiently waiting.

The guard breathed too heavily, like a wounded dog. His skin was pale, slack, and losing cohesion below the eyes. Ian tried not to stare, but even a quick glance showed him the man's brown, half-dead facial muscles around the pits of his eyes. His mouth was similarly slack, giving him the loose-jawed manner of a stroke victim. The whole face looked fake, like a mask. Ian almost wanted to grab his nose and pull.

He held up his card. "The guys who brought me in said I needed to … "

"THIF WAY," the guard said, too loudly.

He snatched the card like an animal taking food. Ian sensed a quick glance at his hand and, a bit ashamed, stifled a flinch. If the guard was working — working *at Hemisphere,* no less — then he was perfectly safe. But Ian had risen through the company quickly and had grown more used to non-necrotics than he'd want to admit. They just didn't earn that well, equality laws or no. When Ian had been in college, it had looked like white Anglo men would stay on top forever. Those old prejudices had given way to disease-based distinctions. In some parts of town, there were even separate water fountains. When necrotics flew on planes, they always seemed to wind up in the back with their own kind, sometimes jokingly referred to as "the dead end."

There was no need to be a bigot. But in secret, it seemed like everyone was.

The guard slid Ian's key card into a machine, pressed some buttons, and handed it back. Ian suppressed doubts that the card would work when it was needed and headed where he was told, toward what looked like a decrepit service elevator at the end of a long basement hallway.

The hallway was lined with doors, each with a wheel-type lock on the front. There were small handwritten designations on dry-erase boards beside the rooms: sequences of numbers and letters, then a large number below. In many cases, the larger, lower number had been crossed out and rewritten one or two numbers lower, like one that went *11-10-8*.

"What are these rooms?" Ian asked, not expecting a response. Either the guard would be too dim to explain, or it would be yet something else Ian wasn't, apparently, supposed to know.

"Tetht animalth."

"Like lab rats?"

"Other kind," the guard said.

Ian was about to ask what that meant, but by then they were entering the elevator, which flashed green on entry, meaning the guard must have properly re-keyed his card after all. Before the elevator's doors opened, one of the wheeled doors began to spin then opened with a hiss. A white-coated scientist emerged wearing a simple paper mask and gloves.

Behind her, Ian saw a line of cages filled with thrashing feral deadheads.

The elevator moved upward. Then it dinged and slid open. Ian found himself facing Paul and Stonegate once again. How they'd entered or why they'd separated, Ian had no idea, but they flanked him and left the guard behind.

The upstairs hallway was significantly nicer than the basement, but the elevator itself seemed dingy enough to have been relegated to rear passages. It took a few turns and another keying-in (still green; good job, dead guard) before Ian found himself in a pristine office hallway with fancy wallpaper and stainless steel light fixtures. They traversed another few turns and finally came to a large, thick-wood door bearing the inscription *ARCHIBALD BURGESS. PRESIDENT.*

Paul knocked on the door.

"This is where we leave you," he said when the doorknob began to turn. "Have a good day, Mr. Keys."

# Chapter Twenty-Eight

## REDEFINING NATURE

ARCHIBALD BURGESS WAS TALL, LEAN, and had what could only be described as a powerful presence. Ian had read all about the man and talked to him once or twice (never intimately, always in a crowd), but it took being with him to appreciate that the rumors seemed to be true: The man was in his seventies, but his movements were as smooth and energetic as someone in his twenties. Archibald Burgess, the press joked, might just live forever.

"Ian! It's good to see you again." Burgess extended a large hand. Ian took it and shook, following rather than leading, wondering which "again" the man was referring to.

"Good to see you too, sir."

"Don't call me sir, Ian. Even my father wasn't a sir, and he lived in Britain most of his life. Call me Archibald. Or, if you insist, Archie."

Ian didn't want to insist. After all his idolizing — and all the idolizing the world as a whole had bestowed upon the man — there was no way Ian could ever call him *Archie*. Or even *Archibald*, for that matter.

"How are things over at headquarters?" Burgess went on.

"They're fine."

"Do you have everything you need?"

"Um … sure."

"You have an open line to me, Ian. I want you to keep that in mind. Anything you need, you just call or send word through Raymond. I try to keep an open-door policy at all times, especially for this company's key lieutenants. But lately it's been tricky, what with all the wolves at the door."

To his right, Ian could just make out the tops of the news vans he'd seen earlier on the front lawn. The Apex was situated so that the only way to look into Burgess's office was to stake out a place off the grounds. Unless they walked to the edges, they were mostly invisible. And of course, if Burgess wanted, he could lower blinds or tint the windows.

"I noticed the wolves at the door," Ian said.

Burgess nodded. He was supposedly a meticulous eater, following most of the diet outlined in Ian's mother's book. His arms were lean. The old skin hung at his neck, but the look wasn't a bad one. He didn't seem old despite his wrinkles and thinning hair. He seemed like an imposing man in sheep's clothing.

"Raymond talked to you about that, I assume?"

"He asked me to review Alice Frank's latest special. The one from Yosemite."

"That's what I mean. I believe in the free press, Ian. And despite all the blabbing you hear today about civil liberties and rights and how Panacea has too much authority, that's one thing that hasn't been stifled. As long as anyone can say whatever they want about those in charge

— or in positions of authority — then freedom isn't threatened. Don't you agree?"

He didn't wait for Ian to weigh in before continuing.

"I actually like Alice Frank. The press sets us up as adversaries. She's 'trying to catch Hemisphere and Archibald Burgess doing something wrong' and we're 'soldiering on and trying to keep saving the world despite the accusations.' But who is the good guy or gal there, and who is the bad one?"

"Maybe it's just a difference of opinion."

Burgess stabbed a finger at Ian. They were ten feet apart, and there Ian was, still waiting for an offer to sit.

"Exactly. That's *exactly* what it is. She's doing her job, and that's watching to make sure no abuses are taken. I admire her for it. I've read much of her stuff. But even so, some of her facts and many of her more subtle implications are simply incorrect, and it would be irresponsible — not just within this company, but to the world we report to as well — to simply let those inaccuracies go. So it's not a war. It's not them against us. This is the natural balance." He walked a few steps closer to the window over the lawn, now seeing the farthest vans. "This is the way of life, of evolution."

Burgess turned to Ian, waiting for something Ian couldn't imagine. A response, or perhaps applause.

Instead, Ian found himself asking his most impertinent question.

"Why did you have people drag me in here?"

"*Drag*?"

"I was on my way to the office. Getting out of my car and crossing the parking lot. They came up and took me by the arms."

"They were asked to retrieve and escort you here."

"They could have asked. I dropped my phone on the ground when one of them grabbed me."

"Were you hurt? Did they hurt you?"

Ian watched Burgess's eyes, suddenly seeing exactly what game was being played. Of course he knew what had happened. There were no mistakes. There was a reason Ian had always idolized Burgess: his unflinching boldness in going after what he wanted, letting nothing stand in his way. Men like Burgess didn't ask permission, or apologize. The company's first stem cell research had taken place in Singapore, where it was encouraged rather than restricted. When he'd opened a subsidiary to use research in America that the States wouldn't have allowed him to gather, he hadn't asked. He'd looked everyone in the eye and dared someone to stop him. Maybe in time, someone would have. But Rip Daddy happened first.

"Of course not," Ian said.

"Was your phone damaged?"

"No."

Burgess's face didn't change, but its question did. It said, *If you're fine and nothing was broken, what are you whining about?*

Burgess turned, paced to his desk, then leaned against it, his posture like a college kid.

"Do you believe in evolution, Ian?"

"Of course I do."

"Don't answer so quickly. We all learned about it in school. Men from apes. Or rather, men *are* apes. Only a fool or a fundamentalist would deny it. But I'm not asking about evolution's past. I'm asking about its present."

"Its present?"

"I began Hemisphere with two premises. The first was that evolution, in modern society, had been stopped in its tracks, and that we as a people have been artificially kept alive by medicine. The second was that without that crutch, we might have advanced again — but that *with* the crutch, we'd never change. Never become what nature intends us to be."

"I don't follow."

"Everything we've made has improved through selective pressures. Capitalism only allows the strong to survive — in this case, strong ideas, strong companies. When media went DIY — independent music, books, movies, and more, at prices that were affordable by anyone — society itself (not a handful of high-powered executives) became the selection force that made art better. The same is true of technology: Only the best were purchased; only the best advanced. Natural selection works for everything, Ian. Everything but us."

Burgess picked up a paperweight, twirled it, set it back down.

"Disease and predators no longer thin the weak and unfit from the human population. It's not only the *best adapted* genes that get passed on to the next generation to make humanity stronger as a species. Now, thanks to medicine, *all* genes get passed on. Our diseases aren't making us stronger. Those diseases are simply being forced to adapt. If they can't kill off our weak, the selective pressures simply need to become stronger. It's almost as if evolution has flipped: instead of improving us, it's improving the pressures allied against us."

Ian shook his head.

"I know you've been talking to the press, Ian."

Ian felt blindsided. He'd settled into Burgess's monologue, and now here was this pat accusation. He was unprepared. His most naked response was unfolding as Burgess watched — surely the old man's intention.

"It's okay. They're persistent, and the best, like Alice

Frank, have a way of finding modes of contact they shouldn't have, to bypass official company channels. I'd never forbid anyone from speaking what they feel is the truth. But it is important to me that if my people talk behind my back, I have a chance to correct any misperceptions they may have first."

"I haven't been … behind your back … " Ian stammered.

"After I watched Alice's documentary about Yosemite, I came away with a few distinct impressions. They're why I asked Raymond to talk to you, and then for you and a few others to decide the best way to respond: overtly, through our PR channels, or subtly, by shifts in direction. We're not perfect, Ian. None of us are, and Hemisphere certainly isn't. But I don't think it's as Alice suggests. If this was about money, we'd charge for Necrophage's base formulation instead of making it freely available. She's pointed out before that we receive government stipends as compensation, but she doesn't point out that those stipends are a drop in the bucket. This company, by all accounts, *loses* hundreds of millions of dollars each year providing the drug. Did you know that?"

"Sure, I — "

"Another thing this misinformed crowd of media folks outside seems to believe is that we're in bed with Panacea. We have partnerships, of course. Panacea's purpose is to contain Sherman Pope, and efficient Necrophage distribution is a large part of that. But despite her allegations in that piece, this has never been a heartless company bent on power."

"I don't think the world sees Hemisphere as heartless, Mr. Burgess. Quite the opposite, actually."

"Of course. But disruption *always* starts small. Evolution again. It always begins with a few individuals and a critical change. Evolution walks hand in hand with chaos. Neither can be contained. But we must try to guide and shape it. Right now, our detractors are a small group. But tell me: After you watched that piece, did you begin to wonder if the way we handle the terminally infected individuals in this country is right? Did you feel for the MP whose job involves escorting hunters who book vacations to hunt people a few degrees farther down the ladder than her?"

"It's the least of evils. I think people understand that."

"Maybe." Burgess shrugged. "But I'm troubled by the direction of your inquiries."

"My ... *my* inquiries?"

"I don't blame you for being curious. But perhaps you can tell me what exactly you think is the matter with our systems? I can tell you all day that this company's purpose has always been to foster humanity's potential — through our non-Necrophage lines as a matter of progress and through Necrophage as a matter of triage — but that means nothing if you believe something different."

"I'm sorry, sir. I don't know what you mean."

"Please, Ian. Don't call me sir."

Burgess picked up an apple from his desk and took a large, crisp-sounding bite. Then he chewed, waiting for Ian to speak next.

"I honestly don't know what you mean. Alice Frank has tried to call me. But I haven't spoken to her. I've hung up each time."

"Why?"

"She should go through official channels. And she's a troublemaker with an axe to grind."

"So says your sense of loyalty. But do you honestly not think she has any valid points?"

"Well ..."

"And the files our IT department tells me you've been browsing and copying. I can't make sense of them, and I'm sure I know the research far better than you could, no offense. I'm just wondering what point you're trying to establish. None of it is confidential, other than the fact that it came directly from our systems rather than the Internet. How do you feel it all connects, Ian?"

"I didn't pick any of it out! It was shoved at me!"

Burgess's face changed. Not to anger, but to a sense of acceptance. Now they were finally shooting straight, no bullshit.

"Is it for August Maughan? Has he been in touch?"

"*August Maughan?* No; I've never even met him. Why?"

"Frankly, he's the only person I can see finding any use for what you seem to be … well, it doesn't matter. If you are talking, please tell him to call me. He was the best, and the conditions that caused him to leave were unfortunate. I question this thing he's supposedly doing now, as a *guru*. But to each his own."

"I haven't talked to him!"

"Or to Alice Frank."

"No." Ian willed himself to calm. If Burgess knew about the calls and the files, what was left to hide? It was all just a big misunderstanding.

Except for the unseen hand he'd felt lately: one incursion telling him to copy, read, and delete, and another somehow connecting his phone to Frank's as if making an introduction. Did Burgess know about that? Should he hide, or volunteer it? He was a company man, not a rat. Hemisphere had nothing to fink on anyway. He could come clean, but said nothing.

"That's good."

Burgess took another bite of his apple, still just staring at Ian. The way he was simply accepting all of this was flat-out emasculating, but Burgess's sense of authority and control was palpable. Ian felt like he'd just run a race, and would be happy to get out of here unscathed.

"Is ... is that all you need from me?"

Burgess answered obliquely. "Do you believe in this company? Do you believe our mission statement — 'Upgrading Nature' — is more than just hyperbole?"

"Yes. Of course."

Burgess nodded, seemingly satisfied. "That's good. I respect you, Ian. Your mother's book is my bible, and the apple—" He held up his own half-eaten fruit. "Does not fall far from the tree. There's a reason I greenlit your speedy climb. Especially today, in this time of rapid social evolution, we need minds like yours to thrive. Survival of the fittest, am I right?"

"Survival of the fittest," Ian parroted.

"As we face opposition, a firm and convicted belief in the mission at hand is the only thing that can keep us on course."

"Sure."

Burgess touched something on his desk. The door opened, and the two black-suited men appeared, as if they'd been waiting just outside.

"Paul and Richard will take you back to HQ. I'm sorry to have occupied so much of your time."

Ian fought the urge to reply that the visit was an honor. He wouldn't kneel that deeply, even though it was exactly how he felt.

"It's no problem," he said instead.

They exchanged a handshake. Then, halfway to the door, Burgess called out.

"Ian."

Ian turned.

"You're a good man with priorities for yourself and

your family firmly in order. I'm glad to hear you're with, rather than against, us."

Ian managed to nod, but it wasn't easy to swallow.

It was hard to forget the manner in which he'd been brought here, and harder not to hear Archibald's parting words as a threat.

# Chapter Twenty-Nine

## PUBLIC RELATIONS

ALICE DIDN'T BELIEVE IN GHOSTS, spirits, ESP, life after death (other than the kind that lived next door), the Law of Attraction, or fate. But she managed to believe in intuition. *That's* what had led Alice to her initial leads in her first story as a reporter. Intuition had steered her toward loose ends in the Rip Daddy outbreak, and had told her to watch closely when it morphed into Sherman Pope. Intuition told her that Hemisphere and Archibald Burgess, though they were the world's darlings, were hiding something — not that they were playing dirty, necessarily, though that seemed possibly true as well. Intuition told Alice to keep picking at scabs when others would give up. There was no reason, not really. Just a strong and unrelenting feeling.

Alice didn't *need* intuition to think that Ian Keys was in trouble.

But it did suggest that whatever had gone wrong, it had to do with her. With this almost-story she sensed just below the surface. To do with Necrophage and its various formulations. That feeling had itched upon receipt of the packet then bloomed when she'd spoken to Nicole about Kelly's condition. Briefly following August Maughan's trail had been part of that errand, and even her last attempts to get in touch with Bobby Baltimore had carried unasked questions about the drug.

*The drug.*

The text, when she'd been speaking to Ian in that strange *who called whom* call, had said, *Ask him about BioFuse.*

And *that* was starting to ring a bell. Something she'd seen. Having to do with the drug.

The text's sender was undefined. In her history, the message seemed to have come from phone number 0804 — not enough digits to be anything beyond meaningless. But she could go into that history and see the way it had perfectly synced with her incoming call from (not outgoing call to) Ian Keys.

*Ask him about BioFuse.*

Whoever had connected Ian and Alice on the phone had sent that text. Someone who wanted them to talk, and was perhaps passing information to Alice that he or she couldn't send directly. Someone with reason to believe that Ian would *want* to speak to Alice if the right conditions arose.

Alice went for her envelope of meaningless paperwork, surely sent by the same person. On second inspection, nothing in the packet was any more helpful. And still, nothing seemed confidential. She could have printed the same pages after a quick Internet search and a visit to Hemisphere's public relations department.

But Intuition told Alice that despite appearances, there was something in those papers worth noticing. A message sent between the lines.

And sure enough, this time one glossy, tri-fold brochure stood out that hadn't before. It looked like something a drug rep might distribute to doctors, for a pill called BioFuse.

As with everything else her Deep Throat had given her, the brochure wasn't confidential. But when Alice visited the Hemisphere website and searched, she found that BioFuse was no longer among the offerings. They no longer sold it, unless it was being vended through channels that weren't on the website. It wasn't mentioned. Anywhere. At all.

The rest of the web didn't care much about BioFuse, either. There were a handful of search results, entirely uninteresting at first glance. It was something that used to be sold, then was ditched after the company's focus turned to managing Sherman Pope.

Alice opened the brochure. There were a lot of smiling people in it, mostly older. One showed a white-haired couple in the park. In the entire brochure, there were no obvious necrotics. And in PR materials, thanks to Panacea's non-discrimination laws, companies were rarely subtle. Almost everything these days featured someone clearly necrotic. You wanted to show that your company embraced everyone, no matter how awkward the photo shoot might look.

The oversight seemed glaring. Alice's eye had grown so used to over-obvious (almost pandering) inclusion of necrotics, this brochure full of uninfected people seemed almost offensive — unintentionally insulting, but insulting nonetheless. Like an early printing of *Little Black Sambo*.

She picked up one of the magazines on her coffee table. Flipped through. Found an ad for a Walmart. It showed a group of people, all smiling. Every box of humanity had been checked. There were men, women, tall people, short people, young and old. There was a large woman in a wheelchair up front. Every skin color under the sun. And off to one side, too far from the group but maybe the best shot the photographer had been able to get, was a half-slouched man, his arms halfway up and dangling like a mantis at the wrists. Mouth open. Facing away from the group, looking like he was trying to escape.

Alice looked back at the BioFuse brochure. Then back to the Internet.

She had it: The brochure seemed strange because it had been published prior to the outbreaks. Before the reintegration. It was hard to believe there had been an America before Sherman Pope, but here was evidence — of that and more.

She opened the brochure. BioFuse appeared to be one of Hemisphere's early patents, meant for the treatment of Alzheimer's disease.

Alice picked up her phone. She tried Ian's mobile again and got voicemail, as expected. But really, what would Ian know even if she could get him on the line? BioFuse was a dead end. They didn't even make it anymore — and by the looks of the exclusionist brochure, hadn't for years. According to what her source had dropped in Alice's lap and what she'd discovered on her own, Ian had been with Hemisphere for five years and executive vice president for just over one. He wouldn't know anything about this old drug.

She tried his home number anyway. That had borne fruit a time or two, proving one level deeper that the source who'd given her the number actually knew a thing or two. She also had a few email addresses, though she hadn't tried them yet.

But this time, the home number just rang and rang.

Alice sat motionless on the couch, knowing all she could do was pass the time. If Ian Keys had been abducted, she could wait for the story to hit the mainstream news. If he'd merely been called aside, which seemed more likely, she could either wait for him to return her call (unlikely) or wait to try again. She'd put out feelers to find August Maughan, but she'd have to wait and see if anyone underground could find a lead. She'd left a few messages for Bobby, so she had to wait for him, too.

Not that Bobby was likely to know anything. He was a hunter. What would he know about Hemisphere? He'd barely known the company's basics when they'd talked at the Bivouac, both on and off the record. And they'd talked a *lot.* Something about being surrounded all night by vast lands populated by hungry monsters loosened lips.

But there was intuition again, suggesting she call him anyway.

Alice picked up her phone and hit Bobby's number.

To her surprise, he picked up, practically screaming.

# Chapter Thirty

## EXTRACTION

BUT IT WASN'T BOBBY. IT was someone else.

"Hello? *Hello?*" The voice was demanding, as if Alice had committed an atrocity with her call. Out of breath. Manic or in a panic; one of the two.

Alice could hear Bobby in the background. There was a mechanical thrumming, very loud. The phone had some sort of noise cancellation, but it was nowhere near adequate.

"Goddammit, Cam, get off the phone and — "

There was the rapid popping of gunshots. Noise cancellation (or possibly maxing out of the microphone) dulled the sharpest reports, but Alice knew guns when she heard them.

"It's *your* phone, Bobby!" said the man, Cam, closer by.

*"DROP IT, AND GET THAT ONE NEAR THE — "*

Someone yelled. It was a desperate, horrifying kind of cry. The thrumming (a helicopter, Alice decided) changed pitch.

*"How about some warning up there?"* Bobby's voice shouted.

Cam must have lurched. Alice heard things shift and roll, as if the space they were in had been turned on end. She heard a muffled *thwump* then a crack as the phone must have run into something hard. There was a burst of interference, then Cam's voice was back.

"Are you still there? Hello? Hello!"

*"Cam put down the fucking phone, and shoot!"*

More gunshots. More chaos. If they were in a helicopter or near one, it sounded like it was trying to take off. Trying and failing.

"Who is this? Our location is — "

Another lurch. Another crack. This time, the phone must have hit the ground. Alice heard the thing slide across the deck — a low, teeth-rattling drag. Then Cam was snatching it back up, yammering about hellos and locations and how they were in deep-shit trouble. He only shut up when something hit something else, hard. One man grunted, probably Cam, probably punched or shoved.

More evenly, just loud enough to be heard over the rotors, Alice heard Bobby say, "Can I trust you to point this and fire? Or do I have to strap you down like a child?"

"Jesus, Bobby! They can't do that! You said they can't do that!" And then Alice, in Cam's pleading voice, could almost hear the *tell-me-it'll-be-all-right* suffix the man wanted to add: *You promised me.*

Gunshots multiplied. Someone said, "There!" Then they multiplied more.

The helicopter's sounds changed again, and most of the chaos fell silent. Alice could hear muttering, possibly relieved, indistinct. Then the phone was back to being dragged. But this time, no one spoke into it.

She heard Bobby say, "What?"

"It's yours," said Cam's voice, now calmer, still low on breath.

"It's mine?"

"It was in your bag."

"Goddammit, Cam. You're supposed to be a professional. You don't make phone calls in the middle of—"

"I told you. It rang."

Without any visual cues, Alice had to guess at what was going on. She could imagine Bobby frowning, sighing, any one of a full deck of annoyed or patronizing expressions. She had a strange impulse to hang up. She'd only placed a phone call; she'd had no idea what she'd been stepping into. But now Alice felt guilty, as foolish as this man Cam.

"It's still connected?"

No response.

Then Alice heard Bobby's voice, full in the mic, the noise cancellation only moderately able to do its job. He didn't sound nearly as out of breath as Cam had. He addressed her directly, apparently having consulted the thing's now-surely-scratched-to-shit screen.

"Alice?"

"Bad time?"

"You might say that. We were just ambushed."

"Ambushed? By whom?"

"Deadheads."

"I thought you said they couldn't—"

"They can't. It was in Purgatory Valley. It's a natural funnel. They just went down, and we walked right into them."

"I thought you didn't go into Purgatory Valley."

"I don't. We were tracking Golem."

"Did you find him?"

Bobby paused for too long. It was a thoughtful pause, as if weighing more than the situation's objective facts.

"Yes."

"And?"

"What's on your mind, Alice?"

There was some static-filled chatter from behind Bobby. Possibly the pilot, assuming the helicopter had extracted them from the ambush as she imagined. Telling them how far it was back to the DCC base, maybe.

"Call me when you're settled."

"I'm fine."

But for some reason, Alice could only picture Bobby as he'd been in her deleted scenes, telling the story about his mother. His obsession with Golem was unhealthy. Golem was a random deadhead, same as Moby Dick was only a whale. And yet Bobby had heaped his carefully hidden pain atop the zombie's shoulders, as if he'd caused every wrong in Bobby's life.

"It's hard for me to talk to you when I know you were just attacked."

The seriousness was already fading. Alice could hear Public Bobby entering his voice. The man with the stubble and hypnotizing blue eyes, always quick with a handsome joke.

"Haven't you seen my show? I'm *always* 'just attacked.'"

Alice shifted on her couch. She hadn't been kidding. Bobby could grant permission for her casual inquiry, but that wouldn't stop it from feeling awkward. It was a bit like calling someone during a funeral by mistake then being told, *No, no, it's fine. What's up?*

She went for middle ground. "What was happening with the 'copter?"

"They were climbing on it. It was quite the swarm. We could take off once most were cleared, but there were some on the tail, too. I didn't really want to shoot at them back there once we were airborne."

"Oh."

"Looks like you called a few times."

"I can call back."

Still projecting his voice over the rotors, Bobby said, "Don't be ridiculous." Then: "What were you calling for?"

"Have you ever heard of a drug called BioFuse?"

"No."

"It was an early Hemisphere patent. One they discontinued. For treating Alzheimer's disease."

"Maybe that's why I don't remember it." Laugh. Pause. Then: "Sorry. No. I don't know it. Why?"

"Just a feeling."

"Hmm. Was that all you needed?"

"I was wondering about behavior. Deadhead behavior."

"I'm hardly the guy to ask. I just shoot them."

But that wasn't true. Thanks to his peculiar obsession, Bobby had, perhaps unintentionally, ascribed all sorts of traits for the deadheads in Yosemite that even the people around him thought were ridiculous. Mostly they were empty receptacles waiting for his bullets, yes. But a few, like Golem, merited personality.

"When you see them turn, how fast does it happen?"

"I'm not Jane Goodall here, Alice. We're allowed to take down the ones that come at us and leave the rest alone. I don't study them, or watch and wait for them to turn."

"What's your impression?"

"Same as everyone's. It happens over time. A few days for the worst of it."

"And they all seem to rage about three weeks after hitting their inflection points?"

"Well, nobody comes here who's not past the inflection point already. But I assume so."

"The deadheads there. Are they treated? With Necrophage?"

Bobby laughed. "What would be the point?"

"Maybe someone didn't believe the doctors or the clarifiers. Tried to bring someone back."

"Nothing can drag someone from the inflection point back to the safe side, as far as I've heard."

"No, of course not." But in the pause of a breath, Alice found herself thinking of Nicole. *Let me know if you ever hear of something that will turn back the clock.* "I just meant . . ."

"What did you mean?"

Alice sighed. "I don't know. I've got a feeling. A hunch."

"I heard that when Alice Frank gets hunches, people get busted."

"It's just a sense I can't shake, but I don't know where to go next. It has something to do with Necrophage."

A new thought occurred to her, along with a sudden certainty that her fears were accurate and that Hemisphere had, indeed, somehow bugged her phones. But whatever.

"Did it ever strike you as convenient that Hemisphere had this cure ready to go when Sherman Pope struck?"

"If they had it 'ready to go,' it was kind of shitty to let Bakersfield happen before unveiling it."

"So it's *not* too convenient."

"They crowdsourced the solution, Alice. They released all of their research publicly. They let everyone play. That feels pretty selfless to me, as far as big, bad companies go."

"But they kept the profits, when Necrophage was ready, all for themselves."

"Necrophage is free."

"Yes, but the designer versions. The ones that do more than halt the disease."

"So what? *Let* them charge for those. If I ever get bitten, I won't need it. My chest is hairy enough."

"Is that something the designer versions do?"

"I'm kidding. I don't know what they do. Don't care. I carry the base shit with me. I get bitten, I'll start taking it then get my bolus the minute we get back. Why do I need all sorts of extra bullshit? I already take a vitamin every morning. Injecting shit with a Gadget doesn't seem much different."

But the sense of a puzzle piece not quite fitting had settled into Alice's mind. If anything, it was bothering her more. What *was* different between the formulations? What was missing here? And what, pray tell, was her anonymous tipster trying to say? Was it just another crackpot — or Hemisphere itself, fucking with the constant thorn in the company's side?

Alice thrummed her fingertips on the coffee table. Calling Bobby hadn't made sense to begin with. She'd just been looking for something — *anything* — to break her stalemate while waiting for Ian, for nothing at all to occur. She should end the call. Maybe go back through his footage, if she needed something to do with the ever-popular web show host. Or wait for Bobby to come east, as he was due back soon. His house was in Aberdeen Valley, just like Alice's, and for similar reasons. She'd wanted to be near Hemisphere's headquarters to keep an eye on their comings and goings. But Bobby, for his image and his popular shows, just wanted to be in Dead City's orbit, at the heart of all things undead.

Obeying another of those troublesome hunches, Alice said, "Bobby, have you ever heard of August Maughan?"

She expected a no. Or maybe a distant yes, in the way people recognized the name of an actor or politician. Maughan was far more of a cult figure than the always-in-the-spotlight Burgess, known mainly by only those truly interested in Hemisphere lore.

Instead, Bobby surprised her.

"I'm seeing him Friday," he said.

# Chapter Thirty-One

## NOT ON THE MENU

AFTER EATING PANCAKES, DANNY AND Jordache sat and drank coffee for hours — long enough that Jordache ordered more sausage. Not pancakes; sausage.

On one level of Danny's mind, the fact that she defaulted to meat more often than not reminded him that she wasn't entirely healthy, that she was infected and always would be. But on his conscious level, the thought barely registered. Jordache was Jordache. She liked eating meat, and every once in a while she staggered a little. Very rarely — and it had become even less frequent since she'd been on PhageX — Jordache forgot things an uninfected person wouldn't. But those quirks were all just parts of her, no different from the single mole on the left side of her neck. Danny could accept them. He already had, wholly and fully.

They sat for a long time because despite their different social standings (Jordache remained poor; Danny's cars and apartments had improved quite a lot lately), Danny thought he might love the woman across from him. And, if she'd admit it, maybe she liked him, too.

But the main reason for sitting so long was cowardice.

Finally, Jordache seemed to remember what he'd said earlier and called him on it.

"Hey." Her mouth and nose wrinkled thoughtfully — something Danny found irresistibly cute on the petite blonde. "You said you had something to tell me."

Danny squirmed. He'd prefer to keep drinking coffee and ordering sausage. Maybe, if they made it until nighttime, he could retire for the day without saying what he had to say.

"I got a promotion."

"Really?"

"No, not really." He folded his hands on the table. That had been a stupid thing to say. It hadn't even been a joke. It had burned another five seconds and maybe tossed a rock to distract her, nothing else.

"New car, though," he said.

"I saw that. And you've already filled it with crap."

"My offer still stands, you know."

"Danny, you're not *buying me a car.* That's just stupid, so don't mention it again, okay?"

"It'd be a loan. You could pay me back." He paused. "If you wanted to."

"I don't need your charity."

Sure she didn't. She only lived in an armpit of a trailer park and rode the bus to work. Probably had to sit next to drooling guys — some twitchers, some just assholes — who kept accidentally brushing against her tits. Her job paid shit, and his paid far better than it should. He didn't feel guilty about selling the extra stock he got using Ian's access codes; Hemisphere had all it needed, and nobody was suffering. But sharing his take beyond just giving Jordache free designer Phage? Well, that would make everything that much more okay across the board, karmically speaking.

"You need a car, Baby."

Danny paused. That last "baby" had felt as wrong on his lips as a left-behind bit of pancake. He wanted to take it back, but Jordache either wasn't taking any of the obvious signs or he'd been deliberately friend-zoned. That felt unfair. A lot of guys just wanted to screw girls like Jordache (her ex certainly had), but Danny wanted more. Of course if there was screwing to be had as part of the package deal, he'd be happy to accept it.

She didn't stutter at his affectionate add-on, but Danny had already decided never to do that again. Some guys could get away with using pet names and terms of endearment, but Danny wasn't one of them. He was a good salesman, for sure. But dating? That was different.

"If I need one, I'll get it on my own. And that's that."

To soften the words, Jordache laid her hand over Danny's. He let it sit there, fighting the urge to make a sarcastic comment and break the moment.

Then her hand vanished, and he wanted it back.

"So." She lowered her voice and did another of those cute things she did: whispered artificially low, as if in conspiracy. *"Where's my drugs, mister?"*

Danny sighed. Jordache's eyes, darkly lined like a cat's, looked up.

"You don't have it," she said.

"I didn't say that."

"But it's true."

Another sigh.

Jordache sat back, affecting a casual expression. It came off wrong. She was trying not to be impatient or angry or disappointed or anything else that might seem like blame laid on Danny, but she was also fighting addiction. Not to the drug itself; PhageX, like any designer, was just Necrophage with enhancements added like mix-ins. She was only as addicted as any necrotic: enough that if she went for too long without what she needed, she'd start to slip until she got more, which was free and available everywhere in its base formulation. What he was seeing now was a kind of psychological addiction. PhageX definitely made her feel better than base Necrophage ever did. She'd grown too large for her old box and was trying not to feel horrible about a fear that she'd be returning soon.

When she spoke next, Danny heard that mixture of emotion. She wouldn't accuse him because that was unfair. But she'd been promised something that wasn't being delivered.

"You said you could get it. You said I wouldn't have to go back."

Danny rushed to reply. "I can! And you *won't* have to go back. I promise, okay?" He took her hand — another calculated, affectionate risk. "I just wasn't able to get any yet. When I went back into the building, turns out Ian had just been through. If I went back in so soon, using his same access code to get more from the dispensary, it might look—"

Jordache's face registered disappointment. It hurt Danny to see. He'd been so eager to check in with Jordache that he'd rushed to call before verifying that he still had some PhageX in with the rest of his samples to tide her over until he could restock. He'd been so sure to hold some back for just such an emergency, but he'd come up empty. The small pack that Danny thought he already had was supposed to get Jordache through the next few days. After that, he *would* be able to hit the dispensary, and fill her medicine cabinet with enough high-end Phage to keep her happy for months. But that was then, and this was now.

"It's just a few days' delay. I can get it Monday."

"Monday?" She looked uncertain. "You're sure?"

Danny squeezed the soft hand between his a bit harder. Her skin was chilly and refused to warm in his grip. The difference was subtle, but feeling it while watching Jordache worried hurt him.

"Do you have enough to get you through?"

Jordache gave a slow, tentative nod. "I think so. I think I have a few days. But *just* to Monday. You're sure you can get in there then? On Monday?"

"I told you, we're good. I still have his access codes. I can get past the new security. I could have got you more today, even. I just didn't want to take the risk. But I *would've* if I'd known—"

Finally, Jordache squeezed back. "No. I wouldn't have wanted you to take any risks."

"It's not just a risk to me. It's a risk to you, too. If anyone figures out that I'm sneaking in there and taking stuff I shouldn't even be allowed to *sell* …"

"I know. I'm sorry. I just get edgy."

Danny nodded. He understood edgy. When he'd first peeked into the breadth of inventory available at Ian's more exclusive access level, he'd practically lost his shit. He'd been so nervous that first time, and had still been nervous every time since. Technically *(teeeechnically)*, he was doing something illegal. And yes, he could stop selling and stick only to giving Jordache what she needed for free, but the perks were too good. And again, who was being hurt?

"Monday then?" she said, trying to smile.

"Monday."

Danny pulled a printout from his pocket. It was squished from their long time delaying the inevitable, but now that the discomfort was over (and a solution was in the works), he could share.

Danny slid from his side of the booth and over to Jordache's. Their bodies touched. She smelled wonderful.

He flattened the paper on the table.

"I printed out the full roster. Do you want to try any of these? Beauty. Truth. Glamour. Why do they all have such pretentious names?"

"Here's one that's less pretentious." She put a finger at a line on the printout. "Genius."

"How is that not pretentious?"

"At least it's not superficial."

Watching her scan the list, Danny thought of saying something about how she didn't need any help with the superficial because she had it all covered. But there was no way to say it without being cheesy, so he let it go, remaining firmly Danny the Rep, Danny the Salesman.

"These are supposed to be good." He pointed at a cluster designated as being part of a class called *augmentation plus.* "Did I tell you about Sully?"

Jordache shook her head.

"Another guy in my department. I know he reps those. Lots of celebrity clients."

"Ooh. Look at the prices."

"That's retail. And besides, you wouldn't have to pay anything."

Jordache looked up. She had pale-blue eyes to accent her naturally blonde hair. She made a little face, and Danny thought he knew what was coming. It was another of those split-morality things. On one hand, she seemed to know it was wrong to allow Danny to risk what he did — for her, for anyone — and that she should protest. But on the other hand, there was her need.

He cut her off before she could speak, returning her attention to the paper.

"Ian's code gives me access to order any of this. He

must be superauthorized to give out samples or something, or to shuttle product around, because it's been six full months now, and I've yet to see any sign that he's expected to balance his requisitions with credits back." He turned to Jordache. "That means turning in the money he supposedly makes selling what he takes."

"I know what it means, Danny. I'm not an idiot."

Danny's jaw slid sideways. He didn't want to say what came to mind: that she most definitely was *not* an idiot, but that nonetheless, she seemed to be further from idiocy than ever before. It seemed like Jordache had been underestimated her entire life. Her parents tossed her out, and a long string of boyfriends used her like a sex doll before getting arrested or (in Weasel's case) shipped off to Yosemite. Nobody ever took Jordache seriously, until Danny. But even he had to admit that something had changed, and that taking PhageX from Jordache now would represent a definite loss, no matter how *adequate* the base drug was supposed to be.

"Anyway," he said. "I can get you any of this."

She sat back and shrugged, the paper apparently dismissed.

"I'll stick with what works."

"Don't you want to try anything new? They're all superexpensive. Seems a shame not to try them, especially given their supposed benefits."

"I like the way PhageX makes my mind work. It's … " she sighed, "… *better.*"

"Better how?"

"All I know is that something is different, Danny."

He held up the printout. "I don't even know what it's supposed to do. It's not classed like the others. It's not an Aesthetic. It's not a Sensory Enhancer. It's not Cognitive Preservation. Sully says some of the guys he sells designers to *swear* whatever they're taking makes their dicks bigger."

"I don't want that one," Jordache said.

"But PhageX isn't even designated. And based on what I see, it only goes to a couple of clients. You know what Sully says?"

"That it makes tits bigger too?"

"He thinks PhageX is ultra-designer. Like, above price. The kind of special thing on the menu you have to know to ask for. You've heard of August Maughan?"

"The healer. The Hollywood guru guy?"

Danny nodded. "I guess the big thing he used to do when he worked for Hemisphere was messing with the formulas to make them … different somehow. Like moving them that last 1 percent, from great to amazing."

"And?"

"Sully thinks PhageX might be the highest of high-class Necrophage. For August as the only recipient. Like he's still working for the company, on the sly."

Jordache smiled. "Then I guess I have good taste."

"*Champagne* taste, I'll bet. You know what it means when there's no price on the menu for that special item, right?" Danny pointed, where PhageX, at the tip of the zenith had no listed retail. Either someone had made a mistake and left the price off … or, more likely, it simply wasn't ever for sale.

It took visible effort for Jordache to say the next thing.

"Maybe I *should* switch to something else. Something as exclusive as you're describing … Danny, you could really get in trouble."

Danny watched her eyes. Her barely affected, chronically underestimated, increasingly intelligent eyes.

"I started this," he said. "What the lady wants, the lady gets."

Jordache looked for a moment like she might protest then wrapped her arms around his slight bicep and leaned against his shoulder.

"I don't deserve you."

Danny didn't agree. Jordache deserved plenty.

But even though he suspected it made him a son of a bitch, he couldn't help feeling that after all the time he'd put in, maybe he deserved her, too.

# Chapter Thirty-Two

## THE GOOD LIFE

AUGUST WASN'T SURE IF HE was being a good guru or a terrible recluse.

Aberdeen Valley had once been a nothing of a North Carolina town centered (in concept, anyway) around a tiny river too pathetic to be much more than a creek. Back then (when August had been part of the fold, and he and Archibald had chosen the company's location together), Aberdeen had been a quaint place. Hemisphere had quickly changed that, and even by the time of August's much-publicized blowout with his partner, the place had been nearly big enough to hide inside.

The pace of expansion had only accelerated, and the growth between then and now had been stratospheric. Soon after ending their partnership, August was already wondering if he should move somewhere where he could vanish — probably LA, where his richest clients lived, Holly Gaynor being the biggest. But then Holly had nabbed her Hemisphere endorsement deal and moved the other direction, to Aberdeen — and by then, August had to admit that, looking around, the place had grown large enough to disappear.

Even so, sitting in the open made August nervous. He'd been watching Holly on the outdoor stage from across the huge, walk-through fountain and could clearly see the way she was being fawned over. She was a featured attraction at the Good Life Awards ceremony, but the attention she was getting from onlookers was disproportionate to her actual role. The Good Life Awards were supposed to be about the recipients. But everyone kept approaching the spokesperson.

It, like the Good Life Awards themselves, was back-handedly insulting.

Holly had been popular before the outbreak and her infection, but even then she'd been a cult celebrity, renowned for her acting chops and range but unappreciated by the mainstream. Once she'd become the poster girl for Sherman Pope (first in films where she played infected characters then literally when Hemisphere had hitched its endorsement wagon to her rising star), she'd started hitting the covers of every magazine. She was the perfect spokesperson for the disease: affected enough to speak for the masses, but mostly unblemished on the surface, so that she was still nice to look at. She'd already been a half-black woman who was white enough for the Caucasian decision makers, and now she was a necrotic who wouldn't offend the uninfected nation's eyes with sagging skin, blackening and receding gums, sunken eyes, and a head that could barely cling to its hair.

Now nobody could stay away from her. It would be insulting if the press avoided Holly, but the lengths to which they went the other direction was condescending.

Like the Good Life Awards.

Like this entire plaza. Like the businesses that didn't exactly cater to the infected's needs, but pandered to their most obvious, most photo-op-ready desires.

August sat on his picnic table, far enough from the crowds to hide from curious eyes but close enough that Holly, onstage, would be able to see him for moral support. He didn't need to be here. He'd been watching the proceedings to see Holly's latest public showing, but he'd been doing so on his tablet. He could look up and see Holly tiny, or down to see her close up, same as he'd have been able to do at home, in his two-floor penthouse with his cat's name on the tenant register instead of his own.

He was doing this for Holly, but he didn't like it.

Holly, who was his responsibility now, one way or the other.

They were in this together, and had been since she'd begun taking Prestige. Neither of them had needed test results to prove the myelin on neurons in Holly's brain had started to regenerate. Neither of them needed scans to show the way her frontal lobe was lighting back up. She wasn't being cured, precisely. It was more that her brain was finding new ways to do old functions — rerouting mental traffic around damaged areas to find new paths. Unsurprisingly, given what August suspected Hemisphere was keeping secret these days, the tweaked Necrophage had lit up Holly's corpus callosum like a twelve-lane expressway. The band of nerves spanning the two halves of her gray matter seemed to be more active than any brain August had ever seen. It might not mean anything; August still didn't believe the disease had an out-and-out cure.

But it could also mean *something*. Or everything.

August didn't exactly work with FDA approval. He was

reasonably sure he was actively disobeying half a dozen Panacea statutes, all of which were supposedly in place to ensure that Sherman Pope stayed stable and predictable rather than being shaken and allowed to mutate in the wild. *Supposedly*, that's what Panacea was in place to do. But to August, who'd grown up skeptical of power, it smacked of fear-based systems designed for control.

When you wanted a nation to obey, you told it a deadly enemy was knocking at the gates.

When you wanted a nation to obey, you told it that without the government's protection, something horrible might break out like wildfire.

*Bullshit.*

But it meant that both of them had a secret, too. August and Holly. She was an unlicensed, unapproved test group of one. And if anyone saw him here, in public, so near Holly, they might connect the dots. They might believe the rumors. Reporters would renew their search for the famous recluse who'd pulled off the wunderkind's greatest trick: getting the world's mainstream to mostly forget about him.

He shouldn't be here. He went out to get groceries, to attend events, to live his life. But to August, Aberdeen Valley was just a place to live. The rest of the world saw its very existence as meaningful, as if living in the halo city Hemisphere created had purpose in itself — the same way people used to think that all who lived in Las Vegas spent their days on the Strip and in casinos. But it wasn't like that. August had stayed because he wanted to be close to the company he'd once been a part of, and because his wealthiest clients lived here or made pilgrimages here. And why not? It was Dead Fucking City, mecca of those that were still tastelessly called the walking undead.

The entire country had non-discrimination statutes,

but Aberdeen had entire industries populated by necrotics. Even *run* by necrotics, in a few cases. Playtime was run by Carol Gartner, who was SP-positive. She'd started the play park franchise with a single location meant to entertain her still delightful but relatively mindless necrotic grandchildren. Carol's incubation was something like a day, whereas her entire brood of grandkids were damn near feral. All they wanted to do all day every day was to jump in bounce houses. But as things turned out, there was a demand for more play parks in Dead City and the rest of the country beyond, and Carol was still plenty adept to be an entrepreneur.

It wasn't just Hemisphere that made Aberdeen Valley home. It was the acres of secondary and tertiary industries Hemisphere's employees and siren song had drawn here. There were independent labs who worked off of Hemisphere's publicly released formulary information. There were pharmacy hubs, mostly overseen by Panacea, who acted like vast distribution centers for the rest of the country. There were the entertainment businesses, who'd come to Aberdeen because the best necrotic talent came to Aberdeen. Able, the computer peripheral company, had come to Aberdeen because demand for modified keyboards and other necrotic-friendly input devices was highest here. Same for Telcot, Moxie Systems, and Next Step Imagery.

More restaurants to serve all of those businesses, all of which preferentially hired necrotics.

More retail stores, dry cleaners, easy-on clothing outfits, coffee shops that never, ever sold coffee hot enough to burn because patrons always spilled, 100 percent of the time.

August pushed his earbud farther into his ear and tilted the tablet for a better view. Holly had been nervous, though to August's eye, she didn't look it at all. But that was Holly for you — so used to pretending to be someone else that few saw who she actually was. And it's not like Holly wasn't used to pandering. She'd been mixed-race in white Hollywood before her infection. She was used to smiling, unsure whether those around her were being genuine or patronizing.

Holly approached the mic. She looked out, away from the camera. August's eyes flicked up, looking across the fountain at the small shape on the stage beyond the fountain's leaping arcs of water. He knew she was looking at him. Trying to draw strength to playact — to play dumber than she was, to feign the uncertainty her handlers always seemed so sure she was.

Holly began speaking, her voice projected by speakers in real time, then a half second later through the earbud in his ear.

"Iffs goot to be here today," she slurred.

In his earbud, August heard the rustle of press. Someone had a camera with an ancient shutter, and he could hear it clapping.

"Hemithpere hathz made a hyooth diffrenth immy life," she went on.

Huge, yes, but it was only part of the story. August watched the screen, watching Holly's face, wondering if anyone was fooled. Holly wasn't the face of Sherman Pope or Necrophage. The guy dragging one leg with his foot canted sideways, his face almost literally half-torn off, who was sweeping cigarette butts near the fountain right now? *That* was closer to the face of Sherman Pope. Some people got lucky, like Holly, and took their major damage below the skin where nobody could see. But most people with a one-week incubation or more were at least a little hard to look at. A lot could die off in a week of localized necrosis.

Holly went on. August watched her onscreen, watched her in the distance, let his eyes stray to the large, fine, new buildings around the clearing. The place hadn't even had a skyline when Hemisphere had come here three years ago, and now its size rivaled that of a medium-sized city. Everything was white and gray and silver and black, its every inch pristine. In the center of the place like this, so near Hemisphere, you'd think the whole city was a marvel and that all this PR bullshit told the whole truth. Never mind the ghettos no one spoke of.

"And to theeth winners of the Good Life A'ars, the ability to live normal lize makes all the difference in'a world."

Not for the first time, August found his mind wandering to those old days, when he and Archibald had been partners. They'd been an odd couple: Archibald the man with the plan, and August a protégé. August had a stake in the company, but Archibald's was a majority, so he could never be outvoted even after Hemisphere went public. August's buyout following their rather loud and public tiff had made him rich enough to never work again and still live as lavishly as he wished. At the time, it had felt more like a payoff than a buyout, like those billions were hush money, even though nobody had made it clear exactly what he wasn't supposed to whisper about.

But of course, Archibald had been right. No matter what else had happened, the plague had been stopped in its tracks. And maybe that made it as his former mentor had said: that the ends really did justify the means, when evolution itself — and the history of the species — was at stake.

Holly, in August's ear, went on.

"I'm proud to share the stage with these amazing,

brave people who've refused to be bound with the tethers of the illness that afflicts so much of us today," she said.

August looked down, feeling something amiss. The camera view on his tablet still showed Holly at the lectern, doing her spokeswoman thing, but her face had gone strange. There was movement to either side, subtle.

August looked up. He was maybe two hundred feet from the crowd across the fountain, but it wasn't far enough for their murmuring to be inaudible.

Holly didn't work off a script. When she'd returned to show business, she'd been unable to remember lines, let alone deliver them flawlessly. Today she could, but she had to play possum and still worked off the cuff, ad-libbing most of what she did.

On the big screen.

Onstage.

And when giving public speeches.

August stood and began walking forward, feeling urgent. There was no way to get in touch with Holly. She was dressed to emcee, and only her manager and security were tapped into communications … and right now, August could see them stirring nervously.

What made Holly endearing was that she talked from the heart, top of mind, without overthinking before she spoke.

And now, it seemed she'd chosen one hell of a bad time to rediscover the trick of proper speech, using clever phrasing and big words.

August moved to slip his tablet into his bag while walking, unsure where he was going or what he was doing. Before he put the screen to sleep, he saw Holly, still camera center, looking left and right nervously, probably realizing what she'd just said.

Not something she'd said poorly, like a mistake.

But something she'd said a bit too perfectly.

Holly's black-suited handlers moved onto the stage. One of them — Cyrus, August thought — took her by the arm. It was hard to tell from so far away, but his body language seemed to be fake casual, pretending nothing was amiss. Holly wasn't going without a hitch; she looked like she might grab the lectern and hang on at any moment.

Her eyes were across the stage, where the Hemisphere security guards set in front of the stage to control the crowd were moving up, coming forward.

August moved faster. The crowd — many of which were far-gone necrotics who'd miss the scene's subtleties — looked around as if confused.

Cyrus pulled Holly harder. Now that August was closer, he could see her nervous smile: all white teeth, still in character. But there was something off about her look. Something that recognized the problem for what it was.

Holly's handlers, pulling her stage-left.

Hemisphere security agents, all of them subtle and without uniforms, coming from stage-right, pressing earpieces with their fingers, receiving orders from someone, somewhere.

"Thank you," said a male voice over the speakers. It was Cyrus, leaning in to speak for Holly. But the farce was paper thin. Anyone paying attention and able to think straight could clearly see what was happening. Holly had, in speaking so well, committed a crime that no one could admit was a problem. The ensuing dance unfolded before August as he paced faster: the Hemisphere agents coming forward slowly because they were pretending they only wanted to talk, and Cyrus and the others pulling Holly away as if they didn't even notice because Holly had, of course, done nothing wrong.

The agents moved a hair faster, surely mindful of the cameras watching the event.

Cyrus dragged harder. Holly, in the middle, seemed torn. She saw the agents and clearly didn't want to face them, but Cyrus wasn't much better. She was pulling away with half strength, still trying to smile at the crowd as if everything was perfectly normal.

Her eyes went where she'd been trying to keep them away from, and Holly looked directly at August.

The crowd turned to see what had captured her attention. As their heads turned, so did the agents who hadn't gone onstage, and were still watching the gathering from the rear.

August stopped. However he'd hoped to help Holly, it wasn't going to work.

Agents approached him, blazers flapping. As the fabric moved, August could clearly see the butts of handguns in their shoulder holsters.

They were Panacea, not Hemisphere — maybe even high-level clarifiers.

With the world's eyes still watching everything that was happening, the parties moved slowly like a dance advancing frame by frame. The first to run would break the stalemate. The first to run would start it all.

August detoured. Slightly to his left, toward a line of cars just past the blocked-off section of walkway, on the street between his position and the fountain, where kids — necrotic and non-necrotic, the picture of Aberdeen harmony — continued to frolic.

The Panacea agents began to jog, seeing the writing on the wall.

But August was too near his target. He yanked open the door of an electric cab, waved his card in front of the sensor, and tapped the digital map to indicate his desired destination — not in the right place, but enough to get the cab moving.

When the cab was away, August turned to look backward.

The agents watched his departure for a few seconds then turned toward the stage, where Holly had no such escape for the crime she hadn't committed.

# Chapter Thirty-Three

## PARANOIA

IAN WAS BEING OVERLY PARANOID. He was sure of it. His meeting with Archibald Burgess was just that — *a meeting*. It was about time he got to meet his highest boss (and, let's face it, idol) in person for more than a few minutes. He'd quickly ascended the company ladder, so it was only logical that he'd eventually end up climbing all the way to the big man's office. Burgess had said he respected Ian's mother's book, and Ian by extension. It was a great, expectation-setting meeting.

It wasn't anything ominous. That was just his earlier unfounded fears. Burgess had requested his presence, and it didn't make any difference that he'd been summoned with rough hands, or that the meeting had ended on that dark little cliffhanger.

*You're a good man with priorities for yourself and your family firmly in order. I'm glad to hear you're with, rather than against us.*

With us.

Not against us.

Priorities in order.

For yourself and your family.

The words kept looping in Ian's mind, and by the next morning he still hadn't shaken them. They'd been in his head all night, robbing him of sleep. They'd been in his eyes when he'd woken, then stared into the mirror to brush his teeth. They might as well have been written on the wall at night, or across the bare flesh of Bridget's sleeping back.

*Everything is fine,* he told himself.

But goddammit, it just *wasn't.* He'd been sure someone was messing with him, but now it seemed that Hemisphere's top brass had been informed. That was a problem even if the original incursions were someone's idea of a joke. It all made his skin crawl. Ian felt like he'd been caught even though he'd never trespassed where he didn't belong. Someone else had started this. Someone else had put files in front of him — and not even *useful* files, as if this mysterious source (or more likely troublemaker) wanted something figured out but lacked the guts to say what needed saying even to the person he or she wanted to say it to.

Ian's toothbrush paused mid-stroke.

Maybe it was Alice Frank.

That made sense. She was a snoop who didn't trust Hemisphere at all, despite the fact that the company had — oh, no big deal — just *saved the fucking world*. She seemed, from what Ian could tell, to have a lot of connections. You don't get into the Yosemite Containment Reserve without connections. Someone was helping her get into places she shouldn't be, and she had every reason to want to be there. Not only had she tried to call him repeatedly (including that strange call where she'd pretended *he'd* called *her*); he'd seen between the lines in her documentary. It was objective on the surface, but tilted to anyone with the least bit of sense. Hemisphere was the bad guy, daring to make a profit, even though it gave out its cure for free. If Alice

Frank had one wish, Ian supposed, it'd be to topple the giant and … well … apparently to go ahead and let the plague break out all over again.

Yes. This was Alice Frank's fault.

Ian couldn't believe he hadn't thought to pass the buck in Burgess's office. He should have blamed her top to bottom. This wasn't Ian butting into places he shouldn't be. It was Alice Frank, known adversary.

Ian spit then wiped his mouth. He met the man in the mirror's blue eyes, running a comb through his brown hair.

"Stop being an asshole. You're not doing anything wrong," he said, reaching into the stream of water.

"About what?"

Ian's gaze flicked up. Bridget appeared behind him in the mirror. He'd thought she was still asleep. They had a fixed schedule: He woke at five; she woke at seven. Today he'd overslept, and they seemed to be meeting in the middle, the clock on the wall fixed at 6:04.

"Nothing."

"Talking to yourself again?"

"You knew I did that when we were first dating."

"Yes. It creeped me out."

Ian turned, a smile on his lips at her effacing joke. Bridget slept only in panties. He was bare chested, and so was she. He stepped closer and reached around to hug her close, but the skin-to-skin warmth lasted only a second. Instead of lingering as they usually did, Bridget only gave him the shortest of moments before pushing past him to reach for her own toothbrush, in her own sink down the counter from him.

Puzzled, Ian looked at his wife's profile. He'd always found her beautiful. She had pale skin and bright-red hair that brushed her shoulders. It was in a mess now, sleep-tousled and bent in odd orange angles. The way it hung mostly covered her face, hiding her expression.

"Did you sleep well?" he asked.

"Okay."

"Why are you up early?"

Bridget turned to face him. Again, her expression was unreadable. Standing there topless as she was, Ian found it difficult not to be aroused. But the look on her face dampened any fire that threatened to rise.

She turned back to the sink. Instead of answering, she made a statement that was almost a question of her own.

"You've been working a lot lately."

"There's a lot going on."

"I tried to call you yesterday morning."

Ian nodded. He'd seen the missed calls once the big men had taken him out and returned him to the other campus, where he'd met his team with tired eyes.

"Where were you?"

"At work."

"I tried your office."

"Why?"

"Do I need a reason?"

Ian couldn't quite get her tone. It was unusual between them. He looked over, but she was again looking down, toothbrush working.

"You must have called when I stepped out."

"That busy, huh?"

She looked up. Ian nodded.

"And working evenings, too. I thought you hated doing that."

"I don't work evenings. It's one of my rules."

"You were in your study watching that thing the other night." She paused, spit, then said, "After taking that call."

"It was a work thing," Ian said, knowing "taking that call" for the violation of his usual rules that it was.

Bridget wiped her mouth then put both hands on the counter. She looked up for a second then over at Ian. Her eyes were soft, hard to read.

"I really like the life we've built here," she said.

It was a strange thing to say. "I like it too."

"I don't say that often enough." She blinked, looked away, looked back. "I just don't want to take it for granted."

"What's this about?"

"We used to be so poor. Just kids."

Ian nodded again. "Sure." He didn't trust himself to say more, strange as this was. Their time as "just kids" held some of his favorite memories. Bridget had been so crazy back then, before the demands of family and marriage and motherhood. They hadn't had money, and he'd had a lot of time. He still had time thanks to his rules (no working after dinner, no working on the weekends), but it wasn't the same. Now everything was scheduled, right down to their sex life.

"But I like things how they are. How they've been for a while now. You could work a little less. But that's just details."

"Bridge—"

"Are *you* happy how things are?"

"Of course. What's going on here?"

She blinked, sighed, shook her head. "Nothing." There was a long pause then: "You got a phone call the other day."

"I get a lot of phone calls."

"On the house line."

"The house … wait, the *wall phone?*"

"Yeah."

"The phone company. Or a wrong number. I don't even know what that number is. Or if it even *has* a number."

"The caller asked for you."

Ian looked up. Then he saw it: somehow, for some reason, Bridget was scared.

"What did they say?"

"'Is Ian there.'" She said it like a statement, not a question.

"What did you say?"

"You weren't home. I said no."

"And?"

"It went dead."

Watching Bridget's emerald-green eyes, Ian heard another voice in his head: *You're a good man with priorities for yourself and your family firmly in order. I'm glad to hear you're with, rather than against us.*

*You're a good man with priorities for yourself and your family firmly in order.*

*For yourself and your family.*

*Your* family.

He was being ridiculous. Being more of that paranoid. But then, who else would call that number? Who else could find that number?

If he'd been alone, Ian would have splashed water on his face and shaken his head. It was moronic. First of all, Hemisphere was a good company — just a company, not some sort of evil genius's underground organization. Second, Burgess hadn't been happy that Ian had been 1) snooping and 2) talking, seemingly, to Alice Frank. Ian had seen it before; Archibald Burgess was all over the media and routinely adored, but strange in person. Clearly there were two Burgesses: a public face and a private one. The latter was far more driven. Far more tuned to mission and destiny. Far more willing to do whatever needed to be done, obstacles be damned.

But he was strange, not intimidating.

He'd spoken of priorities and allegiances and family as face-value items, not something Ian should take as anything deeper.

Not the kind of thing someone would snoop around and get an unknown number for in order to mess with his family, even though Hemisphere was one of the few companies connected enough to Panacea to pull something like that off.

"I'm sure it was just a mistake."

Bridget's hands went to her hips, her breasts still on prominent display. To Ian, her body had never stopped being fantastic. He was confused in two diametrically opposed directions, both turned on and feeling accused.

"A mistake. Is that really your response?"

"What do you want me to say?"

"You don't seem very surprised. By someone trying so hard to get in touch with you in a way that's kind of … covert. Then hanging up when I answer."

"I don't know what the hell it was, Bridge! Maybe it *was* the phone company."

Of course he didn't think so.

Bridget returned to the bedroom. Ian splashed his face and followed. He found Bridget with her shirt back on, looking deliberately away from him. He decided to let her sulk. He'd get to the bottom of this, but the fact that he was somehow being accused of wrongdoing from every angle at once was too irritating to take. The files had been forced on him by, probably, Alice Frank, and Burgess blamed Ian. Now someone was calling the house to intimidate him into keeping his mouth shut, and Bridget was accusing *him?* Ian loved his wife with all his heart, but *fuck that.*

She wasn't going to break the silence. Ian didn't want to play into whatever this was but wanted them to meet Analise in the front room with an angry cloud overhead even less.

"I saw leftovers in the fridge," he said, keeping his voice light. "You went out with Gabriella?"

"Yes." Just one word, but almost challenging in itself.

"How is she?"

"Cheating."

Ian's head cocked. It was a private joke between them that Gabriella — who, Ian had to admit, was stunning — was screwing every uninfected guy she could lure to the house while Jim was away. But her saying it with no mirth felt strange.

"What, does she have new stories?"

"Just stories about how she gets away with it."

"Oh? How's that?"

"She says you just need to know what kinds of things will give you away if you're cheating."

Again, Bridget was looking right at Ian.

"What kinds of things?"

Bridget turned the knob and opened the door. But before heading out to greet the day, she said, "You know how she watches the neighborhood all the time with her binoculars, right?"

"Yeah." They'd joked about that plenty, too, even though Bridget's tone didn't have a single note of humor.

"She said someone keeps coming around. Driving down our street, over and over, slowing in front of our house without ever stopping." Then she turned, shrugged, and gave Ian a fake little smile that didn't fool him at all. "Not when *I'm* home, anyway."

# Chapter Thirty-Four

## MALFUNCTIONS

DANNY WAVED HIS CARD IN front of the swipe sensor to enter Alpha building. Then he waved it again.

Red. And an annoying buzz of rejection, not loud enough to do more than annoy Danny and make him sweat.

He glanced around, surely looking like a textbook definition of guilty. Jordache had texted him a few times already this morning, each time about something inane. She was poking him, and he poked playfully back, but Danny knew what she was trying to do. Each text was open ended, heavy with a question he could answer if he acknowledged it. She'd built herself plausible deniability; later, she could explain each message as small talk. But they were all asking if he'd managed to get the PhageX.

*Just wondering about your day. <3*

To which Danny could, if he'd had the PhageX, answer, *It's great. Got something for you. :)*

Or she'd say, *Do you want to set a time to hang out tonight? Just planning my day.*

To which Danny, if he wasn't being stymied by a

locked door, could say, *Let's meet at five, so I can give you a present.*

Each time he answered the texts' obvious message and ignored the deeper query. He could imagine Jordache getting increasingly nervous. His lack of response about the designer Necrophage was an answer in itself. They both knew how badly she wanted — and, really, probably *needed* — the drug she'd grown accustomed to. It was top of mind for them both, even though Jordache had work and Danny had legitimate clients. He knew how much she wanted the good news he'd promised, and how much he'd want to reassure her once he had it. Saying nothing was an answer. One that had to be making her shake and panic.

*Relax,* he told himself. *It's just a glitch in the door. This isn't Fort Knox. You can still get in. And besides, worse comes to worst, Jordache can go back on normal, base Necrophage for a few days. She wants the good stuff, but it won't hurt her if she doesn't get it. Anyone infected can be completely without Phage for a week or more and fully recover. And this isn't that. This is just stepping down, not going off entirely. It's fine.*

But Danny didn't like that he was rationalizing. It meant part of him had already surrendered. And while it was true that Jordache would be fine on base Phage (and, in all likelihood, that she'd recover any of the perceived gains she'd made once back on X), the idea of having to break the news to her hurt. It was the opposite of bringing a girl flowers. It was more like visiting a girl who already had flowers and ripping them to mulch. Not exactly the way to endear himself to her.

Danny backed away from the door, making himself busy reviewing a Panacea/CDC poster about Sherman Pope safety. It wasn't the sort of thing that Danny needed reminding about. If you were bitten, you needed to get a

Necrophage bolus. If you saw someone who seemed to be raging, you called the hotline.

Beside the first poster, there was a second from the Human Resources Department that covered such delicate workplace matters as when a coworker's fingers fell off. It seemed like a strange pairing.

Halfway through reading the second poster (*If you notice blood in a common area such as a coffee station, call Workplace Assistance, and do not accuse anyone directly*), a tall black man approached the door that had been stymieing Danny and waved his card in front of the sensor. The box flashed green. Danny moved into position behind the man, staying back, and put his foot in the door just before it closed.

Once through, Danny began flicking at the card on his belt, wondering if the dispensary would give him problems, too.

It had to be a problem with the door. The access Danny had coded into the card was *Ian Keys's.* Ian was damn near the top of the company, and could go anywhere. The idea that Ian — who the door had been thinking Danny was for six months now — would be denied access to places and products was ridiculous.

The dispensary would be fine. Ian's card would unlock the inventory same as before. The door was a fluke.

But when Danny reached the automated dispensary window (after looking around to clear the way), he found that Ian — or at least the Ian on Danny's card — was no longer cleared for access. To anything at all.

Danny tried his own card. It opened the pharma inventory here in Alpha to his normal access level. Same as in the dispensary he normally used.

That meant the problem wasn't the dispensary door. The problem was Ian's card. Ian's *access.*

Something had been changed.

"Shit," Danny said aloud.

Why would Ian's code change? He'd been paranoid about that early on, certain that security would shuffle codes regularly and Danny would have to find a way to snag Ian's card and keep ripping new codes on a schedule, but it hadn't happened. Not until today. Not until Jordache was bone dry and Danny needed PhageX most of all.

With his own account in the auto-dispensary still open, Danny scrolled through the list of medications he was permitted to order — but not sell below the table, of course, because Danny's requisitions, unlike Ian's, were tracked and reconciled. Maybe there was something in here he hadn't noticed. Some drug he'd had access to all along that might do in this particular pinch.

But of course, there was nothing. He could order base Necrophage in as large of quantities as he wanted, which meant nothing seeing as the drug was free. The rest of what Danny had access to was useless. He could order samples of the neuroenhancement lines, the depression line, various biotic treatments. Or maybe, instead of PhageX, he could take Jordache something from the Alzheimer's line — drugs Danny didn't recognize, half of which didn't appear to be in production: Fabriplaque, ReWAYS, BioFuse.

Again, Danny swiped his card. The dispensary beeped obnoxiously back.

"Come on. Come on, you piece of shit."

Danny swiped again. The machine beeped.

*"Fucker!"*

Danny brought his fist down on the machine's screen just as the tall black man from earlier was walking by. He slowed to give Danny a sideways look, perhaps remembering him loitering outside the doors, maybe wondering who Danny was and whether or not he was even supposed to be here.

Danny put on his salesman's smile. "Technology," he said, half scoffing.

The man watched Danny for another few seconds then moved on down the hallway.

Now what? Jordache said she had enough PhageX to get her through today but no more. Danny had thought he had stock, but it turned out he didn't. The whole plan — and on any other day, it would have worked perfectly, even if it was to the wire — was to use this machine to get more. Then going so close to the bone wouldn't matter. Jordache would have plenty, and the next time, Danny would be sure to refill far enough in advance to allow for stupid fucking machines with their stupid fucking electronic fits.

But now he was stuck. Even if it was a mistake, there was nobody he could go to for help. He couldn't call tech support because they'd ask for the problem card in order to test the system themselves — and that might not just blow things today; it could blow the last six months wide open. There must be records of all he'd requisitioned, even if the system hadn't required him to settle and show his receipts. Anyone who looked closely would see what he was up to, and then he wouldn't just be fired; he'd probably be arrested. Even his clients might come under suspicion. Jordache might get in trouble.

He couldn't rush into Ian's office for a new code, seeing as he had no business anywhere Ian went beyond the parking lot, and seeing as he'd need to manufacture a new excuse to borrow the card. He couldn't yell at Ian, either: *Hey, asshole, why did you go and change your access codes? Didn't you stop to think about all the illicit users you might be inconveniencing?*

Danny's phone buzzed. He pulled it from his pocket and read Jordache's latest:

*See you tonight?*

*Yes*, Danny thought, *I suppose you'll see me tonight. Empty handed, leaving you high and dry.*

# Chapter Thirty-Five

## DRIVE-BY

PEEKING BETWEEN THE BLINDS, IAN watched a sleek black car pass the stone mailbox in front of his house. He was in his office, presumably working, exactly where he wasn't supposed to be. Bridget had even given him a look for coming up here — *again*, her eyes had said. But in the hierarchy of things Ian needed to be worrying about right now, people stalking his home mattered more than his wife's temporary disapproval.

The car was uninteresting and unremarkable. It could have belonged to anyone, and Lion's Gate wasn't a community unfamiliar with black luxury sedans. Except that this car had a bright-orange license plate — either a New York plate or one of those tattletale plates some states gave out when the owner was convicted of a DUI. It didn't matter which it was. Only that the car was obvious, sufficient to tell Ian it had passed by three times already.

There was a sharp rattling sound. Ian jumped, heart thumping before he realized it was only his phone vibrating on the desk.

He snatched it up too eagerly.

"Hey." Only after his greeting did Ian see who was calling.

"You eating dinner?"

"Gennifer." He exhaled.

"You sound surprised."

"No. I'm sorry. I'm just … " But what was the end of that sentence? Was he worked up over nothing? Nervous for no reason? Guilty for being innocent? Never before had Ian felt so uneasy telling the truth about mundane events. He hadn't wanted to tell anyone that someone had given him publicly available company info. He hadn't wanted to tell his wife he'd spent some time researching the disease his workplace specialized in curing. He hadn't wanted to admit that he'd been forcibly connected to a reporter who'd managed to mine none of his secrets, not that Ian had any. Today at work, he hadn't told anyone about his perfectly normal meeting with the boss, and right now he was hiding up here from Bridget, not wanting to admit that there were cars on the street.

"Tired," Ian finished, knowing it didn't particularly make sense.

"Well, I asked around for you. Shockingly, nobody had anything helpful to say."

"You're sure?"

Gennifer sighed. "Ian, you asked me to see if any projects August might have been involved with were still of interest today. I might as well have been asking whether they'd ever 'heard something about whatever.'"

"What does that mean?"

"Well, what kind of question is that? August was half of this company for a long time. He was *involved*, depending on your definition of the word, with most of what Hemisphere does and continues to do."

Ian's mind ran back to Burgess's office and his

surprising question about August Maughan. Ian hadn't considered Maughan, but Burgess's first thought seemed to be that whatever Ian might be leaking, he might be leaking it to his old colleague. It felt like an itch worth scratching, at least a little, even if it made him feel more like a snoop. More like a liar and traitor. More like the kind of guy a company might send long black sedans to check in on three times in one hour.

"I meant anything he may have been working on when he left, that we might still be interested in today."

"Why?"

"Just wondering about connections, Gennifer." He thought fast, feeling the need to justify some of this. "Everyone seems to think that his leaving was a massive loss."

"I guess it was. But why does that matter now?"

More quick thinking. More manufacturing of bullshit.

"I was watching that Alice Frank documentary about Yosemite. It got me thinking about new directions for Necrophage. The designer versions, I mean. To … uh … address some of the shortfalls Frank identified in current treatments."

Ian wondered if he was sweating. He peeked back through the blinds.

Gennifer, on the phone's other end, sighed heavily. It wasn't a casual sigh. It was the kind of sigh a person makes to tell another person just how exasperating and annoying he's being. Not to mention irrelevant. There was no line to be drawn between Bobby Baltimore's Yosemite special and August Maughan. Now Ian felt stupid having tried to justify it. He was Gennifer's boss. He should be able to ask for something, and she should do it — or pass it down to Ted, Kate, or Gary. Gary would do it without asking questions. If Gary had Gennifer's level of oversight, he'd have gone direct.

"Why won't you just tell me what you really want to know? I might be able to help if you'd say what's on your mind."

Ian thought. Gennifer wasn't the kind of person who stepped far off the beaten path. She was the group's mother. He could trust her, couldn't he?

Ian's eyes strayed to the blinds. He pushed them apart with two fingers and saw that the sedan had stopped directly across from his house, someone's bland face looking out, seemingly right into Ian's eyes.

"It's nothing, Gennifer," said Ian, heart in his throat. "Thanks for your help."

## Chapter Thirty-Six

### BREAKING NEWS

THERE WAS A KNOCK AT the Yosemite Bivouac's open office door. Bobby looked up from his map to see Cindy standing in the threshold.

"Did you see the news?"

"You'll need to be more specific," Bobby replied. There was industry news, network news, the twisted species of underground news Bobby followed on the Internet, and plain old gossip. There was too much to pay attention, so Bobby usually chose to remain in the dark. His producer was more responsible than he was, and while in her care, she always made sure he learned what he needed to know.

"With August?"

Bobby's eyes ticked toward his wall calendar. It was one of those obnoxious Hemisphere feel-good calendars: a Necrophage advertisement in disguise. Every month featured an overly happy-looking necrotic with a stroke victim's smile. May's photo had a mostly decaying torso, but at least whatever it was looked joyous.

"It's July."

"August Maughan."

"What about him? Do I need to cancel my appointment?"

"Maybe," Cindy said. "Seems he's vanished."

"August has been 'vanished' for years." Bobby returned his attention to the blue-and-green map atop the table.

*"Really* vanished."

Bobby picked up one of his highlighters and dragged it along the straight edge of a ruler, connecting one Reserve spot to another.

"I'm sure he has his phone."

"Bobby."

Bobby finished his line then looked up in the quiet, where Cindy was all but tapping her foot, waiting.

"You're not listening to me. Do you know about the thing with Holly Gaynor?"

"What thing?"

"She was giving out some awards for Hemisphere. She suddenly started talking normally."

"Fascinating."

"Bobby, she's practically tipping point. You've seen her movies. You can barely understand her."

Bobby looked back down. Put one finger at the ridge. Another in Purgatory Valley. There was something missing — something he just wasn't seeing.

Barely paying attention, Bobby said, "Maybe she was acting."

"Her being strange is kind of whatever. We've seen weirder things out in the park, honestly. But then everyone kind of got uneasy. Cops or crowd control moved around to settle things, and for a while, in the footage, it's like something bad could have happened."

"Did it?"

"No."

Bobby looked up, not taking his fingers from their

places, and flashed his white teeth at Cindy, lips stretched to his widest smile.

"This is a great story. I love a happy ending."

"August was there. At the awards ceremony."

Bobby's cheeks went slack.

"There with Holly Gaynor?"

Cindy nodded. "Across the street. The cameras pan over when some cops move in that direction. Looks like he's guilty of something, really. He shuffles right into a cab and peels away."

"Why was he there?"

"Officially, nobody's saying anything. But if you look on the boards, people think Holly was a client."

"Big deal. *I'm* a client."

"You want to live forever. If Holly's a client, she just wants to live."

"August does life extension. What the hell would he do with a deadhead as a client?"

Cindy looked like she was about to rebuke Bobby for his borderline slur, so he rushed to beat her.

"She's practically dead, Cindy. Maybe *actually* dead, technically. She must have a two-week incubation. How exactly is August supposed to help someone like that? Necrophage keeps them alive, but it's like treading water."

"I'm just telling you what people are saying. Holly looks right at him, the cops or clarifiers or whoever they are look where she's looking, and then there's this slow-speed chase where everyone looks too polite to run. If you ask me, it seems like they were all curious like you are. What exactly would the world's best-known longevity specialist be doing with a necrotic client?"

"He used to work at Hemisphere."

"He cofounded Hemisphere," Cindy said.

"So? They developed Necrophage. Maybe it makes sense."

"He left before Necrophage. Or during. I'd need to check. Before that, Hemisphere was all life extension."

Bobby tapped the highlighter against his chin. "You know, Alice was asking about him. About August."

"Asking in what way?"

"In the way a reporter who mainly covers necrotic culture and Sherman Pope would ask, maybe." He tapped the highlighter a few more times. "What time is it back East?"

"Seven thirty."

"It's got to be later than that."

"You're a smart guy, Bobby. I don't know why you can't figure out how time zones work." Pause. "What, do you want to do another special? You want me to call her for you?"

Bobby thought then shook his head. "No. I'm headed back to Dead City tomorrow anyway." He looked around the Bivouac. "Which, ironically, is far less dead than what I'm used to."

"I wasn't kidding, Bobby. I tried contacting him for you. I'm getting nothing but voicemail. He hasn't been publicly visible in the best of times, and suddenly everyone is interested in him again, and whether he had something to do with Holly Gaynor's strange appearance … who, by the way, seems to have gone underground as well. Not that I have *her* phone number. But, you know. Rumor."

*"Rumor,* Cindy."

"I don't think August is going to be interested in *restoring your telemetry* if he's — "

"Telomeres."

"Whatever. I love you, Bobby, but let's face it. You pay that man a shitload of money for what are essentially spa treatments. I can't imagine it's worth flying all the way back to Aberdeen for, if he has other things on his mind."

"Our visa is up anyway," Bobby said, his attention straying back to the map. It was circled with five colors of highlighter, each with its own meaning. Bobby hoped Cindy wouldn't look too closely and ask him about it. Given all the detail he'd added about movements, time-stamps, and positions, there was little chance of her believing he was planning locations to shoot on their next visit.

"I can get us an extension. Finish the current season. We need to take advantage and film while the weather is good, Bobby."

Bobby shook his head. "Three goddamned months surrounded by zombies. That's enough. I need a break." Again, his eyes went to the map. *And it's getting inside my head.*

"Two more weeks. Two more weeks on site, and we can have a half year in the can."

"Or we could leave then come back to Yosemite later as planned. We need off-site specials, too. You know our viewers like the hide 'n' seek shows. It's one thing to hunt inside a federal preserve. But it's so much more thrilling when we make them wonder if there are ferals hiding in *their* garages."

"You're not going to find ferals in Aberdeen Valley, Bobby. Nor, probably, in the surrounding land. It's too well controlled."

Bobby thought. Cindy was right, of course. There were a few ferals everywhere, and despite Panacea's control and education programs — *curl into a ball and yell* was the new *duck and cover* — there would always be idiots who got bitten and ignored the infection, or rednecks who kept too-far-gone friends and family in cages or chains. Ratings were always great for Yosemite shows, but the Reserve felt far off and unreal to most people. Closer-to-home scares glued people to their couches, kept them buying supplies and guns, building fences and installing security lights.

Still, the idea of staying on a visa extension was appealing. Bobby almost wanted to believe Cindy — to accept that his appointment with August was off anyway and that there was therefore no reason for going home. These days, he lived at Yosemite more than Aberdeen anyway.

But it only took one look at the map to change his mind. He wanted her to leave so he could finish obsessing. So he could resume searching for patterns, pulling footage from the park's security feeds and watching hour after hour on 5x speed, waiting for one specific deadhead. It was unhealthy. The expired visa had given him an unarguable deadline to leave, and he didn't want to hear about possibilities of staying. He'd lose his mind if he did. Bobby needed saving. From himself.

The ambush had made Cam run, never to return.

It only made Bobby want to dig in deeper, sure it meant he was closer to finding Golem than ever before.

Cindy finally noticed Bobby's marked-up map. She took a step forward, but he swept it away, folding the big thing into a mess.

"Make sure the pilots are ready, here and in Fresno," Bobby said. "You can stay if you want, but I'm leaving tomorrow."

Cindy looked like she might protest, but then sensibility seemed to descend. Whatever she saw on the news had raised her hackles, but Cindy was smart enough to know that he needed to go. A lot of Bobby's success came from being half-crazy; it wouldn't be smart to push him all the way.

Besides, it's not like he couldn't work back in Aberdeen.

It's not like he couldn't watch Yosemite's security footage from afar.

Bobby shuffled his map and stood, trying to convince himself that the revelation about August Maughan and Holly Gaynor held no interest.

August wouldn't have any thoughts about why some necrotics didn't act much like necrotics at all.

Not a chance.

# Chapter Thirty-Seven

## FAIL

THE ROAD BETWEEN HEMISPHERE AND the Sunny Day Trailer Park was mostly flat, but to Danny it felt like a roller coaster.

He'd left work with a lump in his stomach. The second half of the day had been torture. He'd accomplished nothing, and after ignoring the first of Jordache's afternoon texts, she'd sent two more. Earlier, he'd been able to put her off, but things had changed. If he replied now, he'd have to either tell her the truth or lie. The gray area was all gone. He wouldn't be procuring any designer Necrophage in time to keep Jordache from jonesing — let alone the ultra-exclusive PhageX, which he'd never even seen outside of Ian's high-level inventory access. Officially, PhageX didn't exist, so far as Danny could tell. It couldn't be purchased at any price, forged prescription and absurd cost (Danny was willing to pay, if he had to) aside.

But maybe he could buy some of the more ordinary designs. He'd heard good things about Charm and Strange. Even Twisted seemed intriguing; he and Jordache had laughed over that one and its supposed inhibition-lowering add-ins, and Danny secretly hoped taking such a thing would loosen her enough to get Jordache boarding the Danny Express.

He couldn't do it easily, though. He didn't have personal access, even to samples. Asking the other reps might get him busted and get prying eyes where they shouldn't be. He could try to buy some but wasn't sure where — and, again, knew he'd need a prescription. Base Necrophage was like locker room tampons, according to Jordache. Nobody put barriers in front of either because nobody wanted you bleeding all over the place for want of a quarter.

Gross but apt. True Jordache at her most charming.

Thinking of Jordache — imagining her yearning and starting to panic — unseated Danny as his workday neared its end. He'd shoved his phone into a desk drawer and forgotten it. Literally. He hadn't remembered to take it from his desk when he'd left, and now, on the drive, he couldn't get any of Jordache's fearful texts if he wanted to.

When he'd begun driving, Danny's roller coaster had been at a low. He'd have to tell her he'd failed. There was no other option. She'd have to go on base Phage for at least a day or two or three. She'd be crushed. She claimed that PhageX was more than medicine. She said it was like a fresh start in a bottle. It was as if the drug didn't merely keep her decay where it stopped. It seemed to have pushed her further back. Elevated her beyond her old station. She was becoming more interested in conversation. Curious about movies and books.

But as Danny drove, the sinking feeling slowly abated. He began to feel less terrible then actively better. He was making too much of this. He wasn't taking away something Jordache needed; he was taking away something she *wanted*. And while Danny would love for his girl to have all she wanted, the distinction remained exactly that. Maybe there was a kind of addiction there, but it was mental, not physical. Her *burning need* for PhageX, above and beyond the base formulation that would keep her healthy, was all in her head. Jordache would be fine, if she could get over her preconceptions.

Her attachment to the designer drug was psychosomatic.

"Holy fuck," Danny said aloud.

He hit the car's brake. The vehicle behind, despite collision avoidance, nearly rear-ended him, swerving around with a long, braying honk.

Danny turned into the parking lot in front of the white building on Aberdeen's outskirts — something old enough to be pre-Hemisphere but still safely away from the ghettos and the curious breed of crime unique to the poor infected.

He had an idea.

Danny got out, checking his pockets, digging his wallet out from under the avalanche of in-car garbage.

He knew what he needed to do. And if he was lucky, he could probably get away clean.

zombie. And while Danny wouldn't want his girl to have all the scorned, the [illegible] exactly that. Maybe there was a kind of [illegible] then, but it was [illegible] physical. He [illegible] for Phoebe, above and beyond the [illegible] would keep her reality was all in her head, and he would be fine if the [illegible] got over [illegible] pieces.

Her [illegible] to the dead [illegible] was [illegible] [illegible].

"[illegible]," Danny said aloud.

He [illegible] the [illegible]. The [illegible] behind [illegible] [illegible] [illegible] around [illegible] a long, [illegible].

Danny [illegible] parking lot in front of the [illegible] building [illegible] something [illegible] and the [illegible] of [illegible] the [illegible] infected.

He had an idea.

Danny got out, checking his pockets, [illegible] his wallet out [illegible] of [illegible].

He knew what he needed to do. And if he [illegible], he could [illegible] away [illegible].

# Chapter Thirty-Eight

## SKIN DISTRICT

ALICE WATCHED THE SKYLINE DARKEN in the distance. She kept her engine running. The engine was a next-gen hybrid and barely purred, mostly drawing juice at a low idle rather than torque from a loud engine. Still, the vehicle's little sounds were a comfort, making her feel like she could floor it and be gone in a shot if she needed to.

The thought itself was tinged with liberal guilt. Alice had parked on a slight rise, in what passed for a low-rent park, and the surrounding area was mostly clear in all directions. Nobody — and nothing — could come for her without being seen, and that was doubly true because Alice had parked under a large halogen streetlight. Still, the idea that she'd taken precautions (the open parking spot, the light, the running engine) felt wrong. Alice Frank was supposed to be a crusader for human rights — even if the definition of human had changed in recent years. She was supposed to be fighting for the little guys on the bottom rung, casting a skeptical eye at the big boys. Alice had covered little other than Hemisphere since the first big outbreaks, since Bakersfield, since Rip Daddy had mutated into the far more troublesome Sherman Pope. That was supposed to make disenfranchised people of all stripes (but especially necrotics) her peeps. And, in theory, she should be their peeps, too.

And yet here she was, in the most densely necrotic part of town, her windows up, doors locked, engine running, jittering like a scared little white girl in the middle of the inner city.

She forced herself to lower her window. She'd see anyone before they could do anything to her anyway, and if she was politically incorrectly frightened of necrotic criminals, she had even less to worry about. In this part of town, victims often had real advantages over gunmen. It was hard for all but the newest necrotics to use firearms at all, they weren't usually fast, and you couldn't understand them anyway when they said, *Gif me aww jor muddy, or I'll thute.*

The thought made Alice give a shameful, nervous laugh. The park was deserted, and her own snicker seemed to echo back as if off the wall of a handball court. Hearing it, thinking of necrotics playing handball, Alice laughed again. The new laugh echoed back harder in the twilight, and finally her bones seemed to chill. She pressed her lips tight.

Headlights appeared in the distance. Alice swallowed, gripped her steering wheel despite that ever-present guilt, and steeled herself. As the sky darkened and the sounds of night in the so-called Skin District started to chatter, an empty park wasn't a place a healthy lady wanted to be alone. She'd flee if this wasn't the person she'd come here to meet.

She couldn't see the car's cab until the headlights were

eclipsed by her own car's body. But then she saw the face inside and relaxed: a man in his thirties, face stubbled, hair combed in a way that was perhaps overly neat. He had bright-blue eyes just like the few photos she'd found online, and despite the circumstances, he managed a small, attractive smile in greeting.

His window went down. The two cars paused side by side with their fronts in opposite directions, open windows lined up.

"Did you have any trouble finding the place?" Alice asked.

Ian shook his head. "No. It came up in my GPS. I saw your headlights when I came in on the main service road. The gate was closed, but there was room to drive around on the grass."

Alice nodded. "I didn't know they closed it. I've only been here in the daytime."

He swallowed. His Adam's apple bobbed as Alice watched his profile. He didn't want to say it any more than Alice had wanted to admit it to herself, but he was scared shitless. Maybe even more frightened than he'd sounded on the phone when he, for a change, had dialed her number.

"What made you call me?" she asked. He'd been so guarded on the line. Alice felt the same most of the time, but it was strange to see paranoia from someone who lived in Lion's Gate. Ian wore suits to work and probably pulled in around a half-million dollars a year. Alice was used to speaking like her phones were bugged because they probably were. But Ian worked for Hemisphere. Strange that he'd suddenly become afraid they'd overhear him.

"Something is going on. I don't know what it is, but it's something."

Alice wanted to make a sarcastic remark, but now wasn't the time. He was here. He'd made contact. For now, she'd handle him with kid gloves if it kept him talking, grateful that her absurdly priced scrambler would destroy the dialogue for anyone who might be listening in.

"Did you learn something that … that changed your mind about talking to me?"

"Someone's watching my house. I've been … called in."

"When we were talking earlier. It sounded like someone grabbed you."

Ian nodded.

"Why? Where did they take you?"

Ian's eyes flicked around the park. "Not here."

"Why not?" Alice looked toward the road, the direction Ian had come from. "Were you followed?"

"I don't know. I've never been followed before. This isn't something I'm used to. It's not something I goddamn deserve!"

Alice let it go. She could see fear, frustration, anger. Ian wasn't acting like a normal source. He was acting reluctant, as if he'd been dragged here. As if he didn't particularly want to talk but found her to be the least of his pressing evils.

"It's safe here. Nobody can hear."

"It looks bad. What would I be doing in this part of town?"

"Checking in on all the good Hemisphere is doing."

Ian shot her a look.

"Sorry. I make jokes when I'm nervous. You want to go somewhere else, we'll go somewhere else. No problem."

Ian was still looking around. In the distance was a playground that looked a bit sad in the daylight but managed to look menacing in the dark. It was all plastic, all padded, all totally necrotic safe for the little dead children. The city had erected the park two years ago as a grand gesture then forgotten it. Locals had taken it over, some good, some bad. This section had grown decrepit in just two years but was the safest of the lot. There were hideaways among the wooded sections where people traded lost body parts. Not for use. Just for fun.

"No. It's fine. I'm just … I don't like any of this. I didn't ask for it."

"You're doing the right thing."

Ian's eyes became momentarily hard, shadowed under the reflected glow from the overhead light. "I'm doing the only thing I can. I'm not trying to be noble. To be honest, I'm not convinced you're not behind more of it than you're admitting."

Alice decided her best chance was to attack the accusation head on. "Understandable. But you called. You came. So you must believe me on some level. What changed your mind?"

"I saw that it wasn't you staking out my house. It was men. Two of them."

"Maybe they're my cohorts."

"They have Panacea plates."

"Panacea?"

"You know who else has Panacea plates, just for the permissions?"

"You think the people outside your house are Hemisphere?"

"One or the other. But not just anyone at Hemisphere. I have normal North Carolina plates. But I've seen the lines blur before."

Alice had heard rumors that confirmed what Ian was implying — that Hemisphere and Panacea worked together more closely than was commonly accepted —

but it seemed too early in their relationship to be too bold.

"Why do you think they're watching you?"

Ian half scowled. "I don't know." Then he told her a story very like her own: an anonymous source who gave hints but never any real information, nudges from this direction and that without any real help, even a response from Archibald Burgess himself that made Ian's paranoia about being stalked feel valid. To Alice, Ian sounded like a pawn. He seemed to be suspecting Hemisphere plenty, but ironically the company seemed to have caused his suspicions itself. The Ian Keys she'd researched and tried to call earlier had sounded like a Boy Scout, loyal to the end. Now he sounded like a jilted lover. Someone whose dutiful affections had been upended one too many times.

"I think the same person has been leading me," Alice said then gave him her own history, from the anonymous packet at her door to the way her phone had rung, finding herself voice to voice with Ian as if she'd placed the call herself.

But that reminded her of something, too.

"BioFuse," Alice said.

Ian's head flicked toward her.

"I got a message while we were talking. It said, 'Ask him about BioFuse.'"

Ian's eyebrows scrunched together. "What about it?"

"I don't know. I got a pamphlet. A product brochure. And I looked it up online. Seems like it was one of Hemisphere's earliest drugs, discontinued around the time Sherman Pope hit. Does that ring any bells?"

Ian shrugged. "It's like you said. It was one of the lines Archibald believed in most. If not for the outbreak, we'd probably be in the BioFuse business today."

"Curing Alzheimer's," said Alice. She'd had a grandmother who'd died mostly demented, unable to remember her own husband. Nana had gone before BioFuse would have hit prime time, but it felt like a worthy line of research to Alice, for other people's sake. Maybe designer Necrophage (and international distribution of base Necrophage, *just in case*) was more lucrative than their dropped line, but letting it go felt almost offensive.

"It was one of a suite of drugs. Alzheimer's, yes. But there were others."

"Were the others discontinued?" Alice asked.

"I don't know. I'd have to check."

"Why was BioFuse discontinued?"

"I don't know. It's a company legend, but I don't know the details."

"Was it distributed? Did people take it, I mean?"

"Oh, sure. A lot of people, I think."

"Wasn't it profitable?"

"I assume it was, but again, I'd need to ask."

"But other drugs like it remain in production?"

Ian nodded.

"Why just cut the one?"

"I don't know a lot of details."

"How did it work. Do you know? Was it a … " Alice fluttered, wondering why she'd asked. She didn't know the types of pharmaceuticals or what to do with any information he gave her. She was recording on the sly via the digital recorder in her pocket and could analyze anything said afterward (all of this was off the record anyway), but asking-wise, she was at a total loss. "A beta-blocker or something?" she finished, wondering why it could possibly matter. "What did it do to help Alzheimer's patients?"

"I don't know. I'm not a chemist."

"You must know something."

"I'm an executive. I work in an office. When I ask too many science questions, people look at me funny."

"You've asked?"

Ian looked caught. But what the hell; he'd come here to talk of his own free will.

"One of the bits my anonymous tipster was pushing at me had to do with viruses. So yes, I asked."

"What did you find out?"

"Nothing."

"You must have learned *something.*"

"No, nothing!" Ian tipped his head back and peered at the ceiling, looking for all the world like a man resisting an outburst of temper. He looked back over. "I didn't even know *what* to ask — *virology* was all I had. Shit, I don't know about any of this. I was just sitting in my office, and someone started pushing shit at me. Stuff I didn't understand. Told me to copy it, so I did. Told me to read it, so I did that, too. But none of it made sense. The stuff I could understand was all basic company information. Not even confidential."

That sounded familiar. Whoever was playing Deep Throat for them both was inexplicably cagey. He or she seemed unwilling to come out and say what the hell either of them needed to know. Instead, they were being led on scavenger hunts that seemed to be on a collision course … with no useful results.

"All of it? It was all public?"

"What I could understand, yes."

"What about the stuff you *couldn't* understand?"

Ian looked back at Alice, seeming ready to shout and drive away. "I *couldn't understand it,*" he said slowly, as if she were a late-stage necrotic, barely able to tie her shoes.

"Was it about BioFuse?"

"I don't know. Some was about Sherman Pope. Studies on its structure."

"Its structure is established, I thought," Alice said.

"Right. So why give it to me?"

"Maybe someone's trying to get us to connect the dots."

"Well, are *your* dots connecting at all?" Ian spat.

Alice paused, feeling stung, knowing Ian's anger wasn't really for her. And even if it was, she was used to being yelled at, and could take it.

"Okay," Alice said carefully. "I've got the public platform. You have the access. Forget trying to figure out why Deep Throat won't get to the point for a minute, and forget about why he didn't come to me. That itself feels like an incomplete puzzle, if it's a puzzle. I feel like I'm being led to BioFuse. You can't tell me about BioFuse, but you could find out. You could ask."

"Ask whom? And what the hell am I supposed to do with whatever long-winded bullshit I hear that I won't be able to make sense of even if I get it without raising a ton of suspicion … when, I'll remind you, I've already been warned? Burgess sounded like he was making a threat. He had two goddamned *goons* drag me into his office for a lecture on evolution and mission and purpose. Now my wife tells me we're getting strange calls, and there are people watching my house. My *family*. I'm not here because I'm a fan of your work or want to *expose the truth*, as you seem so eager to do. I'm here because I didn't start any of this, and this feels like the most likely way to make it stop."

Alice thought. Ian was being driven by fear. Alice was responsible for a few of those hang-up calls to Mrs. Keys, but the rest sounded like threats, sure and true. Fear for himself and his family would motivate him, but altruism wouldn't. If she wanted Ian's help, the right levers would need to be applied.

"We need someone who can make sense of whatever you find," Alice said. "The missing piece of this puzzle, between the mouthpiece and the guy with access."

"What are you talking about?" Ian asked.

Alice told him.

# Chapter Thirty-Nine

## PLAYING POSSUM

DAMON KEPT PACING. IN HOLLY'S mind, he was dangerously close to making circles around her. Right now she was in her Aberdeen Valley house, slumped in a chair, her tranquil view of the city below mostly unobstructed. Right now, Holly thought she was sitting like she normally would — poor, dumb Holly, pretty and talented in the right ways despite being so fucked up in the head, staring out at the vista her money had paid for. But if Damon began making full circles instead of the pacing half moons he was cutting into the carpet behind her, she might start to feel like the subject of an interrogation. Someone who'd turned like a dog gone rabid, biting the hand that fed her.

No pun intended.

The thought made Holly simultaneously nervous and angry, though she was careful to let neither emotion show, affecting the distant, somewhat vacant expression she'd grown used to wearing instead. She was nervous because if being an August Maughan pharmaceutical success story was a crime, then Holly was definitely guilty. And she was angry because if she *had* felt better recently — if her mind had been recalling much of what had been lost, her mouth relearning the trick of proper speech — then that wasn't something she should have to hide or be ashamed of. In her own goddamned house. In front of the same goddamned people whose salaries she so generously paid.

Cyrus, also pacing, entered Holly's field of view, blocking the hospital and the architectural elegance of the Sherman Pope Memorial Museum. Holly merely looked over, keeping her face overly curious and empty.

"Holly?" he said.

"Huh?"

"I want you to understand something."

"Uh-huh."

"You didn't do anything wrong. Damon and me aren't mad at you."

Holly thought, *"Damon and I," asshole.* Instead, she nodded.

"But we want to understand."

"Umderstan."

"When you were onstage, you sounded … different."

Damon stepped into Holly's view from the other side. "You spoke really good up there, Honey."

"And it's good that you spoke … good."

*That's eloquent.* But from her lips: "Yeah."

"But it was also strange. Because — and I know you're an actor — but it was like … " He looked at Cyrus for help.

"Just say it, man," Cyrus replied.

"I don't want to insult her."

"It's not an insult. It's a fact."

Holly kept herself from looking at the two men as they discussed her. She'd been really playing it up since her slip onstage. That hadn't been close to intentional. For weeks, as she'd been taking August's Prestige drug, she'd found herself increasingly able to think clearly, to solve problems that had previously eluded her (like the bathroom lock; that bastard was *tough)*, and to articulate herself internally, even if it was lost in translation once facing the barrier of her lips. That was still a huge problem, even now; even when she'd been practicing clear words with August, those clear words hadn't come close to voicing Holly's intention. But it was better. Slowly, surely better. In her brain, if not in her body.

But she'd never let that improvement show before today.

Today, it had felt more normal to speak well than in the lazy way her paralyzed mouth muscles wanted to.

Damon and Cyrus had taken her by the arms, and Holly had forced herself to slouch, to drool a little, to affect her usual nowhere expression. On the ride in, she'd played with the door locks as if they fascinated her. And when they'd taken her home and settled in as if they had any reason or right to be in her house, Holly had let them help her with the door. Let them show her to her own damned chair in her own damned living room. She'd grunted a request for a glass of water then had spilled half of it down her front.

Damon looked right in her eyes. "Holly, Honey, you said those words really well. Like … well, like someone who's not different like you are."

*Different*. Holly could almost smell the syrup dripping from his condescending word. Just a minute ago, he'd said she'd spoken differently, when "different" had meant "good." Now different meant something else, something these men secretly felt wouldn't be good for them.

Holly thought, *I've had an elocution coach and been taking dialect lessons since I was a kid, so it's hardly surprising that I can express myself sufficient to satisfy a crowd.* Instead, she said, "Yeah."

"Well, doesn't that seem strange to you?"

Holly shrugged. Only her left arm rose very far. The right was mostly dead and had been for a while. When she went onstage in anything sleeveless, that arm needed makeup. Thank God she had African blood; a white girl would have looked blue.

Damon turned to Cyrus. "She doesn't get it."

"I keep telling you, we have to find that fucking shaman or whatever the hell he thinks he is."

"Sure. I'll get right on trying to call him." Damon rolled his eyes at the edge of Holly's vision.

"She'll have his number. He would have put it in her phone."

A big hand reached out and opened Holly's purse, which she'd left on the coffee table. Then Cyrus was holding up her phone, scrolling.

But of course, Holly had deleted August's address book entry on the drive over after memorizing his number.

"He's not in here."

"Maybe he always calls her. Makes sense, I guess." Damon snapped his fingers to grab her attention. "Holly. You okay in there?"

"Okay," Holly parroted.

"This is important. Do you know how we can find your friend August?"

"She's not going to know *that,*" Cyrus said.

"Don't underestimate her. This girl can still act just fine."

*Yes*, Holly thought, *I sure can.*

"How do we find August?" Damon repeated.

"Afust calls me," Holly slurred.

"If he doesn't call you. If you really, really wanted to talk to him, how would you do it?"

"Afust calls on't phone."

Damon straightened up. Holly saw him give Cyrus a *What now?* look.

"It doesn't matter," Cyrus told him.

"I don't know what to tell the press. Do *you* know what to tell the press?"

"Let Maughan talk to the press. He did this to her."

Damon looked down at Holly as if she were a knick-knack then returned his attention to Cyrus.

"Maybe he didn't do anything."

"You heard her. *Everyone* heard her. That wasn't normal."

"He probably just coached her. As if she were in a movie."

"So you think it's a trick?"

"Why not?" Then Damon bent again to look at Holly. "Holly. Say, 'tethers of illness.'"

Holly saw the trap for what it was. With perfect clarity, she said, "'Tethers of illness.'"

"Okay. Now say, 'The dog ate the bone.'"

"Dog ate't bun."

Damon stood tall again. Holly gazed out at the city in the valley, listening.

"See?" said Damon.

"See what?"

Holly had to fight a laugh. She saw it just fine.

"She can say *those specific words* she said onstage. Coached, like I said."

"She doesn't talk that well in movies," said Cyrus, doubtful.

"Because she's playing twitchers. What, is anyone going to believe her as the first lady?"

"I don't know, man."

"The press wants to talk, let them try and find Maughan. You saw the report. He was there, and everyone knows it. He even *looked* guilty."

"What about the people calling for Holly?"

"Let Laura handle them. She can write up a press release or something. A fancy version of 'No comment.'"

There was a long moment of quiet as the men seemed to consider. Finally, one of them sighed (Holly couldn't see which as she scrutinized the Hemisphere building in the distance) and a hand settled on her shoulder.

"We're going to go, Holly," said Damon's voice. "Got some work to do."

"Okay," Holly said.

"You need anything?"

"No."

"Are you okay here alone?"

"I'm fide."

Another beat of quiet. Then Cyrus said, "You want the TV on or anything?"

Hating herself but wanting to add icing to this particular cake, Holly said, "Zobbie."

Cyrus reached for the TV remote, and Holly watched him navigate to an episode of *Are You Smarter Than a Zombie?* Holly remembered loving this show — not because she wanted to see if uninfected contestants could answer questions better than the show's stable of resident wackos, but because she'd liked seeing the wackos themselves. It was nice to see your people on TV, whether they were the high-functioning Gloria (who'd earned her Ph.D. and had an incubation of sixteen hours), or the comic relief everyone simply called Stump.

Now, Holly found it insulting. And as Cyrus turned on

her screen, Holly kept her gaze out the window, across the city.

Without saying more, Cyrus and Damon walked through the door behind her.

Holly waited until she could no longer hear the purr of Damon's hybrid, auto-drive Daimler, then picked up her phone and dialed the number in her head.

## Chapter Forty

### SPENT CARTRIDGES

BY THE TIME DANNY WAS pulling into Sunny Day and to the front of Jordache's small but neat trailer, he felt much, much better.

First of all, his PhageX problem wasn't permanent. For whatever reason, Ian's access code had changed, but that was a delay, not a denial. Ian still worked at Hemisphere; he hadn't been fired, demoted, or mysteriously gone missing. Ian and Danny were friendly, and Ian seemed to respect Danny's hustle. He'd borrowed Ian's code card once and he could find a way to get it again to siphon off the new code. Danny felt motivated, and Ian had been looking stressed and tired. Ian needed to unwind, and Danny knew he could find friendly ways to make that happen. He needed a week at the most, a day or two being far more likely. Then he'd have his full set of keys again and would be able to get Jordache all the high-end Phage she needed, no problem.

Second of all, as he'd already reminded himself and then repeated ad nauseam, Jordache wasn't actually going without anything she needed. Danny wasn't yet authorized to sell the designer formulations, but he knew how they worked. Base Necrophage kept the disease at bay. Designer Phage had "enhancers" that Danny thought of like mix-ins added to vanilla at an ice cream bar. They made your hair shinier, your eyes clearer and more sparkly, your lips redder, or your eyelashes longer. All were nice for girls like Jordache who'd grown used to the finer aspects of undead life, but none were necessary. There were rumors about some of the designers making users feel smarter or more open-minded, but that was bullshit. Danny had seen the tests; he was a smart kid who didn't want to stay a salesman forever and thought he could move into development, given time. Necrophage — from its base formulation all the way up to the most expensive drug on the shelf — stopped Sherman Pope in its tracks. That was it. You couldn't rebuild parts of a brain that were already dead.

Before killing the engine, Danny bounced a box of brand-new base Necrophage Gadget cartridges in his hand. He still had an empty PhageX box in with the rest of his car's garbage, conveniently filled with spent cartridges. So one by one, he swapped labels on the refills: base Phage covered up by PhageX branding. The labels transferred with too much ease, as if fate wanted this bit of necessary deception. As if it was right, and he was blessed.

She'd be going without something she *wanted*, not something she *needed*.

Jordache didn't need it and wouldn't be going without it for long anyway, so what was the point in her even *knowing* she wasn't taking PhageX? There was zero upside. If Danny told her that she'd need to spend a few days or a week on base Necrophage, Jordache would freak out. She'd panic over her imagined, psychosomatic need. She'd cry, and Danny hated when she cried — not because it bothered him in itself, but because she seemed so ashamed of weakness. Jordache might even be angry, even if she wouldn't want to be. And for what? An imagined temporary loss over something her body wouldn't miss?

But on the other hand, Danny's little white lie would have plenty of upsides. For all intents and purposes, he would have solved her problem. He'd have relieved her, allowed her to stop worrying and panicking. She'd feel better, and he, having *fixed things*, would definitely feel better, too. Life would go on, with everyone happy.

Danny scanned the car for evidence. He tossed the box from the pharmacy, and the old PhageX box was still unbent enough to pass for new. The box itself wasn't dated; it hadn't been prescribed and was, like everything Danny got from Ian's account, just stock.

It was the perfect crime. Danny had a simple cartridge, with zero indication of what it had once been. Jordache would buy it for sure.

Exiting the car and sliding the bottle into his pocket, Danny felt a twinge of guilt. But this was a lie in the service of her best interests. What would be gained by telling her the truth, for either of them?

*Nothing.* And a week or two from now, none of this would remotely matter.

He didn't make it up Jordache's front steps before she was opening the door, her eyes wide, her hair in an adorable tousled mess.

"I've been texting you all day," she said without preamble. It wasn't an accusation, but Jordache was clearly drawn far too thin.

"I forgot my phone at work," Danny said, keeping his expression neutral.

Her face fell. "Oh."

Then Danny smiled his best salesman's smile. He slid the box of refills from his pocket and held it up.

"But I remembered this," he said.

# Chapter Forty-One

## COLD SHOULDER

BRIDGET'S ARM FOUND IAN'S BARE side under the covers. He began turning toward her then seemed to reconsider and turned away. A moment later, she found herself looking up at Ian's shirtless back in the dim bedroom.

"What?" she asked, wondering at the way he'd pulled back.

"I overslept."

"You seem so eager to get out of bed."

"Because I overslept."

Bridget felt like she should return his inexplicably cold (or at least hurried) shoulder with some chill of her own, but the same thing that should have made iciness easy made it difficult: Increasingly, Bridget was sure she was right about what Ian was up to. Right now it felt like she was facing a choice: she could have her pride, or try again to repair whatever had inexplicably broken, and have her husband.

She touched his side, fighting an odd blend of

emotions. The touch was sensual, but Ian stood away from it, fishing through his laundry for a shirt.

"You're not going to kiss me good morning?"

Ian turned. He'd already flicked on the light, and the look in his blue eyes, for a reason Bridget didn't entirely understand, made her sad. The glance lasted only a moment, and he came to her sincerely, sliding beside her but still atop the covers, kissing her with feeling.

"I'm sorry. It's just that I'm going to have to hurry. I don't know why I slept through the alarm."

Bridget had heard the alarm. It had gone off for nearly a full minute before she'd reached carefully over Ian and killed it. She couldn't explain, even to herself, why she hadn't woken him.

"You were out too late."

Ian looked back. She'd only made a statement, not an accusation. He looked like he might respond to the latter with an excuse. But if she was only saying, he didn't need to rebut.

Of course, he did anyway.

"I just had that thing with Smyth."

"He's never made you work late before."

"Well, this thing with Alice … this thing with the Yosemite documentary has caused a lot of problems."

"I haven't heard about any problems on the news."

"Good. That means PR is doing its job."

"You're not PR, Ian." To her own ears, Bridget thought her tone sounded on the verge of pleading. She wouldn't beg. They were only having a discussion, not a fight.

"Exactly. I'm strategy. The people who actually make a difference in what's done rather than just the smoke and mirrors."

"What were you and Raymond working on that had to happen at night?"

"It would bore you, Bridget."

She turned and slid her legs to hang off the bed's edge. Ian was dressing facing away from her, and her pivot turned her away from him. She put on a shirt and slid her feet into slippers. He'd stung in the tiniest of ways. Usually, if Ian used her name, he shortened it affectionately to "Bridge."

"And the nighttime work in your office. Reviewing … videos." Her mind spooled back to the poking around on his computer, the files and history he'd left behind, the drive filled with something that had gone missing. Was it possible he'd been reviewing *different* videos? Or video conferences over a secure connection?

"Will you be working late tonight?"

"I don't know."

"Can we have lunch?" She laughed, pretending this was the light banter it appeared to be. "I think I can clear my schedule here for long enough to come down to Hemisphere."

Ian turned his head, his torso still facing away. Again, she saw that strange expression in his eyes. It looked almost like regret. Or guilt.

"Not today." He paused then said, "Tomorrow?"

Bridget felt herself prying, knowing that each time she added another casual question, everything felt less casual. She was a hands-off wife. She didn't butt in; she didn't meddle; she enjoyed hearing Gabriella mouth off but didn't usually gossip on her own. But there was something else she'd been thinking of lately, though it hadn't bothered her for their entire marriage: She'd given up a career to mind this house for him. At first, when Ana had been small and they'd had less, it almost made sense. But today, with cleaning services and little vacuuming devices and a girl in school all day, she was a woman adrift. It should sound opulent, and Gabriella certainly seemed intent on believing herself to be quite the deliciously kept woman. But for Bridget, it often felt idle and lonely.

Gabriella filled her hours with affairs.

Bridget wouldn't ever do that.

And yet Ian, who was far busier than she was, seemed like maybe he'd found time for one of his own.

Bridget stood. Knowing she should be angry and feeling sad instead, she swallowed her pride and circled the bed, putting her hand on his shoulder.

"I've missed you lately."

Ian's head ticked back to look at her — not full on, but halfway. Then his eyes were forward again, and he continued to pull on clothes for a day that was apparently too busy for her.

He opened the door to the hallway, avoiding the bathroom, probably because she'd be in it.

"I won't be late," he said.

# Chapter Forty-Two

## PLOTS AND SCHEMES

IAN PEEKED INTO THE LIVING room and saw Analise watching TV, sitting on the couch with a bowl of Cinnamon Toast Crunch. They'd told her not to do that. Ana was neat enough when she ate, but she kept setting the bowl on the cushions beside her. Three or four times now, either she'd shifted or one of the adults had come to sit beside her, and they'd had to extract milk from the fabric.

He'd say something later. When he said hello, which could happen around the time he put on deodorant, combed his hair, and brushed his teeth. He felt scatter-brained, unable to find his footing. Every turn inside his house felt like a decision worth weighing, whereas mornings usually happened on autopilot.

Ian backed away from the living room, feeling like a shit for not at least going out and saying hello. It was about the same level of terrible he felt for being so terse with Bridget.

He shook the feeling away. This was a short-term issue. It was for the best, for everyone. Nobody needed to know that the house was being watched, that the phones (said

Alice, anyway) might be bugged, that their computer activity might be getting logged. Bridget already knew some of it, and that had probably been the point. But now that he knew, Ian would do his best to keep it from them.

Nobody would call. He'd already talked to the phone company, and that already-should-be-unknown number had been changed.

Nobody would drive by the house. He'd spoken to the gate guards. Never mind the possibilities that the Hemisphere vehicle (or the Panacea vehicle; the more time he spent in Alice Frank's world, the more he saw the lines blurring like she did) belonged to someone already inside the gated community. Never mind the more troubling possibility: that the vehicle had indeed come from outside, and a bribed security guard was to blame — a guard who, Ian surmised, would let them in again while informing them that Ian Keys was now rather nervous.

So no, Bridget didn't need to know about this. Ana certainly didn't need to catch wind. Somehow or other, this responsibility had settled on Ian's shoulders. He hadn't asked for or instigated it. He certainly didn't want it. But facts were facts. He could either hide while spooks subtly threatened his family, or he could stand tall. Given that he'd already had that supposedly conciliatory chat with Archibald Burgess, it seemed that playing nice with Hemisphere wasn't doing much good.

Secrets were funny things. Once enough people knew them, everyone stopped fighting to keep them suppressed.

Which meant that the faster he could help Alice, the faster everyone could know what Burgess and the strange men didn't want Ian blabbing about. Then it could be over, seeing as it was never supposed to have started.

There was only one problem.

Ian was ready to blow the whistle, but had no idea which specific whistle needed blowing.

He ducked into the den and shut the door. He dialed.

"Ian?" said Alice. "Is something wrong?"

"I thought about what you said. I'm in."

There was a pause on the other end of the phone.

"Are you there?"

"Yes. Sorry. I just thought you were *already* in."

"Whole hog. End to end. I couldn't sleep most of the night then dozed right through my alarm. Do you remember old zombie movies?"

"I think the whole world remembers old zombie movies."

"That's how I feel today."

"Are you hungry for brains?" She paused then said more soberly, "Okay, that went too far."

Ian rubbed his face. He was too tired to feign outrage. Right now, the world's reality felt heavy in all its absurd ugliness. Even feral deadheads didn't preferentially eat brains. It took lots of puzzling to get through that tricky skull problem, so most of them ate arms and thighs, like diners at KFC.

"I just want it all to be over."

"Last night, you thought this might all be a big misunderstanding."

Ian couldn't believe he'd ever believed that. It felt like it had been forever since he'd looked on Hemisphere and Archibald Burgess with the same wide-eyed delight as the rest of the nation. Yesterday morning, he'd set off for work feeling guilty for looking at public information, intent on turning his snitch in for the greater good if he ever discovered who it was.

"If someone's just screwing with us, then worst-case

scenario we just end up asking some questions. Knowledge never hurt anyone."

"If they're telling the truth, then it doesn't matter," Alice said.

"Right."

"But I've got to tell you, Mr. Keys, there's *something* Hemisphere desperately wants to keep from the world."

Ian closed his eyes and pinched the bridge of his nose. "If you say so."

"Anyway, I have good news."

Ian perked up for five seconds of optimism then let his posture slump back to exhausted despair. What could possibly be good enough to matter? As long as someone was watching his house from black cars, there were problems afoot.

"What?"

"You know how I said our mutual friend seemed to be nudging me toward August Maughan?"

"Yeah." Ian wouldn't exactly say the source had nudged him toward Maughan … but Burgess, probably inadvertently, certainly had.

Alice sounded like she was pushing down something very exciting. Ian wished she was in the room so he could slap the enthusiasm out of her, as horrible as he'd felt the past few days.

"I found him."

"Bullshit. Maughan is — "

"Going to be joining us today," Alice finished.

Ian's mouth unhinged. Just last night, they'd been discussing Maughan as a wish-list item, or perhaps as people once discussed the final days of Howard Hughes. It had seemed logical that Maughan would be necessary to complete their conspiratorial triad — the brains required to interpret Ian's insider Hemisphere data into an *A-ha!*

Alice could share with the world — but finding the famous recluse was another problem entirely.

"Turns out we have Bobby Baltimore in common," Alice said, answering the unasked question. "And he saw my documentary about Yosemite. He said something's been nagging him, too."

"Something or some*one?*" Ian peeked out the window, looking for black vehicles with watchers inside. He was thinking of the ghost that had been leading them, and wondering if their mystery person had got to Maughan.

"I don't know. He seemed nervous. You saw the thing at the Good Life Awards? Where everyone is suddenly chattering about him and Holly Gaynor?"

"I saw something." He hadn't had time for the details. Lately, Ian hadn't had time for many of the things that mattered most.

"I should have recorded the call. I've lost most of it in my head. I was really tired. He actually woke me up. But he mentioned Holly. And Yosemite."

"Because of the documentary."

"Because of *Yosemite.*" Alice huffed, sounding frustrated. "I don't remember. But that was important. And Bobby. He says he needs to talk to Bobby anyway. And that *you* might, too."

Ian was still looking out the window. He didn't like this, even though Alice clearly did. Too much felt planned, like a script. Too much felt coincidental. Maybe he was being paranoid, having spent half his sleepless night peering through this same window. But he couldn't shake the feeling that someone was setting them up, arranging three problems in a line like targets in a row.

"He'll join us. Today at noon."

No, Ian didn't like this at all. Not after Burgess. Not

after this overwhelming sense of growing suspicions, and the sudden instability of his world.

"Did you get his phone number? Can you call him back?"

"I did," Alice said. "Why?"

Feeling himself stepping into the middle of this fray he'd merely been observing, Ian bristled from a sudden chill. As if someone was behind him, watching his every move, breathing down his neck.

"Change of plans. I'll meet you at eleven, not noon."

Ian told her a new place. Somewhere that, if someone was playing them all, would be much harder to regroup and surveil in the time between then and now.

Alice, sounding confused, agreed and said her goodbyes.

The feeling of being watched and overheard reasserted itself as Ian lowered the phone, sharpened by a tiny squeak from behind him.

Like the squeak of a loose board in the hallway's hardwood floor.

Ian turned. The study door was slightly ajar, and through it he saw the flash of swinging red hair.

# Chapter Forty-Three

## DAWN

JORDACHE AWOKE IN DANNY'S ARMS.

Morning light was streaming through the window. She didn't remember falling asleep; it had sneaked up on her the way sleep did, taking her away to slumber like a thief in the night.

She remembered what had come before, though. That had crept up on them both, and although it had been something with its own momentum, Jordache had found herself letting go, finally letting it happen. She was hardly virginal by anyone's definition, but with Danny, taking it slow — stalled traffic slow, so far — had felt prudent.

Men lost interest once they nabbed what they were after.

She rolled halfway, careful not to disturb Danny on the other half of the cramped, quasi-queen-sized bed in the tiny trailer bedroom. His always affable, usually laughing eyes were closed. Without them, he looked like a different person.

*Great. Now you've really fucked up,* Jordache told herself.

But then another voice inside said that she hadn't

fucked up at all. Another voice — a naive voice, certainly — seemed to think that maybe now, because of this, he'd be with her forever.

Jordache blinked. Sat up. She remembered she was naked but was amused to realize she'd left her socks on. They were little low-rise things that vanished inside sneakers, but somehow they'd survived her feet's departure from those shoes. Survived the romp. Survived despite Danny's tendency to mock people for things like ... well ... like having sex with their socks on.

She pulled on a huge shirt — one of Weasel's, far too large even for his tall frame. She'd never noticed it before, but a distinct scent of Weasel struck her as the fabric slid into place. It was the difference between him and Danny that made her nose know it. Weasel had had a working man's smell. Danny smelled more like soap and clean living. It wasn't that either was good or bad. They were just different.

Jordache stood, wondering why the hell she was thinking about scents at all.

Probably latent regret. Probably her own baggage, sure that Danny would change like her ex had. Her brain was comparing one guy to the next, certain in its way that they were two links in a never-ending chain of meaningless encounters.

Probably her mind continuing to expand as it had been, too. It was so strange. She wanted to read more. She was more curious. Danny had talked a bit about that last night, oddly enough. They'd discussed "neuronal plasticity" — a phrase he almost seemed to have just picked up from a word-of-the-day calendar, given his careful enunciation. The discussion was almost a lecture, as if he'd just learned it and wanted to tell her how true it was. How the brain, if it had a good enough reason to do so, could adapt in ways that were practically mind-over-matter, no medical intervention required.

*It's not the drug. It's your brain.*

But Jordache had a hard time believing that. She knew what she felt. She also knew, throughout all of yesterday, what she'd feared. The panic of having to step down had only been compounded by Danny's silence in response to her texts. But as things turned out, he'd only been playing. Refusing to respond so he could appear at her door and surprise her.

Dirty trick.

But it had worked. She'd been so happy and so in love with her eleventh-hour savior, she'd fucked his face off.

Jordache snickered at herself in the silent trailer. It was a crude way to put it — more defenses rising into place. There was no need for that now. She'd broken their stalemate by giving it up. Now it was up to Danny.

Jordache stood then padded lightly into the bathroom.

When she looked into the mirror, she saw Weasel standing in the shower behind her.

Jordache spun around so fast, she nearly fell. She stood with her back to the sink, chest heaving gigantic breaths, heart having gone from baseline to hummingbird in half a second.

The shower was empty. Of course. Weasel didn't live here anymore. Technically speaking, Weasel didn't even *live* anymore. He was either dead in the old way or dead in the new way, but definitely one or the other. She'd watched the clarifiers take him away. Once, obsessively watching Bobby Baltimore's hunting show for a sign, she'd thought she'd seen him. Only once. But he was probably still out there somewhere, worse than deceased, shambling along as a ghost of himself.

Not in her shower.

Not influencing her ideas about Danny right now. Not planting subversive thoughts in her head. That was Jordache, and Jordache alone.

She turned back to the mirror, heart still racing. And of course the reflection behind her showed all clear.

Guilt. Not for Weasel's sake, but all on her own.

*You're not a slut. You've known Danny for half a year. Six whole, sex-free months.*

Jordache's eyes closed, like a taunt. Opened. And of course, she was still alone in the bathroom.

*Danny is a good man. He takes care of you. He might even love you. And he still will, even now, even after we crossed that last line.*

Looking at the empty shower, where the second-long, early-morning, foggy-headed hallucination had been.

*Weasel was a piece of shit, and I'm not sorry he's dead. Or undead.*

Weasel's real name had been Quincy, which was why he'd taken on a nickname so eagerly, even as unflattering as it was. He drank hard and, like most of Jordache's in-a-prior-life boyfriends, had good moments and bad. She'd spent much of their time together fucked up, lying on one floor or another, waiting for the room to stop spinning and start making sense. Sometimes, Weasel hit. Sometimes, he wanted to have sex, and Jordache didn't precisely *not* want to but was too high to consent or refuse. In those cases, Weasel's whims won more often than not.

After Weasel, Jordache's appetite for mind-altering substances had left her. She'd finally found herself clean, sober, and (she thought) in with a good man. Things would be different, and thus far had been. She had her temper and her trailer, but with those skins shed, she could be someone else.

No more lost days.

No more bad boyfriends.

No more regrets.

She thought of Danny.

But instead of seeing Danny in her mind, she saw a tall man on a bluff somewhere full of rocks and dust, his hair blond, his frame wide, his eyes still blue, well past the point at which they should have decayed and fallen from his skull.

# Chapter Forty-Four

## FUNLANES

BRIDGET STOPPED IN A FUNLANES parking lot to recalibrate. She could drive while listening to a GPS system, and she could (though she knew she shouldn't) drive while sending texts. But she wasn't used to the FindMe app, and it didn't give vocal instructions for how to reach one phone's owner from another's position.

There was a loud slapping sound against the glass. Bridget jumped. Her head snapped up from her phone in the middle of trying to reconcile Ian's position with her own admittedly limited knowledge of this area — someone had flattened themselves against her passenger window.

The intruder, flesh pressed against the glass, looked to be a girl of about sixteen or seventeen. She had her hair in two brown pigtails — a style that was far too young for her. Bridget gaped, unsure how to respond to the intrusion until a heavyset man rushed to the girl from behind, taking her by the arm and pulling her away. Even through the glass, Bridget heard a soft, wet purring sound as the girl's flesh separated at the forearm, exposing the dead brown muscle beneath.

Also through the glass, Bridget heard the man tell the girl, "Now look at what you've done. Go get your kit from your mother."

The girl shambled away, toward another car in the lot where a similarly heavyset woman was waiting with her hands on her big hips. The last glimpse of her face had shown Bridget a wide, empty smile.

Bridget looked at the window. It was smeared with something brown, like insect guts. The man was still outside, seeming torn between saying something and making a gesture. Bridget lowered the window halfway. The brown goo collected at the bottom, squeegeed off by the rubber seals.

"I'm sorry," the man said. "She's just curious."

Bridget, disoriented from leaving half her attention on her phone's glowing blue dot, blinked up in the brisk, bright morning air. The Funlanes were past the car, where the woman seemed to be unfolding a case to treat the girl's wound. The bright colors hurt her eyes. She'd been inside one before, and they were just as bright inside, overflowing with necrotics who, according to rumor, left digits inside the bowling balls at least 5 percent of the time.

"It's no problem."

"I have Windex." He sighed, looking at the goo on Bridget's side window. "She does that to our windows constantly."

"No. Really." Bridget tried a smile. "It's no problem."

The man gave Bridget a little nod then turned. A second later, she called after him.

"Excuse me. Is that Neerman Avenue ahead?"

The man turned back. "No, that's Fourteenth. Neerman is two blocks farther up." He took a step forward to see what Bridget was looking at, but she slid the phone between the seats. He wouldn't know she was tailing her cheating husband just by looking at the app's screen, but holding the thing made her feel guilty. "Where are you trying to go?"

Bridget stammered. The answer was, *Wherever he ends up*, but she couldn't exactly say that.

"A friend told me to meet them at a hotel, but I forget the name. Is there a hotel around here?"

"Hmm. I don't know. Do you *need* a hotel? Are you just visiting Aberdeen? Because we're from Gregory Village, back that way, and there's a Hilton."

Bridget knew the Hilton. It wasn't close. He was probably making the recommendation in deference to her wardrobe, jewelry, and car, none of which were inexpensive. She'd wanted to be ready to follow Ian when he left, so she'd gone with a predictable reason to get dressed and ready so early: Gabriella had something planned. Given prep time, she'd dress well for any Gabriella errands, and Ian knew it. But she'd only stopped at Gab's long enough to drop Ana off after taking a Zen pill to dull the edge. Then she'd told Gabriella a different excuse than the one she'd given to Ian. Bridget didn't particularly feel like hearing "I told you so" from her neighbor right now, or suggestions on how to get Ian back.

Bridget's head turned anyway. Behind her, she saw only the overpass for the Sherman Pope Memorial Expressway. And a black car that seemed awfully familiar.

"Do you want directions to the Hilton?"

Bridget's head spun back. "What?"

"Or do you want to meet your friends first?"

Bridget looked behind her again. And yes, there was a black car parked one lot over, not square in any particular parking slot, with two people in front, seeming to look right at her.

"Ma'am?"

"Yes?"

"Do you have your bearings now?"

Still looking back, Bridget said, "No problem, thanks."

While she watched, a larger vehicle, like a minivan, pulled up beside the idling black car. It had the same orange front license plate. In the car, the driver raised something slowly to his lips, like puffing on a cigarette.

When she looked forward again, Bridget saw the big man walking away.

Bridget retrieved her phone and looked again at the blue dot indicating the location of Ian's cell. The car had gone a few blocks farther, but the direction seemed to be simple: one block up then many to the right. As long as his phone had a signal, she'd be able to follow without getting close enough to be seen.

Bridget drew a few deep breaths, telling herself to calm down, to stop being so paranoid about simply checking up on her man's comings and goings.

She pulled into traffic.

The black car and the minivan pulled out behind her, making no effort to hide.

# Chapter Forty-Five

## NOT EVER

AUGUST DIDN'T KNOW THIS PART of town and didn't particularly like being here. It was something nobody was ever supposed to say, but most uninfected people found being in the Skin District creepy. August was no exception. The necrotic ghettos were depressing enough, but even the non-ghetto sections had a way of upsetting a normal brain's sense of equilibrium.

The biggest problem was in unstated social changes. Most communication wasn't done in words; it was done in body: posture, eye position, direction and speed of gestures, and so on. That's how animals communicated, but it's how humans normally communicated, too. But bodily norms were among the first things to go when people got infected. Only the shortest incubations kept people quasi-normal, and a few days was long enough for Sherman Pope to make a person somewhat socially retarded. Necrotics stared too long and in the wrong directions. Their disobedient bodies didn't gesture properly or sit right. Their mouths turned up wrong, warping what were supposed to be smiles into toothy, vaguely threatening grimaces.

Just walking around here, where they lived in droves among the thriving businesses designed for them, was enough to make a normal person's skin crawl.

But even beyond that, everything down here had an oddly inflated bizarro vibe. Roads were 15 percent wider to account for a necrotic driver's diminished sense of control when not using auto-drive — not enough to easily notice, but enough to feel distinctly strange. Lights were all too-bright indoors and outside at night because necrotics often (but not always; the disease manifested differently, depending on the person) lost some of their eyesight and required the light to see. Colors were brighter because studies had shown that longer-incubation necrotics, prone to emotional outbursts, were calmed by bright colors. And everything that required dexterity was super-sized: walk-to-cross buttons were the size of dinner plates; door handles had smaller diameters and the doors pivoted nearer their middles rather than at the edges; most buildings used environmental sensors in bathrooms and public areas so that nothing had to be touched.

Most unsettling of all, August thought, were the cleaners. It looked to a naive eye like the district had a penchant for neatness and the tax money to spend extravagantly — but Panacea, not the city, paid for the big cleaners and the many droids and robots that swept walkways and lobbies. It wasn't an epidemic hazard for citizens to bleed and slough body parts as they walked (Sherman Pope was spread only by blood-to-blood contact with a feral), but it did smell awful and tended to attract unsightly urban vultures.

No, August didn't like being here — even if it was the best place to hide from the press, with or without his scheduled meeting with Alice. He understood why necrotics often clumped together like any ethnic group, and why businesses catering to necrotics followed, making the problem worse. But understanding didn't make him enjoy it, or think it was a particularly good idea.

August's phone rang. The caller ID read, *ThruPath* — the switchboard service that funneled his alias phone numbers into his never-distributed real one.

"Hello?" he said, touching the steering wheel's blinking icon.

*"August?"* The voice, Bobby Baltimore's, sounded disbelieving.

"Don't sound so shocked."

"Cindy tried to call you, like, ten times before I left Yosemite. I tried to call a few from the plane. We kept getting your voicemail."

"Oh. You should have left a message."

"I got your decoy message, not your real one."

"Look, Bobby, I'm sorry. I just hooked the number I gave you back in to the service I use. I recently switched phones. I've been distracted."

"So I heard."

August figured that meant Bobby had seen yesterday's news — and, probably, the many speculative reports that had followed. Nobody could agree exactly what August may or may not have to do with the Holly Gaynor mystery, and really, nobody could even agree if there was a mystery around Holly at all. She wasn't talking to the press, on August's recommendation. Her people, now that Holly had slipped away and come to hide with August, weren't admitting to anything, either. Officially, Ms. Gaynor had no comment. Officially, Ms. Gaynor was comfortable in her Aberdeen Valley mansion in the hills … and definitely *not* back at August's anonymous second apartment right this minute.

But speculations were priceless. Holly had managed to say a few unmuddled words in public, and somehow August Maughan had now left Hemisphere in disgrace for conducting mad scientist experiments on necrotic minds.

Ironically, today's reality, with Holly, wasn't terribly far off.

"Where are you, Bobby?"

"Back at my house."

"Outside the park?"

"No, back here in Aberdeen."

"I thought you were shooting?"

"You thought wrong. I was around deadheads too long. It was messing with my head."

August looked through his windshield. There were ropes along the curbs to keep citizens from falling into the street. A surface train rattled by a few blocks down, its front equipped with a triangular cow catcher.

"I know the feeling," August said.

"I assume our appointment is canceled."

August's mouth worked, twitching his little goatee. Given what had happened with Holly and the Prestige drug, events — or possible events — inside the Yosemite Reserve had been heavy on August's mind. It was one of the things he thought might come up with Alice and Ian Keys, and he'd already made a note to ask Bobby. He wasn't a scientist or particularly stable, but he had more in-the-wild experience than just about anyone, other than perhaps those poor bastards still cleaning out Bakersfield.

"Maybe."

"Did you skip town?" Bobby asked. "The news people think you skipped town."

"No, I'm still here."

"Where?"

"Grover."

"What, *downtown?* In the Skin District?"

"You're surprised?"

"Just seems like a place I'd be more at home than you."

Yes, that was true. And as he stopped at a light, August couldn't help watching all of them, thinking how thin the line was between his current world and Bobby's usual one. Necrophage did its little kill-and-swap act just fine, but half of a clarifier's job, when someone was close to tipping, came down to psychology. Decades of zombie movies had told these people what they were, sure as doctors had. The ugly truth was that in Yosemite, most people raged before their medical rage point. They did it because they'd *decided* they were zombies. They were infected; they'd been condemned to turn in a place packed with ferals; they felt their conditions sliding into an abyss. They saw where they were going, and most chose subconsciously to turn in advance — to lose their minds, to shout and growl, to attack what they could and eat its flesh before biology strictly required them to.

"Hey, we're all Americans," August said.

"Right. One nation under the plague. Forget the Melting Pot. This is the *Rotting* Pot." He chuckled. "Hey. I had something I wanted to ask you."

"About your treatments?"

"Actually, about my work. After seeing the thing with Holly Gaynor, I got to wondering if — "

"Hang on, Bobby."

August tapped the wheel to repeat the last direction. The GPS told him to turn right, so he obeyed, driving full manual because he trusted himself not to hit a stumbling necrotic more than he trusted auto-drive.

"Are you driving?" Bobby asked.

"Yeah."

"Where?"

"I could tell you," August said, "but then I'd have to kill you."

"Fine. Be that way."

Maybe he should tell him. Invite Bobby along. He probably would, if this were his party instead of Alice Frank's, and if she wasn't clearly playing things so close to the vest. August didn't understand the last-minute change of venue, but the new location was as good as the original. He'd tag along this time, trusting that Alice wouldn't call press because, if nothing else, she'd want the scoop for herself. The next time they met, if his hunch was right, he could set the terms. And if it made sense, his Yosemite expert could come along.

The GPS told him to make another right. He must be close. The conversation with Bobby would have to wait.

"Bobby, I'll need to call you back. I'm almost to Grover Mall."

"*Grover Mall?* Man, when you want to be around zombies, you *really* want to be around zombies!"

"Ah, *Dawn of the Dead* jokes. Nice."

"It's really more of an insight about consumerism."

Another turn brought the mammoth glass cube into view. As far as the necrotic parts of Aberdeen Valley went, this was the best of them — probably, now that he thought about it, the reason that Alice had chosen it. August could relate. If they had to be three uninfected people in infected territory, it only felt sensible (if politically incorrect) to do so in the polished spots — the kind of place that Aberdeen used as one of its oft-displayed crown jewels for the rest of the country to marvel at.

August eschewed the garage, found a meter, and

opened his door. He had a big hat and, despite recent news events, didn't have a particularly recognizable face. The mall was actually decent cover. If the twitchers here had any emotions about August Maughan after the Holly Gaynor thing, it'd be hope.

August killed the engine, holding his phone to his face as he exited then crossed the lawn.

He saw five men in suits run by him. Not necrotics. Panacea clarifiers.

"Buy me a nice, overpriced shirt," Bobby said in August's ear.

August barely heard it. He felt like he was in a trance, staring straight ahead. He lowered his phone, killed the call without saying goodbye, and slipped the cell into his pocket.

What he was seeing ahead was not supposed to happen.

Not in today's world.

Not in Aberdeen Valley's city limits.

Not ever.

# Chapter Forty-Six

## ORANGE JULIUS

IAN'S PHONE RANG WHILE HE and Alice were crossing into the back of the food court, toward the perfect mixture of public (so nobody could try anything funny) and private (so nobody could listen). The way Ian felt right now, an Orange Julius in the middle of the country's necrotic capital was the perfect spot for a clandestine meeting between three people who didn't entirely trust each other: there would be no bugs or listening devices, there could be no obvious conflict fit to create a scene … and if Ian suddenly felt he didn't want to be part of this anymore, he could always run, and no one would stop him.

They'd met out front. Alice was taller than he'd thought but radiated a more trustworthy vibe than he'd expected — probably, he had to admit, because Hemisphere PR painted her inside the company as a kind of devil. August Maughan, she'd told him, had texted and was running a few minutes late. So they'd gone in.

And it had been fine.

Until it wasn't.

The call showed a nonsensical four-digit Caller ID: *0804*. Ian declined the call, and it rang again immediately.

He declined again. Within two seconds, it rang again. Ian wasn't even sure how that was possible. Didn't a connection need to reset?

A text came in: *ANSWER NOW*.

Alice, watching the telephonic ballet with interest, furrowed her eyebrows. Ian turned the screen to show her.

"It's our tipster," she said.

"It can't be. What, now he's calling?"

*"He?* How do you know it's not a woman?"

Ian was about to dismiss that as the least relevant and most loaded comment he'd ever heard when the phone rang again — number still unknown. This time, Ian answered while Alice pressed close, her face almost against his.

"Hello?" Ian said.

A man's voice spilled from the speaker, rushed, panicked, out of breath as if running, somehow curiously familiar.

"You have to get out of there," it said.

"Who is this?"

*"Get out of the fucking mall!"*

"How do you know where I am? Who are you and why are you—"

"Your wife followed you! Some … some *people* were following her! Now some serious shit is about to happen and *you! Can't! Be there!"*

"Bridget is here? Who's after her?" Ian's heart doubled its pace. His head ticked around, and Alice, doing the same, put her hand on his arm, seemingly trying to quell his rising fear.

"They don't know you're here! They're after her! You have to get out!"

Ian's calm snapped. *"Who the fuck are you, and where is my wife?"*

"Okay," the voice said, clearly still rushing but making an effort to be calm, to get his message across. "You have to understand. This is about more than you. You've been watched, and Hemisphere doesn't want you talking. But they don't want to hurt you. They need you. They only want to scare you and are going to do it through ..." The man swallowed, as if forcing himself past the next bit without riling Ian further. "Through your wife. But it's just a scare. Do you understand?"

Ian looked at Alice. Sensing a question, Alice shook her head.

"I know you," Ian said. "I recognize your voice." But from where, he couldn't say.

The strangely familiar voice — a notch deeper than average, the slightest, almost imperceptible softening of consonants — went on, heedless.

"You're too important. They need you saying the right things, not out of the picture. Same for Alice Frank."

Alice looked at Ian then the phone.

"But *they don't know you're there,* okay? The idea is to make a problem you can't ignore, that you'll take personally. But they don't know you're there, with her, or that you've called August Maughan. And that's why you have to go. Because if they find out, they'll — "

"Where is she?" Ian asked. "You know so much, where is she?"

"There's going to be an outbreak. A choreographed, controlled outbreak centered on — "

*"WHERE IS BRIDGET? WHERE IS SHE, YOU MOTHERFUCKER?"*

Alice grabbed Ian's arm hard then pointed with her other hand.

"There."

Ian turned to look across the food court. He saw a thin redhead dressed too elegantly even for this nice mall. Maybe a hundred feet behind her, Ian saw three men in dark suits who seemed to have entered unseen through two sets of brown utility doors at the building's edge.

They had something with them. Several somethings.

Then they let them go.

## Chapter Forty-Seven

### THREE TALL CLOAKS

BRIDGET WAS LOOKING DOWN AT her phone as she entered the mall through the front doors. Once inside and halfway across the main gallery, she pocketed the thing, figuring she'd do the rest with her eyes. The accuracy wasn't fantastic, and she'd learned what she needed to know, as well as what, frankly, perplexed her.

Who met at a mall? She'd been assuming a motel (a seedy one, surely) all along. Even if Ian and his secret were having a non-sexual date, the mall — the mall *in the Skin District* — was hardly the classiest option. Ian was better than that. Even in college, when they'd been poor, he'd broken the bank to take Bridget to the best places he couldn't afford.

There was a fleeting moment of desperate optimism

*(I guess that means he likes me better than her.)*

And then it was gone.

Bridget looked into the mall. Her Zen pill had taken most of the edge off her emotions, but she could still sense a stew brewing below the surface: nervousness, sadness, anger, betrayal, definitely paranoia after she'd seen that sedan and minivan with the blacked-out windows. But she'd lost the last, and the rest was circling her mind like a plane awaiting the runway.

Of course, she might be wrong about all of this. She didn't know what she'd find here; it was even possible he'd gone shopping for something to give his adored wife. But Bridget had never been a fool, and when something smelled like shit, it was usually shit.

She paced self-consciously through the open space, wondering where to begin. She felt out of place, over-dressed, maybe even a bit delicious in front of all these necrotics.

*They're just people. Same as the bag boy at the supermarket. Same as Terri's cousin Jack. Same as those three people in your book club. Same as, honestly, a quarter of the population.*

But they were everywhere. *Everywhere.*

Bridget kept a neutral, somewhat friendly expression on her face and crossed the floor. She had no idea where to find Ian because he could be anywhere.

And then she saw him.

Right in the middle of the open, near the food court.

Beside a tall, thin woman with short blonde hair.

Pressed close to her, body to body, his face against hers.

Something broke inside Bridget. She'd known this was coming. She'd known for days, maybe weeks. She'd come here to confront him and get proof in her own mind, not to find out. But still, seeing it hurt worse than she'd been able to imagine.

Ian was hers. *Hers.*

They'd been together for fourteen years. They had a daughter. They had a home. They played board games, went for walks in the park, had made love countless times. He'd tallied the freckles on her chest, shared things with her he'd never shared with anyone. Almost literally. Ian had only been with three women before her, and she'd told him she'd been with none. It wasn't true, but she'd said it on impulse and had never been able to take it back.

Maybe this was payback for lying.

Bridget felt her eyes wanting to tear up, but a clanging from behind distracted her. She turned to see three men in suits. The men from the car and the van's driver, probably, not lost after all.

They'd just come through a set of utility doors and were looking right at her. They had something with them: three tall forms, covered in six-foot-tall cloaks, somehow restrained, held back, still invisible to the mall at large.

Across the space, Bridget heard Ian shout. She looked over and saw him with a phone pressed to his ear, the woman pointing right at her, maybe preparing to laugh at all of this infidelity and Bridget's general stupidity.

But Ian didn't look amused, or aroused. His eyes were saucers. Something changed in both of their stares, and Bridget knew that whatever they were looking at now, it was behind her.

*Jesus Christ.*

It all came together with the force of a punch. Bridget spun in time to see the men duck back through the doors with the pulled-away cloaks, three feral necrotics charging toward her.

but he'd never shared with anyone. Almost literally. But [illegible] had been with three women before her, and he'd told him she'd been with three. It wasn't true, but she'd said it [illegible] and had never been able to take it back.

Maybe she was paid back for lying.

Bridget felt her eyes widen [illegible] up, but [illegible] changing [illegible] distracted her. She turned to see three men in [illegible]. [illegible] and the [illegible] [illegible] or last [illegible].

They'd just come through a set of [illegible] doors and were looking right at her. They had something with them, [illegible], covered in [illegible] cloaks, something [illegible], held back, still [illegible] to the [illegible].

Across the [illegible], Bridget heard her shout. She looked over and saw him with a [illegible] pressed to his ear, the woman [illegible] at [illegible] preparing to [illegible] all of [illegible] and [illegible] a general [illegible].

Dunbar didn't look [illegible] or [illegible]. His eyes were [illegible]. Something [illegible] in both of their [illegible], and Bridget knew that whatever they were looking [illegible] was behind her.

[illegible]

[illegible] together with the force of [illegible], Bridget spun in time to see the men [illegible] back through the door with the [illegible] cloaks, [illegible] charging toward her.

# Chapter Forty-Eight

## DENIED

DANNY LOITERED OUTSIDE THE ALPHA Building door, reading the posters long enough to garner a few strange looks. But Ian didn't show, and his usual lunch group (whom Danny knew by sight, but not much better) came out without him.

After a moment's thought and glance at the door, Danny's nerves got the best of him, and he scampered after them, calling to a woman with long, dirty-blonde hair.

"Hey, excuse me," he said.

She turned.

"I'm sorry. You know Ian Keys, right?"

The woman nodded. "Sure."

"Is he coming?"

The woman looked back toward the closed door. Probably wondering whether to take Danny's question at face value. Did he want to get in touch with Ian, or know if he was on his way to lunch?

"He's out for the morning."

Danny smiled into the woman's patient expression. He

felt urgent yet needed to act more casual than ever. He needed to find Ian then get him to come along on a very *whatever* conversational ride. The conversation and subsequent exchanging of key cards had to be very by-the-way and no-big-deal. It also needed to happen RIGHT FUCKING NOW.

"Oh. Do you know when he'll be back?"

"I'm sorry, I don't. Do you have his number?"

"Where is he?"

The woman blinked. He'd not only said it too fast; he'd asked a question he had no business asking. This woman worked with Ian, and Ian himself was near the company's top. The idea that a lowly salesman *(a salesman who wasn't even authorized to give samples of designer Phage,* Danny thought bitterly) would so pointedly demand to know where the boss had gone wasn't just impertinent; it might even be a red flag that said salesman should be avoided.

"I don't know," she said, a trifle more coldly. "You could leave a message at his extension."

Danny smiled wider, twirling his key card on his finger and running his other hand through his messy brown hair. "Oh, no, it's no big deal."

"Can I ask what you need from Ian? Maybe I can help."

"I just thought he might want to hang out."

The woman's eyebrows bunched.

"After work. If he wanted to get a beer with me. With the salesmen. Or maybe just me."

Danny kept his winning smile wide, but he could feel himself falling apart. The clock was ticking with Jordache. He'd already lied to her, and that meant he needed to replace her PhageX to make the lie irrelevant as fast as humanly possible. Especially given what he'd seen this morning. She'd been friendly, even loving, sure. And she'd been her usual witty, adorable, intelligent herself. But she'd also walked right by her car keys twice while looking for them, rammed herself into a protruding countertop, and asked Danny if he'd "heard that" twice when the room was almost eerily silent. He'd known she'd probably slide back a bit to where base Phage should've left her, but he hadn't thought it would happen so fast. Apparently, PhageX really *was* a wonder. She'd improved in ways that had crept up on them both and were now only becoming apparent as they settled back to normal. Danny could tell already, and it wouldn't be long before Jordache saw it too … then started asking questions about what exactly was inside her supposedly PhageX Gadget.

"Okay," the woman said.

"I'll just catch up with him some other time."

She nodded, gave Danny a final, curious glance, and turned to join her waiting group.

Danny stood near the closed Alpha door, suddenly unsure what to do with his hands. He felt lost, uneasy, more bothered than he should be. Ian had taken the morning away from his office. *No big deal.* It probably happened all the time. Danny was a salesman, and Ian raked in the big bucks for steering this ship. He surely had many unknown irons in the fire.

But Danny kept thinking of the subtle differences in Jordache this morning. The small changes that made her somehow different, unusual. He'd been counting on running into Ian at lunch more than he wanted to admit. He'd find a way to borrow (or, hell, *steal)* Ian's access card then maybe leave early to swipe Jordache's stash.

She was on Necrophage, and that was all her body needed. It shouldn't matter, but it did.

There was some commotion down the public hallway, in a lounge. Edging closer, Danny saw men and women in shirtsleeves with their Hemisphere cards on their belts, spellbound by a news report Danny couldn't yet make out.

Before he reached the lounge, his phone buzzed with a text from Jordache.

It read: *I think I met Holly Gaynor last night. How's the weather tomorrow?*

Danny stared at the screen, uncomprehending, until the people in the lounge started to shout.

# Chapter Forty-Nine

## WHISTLE AND THUMP

IAN RUSHED FORWARD BUT ACTUALLY collided with the immovable body of a tall man in a suit — a Panacea clarifier if he'd ever seen one. At first, the man's presence made no sense, like that of the three feral deadheads headed toward Bridget. But then the clarifier asserted himself, extending a hand to push Ian back and turning his body side-on, the side with his gun holster facing away from Ian and Alice lest they try to grab it. Because *that's* what was on Ian's mind right now: confronting cops.

"Stand back, sir," the clarifier said.

Ian's eyes flicked to the side. The man had a partner, a woman with brown hair in a ponytail. Where had they come from? And how had they arrived so fast?

"There's a group of feral—" Ian blurted, trying to point.

"We'll handle it, sir. Stay back."

But the shoppers, from end to end inside Grover's crowded gallery, had seen them and were now screaming.

Those who could, ran. But then Ian realized something horrible: He was in the heart of the Skin District. Uninfected shoppers were few and far between. The mall was a Chinatown market, full of natives.

And deadheads didn't attack the infected.

"My wife is over there! She's — "

"Stay back," the female clarifier said.

Bridget, across the opening, stutter-stepped backward, away from the ferals. Ian's panicked eyes could see two mall cops — not clarifiers, both necrotic — creeping toward the scene from the side, seeming to take their time. Grover Mall was multi-floored, open to the overhead glass cube in the middle. Through the center loomed a wide atrium that spanned all levels, each floor's opening surrounded by a railing. Ian watched Bridget's back touch the railing, inhaled a sharp breath as if he, not Bridget, had just realized she'd come up short.

They were closing in on her: the closest source of warm, untouched blood.

Bridget wobbled. She was in heels, not dressed for flight. One of her feet canted sideways, twisting on the ankle, unseating her. The shoes were loose; Bridget kicked them away and backed in bare feet. The ferals came, slowly. Those who'd released them — clarifiers too, if Ian had seen right and believed the voice on the phone — were nowhere to be seen.

Where was his phone, anyway? Ian didn't know. He may have stowed it without thinking. For all he knew, the caller was still on the line, now listening to his pocket.

But no one would keep him from Bridget when she was the only thing the oncoming deadheads cared about.

Ian rushed the blocking clarifiers, lowering his shoulder as if for a tackle. The woman raised a hand again to try and stop him, but Ian was already through and running around the circle with Alice behind him.

The exit was behind, just to the left of the utility doors where the ferals had come from. A crowd, mostly infected, had gathered, those with higher levels of function with their hands over their mouths. But those outside must not have received the message because they were still entering, pushing past the crowd, annoyed that idiots were blocking the entrance.

A couple bullied their way impatiently inside then took a few backward steps to yell at those who were inconsiderate enough to form their human wall. Someone screamed, too close. Then two of the three deadheads turned, seeing a closer target, then ran at their marks.

They *ran*.

"Jesus Christ, Ian. They're — "

Ian didn't listen for the end of Alice's sentence. He moved faster, pumping his arms, finding the distance around the atrium railing impossibly far. Bridget was accepting the distraction, now edging away in bare feet, but her eyes hadn't left the remaining deadhead. She looked as shocked as Alice sounded. Normally, avoiding ferals, if you didn't get cornered and they weren't in a horde, was simple. They were animated corpses, sometimes able to spring like decayed jack-in-the-boxes but mostly slow like ancient men. But these weren't like that. These were something else.

An eighth of the distance between them closed. A quarter.

The uninfected couple who'd entered saw what they faced. Hands raised, the woman's heavy with a big red purse. One of the ferals was on the man. The other was on the woman, head down, teeth out, hands hooked to straighten their victims' necks, finding an artery and spraying the floor with an arc of red. There were screams until the shrieking stopped, wet sinew coming away like hungry dogs fighting for a bone.

Bridget turned. Saw Ian. And ran.

Footfalls multiplied behind Ian. He heard the lighter click of Alice's flats eclipsed by something heavier and faster, then something grabbed his shirt, his collar, the back of his belt. He was wrenched free of his feet, the floor screaming upward toward his face. Ian managed to turn his head and pull his neck back. His chest struck hard, and his head rapped just slightly softer, the blow cold and flat. His vision spun, but fear cleared it, then he felt and smelled breath from behind his neck as someone planted a knee on his spine.

"I said *STAY BACK!*"

The man was over Ian, now seeming to hold a weapon that his peripheral vision could barely see. Alice, slower on the run, had remained standing but now had her hands up.

"Move, and I'll shoot you."

"That's my wife over there!"

"It's handled, sir! Stay down!"

Ian disobeyed, trying to rise, and the clarifier kicked him back. Ian rolled instead and watched as the woman went ahead alone, her own weapon out. Not a gun. Guns were for edgy humans, like Ian. The most confrontational parts of a clarifier's job required something bigger, more direct.

It looked like a small megaphone, its muzzle belled slightly outward like a blunderbuss. She was holding it with two hands, running now, not approaching Bridget because she'd swung too wide. The two making meat from the shredded dead were the more important target, presumably because they'd killed already and might escape through the mall doors.

The ferals saw her coming. One leaped up and again ran — not away, precisely, but toward an old man with a walker. Slow, weak prey for a fast hunter. Natural selection on display.

The second was still kneeling over the woman's body, its face covered with gore, its banquet surrounded by what looked like a crimson tablecloth. It swiveled toward the clarifier's approach, baring its teeth. There was a short, sharp whistle, and the thing's head exploded, spattering the crowd as it pressed against the wall.

Ian's eyes were on Bridget. She still hadn't run, probably knowing the stalemate was the only thing keeping her alive. Ferals had usually spent at least six weeks dead and were little more than rotted meat with teeth, barely kept alive by Sherman Pope's restorative work. They couldn't run. They could only drag. But these looked younger, healthy by comparison. There were people in Ian's office that were more decayed than these three (well, two now).

If Bridget ran, it would chase her. And with the other clarifier more concerned about Ian, it might just catch her.

And yet the clarifiers were doing nothing, going so far as to wave the mall cops back. There were only two of them. One was on Ian, ignoring the real problem. And the other was trying not to shoot the old man as the feral stalked him. Bridget was on her own.

In his head, Ian heard the voice on his phone from earlier.

*They don't know you're here. They're after her.*

They knew now. They knew, and wouldn't forget — even if it meant letting Bridget die to keep Ian safe and confined, down where he belonged.

Bridget backed away, one hand on the railing. The feral followed. It bared its teeth. Its eyes, decayed around the edges but not at all in the whites, appeared wide and intent.

Another shout. A chorus of screams. The clarifier hadn't found an angle in time; Ian could now see the thrash of raking red hands from his low position, meaning the old man had seen his last birthday. At least he wouldn't need to go on as a necrotic, propped up by Necrophage, same as that first couple. Judging by the amount of blood and ropy, flung gore, all were dead beyond Sherman Pope's ability to resuscitate.

Another whistle. Another dull thump, like a sledgehammer striking a melon. Where the old man had been, the mall's outer wall was now stained in a crimson starburst.

*"HELP HER! Help her, damn you!"* Ian shouted.

*The idea is to make a problem you can't ignore, that you'll take personally.*

Ian was yanked roughly upward. His eyes, jostled from Bridget and the finally approaching clarifier, saw Alice Frank and understood why she hadn't run over herself. Sometime in the last few minutes, while lives had been at stake, the man holding Ian down had cuffed her to the railing.

Bridget's cool broke. She ran.

The deadhead ran faster.

There was a whistle. Then a thump.

Blood and brain sprayed over the railing to fall onto those below like sticky red rain.

Ian's breath caught as Bridget stumbled and fell, unharmed, her eyes wide and vacant.

It was over.

The clarifier unfastened Alice from the railing and secured her hands behind her back. Ian's remained uncuffed, but both, at least for now, were in custody.

"Let's go," the clarifier said.

# Chapter Fifty

21:46

JORDACHE PACED HER LIVING ROOM. When that didn't help, she put on her shoes and went running, which was strange because she wasn't a runner. The neighborhood wasn't the best, but for some reason she felt safe running even while wearing a sleeveless tank up top (her sports bras were in the laundry and regular bras chafed when exercising), girls jiggling and giving a show. There were men who might have given her a problem, but Jordache knew how to avoid them. One was two blocks away, hassling a guy who owed him money. The other was a group of teens hanging out on Emma Pope Boulevard, near the theater. Her most logical running route took Jordache by both, but knowing what was out there made her change her route. Simple. Safe. She wondered why everyone didn't do things this way, or why she hadn't before today.

The run didn't help. She still felt restless. She still wanted to talk to Danny. In fact, now that that particular bubble had popped, she kind of wanted to drag Danny back here, strip him nude, and take another ride. But mostly she wanted to chat. To let him know what was going on. Because holy shit, PhageX had given her some great results so far, but this was another level.

She saw the thing on the news about the mall downtown. And she'd really enjoyed meeting Holly Gaynor. She was pretty sure that hadn't actually happened last night because she'd been with Danny (and she wasn't crazy, ha-ha), but she also understood why Holly wouldn't want all that public attention. Good thing too much attention wasn't something Jordache needed to worry about.

She was hungry.

There wasn't much in the pantry or fridge. She needed to go shopping. She could go to the market. It would be nice to cross it off the list, and she was already pretty sure she'd be calling in sick to work because if she did, Danny could come over again, and that would be good because holy shit, her mind was going a mile a minute, and she needed *someone* to talk to.

Crackers. Peanuts. Spices she'd never really used in cooking, even though the idea of learning how to cook, *right now,* sounded really appealing. In the fridge, she had a few things of yogurt, Greek, vanilla, and some of those little cheese wheel things that came covered in red wax. And two steaks, which Danny had run out for, after they'd had sex the first time but before the second, when he'd been inspired and decided they should celebrate. But they'd never made it that far. They'd fucked with her sitting up on the sink.

Jordache pulled her computer from its little alcove. Found a cooking website. Scanned it. Steak, sure, yeah, she could make steak. But then she got too goddamned hungry to wait and ate one of them raw.

Maybe she should talk to Holly again.

Or the other guy.

Not Weasel. She didn't think she could talk to Weasel, and didn't want to. Fuck that guy. He was out there somewhere, maybe, still alive/dead, whatever it was, worse than she herself was alive/dead, but the right amount according to that clarifier who came by yesterday, ha-ha.

Jordache went to YouTube. She didn't remember which of the Bobby Baltimore videos she'd seen Weasel in, except that she did and it was the fourth from the second season, time index 21:46.

She watched it. Maybe it was him. She could ask. Not Holly. But the other guy. The tall blond guy.

She texted Danny: *I went for a run.*

Danny didn't respond.

That's when Jordache realized people might be coming for her and she might need to hide.

She sat in the back of her little closet, letting the clothes conceal her.

After a few seconds of hiding and becoming increasingly certain that she might need to fight her way out of here when push came to shove, Jordache got hungry again, grabbed the other steak from the fridge, and ate that one, too.





# Chapter Fifty-One

## VOICES

"AUGUST."

"BOBBY."

"I GUESS YOU'RE not still at the mall," Bobby said. "So you're free to talk idly about anything. So. How's the kids?"

August didn't have kids. Neither did Bobby. "Yes. Let's talk about the weather."

"Jesus, August. I saw that shit on the news. Couldn't have been a minute after I hung up with you. That's the same mall you were going to, right? The downtown one, with the cube, right outside of Grover? Skin District."

August exhaled. Bobby sounded more nervous, on the phone, than August felt having seen so much of it in person. When the melee had begun, he'd edged close enough to catch some spray, and now he'd need to toss this shirt. Nothing got out blood, but nothing *really* got out deadhead blood. It was as if that shit set in advance, then clung to fabric for dear life because its old owner had no life left at all … unless you counted the puppetry granted by Sherman Pope.

August might be in shock. In concept, he'd seen something simple: Deadheads had somehow got loose in the mall before being taken down with the loss of only (according to reports) three lives. It was tragic, but small outbreaks were hardly unheard of.

Except that August had never seen one so close up.

Except that outbreaks were never, *ever* supposed to happen inside Aberdeen Valley. They weren't possible with all the city's protections, heavy Panacea presence, and necrotic-specific checkpoints.

Except that (and this was something the news kept forgetting to mention, and so far no video had coincidentally been aired) these ferals moved too fast and seemed too fresh in body to be like anything but … well … *intentionally made.*

"That's the mall," August said.

"How many were there?"

"Just three."

"Three? It said that three people were killed."

"That's what I saw, yes."

"But … " Bobby didn't finish the sentence, but his implication was clear: *How could three shambling, drooling, falling-apart ferals take down even one person in a wide-open space?*

"These were different, Bobby. They were fast."

"Fast?"

"You've seen *Night of the Living Dead*?"

"Of course. Every day of my working life in Yosemite."

"And you've seen the remake of *Dawn of the Dead*?"

"I think I covered that joke when we spoke earlier."

"These ferals were like the latter. They could run."

"How is that … " There was a pause on the line then: "How is that possible? They're … *corpses.*"

"Listen, Bobby. You're in Aberdeen?"

"I am."

"Maybe we should keep that appointment after all. Or move it up."

"To when?"

"Immediately."

"What's up, August? Something tells me you don't want to work on treatments that'll make me glow in my old age."

"Little known secret," August said. "If you treat a necrotic with Necrophage after he's already passed the inflection point, it creates a *fast deadhead* like these. Maybe it's time we compare notes because something is definitely brewing."

"I've never seen any deadheads like that in Yosemite," Bobby said. "I get that people wouldn't believe clarifiers and would try to bring people back anyway despite them being selected against, so of course all sorts of folks would do it. I should see some, shouldn't I?"

"They don't make it to Yosemite. Anyone who's been treated after the IP is summarily disposed of. Quietly, once away from the families."

"They'd still have their minds," Bobby said.

"But they're past the inflection point, so they'll turn anyway. It's not in anyone's best interest to know that Necrophage will keep a body fresh even while the mind decays. And believe me, it's not the only example of Archibald Burgess believing that the ends justify the means. That's why we should talk. To see if there might be another out there that your buddy Alice almost seemed to be hinting at in her documentary, whether she meant to or not."

"Go on."

"In person. I need to make another call. To check on Holly."

August could imagine Bobby nodding, maybe trying to catch his breath. "Okay," he said. "Where do you want to meet?"

"My place." And he gave Bobby the address.

"Okay. Can I text you or just call through your paranoid redirect thingy?"

"Texts will go."

"Then I'll text you after I check some stuff. But tonight for sure."

August said goodbye and hung up. He looked around, still not entirely sure that he hadn't been followed. Hiding after fleeing the mall felt wrong. Panacea had taken Alice and Ian away, and Alice had been in cuffs. The same might become of August if he stayed close, especially after the nothing he'd done in that public video at Holly's event. So he'd settled on being as in-plain-sight as possible, figuring that way he could at least see his pursuers coming.

But the wide-open parking lot around his car was deserted.

When he felt as secure as he was going to get, August picked up his phone and dialed again. Holly answered immediately, sounding uneasy.

"August. Thank God."

"What?"

"I saw the news."

"Hell. I can't surprise anyone today. First Bobby; now you."

"Bobby who?"

"Bobby Baltimore."

"Why were you …"

"He's a client. He's also based in Aberdeen Valley. You'll meet him tonight, in fact."

"Oh. Okay."

"You sound funny."

"Funny how?"

As soon as he'd asked his last question, August had realized the answer. Now the question was almost embarrassing. Holly sounded funny because she didn't sound funny at all. He'd taken her as a client at a time when she'd have said her last question as *Fuddyow?*, but now the words came out polished, her mouth remembering its old trick.

That was Prestige at work, apparently. But what nibbled at August's mind now was that Prestige might not be all that groundbreaking, in the bigger scheme of things. When he and Archibald had formed Hemisphere, Archibald's goal to upgrade nature had been crystal clear. They'd both thought he'd failed. But maybe he'd succeeded after all, appearances to the contrary notwithstanding.

"Just … nervous," he said, sidestepping the topic of her previous mushmouth.

"I was worried for you. Were they really ferals?"

"Ferals, or starving people with terrible manners."

"But how? Ferals *in Aberdeen Valley*, August!"

*You don't know the half of it*, August thought. But Holly didn't need to hear about the fast deadheads. The implications were troubling. He hadn't told Bobby that you couldn't just *give* someone Necrophage past the inflection point to create the creatures he'd seen; you had to *keep* giving it to them to keep their bodies from falling apart as they were meant to. But they'd turn anyway, and the process, once past the IP, took three weeks or so. That meant someone had *kept* the ferals he'd seen. Injected them. Fed them, to keep their bodies whole. Who would do that, and why? Only someone who knew August's secret would be stupid enough to try.

"It's not important right now, Holly. It's over. There were three, and I watched them all killed. Dramatically, in ways Bobby doesn't even kill … " He was rambling, possibly still in shock, unloading things Holly didn't need to know just to get them out of his own head. He reset and tried again. "That's all that's bugging you? Just the news? Cyrus hasn't found you or anything, right? Or the press? You didn't go outside?"

"*You* went outside."

"Calculated risk for a defined reason. And I'm not Holly Gaynor."

"I didn't go outside. But … " She trailed off.

"What?"

"Nothing. Just paranoia."

"Holly … "

"You'll think I'm going crazy."

*You'd be surprised,* August thought. Based on the scans he'd taken of Holly, Prestige had done some interesting things to her neural firing patterns. Just as he'd hoped, and tweaked on a hunch, remembering his former company's original roots.

"Hallucinations?"

Holly sounded reluctant. "Maybe. Maybe just a little."

"It's okay, Holly. I thought that might happen. You had a reasonably long incubation time, so Sherman Pope made the nerves connecting your brain's two hemispheres temperamental. As those nerves started lighting back up, I figured you were bound to get confused. In most people, the left side of the brain controls language. If the halves aren't talking fluidly, it's possible you'd hear something *you yourself* just said with the ear controlled by the right hemisphere, and your brain would interpret it as being said by someone else. Or an auditory hallucination."

Even over the phone, August could hear Holly sigh. "Okay. That's weird but good to know." *Good to know,* said clear as day. No twitches in her speech at all anymore.

"We can talk about it when I get back. I got myself clear across town somehow, but I'm going to make my way back as soon as I hang up with you." *If I can be sure I'm not followed,* he mentally added.

"Because wow, it sure didn't sound like my voice," Holly said, her mind clearly still on her hallucinations. "It sounded like *two separate* voices."

August had been entering his address into the car's navigation system. He was too beat to drive back on manual, and given the light traffic, doing so was patently unnecessary. The car could drive. That's what he'd bought it for.

But what Holly just said made him perk up and look around, still feeling unseen eyes over his shoulder.

"Two voices?"

"A woman's. And a man's."

August looked out across the parking lot at the building beyond, feeling alone. Feeling the emptiness around the car as if it were a pressing thing.

"Really."

"But that's okay. I'm not crazy?"

"You're not crazy, Holly." Then, slowly: "What did the voices say?"

"The woman said she was waking up."

August breathed slowly, watching the distance, feeling as if insects were slowly climbing his spine.

"And the man's, when he heard her, said he was glad."

# Chapter Fifty-Two

## SUDS

AT THE DINNER TABLE, ANA asked Ian to please pass the salt, and Ian handed it to her. Sometime later, Ana asked her mother if she thought they could go this weekend to look at new bikes like she'd promised, and Bridget said, "Maybe" in a way that sounded like Ana shouldn't keep bothering her about it, even though it was the first time, in Ian's memory, that she'd asked. There were five solid minutes of silence after Bridget's single word, and during that time Ian focused hard on his asparagus. It was perfectly cooked and seasoned. But saying so — saying anything at all — felt like an awful idea.

Then Ana asked to be excused to get ready for bed. She said she was tired. It was seven thirty.

After that, Ian and Bridget sat opposite each other, both eyeing the table. An opening conversational salvo rolled around inside Ian's head, going so far as to touch the tip of his tongue. He actually opened his mouth a few times to speak but quickly closed it each time.

Bridget got up and went wordlessly into the living room. Ian cleared the table. Normally, dishes went into the sink for later, but he decided to load the dishwasher in the quiet kitchen. Why not? Ian could look out the window into the backyard — an evening-lit portal into the past, where nothing went wrong. There was no street this way, no black cars filled with watchers and danger. Ana's swing set was out there. She didn't play on it much these days, but it had been quite the hit once upon a time.

A voice came from behind him, his hands slick with suds, wet to the wrists.

"Who is she?"

Ian turned.

"Who?"

"The woman you were with today."

"Bridge. You were just — "

"I know what I was just. Who is she, Ian?"

Ian turned halfway back to the sink. He wasn't sure what to say. The man on the phone still rang in his ears. What had happened seemed to be personal: because of Ian, directed at Bridget. He was being sent a message, but his wife — and, maybe, his daughter — were the leverage. Ian was too important to risk harming. His compliance was necessary, but he couldn't shake the feeling that Bridget's being saved today was a *Sure, that worked out nicely* situation. If she'd been killed instead, it would have been "Oh well, you have to break eggs to make an omelet."

"She's nobody."

"But worth skipping your morning's work for."

"It was a work thing, Bridget."

"Is that why you won't tell me who she is?"

Not Alice Frank, that's for sure. That much, Ian wouldn't say, and Bridget had apparently been too far off to recognize the media personality without his help. If Ian told her that's whom he'd met, she'd have follow-up questions. And given all that man on the phone seemed to know, Ian wasn't confident that someone wouldn't overhear the ensuing discussion. Someone who, having already shaken them once, might not mind breaking eggs the next time.

"Is this really what you want to concentrate on? You were almost killed today."

"Hmm. Yes, I was. And do you know what I saw on my way to the mall? I saw that black car that I mentioned yesterday. It was following me. It and a minivan big enough to ... I don't know ... hold the three things they set loose."

"And why were *you* following *me?*" Bridget was angry at him, sure, but he'd been calm and kind for too long. He couldn't be selfless anymore. None if this was his goddamned fault, and he was tired of being painted as the undeserving bad guy.

"Did you hear what I said, Ian? *Someone set those things loose on purpose.*"

Ian turned fully, snatching a towel with malice, as if it had offended him. "And that doesn't strike you as odd, given what you seem to be accusing me of? Make up your mind, Bridget. Are you saying I'm cheating, or that I'm dealing with murderers? Because I've got to say, that's one *hell* of a fatal attraction if you're combining them."

"I'm saying you're not playing straight. You're keeping secrets," Bridget said, her anger somewhat blunted by his rebuke, now sliding closer to hurt. Seeing it made Ian guilty. It was as if he'd hit her, and now she was flinching back.

"I have reasons."

"What's going on, Ian?"

"I just said I have reasons."

"The people in the car. Who are they?"

"Dammit, Bridge. This doesn't concern you. Leave it alone. Let me handle it."

Ian turned away. Bridget grabbed his discarded towel and threw it hard at his back as if it were heavy enough to hurt him.

"It doesn't *concern* me? I was almost killed today! You saw those things! How did they move that fast, Ian? It's all over the Internet! People are coming out of the woodwork, saying they've seen others, too. Smaller outbreaks, mostly in the country or other cities. People are saying that something is happening. Like maybe the virus is changing. Or that Necrophage is weakening."

"Who's saying that?"

*"People!"*

"And you believe it?" He said it with disbelief, dripping more with condescension than curiosity.

"Why don't you tell me something different then? Why have you been sneaking around so much? Working evenings, going out on weekends, getting calls from strange women … "

"It doesn't make *one goddamned bit of difference* that she's a woman. She just happens to be—"

"Then who is she? Why won't you tell me? She's sure wanted to talk to you a lot, Ian. All those calls and emails and — "

"Emails?" Ian said, feeling a strange sensation rising up from somewhere deep.

*"Emails!* Oh, she's definitely been dying to talk to *you*, Ian."

"You've been reading my email?"

Bridget looked caught. Ian wanted to keep prodding because as bothered as he felt, her own snooping should, if she thought for a second, unhinge her argument. She'd see what they were talking about and know it wasn't an affair

… except that most of the emails he'd exchanged with Alice had been vaguely worded requests and similarly vague rejections. Both of them seemed to know that email was insecure, that anyone might read them.

But the look was only a flinch. Bridget went on the offensive rather than backing down.

"What's she been sending you that you've been deleting? If it's not pictures of her with her tits out, then by all means please — "

"Christ, Bridge. Really?"

"How can I know what you're hiding? If you want to convince me it's something else, just show me. You *used* to trust me."

Ian's temperature was up, but the last sentence popped him like a balloon. Quieter, he said, "It's not about trust."

"I used to trust you, too."

"This isn't fair. There are things I can't tell you, but not because I don't want to. None of this is my choice."

Ian's phone buzzed on the countertop. He looked toward it, but Bridget grabbed it.

"'Alice,'" she said, reading the display, her mouth twisted.

Ian found himself wanting to tell her everything, safety be damned. Things had been good for the past few years, but their marriage had seen its troubled times, too. They'd pulled through it with honesty and love, and right now felt like neither. Maybe Hemisphere was the bad guy. Maybe they were all in danger. But right now, all Ian cared about was erasing that loathing, distrustful look from his wife's face. He'd never loved anyone like he loved Bridget. Peril mattered little. He just wanted her back by his side, giving him a solid foundation from which he'd be able to fight whatever might be coming.

She could connect the dots. Alice Frank was well

known. Bridget hadn't been close enough to see Alice properly at the mall before Alice had been taken away and Ian had been rather coincidentally freed, but she'd seen the basics: tall, thin, blonde, more no-nonsense attractive than strictly pretty. If Bridget's mind cobbled the puzzle together now and asked him if he'd been chumming with Alice Frank, he'd confess it all. He'd tell her everything, hold nothing back.

But Bridget's green eyes were hard and accusing.

The phone stopped vibrating and died. Alice didn't leave a message. Maybe she couldn't; maybe Ian's lack of answer had wasted her *one jailhouse phone call*. Did they let you call from your cell? Ian had never been arrested. He had no idea.

"She can't be without you for a minute, can she?" Bridget slid the phone toward him.

"I'd tell you if I could."

"Then tell me."

*"If I could."*

"Why can't you?"

But Alice, failing to reach him, must have turned her call to the third member of their party because now Ian's phone began to vibrate. *Blocked Caller* filled the screen.

When Ian didn't answer, declining the call and staring wordlessly at his wife, the Blocked Caller sent a text.

From August Maughan. With an address and a time to meet, immediately.

Bridget's hands moved to her hips.

"I have to go," Ian said.

"Of course you do."

"I don't have a choice. I promise I'm doing this for all the right reasons."

"Reasons you won't explain. Involving someone whose name I can't know. Except that it's *Alice.*"

"Bridge … "

"Go, fine." She turned to leave.

"I'm doing this to protect you. And Ana."

Bridget turned back. Her eyes were angry, hurt, uncomprehending, crushed.

"If you want to protect us," she said, "then stay."

"I can't. I have to … "

Bridget shook her head then left the kitchen, leaving Ian alone with his impossible choice.

The best chance for keeping his family safe seemed to be to leave them defenseless, hating him for his abandonment.

# Chapter Fifty-Three

## NEWS

HOLLY TURNED AUGUST'S TV OFF, unable to take it anymore. She was no stranger to media manipulation; she'd been its subject (both from her managers' perspectives and those of the media themselves) since before she'd become the darling she was today. But this was different. This felt like … like *falsely modest* news. There were sly-sounding reports surrounding the Grover Mall incident, but even though it looked like a cover-up, it was very much not. Video footage was being withheld, but Holly got the distinct impression that the withholding itself was supposed to convey a message:

*Yes, a group of ferals attacked and killed several people in the mall today, and yes, they were "something different" (maybe even "something alarming") as far as ferals go. We all know it. But we're holding back footage so you can use your imaginations … but no, nobody is denying anything. Wink-wink.*

Holly had felt increasingly insightful since beginning August's Prestige drug, but her insights into the news reports went further. It was as if everything was glass, and she could see through it all.

It all felt like one of her performances. Something meant to make a point, controlled and orchestrated from the get-go.

That's what the man whose voice she kept hearing seemed to feel, anyway.

Holly blinked the idea away. August had explained that. Prestige did some magic juju on her brain that even the Stardom formulation didn't — testament to the fact that Damon and Cyrus were wrong, and what Holly paid August was money well spent. He wasn't just a genius; he'd begun his professional life side by side with Archibald Burgess. Hemisphere, August said, had wanted to upgrade the human brain, and that might just be what was happening with Holly. There were bound to be some growing pains. Like hearing her own voice as auditory hallucinations, thanks to her brain's temporarily crossed wires.

Never mind that the voice was a man's.

And never mind that there was that other voice too: new to the world, waking up, feeling (in Holly's mind and apparently the unseen man's) like a bright light in the darkness.

Growing pains. That's all it was.

But Holly still stared at the dark screen for a few extra seconds, letting the news report settle. She let the feeling of transparency settle. She let the feeling that she could tell more about those reports than she was supposed to dissolve into nothing.

She heard the sound of a door latch opening. She turned on the couch to see August enter, looking frazzled, carrying a box overstuffed with paraphernalia.

"Iss late," she said, her voice tending toward its old slur.

"Okay, Mom," August replied.

Holly waited until August looked up. Then he said, "Sorry."

"I's worried."

"I needed to pick up some supplies from my other place. I wanted to make sure nobody spotted me."

"Nod worried furyu."

August looked at her, and Holly moved her tongue inside her mouth, trying the strength of her lips. If she couldn't control her mouth by force of will, how could she control the disconcerting sense of connection and chatter she seemed to sense in the air all around her?

"I'm not worried for you," she said, trying again.

"Why? Have people come or called, looking for you?"

Holly waved dismissively. The movement was still clumsy. She'd been lucky; Sherman Pope hadn't given her much facial palsy, and her speech was now increasingly coming under control. But so much of her body was still dead and would be forever.

"Nothing like that. I don't even think anyone cares about us anymore."

August saw her glance at the television.

"They're talking about the mall."

"And others. Small outbreaks, from over the past weeks and months, somehow all very interesting now. There's *leaked video* with some. Everyone is afraid."

"People are jaded, Holly. They'll be fine."

But Holly knew that wasn't true. People *were* afraid. She could feel it around her like mist. Yet another thing she had no business believing, another glitch in her increasingly cross-fused brain.

She watched as August set the box on the kitchen countertop. "What is that stuff?" she asked.

"A joke of a lab. All I have that's portable."

"Why?"

"We're having company tonight."

"Who?"

"Someone from Hemisphere." August looked like he might keep the next thing to himself, but then he said, "What happened in the mall was intentional. You know as well as anyone, ferals are supposed to be slow. Because they're basically corpses. I have a theory about why the ones today were different, and it's something that's been bothering me for a while now. And after this, I'm afraid I might be right. Alice says this Hemisphere guy, Ian, has something I might need to hear, and I want to be prepared." He nodded toward the box of glass, plastic, and electronics.

"*What* do you think you might be right about?"

"Let's perform our due diligence before jumping to conclusions."

Holly watched August unpack the box, creating a miniature version of the lab in his other apartment. She wondered how long they'd be here. She wondered how much Prestige August had for her once her current supply of infusions ran dry, and if he'd be able to make more.

She didn't want to think about that, so she turned her attention to the bright, glowing light inside her mind. *The awakening,* for whatever it was worth.

Holly saw a dark place, draped with cloth.

She felt sadness, desperation, the eclipsing of a black cloud.

And she heard three words:

*Danny, please hurry.*

# Chapter Fifty-Four

## THE MOON

JORDACHE'S TEXT MESSAGE TOOK JUST sixteen letters, two spaces, a comma, and a period on Danny's screen. But he stared as if it were a cancer diagnosis.

*Danny, please hurry.*

Danny's thumbs moved quickly, stabbing out a reply. But halfway through typing, he wondered why he was being an asshole and made a call.

"Who is it?" Her voice was hurried, edged with panic.

"Danny. It's Danny, Jordache." Repeating what she'd already know, just by looking at her phone's screen — the same screen she'd have touched to accept his call.

"Danny. Thank God."

"Are you okay?"

"I'm hearing things. I'm hearing someone call. You, Danny. I can hear you calling."

Danny's skin crawled. "I'm calling you right now."

"All day. All day I've heard you calling. I want you here again. Come back to me, Danny."

Danny looked around his car's interior, littered with debris and garbage, the shadow from a huge elm throwing the vehicle into shadow. It was late to still be at work — or, in Danny's case, in the parking lot. It would be dark soon.

"I can't come over just yet."

Danny waited. He thought she'd ask why, and he wasn't sure what he'd say. He'd promised to come over later. He couldn't admit that he was still desperately hoping that Ian Keys would walk through that door, having pulled a later-than-usual shift. Because officially, as far as Jordache was concerned, Danny didn't need to "hurry" to do anything other than return to her side. She had her PhageX, supposedly. It wasn't something he'd lied to her about, and that he was now frantically chasing like a junkie after his habit.

He looked at the doors, waiting for Ian. But Danny doubted he'd emerge. Ian was a Boy Scout when it came to work/life balance. They'd covered Ian's unwillingness to burn the midnight oil the last time they'd spoken. So no, Ian wasn't still in there, as much as Danny wanted to believe he was. The only conclusion was that for reasons unknown, Ian simply hadn't shown up for work.

But instead of asking Danny that tricky question, Jordache said something else.

"We've been watching the moon," she said.

Danny looked up. It wasn't dark yet.

"Who's there?"

"Nobody's here. When can you be here? I need you here."

"I — "

"I love you, Danny."

Danny stopped, unable to speak. She'd said that last in a slightly different voice, rushed, as if she'd forced it past her lips. He should respond in kind, but for the moment, he had no idea how.

"I'll be there soon."

"When?"

"I just have another stop to make," he said, already starting the engine. Fortunately, Ian's old card still had enough mojo to have admitted Danny into his personnel file, and he'd already entered Ian's address into his GPS. He'd hoped it wouldn't come to this, but there was no other way. He'd have to go now, and hurry. Because he actually had *two* stops to make, and the second was back in the same lot he was now. The doors and dispensary wouldn't care what time it was. Tomorrow, if anyone had a problem with Ian Keys entering and requisitioning stock after hours, Ian could deal with it.

"I'm afraid."

Danny forced a smile, hoping it would show in his voice. If he kept marching, this had to work out fine. This couldn't have anything to do with PhageX — something most of Danny thought was bullshit, given the way he'd spent all day trying to get more. But there was no logic to any of this. She'd been on Necrophage; now she was on Necrophage. Add-ins in designer formulas were irrelevant. People went on and off the designer drugs all the time. This had to be in her head.

"Don't be," he said, trying to keep his tone light. "I'll bring a pizza."

"I'm slipping. Holly thinks so, and so does he."

Danny's brow furrowed, not understanding.

"I can't get comfortable. It's like my skin is trying to get away. I've been under the bed for hours, then in the closet."

"In the — "

"I opened my plumbing access. I went under the trailer, to clean, to see what was there. After my run. I stayed for hours because it was so nice."

Danny wiped his forehead.

"Jordache. Maybe you should go to a clinic."

And tell them what? That everything was fine? He'd seen her infuse the Necrophage with his own eyes. Which part of Jordache going to a clinic would help anything? The part where they gave her more of what she already took, in compensation for withdrawal there was no logical reason to have? The part where, maybe, blood tests revealed the presence of a designer Phage formulation, and implicated her maybe-boyfriend who worked at Hemisphere and had no business dealing it? The maybe-boyfriend who, as things turned out, had been spending more money than he should?

"I got afraid. I went to the store. I got more Necrophage. The base stuff. And I took it. I asked the pharmacist if I could take more, even if I'd already taken some today, even if my usual wasn't a base formulation at all. And he said yes. More makes no difference. So I took two infusions, to be sure. He helped me. He had blue eyes. His name was Marvin. The pharmacy's hours were six to eleven. Its phone number is—"

Danny cut her off, feeling cold. She hated the idea of taking base Phage, yet she'd done it today despite already having had some this morning in the guise of her own PhageX.

It was an impossible situation. He needed to get more of the drug, but right now, Jordache seemed thin enough to snap. He'd have to run back to her then leave again and lower his standards on how *ideal* these events could turn out.

"I'll be there as soon as I can."

"Hurry," she said.

"As soon as I can. I promise."

"The moon," Jordache said. "The sun is out, and I can see the moon."

# Chapter Fifty-Five

## A-LIST

THE MOMENT WAS SURREAL. IT was dark through the large windows with their fine but anonymous view of the city below. Ian was watching a comedy flick with a name he hadn't caught and a plot he hadn't been remotely paying attention to. To one side, on a plush couch, was the actress Holly Gaynor — who, it turned out, must only put on her famous necrotic accent because she had none of it in person. To the other side was Bobby Baltimore, famous deadhead hunter.

He'd heard August Maughan was connected, with a roster of A-list longevity clients. But he hadn't expected a Who's Who to be here tonight, nearing ten o'clock, while Ian feared for his family — and, honestly, feared his wife a bit, too.

He checked his phone. Still no returned text from Bridget or missed call. No new voicemails. Or emails.

He could try again. Maybe he even *should* try again; incessant, never-give-up attempts to contact someone stopped being stalking and became proper when trying to heal an argument with your wife. But Ian didn't, partly because he'd need to do it on the sly. He might even need to leave the room, in case Bridget miraculously answered.

But mainly he didn't try again because he knew she wouldn't take his call. She wouldn't respond to a text. She'd keep ignoring him, as she'd been doing since he'd left home hours ago to meet August.

Unless Bridget was dead, of course. Bridget and Ana both.

Ian felt restless. He couldn't get comfortable. There was no proper answer. August would only talk to Ian in person, and their talk had been revealing … to the scientist, anyway. But that had been a while ago now, all four of them pow-wowing to reach conclusions that only August, with his insider knowledge of Archibald Burgess, already knew. He'd gone into his ad-hoc lab. To his computer, with all of the information from the thumb drive, public and general consumption as it seemed to be.

Ian could probably have left after that. He wanted to, but he also felt sure he shouldn't. This was bigger than his family. This might be the whole world.

He stood. Bobby's eyes followed.

"They'll be fine," Bobby said.

"You don't know that. Hemisphere doesn't want me talking, and sicced three ferals on my wife today to prove it. And now that I'm here, they —"

"Are still being watched by my buddies."

Ian sighed.

"Do you want me to text them?"

"No. It's fine."

"I'll text them." Bobby's phone appeared, and he dictated a message. The response was immediate. Bobby held the screen toward Ian, who of course couldn't read it from where he was sitting.

"She went to bed ten minutes ago. Nobody's come knocking."

Ian closed his eyes and breathed deeply. He didn't love the idea of Bobby's hunter friends staking out his house and watching the windows. Seeing Bridget's light go off as she went to bed alone, far earlier than usual. She was probably lying under the covers, watching TV, feeling nervous and betrayed, with no husband to hold her in the aftermath of her harrowing day.

Ian was about to make an announcement — perhaps that he was leaving and would return in the morning — when August emerged from the kitchen, where he'd set up his lab near the closest water supply.

"I've got a Play-Doh Fun Factory in there and need proper equipment to be sure," he said, removing his little glasses and rubbing his eyes, "but what I'm seeing fits what you told me, Ian."

Ian looked at Bobby and Holly. Had he missed something while he'd been busy missing every word of the movie?

"I didn't tell you anything."

"The files you gave me did. Plus what Alice led me to, the stuff she was given by your tipster."

"There was nothing in them," Ian said. "Same for what he gave Alice."

"I understand why you'd think that," August said. "But all those public studies and reports on the drive had information hidden in the metadata."

"I didn't know that," Ian said, wondering why anyone would do something so obtuse. "How would you even know to look?"

"It's something we used to do when I was at Hemisphere. Archibald is paranoid. It's not enough to obscure information. He was always hiding it in plain sight. Like this."

"You're saying those files contained Hemisphere secrets from years ago that they forgot to — "

"No," August said, cutting him off. "Archibald is both paranoid *and* wicked smart. He wouldn't be that sloppy. What was on those files was put there by your source."

"What the hell would make him think I'd even find it?"

"I don't think you were supposed to. He hid what we needed in the metadata then sent it through you because you have access inside the Hemisphere firewall. But what was in there was, I think, always meant for me."

Ian blinked around at the others, but this part of the discussion meant nothing to Holly and Bobby.

"If this guy wanted to talk to you, why didn't he just contact you and leave me out of it?" The question made Ian resentful. He hadn't asked for any of this and didn't deserve any involvement in this mission of espionage.

"If I had to guess, it's because your access is needed. You and Alice were both nudged toward me."

"But nothing direct. Of course."

"I suspect this is the work of an insider at Hemisphere, like you. Maybe he saw something but didn't know what it was, and can't investigate because he fears for his safety."

Ian huffed. Fuck his safety. What about *Ian's* safety?

Bobby was watching August. There was much they'd discussed earlier, before August had disappeared into the kitchen, about Yosemite. About evolution. About things Bobby may have seen — things, as it turned out, that had been bothering Bobby for a while about the aged dead-head population: a population that refused to die, and became harder to kill the older it got.

"What did you find, August?" Bobby asked. "You found something, didn't you?"

August nodded.

"Sherman Pope appears to be a modified version of a Hemisphere gene therapy virus called BioFuse," he said.

Ian sat up.

"Hemisphere had the cure," August went on, "because Hemisphere caused the plague."

## Chapter Fifty-Six

### WEASEL

"HE'LL LEAVE YOU," WEASEL SAID.

"Shut up," Jordache replied to the unseen speaker, huddled under her covers, totally in the dark, too hot, not caring.

"He got what he needed from you. Same as I did. Same as any guy gets what they want before bolting. Because you ain't worth shit other than that honey trap between your legs."

Jordache tossed the covers off and sat up on the bed. She was naked. She'd met Danny that way because it felt right, but now she could only see her nudity as proof that Weasel had a point. But fuck Weasel. He didn't get to have points anymore. She'd seen him decay. She'd seen him die. She'd seen him taken away to Yosemite in a black van after he was dead, watching him kick and scream. She'd seen him on Bobby Baltimore's program, Season 2, Episode 4, at 21:46. But somehow, she'd also seen him shot, in the arm, in the torso, not in the head. That little video seemed to come from behind her own eyes as if projected there by someone else, by a tall man with a cold voice that didn't warble like it should. That video of Weasel being wounded, savaged, dragging his sorry undead ass to safety like a coward.

He was in Yosemite. Not here, in her trailer.

But Jordache saw her ex right where she nonetheless expected him to be, given the direction of his voice. His arm was tattered flesh, black at the edges, bones protruding. His face was half sloughed away, his teeth exposed even when his lips were closed. His eyes had receded too much around the eyeballs, making him look too intense, like he was paying an insane amount of attention. But his stupid little mustache still seemed to be there — testament to the fact that even after he'd died, he hadn't given up on being trash.

"Come over here, Sexy," he said, watching her, looking down at his lap. Whatever might be there was sluggish. He dripped black clumps of something on her clean floor, as if leaking from a sprung hydraulic line. "I'll still take what you got."

"You're not here," Jordache said.

"No. I'm here. Danny's the one who's not."

"He had to go. He needed to take care of something."

And he did, too. He'd come. She'd tried to attack him and tear his clothes off, but Danny had actually pushed her back, his eyes almost afraid. She was in bed now because he'd put her there. Because he'd said she was unwell even though she felt stronger and smarter than she ever had. She'd heard Danny coming five minutes before he'd pulled up in front. He'd blinked 430 times that she'd seen in the thirty-six minutes his head had been facing her. That was way more than he normally blinked. It made her think of an apple she'd eaten once, when she'd been four, when she'd bitten too far into the core and swallowed a seed. Her friend Ginny had told Jordache that apple seeds contained cyanide and Jordache had tried to throw it up, found herself unable, and had spent the night expecting to die.

"If he wanted you," Weasel said, "he would have stayed."

"He got a text."

"He faked the text, and you know it."

It was true. Of course she knew it, though the last person she wanted to hear it from was Weasel, who wasn't even here.

"You should eat something," Weasel said.

"Go away."

"There's not much left. Maybe you could eat your own arm."

"Danny will be back soon. Or in the morning, if he needs all the time he thinks he might."

"Danny is gone. Forever. Where would he need to go, then come back? Except, of course, to fuck someone else."

"Danny's not like that." Jordache got up and began dressing. She put on her shoes first. Then took them off. Then put them on. Then took them off. Then put them on. Then she remembered that socks went before shoes and gave up, all of it too overwhelming.

Her eyes went to the clock. It was 10:35.

Weasel laughed.

"You'll never make it until morning," he said.

# Chapter Fifty-Seven

## THROUGH THE DARK WINDOW

BRIDGET WOKE TO THE FEELING of someone climbing into bed with her. For a delirious, half-asleep moment, she thought it was Ian (and not just *Ian*, but *Ian before things started getting ugly)* and let herself relax. But then the someone merely sat on the bed instead of getting properly under the covers, and Bridget realized it was Analise, shaking her without so much as turning on a light.

"Mom."

"Baby? You're too old to sleep with me." The second she said it, Bridget wished she hadn't. Now, Ana would need to push for comfort if she still meant to get it, and at eleven years old, that seemed increasingly unlikely. Bridget *wanted* to say yes. She wanted the warm body herself.

"I heard something outside my window."

"You're imagining things, Sweetie. Go back to bed."

"I looked out, Mom. I saw something, too."

The cobwebs were slow to leave Bridget's mind. She was tired and disturbed by the day's events: not just the mall attack, but the fight with Ian that followed — that, judging by the bed's empty half, was still in progress. She'd been woken from a dream where she told Ian her secrets and he accepted them all. But mostly, Bridget suspected she was fighting the Zen she'd popped before bed. She didn't like to take two in a day, but recent events merited extra measures. And then, after she'd swallowed, she'd seen that the vial only contained one last pill. So she'd taken that one, too, to make things neat.

But with the haze departing, Ana's words kissed her skin like a cool blade.

*Something outside.*

Lion's Gate was a gated community, but it's not like people couldn't crawl in from the edges. It's not like people in black cars couldn't bribe their way inside. There were supposedly body-temperature sensors all over the city and extras around communities like this, intent on tracking anything that moved without generating much heat. But if today had shown Bridget anything, it was that the usual rules of safety and peace inside Aberdeen Valley — pacifying pills notwithstanding — weren't as immutable as they were supposed to be.

"I'm sure it's nothing," she said, less sure.

"In the bushes. I'm scared, Mom." She hugged her mother's arm, years dropping from her age in seconds.

Bridget stood in the room's darkness. Ian had guns somewhere, but Bridget had no idea where, how to get at them, how to load them, or how to fire them. Ian hadn't been a gun guy before the plague, and it had been her own urging that had made him arm up. She'd asked for protection with a smile, pretending it was all silly but that she'd appreciate his indulgence, not feeling it was silly at all.

"Is Dad home?"

"Not yet, Honey."

Ana's head swiveled to the nightstand clock. Bridget took Ana by the arm and pulled her away. The girl had enough to worry about without wondering at her father's whereabouts so late.

"Come on," Bridget said, summoning confidence she was nowhere near feeling.

They crossed the hallway to Ana's room. Bridget pointed at the side yard window, the blinds partly drawn. There were plenty of streetlights but not on the home's side. Bridget wished Ana hadn't raised the blinds. Now she'd have to put her face to that blackness, eye to eye with anything that may have climbed a story to peer in unseen.

Still pointing, Bridget gave her daughter a look.

Ana nodded.

Bridget slowly crossed the room, leaving Ana unmoving in the doorway. She fought an absurd urge to grab something: a lamp, a gymnastics trophy, maybe the damned clothes tree. She felt naked unarmed, but what did she think could possibly happen? Would the window burst when she got close, some unknown horror springing in to do battle?

"It's probably just a dog," Bridget said, her voice too low.

Ana was still, arms crossed over her waist. She nodded.

Bridget neared the window and could see nothing through the glare of the small night lights in the hallway.

She moved closer.

Closer.

With a glance back at Ana, who nodded encouragement, Bridget put her face to the glass and cupped her hands around her cheeks to peer out onto the lawn below.

She found herself staring at a yammering horror, its face decayed, its eyes wide, its teeth exposed to bite, tensed, moving to leap —

And then it was just the trellis running up the home's corner, green ivy swaying in the breeze.

She forced herself to scan the dark lawn. Her glance was quicker than it should have been, but Bridget saw nothing.

Her heart descended from high alert. She turned, backing away from the window to face Ana with an awkward smile.

"Nothing there," she said.

Then the booming began.

# Chapter Fifty-Eight

## MECHANISMS OF DISEASE

"WE NEED ALICE FRANK," AUGUST said.

Ian watched him, unable to believe his ears. *Hemisphere caused the plague?* It was the stuff of paranoid, deep-web theory. Not the sort of thing that happened to loyal, law-abiding employees like Ian Keys.

Bobby cleared his throat. "Go back, August."

But August was pacing. As uncomfortable as Ian had felt moments ago, worrying about Bridget and Ana, August now looked twice as terrible.

"We need Alice. We need to break this open, and now. Hemisphere is having their family picnic in the park tomorrow."

Ian watched August, wondering if the goateed scientist had ever been a part of one of the events. They were more like free concerts than picnics, but at the start, supposedly, the events had been small and intimate as their name implied. A time to get together with the community. A time to give back. A time to quietly lobby for federal funding, like an in-public performance review in front of the world's eyes … and Panacea's.

"Maybe you should explain," Bobby said, "before slandering the world's richest company."

August settled with effort, perching half-atop one of the low upholstered chairs.

"You know Hemisphere's tagline," he said.

"'Upgrading nature,'" Ian recited. He'd been reminded of that one rather recently, and under decidedly intimidating circumstances that made this all just a bit easier to believe.

August nodded. "And you know the company began life in longevity research. That was my day. Archibald lost his parents young, and it gave him a drive that was close to an obsession. But there's an expression: 'Obsession is what lazy people call dedication.' And so that's how I always saw that mission: as one we were dedicated to, come hell or high water. It's something I'm still preoccupied with today." He tipped a look at Bobby, who Ian surmised must be one of his independent life-extension clients, in August's post-Hemisphere days.

"Most of what I do today, I learned as Archibald's protégé. The man is brilliant, and driven. He has a passion for discovery I've never seen matched in anyone else. But the longer I worked with him, the more I wondered what mattered most: reaching the destination, or building a stable foundation. But being stable isn't exciting, see. So we became yin and yang: he was yin; I was yang. He pushed every boundary in the lab — it was my job to rein him back in. You probably know that Hemisphere's stem cell operations started in Singapore, for instance. And I can promise you, now that my NDA is pretty much moot, that what his team learned there, he brought back stateside, legal or not."

Holly shifted on the opposite couch. She was wearing jeans and a tee, beautiful but not remotely Hollywood. But of course, her speech and manner (so long as she stayed sitting) didn't seem necrotic at all, either.

"The BioFuse drug you mentioned, Ian. The one your anonymous source pointed both you and Alice toward. It was a gene therapy treatment for Alzheimer's disease — a neutered virus that produced a protein in the brain, meant to clear out the neural plaques thought to cause Alzheimer's symptoms. We wanted to force the brain to adapt and create new pathways in the damaged brain — a way of *detouring* around the damage caused by Alzheimer's. And it worked fairly well. Not perfectly, but well. I was there during the initial development and trials. For a while, it looked like Hemisphere was on its way to eradicating one of the world's most devastating diseases. Becoming the heroes then that they are to most people today."

"But you left," Ian said.

August nodded. "In the middle of the BioFuse heyday."

"Why?"

"Because it was a failure. We saw the writing on the wall early, before the public, and it became apparent we'd need to pull the drug and start over. Our first trials were promising, but then nature — which tends to resist being upgraded, except by its own hand — adapted. The plaque-clearing protein worked okay, but only about half the time did patients' brains know what to do once the way was clear. The process was slow, and a myriad of other problems plagued the frustrated scientist."

August sighed and went on.

"The FDA was preparing to pull our approval. Hemisphere was headed for the shitter, and lawsuits, from the patients who weren't healed and somehow felt damaged by our treatments, were a given. Archibald was livid. But not just livid — *indignant.* He said a lot of things like, 'How dare they?' He tore up a lab while I watched. He'd worked too hard and had only tried to do what was best for the people Hemisphere wanted to help. And now those people were going to turn on him and ruin his legacy? Destroy the company he'd started in his parents' memory, to make humanity's lives better and longer?" August shook his head. "It made him so angry. Reckless."

"So you jumped off the sinking ship," Bobby said. Ian wasn't sure if it was a judgment or not.

"It wasn't the failure that bothered me. We had other lines. We had venture capital and a few angel investors ready to dig us out. To me, failure has always been a stop along the road to success — sometimes, *many* stops. But Archibald took things personally. He started to talk about ways to save the situation. Options we'd discussed and dismissed. Things like de-neutering the gene therapy virus so it would be self-replicating. Things like injecting into the body as well as the spinal column, finding ways to work around the blood-brain barrier — which keeps stuff from the body from entering the brain and vice-versa — so he could use stem cells from a person's bone marrow. Tactics we'd considered and rejected because they kept things in the body alive a bit *too* well."

"How can something be kept alive too well?" Holly asked. "More life is good, right?"

"Cancer," Ian heard himself saying. "Cancer is just a cell that doesn't know to die."

August nodded. "I'll have to investigate more to be sure, but once Ian told me what to look for, I found it easily enough and feel confident about what I'm seeing."

"Which is?" Bobby asked.

"I think that Archibald continued BioFuse trials after I left but did so without me being a wet rag on his best ideas. But it still didn't work, and somewhere along the line he must have realized he could go a different direction with those same game pieces. A direction that would save the company by making something that everyone, everywhere, would want to buy."

He looked at Ian, Holly, and Bobby.

"Sherman Pope is the success BioFuse wasn't. A few small tweaks to the therapy virus, and it looks to me like suddenly it was replicating everywhere, in and outside of the brain. Not just breaking up plaques that caused Alzheimer's, but breaking up everything, everywhere — and then replacing them with madly proliferating stem cell counterparts."

Holly looked like she wanted to grab her own head, her own arms and legs. August was describing a parasite, and Holly was filled with it.

"The computer models I've run suggest that Necrophage — which contains an artificial cell receptor as one of its components — bonds with the Sherman Pope virus about as well as it does with BioFuse. No wonder it was developed so fast. Hemisphere was creating a biological match to its own creation."

Ian leaned forward, feeling uneasy. He put his head in his hands, the weight of the modern world somehow settling unfairly atop his shoulders."

"Archibald failed to create a brain that could heal itself," August's voice said from above, "but he succeeded in creating a body that healed fast enough, despite the decay, that it couldn't die."

# Chapter Fifty-Nine

## KNOCK KNOCK

BRIDGET TOOK THE STAIRS TO her ground floor as quickly as a girl rushing to the living room on Christmas day. Only halfway down did she remember the black cars and the ferals released at the mall then consider that this might be a mistake.

She stopped. Analise, four steps behind her, crashed into her back. Bridget swayed, but she'd been holding the banister and stayed in place.

"Go back upstairs," Bridget said. She felt foggy. Too much Zen. Her mind wanted to slide into heaven's abandon while its animal depths were teeming with fear and adrenaline.

"I'm not going back upstairs!"

"It could be a trap."

"Mom?"

"Go upstairs, Ana."

But the booming on the door continued. And the same voice they'd heard all the way upstairs, shouted in a way that was far too loud, for Lion's Gate, after dark.

"Mrs. Keys! Open up, please!"

"Who is it?" Ana asked.

"I don't know," Bridget answered.

"We were sent by your husband! We need to talk to you, ma'am!"

Ana came halfway around Bridget's body. "Dad sent them."

"That's what abductors always say. Don't you remember what we taught you about stranger danger?"

Bridget looked down. Ana was looking up at her, halfway under her armpit.

*"Abductors?"*

"We don't know who's out there," Bridget said.

"Someone Dad sent." Ana skipped past and moved toward the door.

It seemed like a terrible idea to Bridget. Aware she felt a little high and was perhaps not reacting in the most sensible manner, she called after Ana.

"There's stuff going on you don't know," she said.

"Like what?"

*Like the fact that someone has been watching the house. Like the fact that I was almost killed by three ferals that — and I don't think I'm being crazy here — sure seemed to have been deliberately sicced on me. Like your father's strange behavior, as if this wasn't as surprising to him as it was to me. Like the way he's been running around with strange women, doing odd deals, getting us all in a lot of trouble with people who are willing to fight dirty. Like the fact that the world, dear daughter, isn't quite what we thought it was yesterday.*

But she couldn't say any of that. So instead, numb, she watched Ana touch the doorknob and impotently said, "Don't."

"Relax, Mom."

Ana opened the door.

Bridget braced herself, eyes searching for something she could use to brain late-night intruders. But instead of facing men and women with guns or rabid necrotics, she found herself looking at a pair of rather ordinary-looking men in camouflage hats standing beside a tidy woman in a no-bullshit pantsuit despite the hour. There was a new vehicle on the street with its dome light on and door ajar. A man in an open-throated dress shirt was being held in the group's middle.

The restrained man was tall, lanky, and had a messy head of brown hair. Despite the harsh shadows of the Keys family porch light, the man struck Bridget as overly friendly, with a wide smile on his face.

"Sorry to bother you, ma'am," said one of the men. "We saw this guy creeping around outside your house."

Bridget looked again at the man. If he'd been creeping around outside, it looked like he must have been doing so in an attempt to covertly sell her a vacuum cleaner. If he'd shown up alone, Bridget wouldn't have flinched. He was one of those people who, no matter what they did, looked harmless.

"Who are you?" Bridget asked.

Everyone answered at once: the man who'd spoken, the tall captive, the woman in the pantsuit. A mishmash emerged, so the woman glared at the others until they were quiet, then addressed Bridget.

She extended a hand.

"I know this must look strange. My name is Cindy Benson. I work with network personality Bobby Baltimore, and — "

Ana interrupted. Judging by the way Cindy's head flicked down to her, her presence had thus far gone unnoticed.

"You know Bobby Baltimore?" Ana asked, eager.

"And he asked us to keep an eye on your house."

Bridget felt like her mouth must be hanging open. She

looked at each of the people in turn. The tall man smiled again, looking sheepish.

*The famous YouTube zombie hunter guy sent us here to keep an eye on you.* Made sense.

"Okay."

"Bobby is with your husband."

"Sure."

The tall man must have decided the situation was strange enough that he couldn't make it worse. He stuck out a hand, which Bridget ignored.

"Hi, Mrs. Keys. My name is Danny Almond. I work with Ian."

Bridget still couldn't say anything.

"This is all just a big misunderstanding. I needed to talk to Ian, and these … these *people* just came rushing at me out of the shadows like Rambo."

"At eleven o'clock at night," said one of the men.

"Prowling around the entire house," said the other.

"I wanted to see if any lights were on before knocking. I didn't want to disturb you if you were asleep."

"Good job with that," said the first man.

"Hey. Nobody asked you," Danny said, turning as far as he could in the man's grip. "Who are you anyway?"

"We're the neighborhood watch."

Cindy spoke up. "I'm sure this is strange. I can explain it all. May we come in?"

"Maybe you can explain it all right where you are."

"I'd rather be in or out. There's another car of our people out there, but there's also reason to believe you might be in danger, and …"

Bridget's arm went around Ana, automatically pulling her back, her hand going to close the door in her visitors' faces.

"Wait!"

"Thank you for saving me from this nice young man," Bridget said.

Danny turned then wrenched free with malice. He put a hand on the door, keeping Bridget from closing it.

"Ian knows me. He'll understand. I know it's late, but this is important. Can I talk to him?"

Bridget wasn't sure how to respond. Somehow (and this was sublimely creepy), most of the gathering knew Ian was gone. Still, she was hesitant to confirm that she was a woman home alone with her eleven-year-old daughter.

"Please. I wouldn't come if it wasn't important."

"Shut your mouth, creep," said one of the camo-hat guys, grabbing Danny's arm.

Danny shook him off, appealing to Bridget. "Please. It will be quick."

"Ian's not home."

Danny sighed. "He left something at me for work that I really, really need. I just … did he leave his key card?"

"That's enough," said the other man, pulling Danny back.

Cindy stepped forward. Her eyes ticked to Ana, apparently trying to decide if she should continue. She noted the way Bridget still held the door's edge and met her eyes.

"I'm sure this is all very strange." She held up something that looked, on a fast glance, to be a press ID. Then she flipped to the next card, which was imprinted with her photograph and the logo from *The Bobby Baltimore Show*. "I can call Ian for you, and he can confirm."

Bridget had her husband's damned phone number and very much didn't want to call it. But he'd texted something a while back that she'd mostly ignored, and now that the haze was clearing, it struck her as the oddity that it had seemed on arrival. Something about August Maughan, from the news. And Bobby Baltimore, from the small screen. And … someone else? Someone famous?

"Why are you here?"

"Ian believes you may be in danger."

"And he didn't call the cops?"

"It's complicated, Mrs. Keys."

Bridget stared out into the black night. Her fears had returned with interest once darkness descended, and now they were creeping back at the thought of sending these people away.

Bridget reached for her phone. Keeping a wary eye on her visitors, she texted Ian one-handed.

He replied almost immediately.

Bridget looked down at her daughter. "Baby, go get dressed."

"Why?"

She looked at Cindy. "Because these nice people are going to take us to your father, whether they want to or not."

Five minutes later, a slow procession of vehicles left Lion's Gate, bound for places unknown.

A black vehicle followed, headlights off.

# Chapter Sixty

## VISITING HOURS

ALICE PACED HER CELL. SHE was apparently in custody, but there had been little ceremony about any of it. As a boundary pusher, Alice had been arrested before. There were always certain touchstones to the process: the reading of rights, fingerprinting, a single call on a station phone. But she hadn't been read her rights — something Alice was holding close to the vest like a literal get-out-of-jail-free card. She hadn't been fingerprinted. And the phone call (first to Ian then to August when Ian hadn't answered) had been conducted on her phone, right from her pocket, before its confiscation.

Since then, she'd been left alone. Entirely, silently alone.

This wasn't police. This was Panacea. And the minute Alice got out of here, she had one hell of a damning exposé to write about them.

She heard a lock turn. The door at the room's far end opened, past the only other cell in the small space. A man came forward who looked nothing like an agent. He was maybe fifty, slightly overweight, with blond hair and soft, intelligent eyes.

He stood in front of Alice's cell then reached up and unplugged something on the overhead security camera. The red light went dead.

"So you're Alice Frank," he said. "You seem taller in person."

Alice's eyes went to the camera. Was he planning to beat her up? Kill her? What didn't he want surveillance to see, and would they simply not notice the missing feed?

There was no reason for timidity. She'd done nothing wrong. She'd been well within her rights as a member of the free press right up until the moment someone had released ferals in front of her. If they meant to silence her as *extraneous* to Ian Keys's *too important*, she wasn't about to die on her knees.

"And who the hell are you?"

"My name is Raymond Smyth."

Alice's forehead wrinkled. "I know that name."

He nodded. "I'm Ian's boss. I'm also Hemisphere's liaison with Panacea. I imagine you came across my name in the documents I sent you. Or maybe the files I sent to Ian."

"That was you. On the phone."

"It was."

Alice looked at the camera. At the cell. At the door to the outside hallway, firmly closed.

Smyth followed her eyes. "I'm not worried about us being overheard, if that's what you're thinking."

"Why not?"

"This is a holding cell, not a jail. Everyone's gone home for the night. It's just me and you."

"Why am I being held?" Alice demanded.

"Because you're an enemy of the state, Ms. Frank. I'd

have thought you'd've figured that out by now." He gave a little shrug. "That's also why I didn't carry the ball myself. I didn't particularly want to be in there with you."

"So you just wanted someone else to do your dirty work."

"It's bigger than just me, Alice," Smyth said, pulling a metal chair from a corner and sitting on it opposite her. "If someone was going to bring down Hemisphere, it couldn't happen from the inside."

"Why not? You recruited Ian."

"Ian was necessary. He has access to the information I needed to push at him, in which our mutual friend August will find more than meets the eye. That information needed to be *carried* out of the building, not sent, or it'd have been detected. Ian has sufficient access to get whatever else August may need to make his case. And Ian can get him into the labs, where he can confirm it."

"Why not you?"

"Because I'm necessary, too. We all have our parts to play. And when the three of you tell the world what it needs to know, I'll be right where I need to be. Because the truth will come out, but Hemisphere is, to borrow an old expression, 'too big to fail.'"

Alice exhaled, unsure what to say. She held the cell's bars, wanting to shake them, to demand more information from this maddeningly calm man.

"How are we going to bring it down, then?" Alice asked.

"About a half hour ago, Ian Keys's access signature was used to gain entry to our modeling software. We both know that you sent Ian to August earlier tonight, so that's August's hand inside the system, not Ian's. It seems August is as brilliant as he always was. I've tried to work out what exactly Archibald was hiding, but I'm not a scientist.

August went for the throat from another angle, once he knew it had something or other to do with BioFuse."

"You said something about that earlier. About BioFuse," Alice said, more intrigued than angry — and less mad than she wanted to be. She'd been sure for years that Hemisphere was hiding something, that their swooping in to save the day and make their hundreds of billions was too convenient. She wanted to know the story's resolution, even if she'd been pinched in the process.

"Yes. That's all I knew: that there was something concealed and that BioFuse was part of it. And that Archibald buried those nuggets deeper than the rest. I've grown to know him quite well and can read him like a book. But he can read me, too. I couldn't ask. I couldn't dig. I don't have the science to understand it anyway. But August could. And you could blow the whistle while I stayed close."

"Close to Archibald Burgess?"

"Yes. The shell of this company will need to survive, and the brain behind it needs to stay on call. Because the world relies on Necrophage, right or wrong."

"Wrong," Alice said, waiting for more, asking a question without asking at all.

"August has concluded that Hemisphere engineered Sherman Pope. That it modified our earlier drug BioFuse to do more than repair Alzheimer's — to repair bodies and brains even as they fell apart and went mad. It makes sense. Even the worst ferals only decay so far. We've seen it in Bakersfield and in Yosemite. They reach a point of stability, where the disease props them up just as quickly as it dies."

Alice felt her legs want to wobble. Somewhere deep down, her gut had suggested something this dark, but that was only morose fantasy. Hemisphere had saved untold millions of lives with Necrophage. But it had killed just as many before the cure had been found … or, more likely, before it had been released, ready to sojourn into the world and usher in profit.

Alice looked at Smyth then around at her cell. The unspoken question finally fell from her lips.

"Are you going to let me out of here?"

"No."

Alice blinked. "What? Why not? I thought you were one of the good guys. You started this. You stuffed me and Ian together so I could blab about whatever he and August found. You turned off the goddamned camera when you came in here, for Christ's sake!"

Smyth seemed analytical, unconcerned. He crossed his legs and said, "When you came in here, did they offer you a phone call?"

"You just said that I 'sent Ian to August tonight.'"

"So I surmised. But I didn't ask if you called anyone. I asked if it was *offered.*"

"It was offered. But I wasn't read my rights, and that's … "

Smyth looked disappointed. Alice trailed off.

"What?" she asked.

Smyth seemed to search for a place to begin. Then: "There's a rather strong partnership between Hemisphere, who manufactures the drug that keeps the infected safe, and Panacea, who does its work more directly out on the streets. That partnership kept the outbreak inside US borders. Hemisphere's knowledge and Panacea's muscle established the Yosemite preserve. They kept the public's hearts and minds on an even keel. My job is to lubricate that partnership. But recently I've begun to fear that something is changing."

"Changing how?"

"They let you make that call to August, about Ian. I'm sure you were careful with your words, but the fact that they let you make the call at all — that they practically *requested* you make it — makes me wonder what Panacea knows and where their allegiances lie."

"You think — "

"Panacea should feel the same as Hemisphere. They should want the truth about the disease's origins concealed. But lately I've seen signs that they feel differently. Prompting your call, perhaps with knowledge of what you know and are attempting to do. Allowing you to use your own phone, which would suggest to August that you were free to speak, at least to some degree. But there's more. Things like this attack, in the mall. It's not the only one there's been, you know."

"There have been other outbreaks?" Alice shivered. Of course; there were always small fires that Panacea was sent into the wild lands to quell, or into urban areas to extinguish. But never inside Dead City itself. And never …

Alice almost didn't want to ask.

"Outbreaks like that one?" she finished.

Smyth nodded. "They have to be grown that way. Kept chained and untreated then injected with Necrophage after they've passed the critical inflection point and can no longer be saved."

"Why would anyone do that?"

"Because Necrophage halts degradation and makes some repairs, essentially ticking the clock backward on decay by a few days or a week after the first bolus. In a percentage of cases, those treated after — but very *recently* after — their point of no return retain enough bodily strength to do what you saw earlier today. They can run. And fight."

Alice felt a charge fill her. She had to get out of here.

The public needed to know all of this, regardless of which pieces she could prove.

"And there have been whispers from my contacts on the Panacea side about solutions to a problem at Yosemite that isn't being shared with me. Rumors being spread about Necrophage itself: that its effectiveness may be diminishing. Which, to my knowledge, is entirely false. But it seems to me that Panacea is trying to do something, and that it's seeding fear as a weapon."

"So let me out. I can time a release for Hemisphere's big feel-good press event tomorrow. Let me blow the whistle."

"Not just yet," Smyth said, falling into a fugue of concentration.

"Why the hell not?"

Smyth stood. Then he turned and left, leaving the camera disconnected.

Alice started screaming.

# Chapter Sixty-One

:)

DANNY'S CAPTORS WERE INDECISIVE.

THEY weren't cops or clarifiers or anyone official; he'd worked that out pretty quickly. His own sense of guilt had kept him quiet at first (he wasn't used to prowling dark houses looking for quiet ways inside, and justifying it wasn't easy), but once they'd shoved everyone into vehicles and left the community, Danny had become vocal. He'd pointed out that, appearances to the contrary, he'd done nothing wrong. He'd said "my lawyer" a time or two, even though he didn't have one. And he'd tried to charm Ian's wife, Ian's daughter, and the stern-faced producer-turned-SWAT-leader into seeing things his way.

*Hey, I was just looking for my beer buddy near midnight and thought he might be hiding outside his house in the bushes. What's the big deal?*

Danny didn't think anyone bought what he was shoveling, but they also had no authority. Near as he could tell, these were TV hunters — or, more likely, wannabes to the real TV hunters. This was a businesswoman and a few idiots with guns. If push came to shove, Danny could request a formal arrest. And then whom would the cops want to talk to?

After a lot of posturing and hemming and hawing and promises that he'd be in big trouble if he messed with anyone again, they dropped Danny off at a bus stop near the Skin District. His car was back at Lion's Gate (ironically outside the gate), but he wasn't going to push. He was free, and Jordache still needed him. This would have to be close enough.

He waited for the bus beside six twitchers so far gone that Danny spent the wait with keys clenched in his fist. He didn't even try to hide it. Let these lowest-on-society's-totem-pole try to snack on him. As rank with decay as these people smelled, he wondered if he could smash through their skulls with his hand.

He rode the bus in dark silence. He made the mistake of sitting by the window, and a woman with her face halfway off sat beside him. She either fell asleep or died then bled all over him.

Disgusted and increasingly fearful, Danny rode to the center of town and hailed a cab. The driver was necrotic, too, and Danny, in his frustration with the world, had to fight a biting comment about how the driver had better not snap his fucking foot off on the pedal. If that happened, Danny planned to haul his ass out into the street and drive the cab himself.

It was one in the morning by the time they approached Jordache's neighborhood. Everything was quiet. His phone vibrated in his pocket.

A text from Jordache: *Feeling better. Going to sleep. See you in the morning.*

It buzzed again: *Not before 9 a.m. :)*

Danny stared at the smiley face. He wasn't sure if he

wanted to shout at it or kiss it. Seeing as he was in the back of a cab, covered in dark blood, exhausted, and on an adrenaline hangover that made him feel weak, neither felt appropriate.

Maybe it was fine.

In fact, it almost certainly was.

*Feeling better.*

Danny's eyes flicked to the second message.

*:)*

It was one thing to stop sending him things that seemed crazy and deranged and full of hallucinations. It was better to get a text indicating that everything was, somehow, working out after all. But a smiley face? That wasn't just not bad. That was almost happy.

Danny closed his eyes, feeling bone weary. He truly *was* exhausted. He really could do with some sleep. When he'd been by earlier, Jordache had been like a sick patient who needed chicken noodle soup and comfort. And he could provide both much better if he didn't feel like the walking undead himself.

He spoke to the driver, giving him a new destination. The driver grunted. Or maybe it was a groan. This late, most of the workers were deeply, almost hopelessly necrotic. They barely needed sleep, seeing as they were practically dead.

Jordache was fine. Truly, she was. The more Danny said it inside his own mind, the better he felt. Because it was true. *Of course* she was fine. Why wouldn't she be? She was on Necrophage and had never stopped being on it. Whatever had happened before now had been … some sort of a hiccup, perhaps. Now she was settling in. She wouldn't have her PhageX glow until Danny managed to reach the absent Ian Keys, but he could do that later in the week. No rush. Because after a brief and rather intense scare, she was fine.

He could sleep.

And see her in the morning, cleaned up, happy, and fresh as a daisy.

## Chapter Sixty-Two

### BACON

IAN WOKE TO THE SOUNDS of popping and the smells of bacon.

At first, he didn't know where he was. The ceiling above him was wrong, too white and too far, as if he were too low to the ground or it were too high. Both were true. Ian made a small fortune each year and lived in a helluva house. But even August's throwaway second residence made Ian's McMansion look like a hovel.

Ian sat. The couches opposite him in the living room were empty. He'd kicked his covers to the floor. He'd slept in his clothes because Bridget hadn't brought him anything new. She *had* brought clothes for herself and Ana — just a little campout with a famous recluse at destinations unknown. But she and Ana had slept in a sort of second office with the door closed, on a fold-out futon while Ian was out here, alone, in the middle of Grand Central, uninvited.

He stood and ran his hand through his hair. He felt gross. There was a bathroom between him and the mysterious bacon smell, so he stepped inside, found a small tube of toothpaste, and used his finger to smear it around until the bad taste went away. His hair didn't have a lot of character on its own and laid obediently down with a bit of work. His eyes weren't as compliant. Looking in the mirror, Ian realized for the first time that he was no longer precisely young. He wasn't yet old, but he'd never again be denied service in a bar for want of an ID.

Ian found Bobby Baltimore in the kitchen, alone, working a cast-iron skillet.

"Oh, hey," Bobby said, turning at the sound of footsteps. "Did I wake you?"

Ian shook his head. "I thought you were August."

"I do a great August impression. That's probably why."

"Where is August?"

"Dunno. His office light is on under the door, though, so I assume he's still working."

Ian looked at Bobby, the pan, and around the kitchen. Bobby watched him look.

"What?" Bobby asked.

"I'm just wondering what made you go into someone else's kitchen, get bacon out of the fridge, and fry it up for yourself."

Bobby speared a few pieces of bacon and dropped them on a paper-towel-lined plate beside the stove. He pushed the plate toward Ian. "It's not only for me."

Ian leaned against the counter, looking in the living room's general direction, waiting for the bacon to cool. He realized he hadn't eaten much at dinner last night and had put nothing in his belly since. He'd always meant to go home. The hours had dragged and dragged, and then just as his eyes were getting bleary Bobby's people had shown up with Bridget, Ana, and a story that sent a chill up Ian's spine. He'd been wrong to leave them alone after all, and now someone else had needed to save them. Bridget hadn't met his eye. She'd merely accepted August's unsurprised hospitality and gone straight to bed. It was all matter-of-fact, this giant slumber party unusual to no one.

At least Alice wasn't here. Even Holly had gone to bed after pointing out that none of them had any business still being ambulatory. Tonight, at least, Bridget could see that Ian wasn't cheating. Just lying. Just acting in a way that expelled them from their home, probably cost them their sole income, and endangered all of their lives. She hadn't even asked for an explanation. That's how moot his excuses would have been.

Ian munched a piece of the bacon. It was crunchy, salty, thick-sliced — in some strange way, rich man's bacon. It settled into his stomach with a gurgling and only made him hungrier.

"So how do you know August?" Bobby asked, removing more bacon, adding more raw pink strips to the pan from an open flower of butcher paper.

"I *don't* know August. Alice — Alice Frank? — she's the one who knows August."

"Oh yes. I know who Alice is."

"That's right. The documentary." *Explaining Alice to Bobby Baltimore?* Hadn't he just watched the Yosemite piece? Hadn't the whole world just watched that piece? He must be tired. Either that or slowly losing his mind, giving in to the voices Holly had admitted to hearing in her head.

"So you work at Hemisphere."

Ian nodded, chewing.

"This is all news to you?"

"It's not something they put in the annual report."

"Did you hear anything around the office? Murmurs? Rumors?"

"We're as pro-Hemisphere at Hemisphere as the world is."

Bobby's eyes ticked toward a screen mounted among August's cabinets. It was off, but there was a control panel on the wall, within reach.

"You should see today's news. It's not just Shangri-la right now."

"Why, what's happening?"

"More people mouthing off with their theories, is all." He half laughed. "It's amazing what we've gotten used to. When I was a kid, half of the people I now pass on the streets would have been called monsters."

"Is that why you hunt?"

"Some of it. When they flip, they're just animals. Believe me, we're doing them a favor." His bright-blue eyes seemed to darken, as if realizing something he'd forgotten. His spatula, in the pan, ceased moving.

"What?" Ian asked.

"You know, it's funny. I just told you exactly what people expect me to say. But I don't actually feel that way anymore. It just came out. Isn't that weird?"

Ian shrugged, not understanding.

"We grew up with zombies, right? People started drawing comparisons even when Rip Daddy hit. And then Sherman Pope? Hell, the dead walk among us. It's like the Internet had been waiting for it, with the labels all ready. Everyone knew just what to do. They're slow, so don't get cornered, and you'd be okay. They're mad, so you have to destroy the brain. Fucking disease is freaky. The first time I saw a torso with a punched lung dragging its ass after me, I thought I'd died myself and gone to Hell. I don't know how they can function without blood and air, and I guess they can't always, at least not for long. But it's still like seeing a cockroach keep walking after its head is cut off." He shivered.

Bobby's eyes flicked to Ian's face. He looked almost offended, and Ian realized he was smiling.

"What?"

"It's just strange to hear a famous deadhead hunter get freaked out."

"They're *zombies*, man. That never quite settles, no matter how much you see." Bobby took a piece of his own bacon. "Did you know that early on, it was common for the bitten to turn immediately? Except that they didn't really turn; they'd just kind of convinced themselves that was what happened when a zombie bit you?"

"Bullshit."

Bobby smirked, turning back to his bacon. "I've seen it happen. Even with skilled hunters who should know better. Guys who act tough, but then you realize they hunt because they're terrified and prefer action to sitting in the corner slowly going crazy. Happened once with a group I was leading. Motherfucker actually bit me." Bobby pulled up a sleeve, showing Ian his shoulder. "Didn't break the skin because I was wearing a bite shirt, but pinched something bad enough that it never quite faded. We had to hold him down. Gave him the medkit infusion from the big Gadget then made him stare at the empty cylinder until he calmed down. But if we hadn't done that, reminded him that there's a cure? He'd have gone out into the park and gone instantly feral, I swear."

"Could he have infected others, that early?"

"Oh, sure. But if we'd let him get away, there'd have been no doubt about his status. The first group of ferals he ran into would have shredded him. They can tell the difference, you know. They only attack the uninfected or newly bitten, like, within maybe a day. You knew that, right?"

Ian nodded. He'd been at the mall yesterday … and oh God, had that been only *yesterday?* He'd seen the way the ferals had avoided the mostly necrotic shopping population in Grover and gone straight for the uninfected. Straight for his wife.

"You wouldn't believe the things I've seen. I guess that's why August invited me to this shindig." He tipped his hand toward the sizzling pan. "First science sleepover I've had, you know. Discoveries so riveting, you'll stick around for bacon in the morning."

"What *have* you seen out there in Yosemite?"

Bobby sighed. Ian got the impression of Bobby holding back something he believed, while doubting that Ian would share his faith. The kind of thing a person tires of voicing to mockery.

"They're not as mindless as people say," he finally said.

"Who?"

"The deadheads in Yosemite."

Ian nodded. "I guess I got that from Alice's documentary."

"You heard the tip of it. I only told Alice so much on the record because nobody wants to hear what I really believe."

"And what's that?" Ian asked, taking another bite.

"Golem," said a voice behind them.

Ian and Bobby turned to find Holly standing in the doorway.

"He knows the name you have for him," Holly said. "And he says a change is coming."

## Chapter Sixty-Three

### COFFEE

AUGUST REMOVED HIS GLASSES AND rubbed his face with a handkerchief. He was exhausted *and* energetic. He was his own species of walking dead, animated only by burning curiosity.

He picked up the phone and tried to call Alice Frank. Again, his attempt went straight to voicemail. It occurred to August that he was only tightening a noose — that if Alice was still in custody, which seemed certain, he was only making it clearer how badly their little anti-Hemisphere underground needed her loud mouth. But August couldn't help checking in. He barely knew Alice beyond the way anyone knew a public personality (the way she probably knew him, come to think of it), but simple humanity begged to know she was okay. That she hadn't totally vanished or been removed for knowing too much and threatening to blurt the truth.

Of course, if keeping beans in the can was Hemisphere's aim, they'd missed their mark. August was the one unearthing damning connections, whose computer models showed the way Necrophage's two components seemed to fit both BioFuse and Sherman Pope like a key in a lock.

He set the phone down. It was fine. Not only was it early; she shouldn't have been able to call from her own phone anyway. If he wanted to track her down, he'd call the cops. Or Panacea. Or Hemisphere. They all felt the same right now.

He left the office to find Ian, Bobby, and Holly standing in the kitchen, staring at each other as if someone had told a highly inappropriate joke.

"Who made bacon?" he asked.

Bobby looked up, spatula in hand. There was that answer, anyway.

"Do you know how expensive that bacon was?" August went on.

"Are you seriously bothered by this?" Bobby asked.

"Just trying to break the mood. Do you people have a cat-and-mouse thing going on here? Should I leave you alone?" He pointed to the living room. "I'm going in there. You can follow, or you can resume your pork standoff. Cool? Cool."

August plodded into the living room, suddenly feeling the past day droop its full weight onto his shoulders. When his ass hit the couch, it seemed to declare its intention to stay. But then Ian was coming around from the other end, followed by Holly. Bobby arrived a moment later, carrying a plate full of grease.

"Have you been up all night?" he asked August.

"Pretty much."

"Find anything new?"

"I still need a real lab. I can only theorize. But I've made more guesses, yes."

"Such as?"

August forced himself to sit up, to take one of the offered strips to feed his tired mind and wake him up.

"I remember Archibald used to talk about helping humanity evolve. It was drunk talk, though, even when we weren't drinking. Maybe stargazing talk. The kind of thing nobody really expects can happen, but 'Wouldn't it be nice if.'" August yawned. "The phrase that kept coming back to me all night is 'designer brain.' He wanted to create a designer brain."

"Like in *The Beam,*" Bobby said.

"No, without technology. An enhanced organic brain. He really thought he could move evolution's needle. That he could really 'upgrade nature.'"

"Like *X-Men,*" Ian clarified.

"What I keep coming back to is, why BioFuse? It's clear it interacted somehow with the Rip Daddy virus, maybe as a weird kind of vector. But if Archibald meant to inject money into the company by creating a for-sure profit center, why was it this one?"

"Why not?" Bobby asked.

"It's unnecessarily complicated." He shook his head. "I don't know. It's all making a jumble. I need sleep."

"Get some then," Ian said.

"When we're done."

Ian looked around the room as if he was waiting for someone to arrive. "Done with what?"

"Ian, is there any reason your key card wouldn't work at Hemisphere HQ today? There was that attack yesterday on your wife, but what's your gut feel … do you think Hemisphere has cut you off?"

Ian shook his head. "I logged in last night. It's the same code for remote access as for the doors. Why?"

"Has anyone heard from Alice Frank?"

Heads shook.

"Someone is trying to shut her up. Just her. Ian, that guy on the phone said they only want to scare you."

Ian's eyes flicked toward the closed study door, where his wife and daughter were sleeping. Safe, at least for now.

"That's what he said."

"Shut Alice up, keep you in line. Alice was supposed to do the broadcasting, but for now at least, she can't. And we can't tell her what to say, either. So that means it's up to us."

"Us?"

"You and me, Ian. Your guy pushed us together so we could find what I've found. Alice was supposed to be our third, but she's not here. That means we have to do the rest ourselves."

"The rest? You mean … what … broadcasting?"

"Maybe I can help," Bobby said. "YouTube and all."

"Thanks, Bobby." August turned to look at Ian. "But first I need to confirm what I think I know. For that, I need a lab."

Something clicked in Ian's eyes. To his credit, he didn't protest.

"When?"

"As soon as possible. Unless Hemisphere has changed a lot since my day, I'm thinking people don't really start arriving for work until eight or so." He looked at a sleek black clock on the wall. "It's 6:15 now. We can get across town and sneak inside. I know there are cameras, but I doubt anyone will be watching too close because they'll expect you to lie down after yesterday. Give me a few hours to work. I'd like more time, of course, but details can come later."

"Then YouTube," Bobby said. He looked at Ian. "It's best from you two, right? With my introduction, on my channel? Don't worry about spread. It'll go fast, if you're going to say what I think you will."

"I'm actually thinking of something else. Ian, you need to act like business as usual today anyway, right?"

Ian closed his eyes and nodded, another understanding settling. "The picnic. You want me to go."

"Archibald will speak. After that, it's open mic for people to tell their stories of how Necrophage saved their lives. Nobody would question it if you wanted to speak, too. Archibald might even expect it."

"Why would he expect it?"

"You said he talked to you about loyalty. Now they've sharpened the point when you met with Alice. Now that they've gone to your house and scared your wife and daughter. If you show up tomorrow ... " August trailed off.

Ian's head again flicked toward the study door. "Oh. No. No way."

"It'll be fine, Ian. Archibald needs you, remember?"

Holly sat up. She'd been so quiet, August had practically forgotten she was there. Her body still tended toward laziness, due to her necrosis, and she'd been like a silent hole in the room. But damned if it didn't seem as if her body, like her brain, might be healing, too.

"What are you two talking about?"

"He wants me to take my family to Hemisphere Picnic."

"Why would you do that after last night?" She looked at August. "Why would he do that, August?"

"Because it's exactly what Archibald expects. Hemisphere threatened them so he'd be quiet. If they all show up as they're expected to, nobody will question his taking the mic. It's the perfect venue."

"But they'll be in danger!"

"In the middle of a televised event? Surrounded by stable necrotics who won't like Ian's message? Nobody will touch his family. They wouldn't dare. They'll already be on the defensive. They might drag Ian off stage, but I imagine a lot of ire will turn on the Hemisphere officials. There won't be much security. It's a *picnic*, for shit's sake."

"We can watch them, Ian," Bobby said. "Just to be sure."

"No way."

"It's the best option."

*"Recording something and uploading it to Bobby's YouTube channel* is best," Ian said.

"I'd be shocked if Bobby's channel isn't being vetted, especially after the documentary he did with Alice. If we try that and they block it before it goes live, our hand will be played. They'll know we know. And *then* how safe will Ian and his family be?"

Ian, across the circle from August, looked trapped. August felt a moment of sympathy. He'd helped create BioFuse and was, in some small way, responsible for all that had happened. Bobby made his living in the public eye. But Ian was just a loyal executive, living a nice, comfortable life playing by the rules. He'd never wanted to rock the boat.

Holly and Bobby were looking at each other, some ghost of their interrupted conversation from earlier perhaps resurfacing. But Ian was staring straight at August. Almost begging.

"Nobody's forcing you to do anything, Ian," August said. "But for better or for worse, you and Alice came to me."

"I need time to think," Ian said, his voice smaller than before.

August stood. He looked at Bobby.

"Bobby, did you make coffee to go with that bacon?"

Bobby shook his head.

August nodded at Ian. "I'll brew a pot, so that's how long you have to decide."

# Chapter Sixty-Four

## FIVE MINUTES

BRIDGET WOKE TO THE FEEL of being gently shaken. She opened her eyes and saw Ana sitting up across from her in the foreign room. Then she saw something even more foreign: Holly Gaynor with her hand on Bridget's arm, waking her up like maid service. She'd known Holly was here from what Ian had said at her last night (not *to* her; Bridget hadn't wanted discussion from Ian, and the factoid had merely been spoken at her turned back), but seeing the star of stage and screen in front of her now was downright surreal.

"Good morning," Holly said, every trace of her famous necrotic accent gone.

"Um, hi."

"I'm Holly."

"I know. I'm Bridget."

"Nice to meet you."

Bridget looked at Ana, who was positively vibrant. She'd never met anyone famous in person, despite Aberdeen Valley hosting more than its fair share. Her lips were pressed tightly together, her whole body bouncing atop folded legs, her eyes giddy.

Then she looked up at Holly. The situation's bizarreness struck her hard. She sat up, pushing at her surely mashed hair to make it hopefully presentable in the presence of celebrity.

"Nice to meet you too."

Holly's soft brown eyes flicked toward Ana then back to Bridget. "I'm sorry to wake you. But we need to talk, and I only have five minutes."

"Why only five minutes?"

"Please."

Bridget looked at Analise. "Ana, honey? Why don't you see if you can find some cereal? I'm sure Mr. August has something." Although she wasn't sure. August Maughan was almost as famous as Holly, just as bizarre an addition to her recently strange life. What did famous people eat? Organic granola? She doubted they stocked Lucky Charms.

Ana sighed with disappointment at being excluded, but August's geeky breed of fame wasn't the only one out there. There was also Bobby Baltimore because this almost-abduction was a star-studded affair. She left, closing the door behind her.

"Did your husband tell you what they discovered last night, about Hemisphere and Sherman Pope?"

Bridget nodded. She'd tried to shut it out, seeing as it was Ian who'd said it at her, but she hadn't been able. Her entire night had been filled with nightmares.

"August has asked your husband to make a public statement. Today. At the Hemisphere Family Picnic. The event will be televised."

"Why Ian? Why not August?"

"August has an axe to grind against the company in

most people's eyes. I could do it, but they think what happened the day before with me will cast suspicion on anything I say. People don't know who Ian is, but Hemisphere is a public company, and they can look him up. He's never made waves and seems to always have been loyal. He's right at the top, not far down from Archibald Burgess. He's the perfect whistleblower. If he talks about this, people will listen."

"O ... okay," Bridget said, trying to wake up.

"But there's something else you need to know."

"Me? Why me?"

"Because you need to be there, too. I know how that might feel, but it's the safest place for you, and Bobby's people will be there. They'll be armed. Nobody is searched. There's no reason."

*Except in the event that something like this happens,* Bridget thought but didn't say.

"I want to tell Bobby, but I can feel something telling me not to. I mentioned it a bit ago, in the kitchen. His wave of obsession almost knocked me over."

"What are you talking ab—" Bridget tried to ask. But Holly went on.

"Bobby is compromised by his own fixation. Ian is worried, almost entirely about you and your daughter. He won't hear me, and even if he does, it'll be so far down his priorities as to not matter. August won't be on site at the picnic. You'll leave soon, and August will be inside the lab, making confirmations, and will stay there, cleared by Ian's codes, until after the afternoon picnic is over. I'm not going; I'd only draw attention. That leaves you."

"I'm not going," Bridget said, thinking of last night. Even if the mysterious Danny Almond was on his own, there was no question she'd felt Hemisphere's pressure. She felt it right now, and here she was in the thick of it: her home dangerous territory, her husband about to lose all he'd built, and her without the luxury of Zen's calming influence. Her brain was too loud, too busy.

"You *have* to go."

"Why?"

"Because you're the only one who knows what I'm about to tell you."

From the front room, Bridget heard someone say, "Where's Holly?" And Holly, minding the time, glanced at a clock on the bookshelf.

"What do you need to tell me?"

"Something will happen today. Something bad."

"How can you know that?" Bridget heard the pleading in her voice, not so much disbelieving Holly's impossible statement as asking her to make it untrue.

"I can hear it."

"Hear what?"

"I can hear the others. In my head. August says it has to do with the way my brain is changing as I take something he makes for me, a modified Necrophage. It doesn't matter if you believe me."

"I … I believe you." She did, too. Maybe it was because she was tired, or maybe something August had said last night about the way Sherman Pope appeared to rewire the brain the way a longevity treatment was once intended to.

"I hear one voice above the others. Then another voice, somehow different, somehow important as if a light shines upon her, below that. And all around it I get this sense. Like a feeling, but something I can't change or join, and can only listen to. They *know* something."

"*Who* knows something?"

There was a knock on the door then Ian's voice, hesitant. "Bridget? Can I come in?"

"Just a minute!" she shouted back.

"There's a group of ferals like those that attacked you yesterday. I know they're close. They'll be at the picnic."

Bridget gripped Holly's arm. Holly flinched then silently apologized, her look understanding.

"You have to go," she repeated.

"None of us should go. Not if what you think is going to happen will actually happen."

"You have to. All of you do. August might understand why. Maybe even Bobby. But they might not, and they might call it off. But …" Holly closed her eyes, seeming to reach for the best way to articulate what she was feeling. "It has to begin before it can end."

"No."

Another knock came on the door. This time, the voice was August's.

"Mrs. Keys? I'm sorry to bother you, but is Holly in there?"

Bridget said the first thing she thought might make him go away, as bizarre as it was: "She's helping me change."

"Please send her out when you're done. We're in a bit of a rush," he said then retreated.

"You can't tell them, Bridget," Holly said, her voice now hurried, still perfect, still giving no trace of her famous disease. "You have to let it happen. It can't go the other way. Things will change on our terms or on theirs."

"Whose?"

"They know something. The ferals I can hear in my head. I don't know what they know, but it's an ace. This can't be stopped. But you have to know, so you can protect them when it's time. Or direct Bobby's people to protect them."

*"Me?"* It was a joke. She couldn't protect anyone. She couldn't even keep her shit together without her precious

little pills. She liked her expensive tees. She had machines to clean for her and spent her days talking to her philandering neighbor, trading binocular-gleaned gossip.

Another knock. Again, Ian.

"Bridget?"

To Holly: "Call it off."

"If you call it off, more people will die than have to."

*Than have to.* The words made Bridget's skin go cold.

"Bridget? We need to go somewhere. Can I talk to you?"

"He wants you safe," Holly said, "for reasons I'm not being told."

*"Bridget?"*

"He says to tell Bobby and his people," Holly continued, rising and moving backward to open the door, "to find a group of uninfected people at the picnic, and use them like a shield."

# Chapter Sixty-Five

## KOJAK

THERE WAS A SURPRISINGLY COMFORTABLE cot in Alice's cell, so after making use of the rather public toilet beside it (which wasn't terribly shabby so long as the room otherwise remained empty), Alice had decided to sleep. After lying down, she'd discovered something that didn't seem prison-issue between her bed and the toilet: three bottles of water. She'd drunk one and slept surprisingly well, given the circumstances and the general mystery of it all.

She awoke at a time that felt early, repeated the toilet act immediately in case she had morning visitors on the way, and drank another bottle. One remained. The fact that nobody had shown up with snacks felt like an annoying oversight, so hopefully at least more water was coming.

There were no windows to the outside. She'd been steered past a bunch of clarifiers on her way into the room, but there had been many twists and turns to kill her orientation. She only knew that as much as this was about

Hemisphere, *Panacea* was holding her. Which made sense, given Smyth's supposed position between the two.

Speaking of Smyth …

Alice's throat still felt hoarse from yelling after him last night. She couldn't decide if he was friend or foe. When he'd appeared to discuss conspiracy, she'd assumed he'd spring her, or at least let her know when and how she might be sprung. But that hadn't happened. Instead, he'd walked away and left her like a giant asshole.

Her eyes went to the security camera, now plugged back in. She wanted to wave, but the door at the room's far end opened before she could. A clean-cut man with a clarifier badge hanging from his belt walked briskly through then did a double-take as he saw Alice in her cell. He looked back before exiting the far end, eyes squinted as if trying to place her.

Another man walked through.

Then two women.

Everyone seemed to wonder who Alice was and why the hell she was where she didn't belong.

In the rooms beyond this one, she became aware of voices and the hum of activity. Maybe food was on its way. Maybe someone would finally read Alice her rights. Maybe someone would finally tell her why in the hell she was being held, and what she'd supposedly done wrong. And maybe it was time to call some lawyers, and film some inflammatory blog content.

The door opened again. This time, a short Hispanic woman with a stern expression walked in flanked by Big Old Asshole himself, the elusive Mr. Smyth.

"Finally remembered I was here, huh?" said Alice from behind the bars.

The woman, not Smyth, answered.

"Alice Frank?"

"Ah. You know my work."

"You're free to go. We're sorry for the mix-up."

The woman opened the door.

Alice's eyes went to Smyth, who was giving her a look. As much of the evening as she'd spent annoyed at her supposed co-conspirator, something told her to keep her mouth shut about him and any likely double-dealing.

"That's it?" said Alice, not exiting.

"We regret any inconvenience we may have caused you."

Alice looked again at Smyth then the woman.

"'Inconvenience.'"

"Yes, ma'am," said the woman.

"Arresting me, if that's what you did in bringing me here. Ignoring me all night for reasons unknown. Violating my civil rights to — "

"Our officers believed your case to be a matter of utmost security, which allows immediate intervention and the dismissal of certain protocols. We are permitted to hold you for twenty-four hours. Again, I'd like to offer my apologies."

Alice stepped out of the cell. "If I may ask, what danger did you think I was to … well, to anyone?"

"I'm afraid that's a matter of Panacea business."

"And why am I no longer a danger now?"

"Same answer, ma'am. If you'll follow me?"

"Luisa," Smyth interrupted. "I can take her. Go on ahead."

"You're sure?"

"I'd like to extend Hemisphere's apologies as well."

The cop — or whatever she was — shrugged. She left via the opposite door, leaving them alone.

Smyth reached up and unplugged the camera again,

but barely lowered his hand before Alice began hitting him.

"Hey, relax!" he said, blocking.

*"'Relax'?* Fuck you, buddy! You just leave me here all night? No food? No word? And then you show up in the morning, and it's just 'we apologize for the inconvenience' and I get to go? And I'm supposed to *trust* you? I'm just supposed to walk home?"

"Will you stop for a second and listen to me?"

"Oh. I'm *through* listening to you. Hints and double talk. Hiding while I do all the dirty work, then letting me rot in jail like a lowlife. Not so much as answering my questions, while I've run all over the place, risking my life, to — "

"I had to know why they let you make that phone call," Smyth said. "Until I knew, I couldn't risk upsetting things. Because officially, this—" he pointed back into the empty cell, " — is where they should want you to be. Once you're out, you're a huge problem, knowing what you know, same as August Maughan and Ian Keys. Hemisphere and Panacea. Panacea and Hemisphere. Two hairs in a braid, the pair of them. But instead of acting like Hemisphere's partner, they brought you here and let you add your stamp of approval to the other two, to keep them on the case."

Alice's eyes ticked toward the unplugged camera. "The cut video feed is a little conspicuous, don't you think?"

Smyth shook his head. "I think they know about me, too. At least partway. But I'm like Ian. They need me where I am, and they think they know what I'm saying to you right now."

"What's that?"

"I imagine they think I'm telling you to rush back to August and Ian now that you're free."

"But you're not telling me that," Alice said.

"I am. But I'm telling you something else, too. I think I know now why they let you make the call."

"Okay. Why?"

"I told you about the ferals at the mall. How they were created, not natural."

"Yes."

Smyth's head looked from one closed door to the other. His voice turned lower, more urgent. "They have others. *Many* others. Hemisphere knows about some of it because frankly a few smaller outbreaks here and there are good for business. But those outbreaks were controlled, with necrotics who'd gone feral naturally. This is new. People are used to too much, and fear sells. I had to pull strings to find out what I did. But right now, my best guess is that they let you call August in because they want him out of hiding, so he can announce his discovery. He'll have to do it himself without your public platform. Him or Ian."

"But I'm out now. Free to go, apparently."

"It's too late. Ian's wife was followed. A group took her to Maughan's second residence, and surveillance says they're preparing to head into Hemisphere HQ right now."

"To HQ? Why?" A chill ran through Alice with a question. "Why did you mention the feral necrotics?"

"August will use the lab. Ian is going to make some sort of public unveil. They think nobody knows, but Panacea does." He swallowed. "As to the ferals? They've been planning a larger spectacle. This is a case of several birds and a single stone."

Alice shook her head. There were too many moving pieces. This wasn't how you murdered someone or even shut them up. This wasn't how you made an example. Smyth's information, if he was telling her the truth, was probably correct. But his conclusions felt gossamer thin.

It didn't matter. Panacea was shooting; they could all ask questions later.

"They're going to release more ferals at the picnic."

Smyth nodded.

"How many?"

"At least fifty. The idea is to cause a public panic, but it's icing on the cake if they can take Ian, August … or, hell, you. If they send that many and they're sprinters like at the mall, the chances are even decent because they'll gravitate toward uninfected people and it's a necrotic-centric event. It's not to keep you quiet anymore, though. Just to twist the knife: If this can happen to people of prominence, it can happen to anyone." Smyth paused then tipped his head and said cynically, "But I guess it's nothing a new and more expensive Necrophage won't fix."

"When?"

"The picnic is at ten."

"What time is it now?"

"After eight."

"You said they're getting ready to leave?"

"I'm sure they've arrived. I had to play my part with Luisa between finding out and telling you. That information is over an hour old."

Alice tried to do the calculations. Assuming she could haul ass out of the building and grab a cab immediately, she could be at Hemisphere by eight thirty at the very earliest, probably closer to nine. The traffic, which took her out of town rather than into it, wouldn't even be bad after the first few miles. It would be tight. But she could do it.

But of course she couldn't get a cab. Not now, not at rush hour.

"Call them," she blurted, obvious realization dawning. "Warn them."

"I can't."

"Bullshit! You had Ian and me call each other! You hacked our email and our texts!"

"From a secure location," he said, his falsely calm voice trying to counter her increasingly frantic one. "I can't do that kind of thing from my cell. And if I call them direct, there will be a record that I did it."

Alice glared at Smyth. She wanted to shout at him, to hit him again, to swear and call him a coward. But doing so would be indulgent. The situation was nonnegotiable. Smyth had already proved the lengths he'd go to remain anonymous as a source because Hemisphere was, in his words, "Too big to fail." Yelling would change nothing.

"Then get me *my* phone."

"I don't know where it is."

*"Ask!"*

"You'd need to do it. It's not my place to track down detainee belongings. It would raise eyebrows."

"You're escorting me out!"

"You don't understand. I can't raise suspicions, no matter what. It's too fragile here, especially given what's shaping up to happen today."

"Jesus Christ, Kojak! You're one hell of a secret agent!"

"I've told you all you need to know. It's in your hands."

Alice wanted to shout, but she kept her mind on the ball. She had plenty of time to get there if she didn't dally. And if she could find her phone, all the better. But Smyth had just said Panacea *wanted* the great Alice Frank covering this event, and that she might even be a target: the vanguard of necrotic rights ripped to shreds by those she wanted to help. Oh, the irony.

She could ask around for her phone. But if Panacea was releasing her so she'd do something foolish like rush to Hemisphere, Alice doubted anyone would be able to find that phone. She also doubted anyone would know Ian's office or mobile number, or one for anyone else who'd help. Not in enough time to make a difference.

"I'll never get a cab in time," she told Smyth.

Smyth dangled a set of keys in front of Alice's eyes. "The agents who arrested you might have brought your car here and placed it in space A-7 by mistake."

## Chapter Sixty-Six

### MAIL CALL

JORDACHE WAS SITTING AT HER small table, listening, waiting for a sign.

It wouldn't be long now. There were only a handful of voices she was able to talk to without using her lips, but there were also untold millions she could hear like a hive of insects. Above the buzz was the sense of one group nestled within another. Maybe a hundred minds, maybe less, maybe more. Maybe a hundred who knew what they were supposed to do, yet planned something else entirely.

"You feel better now," Weasel said, sitting at the table across from her.

Jordache didn't answer. For one, it wasn't truly a question. It was closer to a statement — and, she'd decided, a statement she was telling herself. She wasn't talking to Weasel in the way she talked to the one who called himself Golem — a human name, in a way, despite it sounding distinctly inhuman. Golem was real, as was Holly Gaynor. Those were real people who were as close to Jordache, at times, as Weasel seemed now. But Weasel was only a figment. A part of herself that was speaking while a different part listened.

"Better," Jordache said.

"Because you see."

"I see."

"But you still don't understand it all. You're better, but still can't fully grip it."

Jordache stood. She was still nude. Her front was covered in blood. The mail had come early. The man had rung her bell, and Jordache had opened the door, naked like now, to ask him in. Once he'd been inside, she'd ripped the head from his shoulders. That head was on her bed now, upside down with the ragged neck pointing toward her ceiling. Normally, when you tore a man's head off using your teeth, it stopped screaming. This one hadn't. Instead, it had kept on, trying to exact its bodiless revenge with its teeth. She'd beaten it until it had stopped moving. The sheets were a Christmas red. It was all very interesting.

"I understand enough."

Weasel laughed. It annoyed Jordache, so she concentrated until he went away and she was alone in her trailer. Well, unless she counted the mailman's body on her bed, along with all his various bits and chunky spatter.

A noise came from the front room. Jordache felt like she could hear something before the noise began — like a shout coming to her through the air itself. But it was only her phone, ringing faithfully just once.

The screen read, *I'll be there in a half hour with donuts.*

Jordache picked up the phone. It was hard to work through all the blood her thumbs painted onto the screen, but she managed to send her reply:

*Hurry. I'm hungry.*

# Chapter Sixty-Seven

## JUST ANOTHER DAY ON THE JOB

IAN COULDN'T HELP HIMSELF. HE looked around for Danny Almond when they arrived at Hemisphere.

Bridget's story was too bizarre. He didn't precisely *not believe it* in the usual sense of the words, because as pissed off and agitated as she seemed, he didn't think Bridget was delusional or lying. And besides, based on the description of Bobby's people, the man who'd been stalking his bushes last night sure sounded like Danny. But why? And what of his story? Was it possible Danny really did "just need something" and that it was all somehow a mistake?

Ian hated that he thought it might have been. It indicated denial so deep, you'd need a pressure suit to enter it. But really … *Danny?* Danny wasn't a creep. Ian had risen through the ranks in college and at Hemisphere in large part due to his excellent eye for character. And while Danny might seem a little mischievous, he definitely hadn't struck Ian as anything but a nice guy who'd ultimately do what was right. Or at least what was best, which was slightly different.

But Danny wasn't hanging out in the coffee room. His

car didn't seem to be in the parking lot. He wasn't in the sales department when Ian just so happened to walk through it for no particular reason.

"Hey," said a familiar voice. "How did *you* get the day off yesterday?"

Ian turned to see Ted Doyle behind him, taking a bite out of an oversized plum.

"Oh. Hi, Ted."

"Are you fucking Gennifer or something?"

"I'm *Gennifer's* boss," Ian said. "That would be backward."

"I didn't ask who was whose boss," Ted said, chewing.

Ian turned and began walking back to Alpha building. Ted followed.

"Seriously. What's the trick to getting the day off?"

Ian felt caught. He didn't want to talk to Ted. He liked Ted, but this wasn't just another workday for Ian Keys. There was betrayal afoot. In just over an hour, the entire staff, minus essential personnel, would be excused from work for an hour and a half so that visiting dignitary/boss Archibald Burgess could stand behind a lectern on the wide, downward-spilling front lawn and crow about Hemisphere's greatness and how much the company loved the people it had saved from certain undead doom. It all felt so transparent, Ian wanted to vomit. Just a few days ago, he'd been thinking how noble the event was: important Archibald, taking time out of his packed schedule to shake hands with the people who'd received what he'd selflessly given for free. But now Ian could only see a big, phony photo opp. A natural sales funnel rich with upsells, government subsidies, protection from Panacea, favors, lobbies before congress … *all the dirty-dealing worst.*

"Not right now, Ted."

Ted had come even with Ian. He moved in front and

turned, stopping him in his tracks. He leaned against one wall and took another bite.

"Hey. Meant to tell you. I took everyone's message to heart. I'm going to drop my remaining prejudices."

Ian saw the punch line coming but was unable to duck.

"I asked Sarah out. You know, the temp who's a twitcher?"

"You're unreal." Ian skirted Ted and kept walking.

"I know, right?" He eyed Ian. "Hey, you still seem worked up. What's up, boss? And what was up the other day? I saw you talking to Gennifer." His face clouded. "That wasn't about me, was it? Because, dude, I'm just kidding. Or was, the other day. Sarah actually seems really nice. And I did ask her out."

Ian wondered if it would be fastest and easiest to deny he'd been uneasy the other day, explain that he'd asked Gennifer about virology and various other things Ian had no reason (or knowledge) to be asking about, or tell Ted that he was the boss and didn't need to explain himself to those below him in the command chain.

He opted for none and resumed walking. Ted lagged, then finally stopped and shouted from behind.

"Well, okay. See you at lunch?"

Thoughts tumbled in Ian's mind as Ted's voice echoed past him.

He'd let August Maughan into a lab he had no right being in and that company lore said he'd been exiled from, for the purposes of driving a stake through Hemisphere's heart.

In just under an hour, Ian was supposed to deliver the basics of August's findings to the world, through a microphone on the sprawling lawn, in front of a sampling of the people Ian had, in his own small way, helped Archibald Burgess betray.

His wife was outside, ready to spread a prop of a blanket for Ian near the lectern, surrounded by men with guns — because someone from Hemisphere (or maybe Panacea) had just tried to kill her.

Alice Frank, who'd recently become Ian's ally, had been hauled off to places unknown and was still missing.

And last but not least, Ian had come down to the sales department to find his supposed friend Danny, who'd spent last night stalking Ian's house, peering through his windows from the bushes.

Ian wasn't sure if he felt angry, guilty, nervous, terrified, or traitorous. Probably, he felt all of those emotions and a few others, mostly unsavory.

"I doubt I'll be in the cafeteria today," Ian said, projecting his voice down the hallway to Ted.

"Oh right!" Ted shouted back. "That thing is today! I'll save you a spot on the team's blanket for your picnic basket!"

Ian kept walking without responding, feeling the ticking clock, the bomb of the unwelcome scientist conducting his subversive research in the lab above.

*Just under an hour.*

And when those sixty minutes were up, Ian didn't think Ted and the others would want to be anywhere near him.

## Chapter Sixty-Eight

### BLOCKED

"SHIT."

ALICE HAD GROWN USED to the idea of touching her steering wheel to make calls, but it was useless without a paired phone. She hadn't bothered to ask for hers, figuring it would only draw attention to the exit Smyth had made possible. The people she asked for her phone back might be some of the same people who wanted her released from custody to open her big mouth … but only so long as she reached the decade's biggest story too late.

Without her phone to yell at, Alice couldn't ask for a detour around the roadblock she'd rather interestingly encountered on the otherwise lightly trafficked roads.

But even if she had her phone, Alice thought the roadblock might move anyway. There were more Panacea agents than there were Alice Franks in the world, and their task was easier. While she tried to race through obstacles to Hemisphere HQ, they merely had to stay in her way for another hour or so.

Alice looked at her dashboard clock.

For another forty-five minutes or so.

"Shit. Shit. *SHIT!*"

Maybe she could get out of the car. Maybe she could borrow someone's phone, ask for directory assistance, call the goddamned Hemisphere switchboard if nothing else. Bridget Keys would have a listed number, right? Except that Smyth had already established the phone access Panacea could get if it only tried, and Alice sort of thought her calls, no matter how ingeniously concocted, wouldn't do the trick.

If Smyth's information was correct, Panacea would release fifty or more fast ferals on the Hemisphere picnic, and her friends were about to find themselves in the middle.

Unless she could get there, *and fast.*

Alice looked at her dashboard clock.

It was 9:31 a.m., and the barricade ahead showed no signs of moving.

She wrenched the wheel around, weaving around the other cars on the berm, saluting angry honks with her raised middle finger.

She hoped Archibald Burgess was the kind of guy who couldn't manage to be on time, or that Ian would at least grab the mic and begin shouting right away, before the horde was released. But it didn't seem likely.

Minutes ticked, vanishing like water down a drain.

# Chapter Sixty-Nine

## CLARION CALL

HOLLY STOPPED MID-STRIDE. SHE'D learned to favor her lazy right leg over the years — a way of dragging along that made her look and feel like a monster cliché. But this time, she stopped for reasons that had nothing to do with anatomy.

She was holding two slices of American cheese. In the pan on August's stove were two slices of white bread, buttered sides down. The burner was on medium, the odor of toast wasted on Holly's dead sense of smell. Soon, it would begin to blacken and burn, like a body on a pyre.

A slice of cheese hit the floor. It made a wet smacking sound.

*Concentrate.*

A voice not meant for Holly's ears, if it had been her ears that had done the hearing. Meant for someone else, from someone else. Holly was a snoop on a party line, listening in to other people's conversations.

*Know who to take. Know what it means.*

And a sort of rumble in answer. An understanding that

wasn't comprehension. A sense of knowing that wasn't like knowing at all.

"Miss Holly?"

The girl's voice was like an ice pick, intruding on Holly's auditory theater. For a second — *only* a second, and then only on the level of impulse — Holly imagined herself ripping the girl to pieces. Then the feeling was gone, and the voices snapped off, and she found herself looking at Analise Keys.

"Are you okay, Miss Holly?"

"I'm fide."

But the word came out wrong. Not *fine* but *fide*, as if she had a cold. As if her lips wanted to remind her who she truly was, and whose side she was supposed to be on.

"You're sure?"

More certainly, with more effort at control, Holly said, "Yes. Yes, Ana, I'm sure."

"The grilled cheese is going to toast all the way without any cheese in it," she said, looking at the pan and then the yellow square on the floor.

Holly forced a smile. "Grab me another from the fridge, will you?"

Ana watched Holly warily for a moment then turned to go.

In the seconds that followed, Holly seemed to see her body's own cells, the cells of others, *inside* the cells, to the soup beneath the fluid membrane.

She saw molecules like little Pac-Men, dutifully gobbling troublesome pellets.

She saw blood.

She saw more molecules than Pac-Men, overwhelming them, making them pop.

A spotlight in the darkness.

A man on a bluff.

And even more blood, red like a harvest moon.

"You're *sure* you're okay, Miss Holly?" said Ana's voice from behind her.

Holly felt regret that wasn't her own.

She felt hunger and anger. She could hear a clarion call like a wail in the night.

Something was coming.

And action would need to be taken.

## Chapter Seventy

ROCKWELL PORTRAIT

IAN CHECKED HIS PHONE. HE checked his phone again.

"Stop it," Bridget said beside him. "Your stupid compulsive checking is making me nervous."

Ian wanted to snap back at her, just as he'd nearly snapped at Ted. She'd been edgy all morning, her nerves seemingly tissue thin. But rather than feeling for Bridget, Ian could only feel for himself right now. She wouldn't have to nudge her way onstage. She wouldn't have to say anything outrageous — something that would ruin her, might get her arrested, might get her killed. He was doing this for her and for Ana in the first place. How about a little sympathy? How about some appreciation?

"I just want a text that gives me a thumbs-up. A green light. A go-ahead," Ian said.

Bridget shifted on the picnic blanket. It was red-and-white checks. They actually had a picnic basket in the middle, like something out of a Norman Rockwell illustration. Ian's work family — Gennifer, Ted, Gary, and Kate — were around them in a ring, forcing Ian to watch his words when discussing August and his plan. He wouldn't have wanted to sit so close — or, really, to sit with Ted at all. Normally, Ian liked Ted, but today he had no patience. But Bridget had insisted. She, unlike Ian, had never really liked Ted. And yet she'd forced her way into the work group's middle, making Gary and his wife pick up their own blanket and shuffle back to accommodate.

*"Supposedly,"* she said, dragging the word out, making it feel belabored, "you have the go-ahead unless you hear different."

"I want proof. If I'm supposed to get up there and talk, I'd at least like an indication that he has some *firm goddamned proof.*"

"Proof of what, Ian?" Kate asked from Ian's right.

"Nothing." Ian tried to smile.

Bridget leaned close and whispered. "You think I like this any more than you do? You want my opinion, really? I say you call this off. Because what if August *can't* really prove it? You'll just look like an idiot." She craned her head and looked around. "Do it later if you have to do it. After you find Alice."

"So now you're *for* me finding Alice?"

Bridget's breath was hot in Ian's ear — a distinct change from her usual sweet self, as if she'd somehow come unhinged. Like Ian felt.

"I'm not apologizing again, Ian. Just because you're not having an affair doesn't mean you're not fucking someone."

"Who? *Who* am I fucking?"

"Me. Us."

"What the hell are you talking about?"

"Why do *you* have to be the one to do this? Why here and now, so publicly? Maybe August will find what he's after in the lab and maybe he won't, but you shouldn't have to be the one to blab about it. Let him, or let Alice. You've done enough. And what about me? Do you have any idea what I've been through for all of this?"

Ian rolled his eyes, but she was too close to see it. Of course he knew. Of course he kept thinking of it *over and over and over* again. Didn't she know that what had happened bothered him even more than it bothered her? She'd almost died, but *Ian* had almost killed her. This was the only way. Everyone agreed waiting for Alice to show might mean missing their only chance. This was like ripping off a Band-Aid: one swift motion to end it all. Sure, his job would die with the rest of Hemisphere. Sure, they'd have to start over. But what was the alternative? To keep hiding? To keep worrying? To keep going to work day in and day out, knowing the evil he was helping to perpetuate?

"I don't have a choice, Bridge. It's gone too far."

"But Alice … "

"We don't know where Alice is. We wait, it's more dangerous. For all of us."

Bridget's head popped up. Again, she scanned the crowd edge to edge, as if searching for something.

"What the hell do you keep looking around for?" Ian demanded in a harsh whisper, his nerves worn and patience gone.

Beyond Gennifer's blanket, the group of Bobby's hunters looked over, out of place in their long jackets, weapons beneath, bags that were clearly not holding crackers and cheese, looking for all the world like people to avoid rather than trust.

Someone to the hunters' right shushed him.

Not far ahead, a balding man in his seventies was taking the stage, his carriage and manner far too upright for a man of his years. Tapping the microphone too casually for a man whose fingers seemed suspiciously free of arthritis, too rejuvenated — as if by a longevity drug that had been weaponized into a plague. Smiling too broadly for a media darling with a genocidal secret.

"Too late," Ian told his wife, his eyes still on Burgess, his mind recalling the quiet threats Hemisphere's CEO had made the last time they'd spoken.

Around the stage and the several hundred people spread across the lawn, a ring of Panacea agents moved into position, perhaps to keep an eye on the few dozen strangers Ian could now see approaching from the property's edges, almost too far back to be seen.

The strangers stopped suddenly as if tethered, their body language impatient.

Bridget, watching them, gripped Ian's arm.

Archibald tapped the mic again.

Ian's phone vibrated in his hand, displaying a text from August: the permission he needed.

Ian's heart rate seemed to double.

Opening remarks at the annual picnic were always brief, lasting only a handful of minutes.

It was do or die after that.

# Chapter Seventy-One

## CHRYSALIS

FUCK WORK.

MAYBE HEMISPHERE DIDN'T know that Danny was depending on its auto-dispensaries to deliver his livelihood, but in Danny's opinion that didn't excuse it from holding out on him. Last night hadn't been fun. He'd gone through a roller coaster of emotions the entire workday then had endured more ups and downs in the evening. He'd ended the night panicked, resorting to trying to break into a man's (a *friend's)* house to … let's face it … get the drugs he needed. It didn't matter that Danny wasn't a junkie. Drugs were drugs.

Now, in the light of day, Danny figured Hemisphere could eat shit. Not in the long term, of course; Danny would need more supply soon (once he got another key card; Ian might have filed a restraining order by now), and he was also a loyal guy. He made fat stacks selling what the company made, but that didn't mean he was too good for his job.

But for today? For this morning, at least? Yes, Hemisphere could eat a big fattie.

Danny called in sick. He slept in, to make up for the sleep lost and the night's general trauma. For the first time in what felt like forever, he could relax.

He *wanted* Jordache to have what she'd grown used to. If there was one thing hotter than a girl who dressed like Jordache, it was one he could talk to. And there was no doubt her drug of choice had helped in that department. But she'd be fine for now. Jordache was over her hump, her body acclimated to plain old Phage like the rest of the necrotic world. Resupplying with the good stuff could come later.

Jordache laughed when Danny talked about the future, but he could see himself with her. For sure.

Danny languished in bed. Stretched. Watched some TV. Then he got donuts because Jordache loved them. The girl had a stomach you could bounce quarters off of (it was often exposed, and Danny had literally bounced coins once), and yet eating junk food was just about all they did together.

With that one exception. And soon, he hoped, they'd do more of the other thing.

When he knocked, she answered from far away. As if she heard him but wasn't on the other side of the door to answer.

"Go away," she said.

"It's Danny."

"Go away, Danny."

Danny backed up a step. His brow furrowed. He moved down the trailer's body, toward the source of her voice. A window was open to the screen. He peeked in, catching a whiff of something gone bad, like garbage left in the sun. He peeked around for a few seconds and almost jumped when he saw her staring right at him from between a tangle of clothes in the shadowy closet. Somehow, her eyes were piercing the gloom. They were usually blue, but from where Danny was standing, they looked almost iridescent except at the edges, as if her irises had been bleached by the sun.

"Jesus," he said, meeting those staring eyes, unable to see most of the rest of her. "You scared me."

"Maybe I *should* scare you."

"Hey." He raised his box and shook it. "I got double chocolate glazed."

"I don't want any."

"Oh, come on."

"I'm scared of you, too."

Again, Danny's brow furrowed. "Are you feeling okay?"

*No*, he told himself. *Obviously not. Dumbshit.*

"I can smell you."

Danny made a comical show of sniffing his armpits. He watched her eyes to see them change, ideally with mirth. But they didn't even blink.

"I'm scared."

"You don't need to be scared. Let me in."

"I've made a horrible mess in here."

A waft of breeze sent the smell back in Danny's direction. Maybe she was the one who stank and she was deflecting. It was okay. He'd be happy to shower her from head to toe, spending extra time cleaning whatever she wished.

"Let me in. I'll clean it up for you."

Her eyes finally closed. Seeing them blink and shift made the eyes-only illusion far more disturbing. He'd almost convinced himself that the ghostly blue-white circles weren't Jordache's eyes at all but some trick of the light. Now they were real and impossible at once.

Then he saw her wipe them. She sniffed, as if starting to cry.

"I keep hearing him," she said.

"Hearing who?"

*"Him."*

"Hmm. Okay. Well, tell him hi from me."

"And there are others. People different from me."

"From all of us," Danny said, unsure where this was going.

"From me."

"Okay, from you."

"I don't know what they're going to do, but I can hear him telling them what he wants. It's horrible. I don't want to listen, Danny."

Danny moved back to the door and yanked the knob. The door remained closed, but then he realized he could pry open a small screen. It was gloomy inside the trailer, so he put his face to the dark slit. The eyes appeared again, very close. When she spoke, that putrid scent came at him strong, as if it were on her breath.

"Let me in, Jordache. Seriously." He yanked again.

"I'm afraid I'll hurt you."

"I told you. I'm a big boy. I like you. And I don't think you want to hurt me like other guys have hurt you."

"You're wrong," she said, her voice somehow wet with tears.

The eyes moved away. In the shadows, Danny could almost make out her shape, crawling on all fours, burrowing into a pile of something like a dog into blankets.

"Come on. These donuts are getting cold."

"Go away, Danny. Don't come back." Then weaker: *"Please."*

"This isn't funny. You're not well. I thought you were better, but you're not. We need to go."

"Where will we go?"

"I want to take you to an urgent ca —"

Jordache cut him off, providing her own answer: "Hell?"

"Christ. Open up. Okay? I'm not kidding. If you don't unlock this door, I'll break it down."

"Break it. Bend it."

"I'll count to three, Jordache. One … Two … "

There was an animal sound, as if a sick dog had run by unseen.

"What the fuck was … " Danny trailed off, stooping. There was a puddle of something on the stoop — red and tacky to the touch, like partially dried glue. "Did you spill something out here?" he asked, already feeling his heart speed its beating.

"I got a special delivery today," she said.

There was another of those animal sounds, closer.

Danny tried the door again, knowing it wouldn't open, increasingly afraid he knew what was happening but unwilling to think of it.

"Oh yeah?" Rubbing the red substance between his finger and thumb, watching it turn from brick red to crimson. "What did you get?"

"A revelation."

She probably kept a key under the mat. Didn't everyone do that? Danny, still crouching, searched.

"You don't see enough of those in the mail these days."

"Do you know what I realized?"

"What?"

"I've been this way all along."

"What way?"

"Like you made me."

"You're welcome?" Danny said, unsure.

Silence chased the words. Danny kept searching, came up empty. He had to get her out of there. There must have been something wrong with the Phage, though there hadn't ever been a reported case of that happening, so far as Danny knew. He'd picked up a separate batch last night when she'd been so odd, from a separate place, and watched her infuse that one, too. She was fine. She had to be. This was something else.

"Like a butterfly, changing on the inside while the outside stays the same."

"A little butterfly," Danny said, playing along, now searching a potted plant, a light fixture, a ceramic statue of a cat. There was no spare key. He'd have to break the lock, or a window.

"I know what they'll do," she said, "when the time comes for them to do it."

"Who?"

"And I know what *I'm* supposed to do, too."

*"Okaaay . . ."*

"All that's stopped it from happening before now is instinct. And choice."

"Jordache, do you have a . . . " Danny stopped, realizing how stupid it was to ask for a key from someone trying to keep him out.

The door clicked and sighed open before he could finish his sentence. The rancid odor hit him like a wave, but he couldn't see its source. The trailer's lights were all off. And except for the window he'd spoken through earlier, the blinds were all drawn.

"Go away, Danny," said her voice, clearly conflicted, clearly not wanting him to leave. "I'm afraid of what I'm being told. I don't want to hurt you." And there was a small sob.

"You won't hurt me," Danny said, his heartbeat uneasy.

He stepped inside, into the darkness.

# Chapter Seventy-Two

## HUMAN WEAPONS

TWO MORE SUSPICIOUS ROADBLOCKS, ONE official and one where some asshole had overheated in the middle of the road and not bothered to move. Traffic had crawled around it, and when Alice reached the obstruction, she'd found it to be a woman in a suit who somehow looked plenty capable of cooling a vehicle, changing a tire, or replacing an engine. She watched Alice as she passed, not smiling behind dark sunglasses.

By the time Alice reached the Hemisphere campus, she was uneasy, sweaty, and sure she'd arrive at a bloodbath. Only once parked did Alice stop to wonder if she was being played. Not by Hemisphere, but by Smyth.

She was only here because he'd given her keys and let her go. She was only involved with Ian and August because Smyth had shoved them together. He'd warned Ian about the first attack, but he couldn't have warned him if he hadn't known … and lo and behold, despite the warning, the attack had happened anyway.

But she tossed the idea away. Smyth's info had all been public — and now that she thought about it, avoiding

Alice's skepticism about her source was probably the reason he'd snitched in the precise way he had. Everything he'd given her was true, all easy to verify. He'd told her there was a meaning in the message that Maughan, once located and brought into the mix, would be able to read. But beyond that, the raw materials Maughan needed in his investigations were things Hemisphere had told the world themselves … or done to it.

*Hemisphere caused the plague.*

*Because Hemisphere had the cure.*

She'd had a gut feel about Burgess and his company for years but never thought she'd ever find the big, bad story she'd been slobbering for. Now she was a dog who'd finally caught a car after chasing it for blocks. What came next? She had no idea.

She'd get the full story later from August or Ian, if they were still alive. One more incentive to do this thing right.

Which now seemed doubtful in a very specific way: She reached the parking lot at the lawn's far edge while Burgess was finishing up, leaving the stage with a crowd-pleasing smile and inviting others to speak on the cause's behalf. There were Panacea agents there, too, and those close by had turned to watch Alice approach.

She felt a chill, watching those heads swivel toward her.

*They're waiting for you.*

But that was ridiculous. Alice wasn't in the spotlight here. Archibald Burgess and the other speakers were. And yet it was apparent that Burgess had been speaking for a few minutes, and still that outer ring of dark figures waited. For something.

Keeping her eyes forward, Alice reached through the car's open window into the backseat. Smyth had somehow arranged for her camera bag to be placed there; she'd seen it while facing one of her three obstructions on the way here. Or someone else had, so she'd be able to record all that happened from where she was standing.

Before walking forward, Alice hung her 35MM around her neck. The telephoto lens was in place. She raised it and looked through the viewfinder at the closest suited figure.

The three others around him were ferals, kept mostly inconspicuous from the crowd's eye. Alice saw masks that covered the lower halves of their faces. She saw leashes. She saw heavy gloves on the handlers' hands. And when the handler turned his head, Alice saw a wound on his neck — the handlers were probably necrotic themselves. It made sense because it made the ferals obey: *infected didn't attack the infected.*

Alice moved slowly forward, knowing she should shout but unable to do so.

Burgess was standing at the lectern's side, watching Ian behind the mic, his smile uneasy, his arm flicking toward unknown others to do … something. But Ian was still speaking, spewing disconcerting words, while the crowd grew restless.

The handlers held their human weapons. And let it happen.

Alice saw it all at once. She saw why she'd been obstructed but not blocked all the way. Why she'd been detained, then released exactly now — sent to the picnic, but not early enough to warn anyone.

She knew why, when she'd been taken in, she'd been allowed to make those phone calls. Why those in charge were playing both sides.

They weren't waiting for Alice. Not *just* Alice, anyway.

They were waiting for Ian.

Alice ran, yelling at the top of her lungs.

# Chapter Seventy-Three

## INTUITION

BOBBY SHIFTED ON THE LAWN, unable to get comfortable. Part of it was the heavy gun on his hip. Part of it was the way he felt compelled to keep a hand on the blankets obscuring the shotguns they'd brought with the props. But most of it was an itch. A hunter's intuition that something was going wrong, and that the prey had gained the upper hand.

He'd felt it in Yosemite, when the army of undead had ambushed them. That had been Cam's assessment: *ambush*. Bobby had played it off, saying things he himself had already stopped believing but still recited for the benefit of the others. Things like, *They can't ambush because they can't think* and *They don't even communicate with one another*.

This was different, of course. There hadn't even been gate security. Part of Hemisphere's *open and honest* image was an open-grounds policy. The extensive green area was used by walkers every morning, and nobody started checking IDs until you tried to enter one of the buildings. And while there might be trouble, it would be the administrative kind. The kind where Executive Whatever They

Ares got fired for loose lips. The kind where everyone got mad at a company who'd made them sick so it could profit from the cure, but where the crowds weren't quite big enough for a riot and were armed only with peanut butter and jelly sandwiches.

And yet Ian's wife had plunked her blanket in the middle of a halo of others like a queen before her court. From where Bobby was sitting two rows back, she seemed positioned like an animal protecting its soft belly. She kept scanning the crowd, craning to look around. And although Bobby felt uncomfortable, Bridget looked ten times worse. Like she expected death rather than trouble.

Intuition prickled his neck. The guns were insurance, just in case anyone tried to shut Ian up before he said what needed saying or tried to drag him away like he said they'd hauled off Alice Frank. But he couldn't shake the feeling that he'd need every one of them and that the hunt wasn't over because he'd been lulled into believing it hadn't yet started.

"Bobby?" whispered a man to his side — a man named Jason, whom he'd hunted with before. "What's up?"

"Nothing."

But Jason's hand was under the blanket, too. Gripping the butt of his shotgun.

Ian, at the mic, was picking at his collar, the nervous sweat on his forehead practically visible from where they sat.

"Just make him a hole when he's finished," Bobby told Jason and the others. "He runs to us, and we make sure he gets out. That's all."

Ian spoke into the mic, his voice unsteady.

The crowd murmured, looking around, shuffling, unnerved by his words.

Burgess turned toward Ian, walking too fast, waving to the event's few security guards stationed around the stage.

Bridget stood, eyes turning toward the back, toward a commotion. Her face was paper white.

Someone was shouting, running forward.

And then it began.

# Chapter Seventy-Four

## SCRIPT

IAN FOCUSED ON THE SCRIPT.

With his lips practically kissing the mic's black windscreen, he fought the nerves threatening to buckle his knees and forced words to form. There was no need for eloquence. He wasn't here to make an announcement, not a speech. To tie his own noose, bankrupt his family's only source of income, and slay the golden goose he'd spent his career caring for.

His eyes stayed on Bridget, who looked absolutely terrified. Why was he doing this to her? He needed to do what needed to be done, but why was he forcing her into a front-row seat? Was it really needed for appearances? Was it really necessary as an *I'm-playing-ball* gesture to get them into the building? Maybe he could have arrived as a dissident rather than a two-faced liar. Maybe he could have come to the Family Picnic without his brood and still achieved all that he needed to, taking the mic as a loner who didn't play by the rules.

He told himself there was no other way. It had to unfold on a public stage — and that by taking Alice out of circulation, Hemisphere had thrust that duty upon him. And on Bridget to be here and watch.

He wasn't harming his family. He was saving them.

He wasn't betraying a friend, in Hemisphere. He was exposing the devil.

He tried not to look up, focusing on the script he'd written for himself, that August had approved.

*BioFuse was modified after it was approved by the FDA,* and he gave a date.

*The new version was used in trials without approval,* and he gave another date.

*Here's what worked with the new drug,* and he used some of August's terms.

*But here's what went wrong.*

Thirty seconds. He'd timed it. Enough time to rile everyone from Hemisphere behind him, including the man who'd quietly threatened Ian's family. Enough time to make a case and tell the cameras where they could find the Internet dump August would make, which proved it all.

"Hemisphere saved you from Sherman Pope," he said, feeling the press of angry bodies from behind, the rising of angry bodies from the lawn, "but they gave it to you first."

Ian turned to find himself facing Archibald Burgess, who grabbed his arm. Ian tried to yank away, but the man's grip was too strong. Only when someone began yelling from the lawn did Ian finally pull away. With shock, he realized the runner was Alice, waving and screaming, gesturing toward dark figures encroaching from the lawn's edges.

Ian headed for Bridget, who wasn't running at all. She was waving Ian forward, into the circle on the lawn. Toward Bobby and the others, who still hadn't broken rank enough to raise their weapons.

"They're going to release ferals!" Alice shouted. "They've got ferals and they're—"

There was new movement as a man emerged from behind a tree and seemed to release something, same as yesterday in the mall.

The deadhead came forward exactly one step, toward the crowd's uninfected.

Then it turned around and bit the man who'd let it go.

Ian saw an arc of blood as the thing hit an artery.

Then the handler turned and attacked someone new.

"They're going to release Faisal!" Alec shouted. "They've got Faisal and they r—!"

There was new movement as a man emerged from behind a box and seemed to release something, same as yesterday in the mall.

The deadhead came forward exactly one step toward the crowd's uninfected.

Then it turned around and bit the man who'd let it go.

Dan saw an arc of blood as the thing bit an artery.

Then the handler turned and attacked someone new.

## Chapter Seventy-Five

### WATCH HIM WITH THIS

FOR THE SCANTEST OF MOMENTS, Bobby felt relief. His shotgun came up, and he waved it to clear a half circle, but nothing was coming for them. Not yet. Instead, the action was sticking close to its sources. Ferals turned on their handlers rather than the crowd then entered the masses, taking down the slow and weak, like cheetahs chasing the least-fit gazelle.

Natural selection at its finest. And luckily, Bobby and the others had come prepared. Behind them, Ian, Bridget, and Ian's knot of colleagues were quickly descending into hysterics. But they'd be fine. Bobby was a hunter, and his people were adept. They weren't the least fit. They were the *most* fit.

But the fallacy hit him almost immediately.

A woman in a blue blouse came screaming toward him. She tackled Bobby hard, her neck spouting blood, her shoulder's exposed tendons like wires inside a busted radio. Bobby firmed up, ready to pass her behind him to join the group he'd protect on the way out. But she didn't go easily.

She grabbed his arm with both hands like a hungry man grabs a chicken leg.

Bobby pivoted and swung his elbow in a short, hard circle. The woman staggered back. When she came at him again, Bobby raised his shotgun and cut her almost in half. The top continued to snarl and crawl forward.

"What the *FUCK?"* said Jason, backing up.

"They're biting the infected. It's — "

"They don't bite people who are already infected, man!" Jason shouted over the growing melee.

An old man shambled forward, hobbled but too fast, his eyes turned and mouth open. A seeping wound marred his arm. There was blood in his mouth, teeth dangling something wet. Bobby fired, this time at the head.

*"Don't fucking argue with me, Jason! Just shoot!"*

A kid came at Jason with a feral growl. He let him charge, not so much as blocking. He seemed to get out one word before the kid raised a knife and buried it in Jason's stomach. The group staggered back before anyone could stop or correct it, and as the gap closed, Bobby watched the kid slice in farther, pulling Jason's innards out with his hands, raising the meat to his lips.

"What the fuck is going on?" said one of the others, not turning, keeping his weapon pointed outward to protect the group's core. The melee shifted and changed, forming huddles and similarly open areas. "That kid … he came at Jason with a knife!"

Bobby looked behind the group, his gunmen at its front, nudging them back. They reached a small, temporary oasis in the trees. Screams filled the air. He'd seen Alice when it all started but had lost her since.

"What the *shit*, Bobby?" said the man who'd spoken earlier — one of the men who'd been watching Ian's house, a man named Mason. A good hunter, better than this panic. Behind them were the unarmed civilians. If Mason broke, everyone would.

"They're biting people who are already infected. Ferals biting necrotics."

"But they don't—" Ian began, clutching his wife by the hand. Bobby cut him off.

"Apparently, they changed their minds." But that's not the whole of what Bobby was thinking. In practical terms, ferals weren't supposed to *have* minds. Nor were they supposed to move like sprinters, or communicate with each other. Yet all of these deadheads had the same idea in advance, as if coordinated. And judging by the fact that the ferals' first bites had been on the apparently necrotic handlers who'd brought them in, it hadn't been the handlers' idea.

"They're—" one of Ian's group began, an attractive dark-haired woman with pretty eyes. Bobby cut her off too, raising his shotgun, too late.

"Look out!"

A man with blood-mussed hair and a face made of gore came from behind one of the trees and took the curly haired man Ian had called Gary by the shoulders from behind. The thing sank his teeth into Gary's trapezius like biting into a half moon of watermelon.

Gary screamed and thrashed, but the thing had him in a grip. Bobby couldn't fire; they were enmeshed. So he kicked at the attacker, which held its pit bull's grip. Blood gushed from the wound. Muscle and tendon between its teeth elongated like a pull toy in a locked jaw.

Bobby kicked again. The thing was as strong as it was fast, particularly in the jaw muscles. It finally came loose and fell back. Two of the other hunters stepped above it and turned its head to paste.

Gary was gripping his shoulder, moaning, looking faint,

somehow staying on his feet despite the pain. Bobby flicked his barrel up, level to Gary's disbelieving eyes.

"What the hell?" he grunted, still swooning with his hand on his shoulder.

"Bobby," said Ian from behind.

Bobby trained the weapon. Waiting. Finger on trigger.

"Put your goddamned gun down!" the wounded man said, slapping at the barrel. Again, Bobby brought it back, holding the muzzle six inches from Gary's face with his eyes narrowed while the others watched and screams filled the air around them.

Bobby lowered the weapon.

"What was that about?" Ian asked, his breath unsteady.

Bobby's calm snapped like a twig. Why were they all so stupid? Hadn't they seen what he'd seen? Had they really been fooled as everyone seemed to be? People called Bobby crazy for his obsessions and theories, but he wasn't crazy; the world was blind. Even now. *Especially* now.

"Goddammit, pay attention! They're turning out there!" His eyes flicked toward the lawn, just beyond the trees. The grass was covered in blood and moaning, wounded people. Ferals — both new and old — ran across it like kids on Halloween. They didn't have long. They'd need to move soon, *and fast.*

"Turning?" said one of the hunters. "How can they turn as soon as they're—"

Bridget answered: "Holly told me this would happen."

*"Holly?"* Bobby demanded. But of course. She'd known more than she should have, and he should have pressed. She knew Golem, seemingly like old friends, definitely by name. How had they communicated feral to feral? This was the answer.

"What did Holly say, Bridge?" Ian moved in front of her, stooping slightly, taking her by both upper arms.

But Bridget seemed to be finished. She looked at the dirt, no longer searching the crowd. Whatever she'd been anticipating had happened, and now she seemed content to let it end by proxy of fate.

"They're biting people who are already infected, and those people are turning right away, maybe because their bodies are used to equilibrium and can't take a new hit of disease. It doesn't matter why it's happening, just that it is. The old rules seem to apply when they bite people who weren't already being treated." Bobby jabbed a finger at Gary, speaking to Ian. "But you watch him close, you hear me?"

Ian hesitated then nodded. He gave Gary an apologetic glance then asked the logical next question.

"And if he starts to turn?"

Bobby pulled his handgun from its holster and slapped it into Ian's palm.

"Watch him with this," he said.

# Chapter Seventy-Six

## BIRD'S-EYE VIEW

AUGUST SAW THE TIDE TURN from inside the lab. Whatever was happening on the lawn, as seen from above, looked like something highly coordinated gone severely awry.

He couldn't see too well without binoculars (which, shockingly, the biochem lab had in short supply), but he'd started watching the picnic after sending Ian his text. He'd already made the web dump then verified that it ended up where it should be and that the firewall hadn't blunted its exit. With his part done (for the time being, anyway; once the news was out, he and everyone else would use legit labs to learn the rest), August turned on the lab's TV and watched in stereo: live view through the glass on the left, close-up view with sound on the right.

August kept waiting for someone — Panacea, probably — to kill the broadcast. But just as the evidence archive had passed the firewall without incident, the broadcast stayed on-air. As if nobody cared what August had done and Ian was doing, or was willing to stop it.

He saw the dark-suited agents surround the park from

above. At first, he assumed they were security, but then the ferals were loosed and the melee began. A repeat of yesterday's mall incident, except that this one was bigger … and, according to the monitor on August's right, was being televised.

He saw the ripples below as the violence spread. It took a while to sort, but soon he saw that the ferals were preferentially attacking the least-likely targets: late-stage necrotics, who couldn't stagger quickly enough to get away.

The necrotics instantly turned. August watched, safe in the locked lab, alone in the building as far as he could hear. He watched through glass, unable to help, able only to fear the chaos below.

He lost Alice, who'd come in from the far left, from the parking lot.

He'd lost Bobby, Ian, Bridget, and the others, who'd backed away in a knot. Accidentally or on purpose, they'd found the perfect strategy, with what August judged as the best chance of escape: stay in a group with other uninfected. If they were bitten, at least they wouldn't turn.

He'd even lost Archibald Burgess, who August was a bit ashamed to admit he'd been hoping would survive once the bloodbath began. Archibald was ambitious — too much for his and the world's own good, apparently. But it was hard to shake the feeling that he meant well — that in the biggest picture, he was only doing what he felt what was best.

The feeling of lost control crept across August's skin when the snipers showed. When the shock troops, with their Plexiglas shields, stormed the lawn.

Someone had started this. And judging by the way they'd had snipers and a riot squad lined up and ready, they'd probably always intended to stop it quickly. Just a little show. A bit of blood and horror to add an exclamation point to what Ian, August, and the others were trying to prove to the world today, as if they were all sharing a side.

But as ferals multiplied, the snipers found themselves with too many targets. There weren't just the few dozen they'd loosed upon the crowd. There were hundreds, every available necrotic turned deadly.

The worst of them — those lunging and shambling before being bitten — turned with what seemed to be a partial second wind. Others were taking longer, the virus needing time to undo what civilization had done.

The riot squads were overwhelmed. Men and women taken down, gear ripped from their grips, bodies ripped open. The uninfected didn't get back up. Shots came. Batons were used, and August wondered why, in today's world, they didn't carry blades. The snipers picked off what they could, but the surge kept coming.

August watched from above, gripping the windowsill with white-knuckled hands.

little things. A bit of blood and horror to add [illegible] and panic to what [illegible] Angus and the others were trying [illegible] to the world [illegible] as if they were all slightly [illegible] sick.

But as [illegible] multiplied, the [illegible] found themselves with too many [illegible]. There weren't just the few dozen [illegible] upon the crowd. There were hundreds, every available [illegible] turned deadly.

The worst of them [illegible] those burning and [illegible] before being [illegible] with what seemed to be a [illegible] second wind. Others were taking longer, the [illegible] needing time to undo what civilization had done.

The riot squads were everywhere[illegible]. Men and women taken down [illegible] from their [illegible], bodies ripped open. The [illegible] didn't [illegible] Shots came [illegible] and Angus [illegible] world, they [illegible] The [illegible] picked off what they could, but the [illegible] continued.

Angus [illegible] down [illegible] the [illegible] with some [illegible]

## Chapter Seventy-Seven

### DECAY

THERE WAS A PATTERN.

BOBBY moved the group when a wave came. There were too many, and two were lost: the woman called Kate, and another Bobby didn't know. But they made it away, leaving the others behind. It was necessary triage. Gary, who'd been bitten earlier, tried to go after the others even though they were almost surely dead. There was a snarl and a ripping sound from the rear, and Gary didn't return.

He pulled them back into another temporary space away from the fray, and watched the pattern.

"Bobby," said a large woman, Iris, who carried a specialty weapon Bobby had only seen in use once before today. It was called a Decimator and wasn't overly large, but heavy as hell. She could only fire it when there was nothing remotely in the way that anyone wanted to keep breathing after the shot. "You know I hate to say this, but we should just run."

"We're surrounded by fences," Bobby said.

"We can cut through them." She hefted her weapon. "With this."

Bobby shook his head slowly. "If we make a hole, we'll let them out."

And despite the situation, now that Bobby was finding his natural rhythm as if in Yosemite, that felt like an unacceptable solution. This was a new kind of plague, spreadable from one infected to another. It had to end here, and now, inside these fences. There was only one gate, and it was in the other direction. Deadheads weren't supposed to be fast, or know how to use tools like that kid had used his knife. But so far, Bobby hadn't seen any with bolt cutters, and the tops of Hemisphere's open and honest fences were wound with razor wire that would turn deadheads into diseased meat.

"They'll contain it," Iris said, nodding to the clearing. The riot squads were making slow but steady progress. There seemed to be sniper fire out there as well, which was a curiosity of its own. Why were there snipers, unless they'd meant for this to happen before stomping it flat?

"It's contagious."

"Yes," Iris said. "But barely."

Bobby looked at Iris. He was chewing on a sprig of grass — something he did in Yosemite despite warnings that one of these days he'd ingest spilled necrotic blood by mistake. Iris was the largest, strongest hunter he'd ever worked with, and he'd never worked with her in Yosemite. He was struck with a sudden urge to invite her, to add her to his crew's deck of cards like a secret weapon.

She was right. They couldn't open the fence because it might cost a few lives, but that was the pattern he'd noticed earlier. This looked horrible, and between the turned (now incurable) necrotics and the dead, there would be many families mourning tomorrow. But it wasn't like wildfire. Bakersfield had been far worse because you couldn't know who was infected and who wasn't until they got sicker, and by then there were too many. That was before Necrophage. This would require a formulation tweak, for sure — maybe more Necrophage for your buck, to protect against secondary bites. Once quelled, this outbreak wouldn't be a problem. But for now, until the final body fell, it very much was for all those inside it.

"We can wait it out," Bobby said.

"Or we can run. Ain't no shame in running, Bobby Baltimore."

Bobby actually laughed. Gennifer, the tall blonde who worked with Ian, gave him a reproachful look.

"I'd run if I had to. But I don't. Look."

Bobby pointed. Beyond the trees, a group of mindless ferals were ripping some poor necrotic to shreds. Their body language was angry, as if they were punishing more than trying to hurt.

"The new ones can't spread it," he said. "Not yet, anyway."

There were three rapid shots. Bullets must have rained from somewhere because all three ferals fell to the ground, leaving their victim to scream at nothing. A fourth gunshot stopped the screaming.

A squad in riot gear passed. The line remained intact, unassailed.

"It's almost over," Bobby said.

Iris kept her weapon high, swinging it side to side, waiting to prove him wrong.

# Chapter Seventy-Eight

## RIGHT THIS WAY

ALICE RAISED THE HANDGUN SHE'D liberated from the cut-in-half policeman. She'd fired it only once, and when she had, the kick had practically slammed the barrel into her forehead. The report had earned her attention from the feral she'd been trying to hit, but its head had inexplicably exploded when it turned, spraying Alice, the grass, and the rock she'd been hiding behind with blood and flecks of blackened gray matter. She supposed someone must have shot it, but she had no idea where the shot had come from, or how she'd been so lucky as to earn its protection.

She felt like a coward. The rock, near the lawn's rear, had proved an overly nice hiding place, so she'd stuck to it. Once she had the gun (more as a high-caliber security blanket than a means of protection), the rock's shelter had felt doubly nice. She kept telling herself to move — to go out there and save her friends' lives. But in the ensuing mental debate, sense won out over moral imperative. If she broke her cover, someone would break *her* for sure. Alice waged her battles with a pen and a keyboard. She wasn't a flesh-and-blood fighter and never would be.

But now, as the shouting and screaming and sounds of slaughter diminished, she decided to stand. She'd left everyone else to fend for themselves and that would always make her a little ashamed, but she wouldn't be rescued. Alice wouldn't end today with a policeman's or clarifier's hand in hers, as he pulled her from to safety from a coward's hidey-hole.

The gun was heavy. She was terrified of its recoil, sure that she'd brain herself if she pulled the trigger again. But still it felt good. Like she was in control, whereas she very much was not.

There was no one past the rock. Nothing but bodies and — she felt a retch — body parts. It was easy to tell the ferals (or, astonishingly, the ordinary necrotic citizens who'd been *turned* feral) from the uninfected bodies.

The uninfected looked chewed.

The ferals didn't have heads because stopping them had required blowing those heads off … or at least perforating them with giant holes.

Alice crossed the lawn, gun out. There were riot squads at the far end. She heard a few shots, far off like the pop of fireworks. Something grabbed at her ankle, and she kicked away, panicked. She looked down to see something that was barely more than arm, shoulder, and head leering at her, its face almost entirely gone.

At the clearing's other side, past shredded and gore-stained picnic blankets, Alice found a line of black backs: clarifiers facing something, putting it down.

If they saw her, she'd be arrested for sure — maybe this time for real. Same for Ian Keys, and August Maughan, if he were here. Alice wasn't sure what crime they'd committed, but they'd done *something* for sure.

She turned and found herself facing a pair of clarifiers.

"You're Alice Frank," one of them said.

Alice considered her weapon. Would they shoot her out of hand and claim self-defense? Should she try and threaten her way past?

She felt her arms lowering. Then, without even looking in her handgun's direction, the clarifier who'd spoken pointed toward the parking lot, away from the finished fray. At the end of his gesture, Alice saw a group of uniformed police steering a tall balding man through a sea of what appeared to be reporters.

Archibald Burgess, being led away in handcuffs.

"Right this way, Miss Frank," said the clarifier, moving to escort her toward the media circus.

# Chapter Seventy-Nine

## UPGRADES

ALICE CLOSED HER LAPTOP AND set it aside. Then she stood and opened the blinds all the way around the room. Morning had evaporated like something volatile, and she'd been working since before first light. But now that her work fugue had snapped, the room's darkness slapped her like an open palm. She didn't like being in the dark. Not for a week now.

The day was bright — and, when she opened the sash, Alice found it brisk as well, the North Carolina late summer beginning its slide into a moderately cool autumn. She took a moment to feel the sun on her face, to breathe deeply. Only then, her body assured that morning had come again with its innocent light, did she feel steeled enough to make her call.

Her party answered on the fifth ring — enough that Alice was about to hang up, glad to forget about all of this for another day.

"Alice?"

"Hey, Ian."

"Wow. Feels like it's been forever."

"It's only been a week."

"I know. That's why I said 'feels.'"

There was a long pause on the line. Alice wasn't sure why. She'd covered the plague from the beginning, and she'd seen horrors in Yosemite. She, Ian, and August had blown the lid on the biggest story of the century — maybe ever — and all she could feel was a throbbing sense of regret or loss or odd malaise. As if they shared a horrible secret and vowed never to speak of it again.

"Have you been to work?" she asked.

"I have. It's interesting."

"Since the takeover, you mean."

"Yes. But I guess it's for the best. Panacea doesn't care about making a profit, but it's like the damage is already done. It kind of sucks. None of us had anything to do with Sherman Pope, but it's like we all feel guilty anyway. You should see the morale around here."

Alice could imagine. She also happened to know that nearly a third of Hemisphere HQ's employees were dead, but had left jobs that still needed doing. Panacea had filled those slots with efficiency not typical of the government, but then again Hemisphere wasn't just another company.

Smyth's words followed the thought, clanging in her head like a bell: *Hemisphere is too big to fail.* It had, in the new zeitgeist, become the perfect embodiment of *necessary evil.* The company had been gutted, all of Burgess's systems dismantled, scientists of every stripe poring over Necrophage's now open-source documentation, Burgess himself apparently in protective custody in a prison somewhere. Everyone understood that the rank and file had had nothing to do with what Burgess's actions, and everyone knew Necrophage still needed to flow for untold millions to survive. That surely didn't stop employees like Ian from getting the evil eye wherever they went.

"How are … things?"

"You mean with Bridget."

"I mean *things.*"

Ian laughed without humor then repeated, "You mean with Bridget."

"I — "

"She's right here beside me. She's not threatened by your calls these days." He laughed again, but this time it felt forced. The kind of uncomfortable laugh that follows something a person wishes he hadn't said to a person who probably won't find it funny.

Alice heard the movement of fabric and the brush of skin: Ian likely standing, moving away from Bridget, uneasy or because he needed to speak freely.

"Okay," he said a moment later. "Not good."

"What do you mean?"

"She has nightmares. She's always edgy."

"It's only been a week. That's understandable."

"She'll barely talk to me. Like it was all my fault."

"Ian — "

"We're going to be moving, too," he said, interrupting her.

"Oh."

"To somewhere more affordable."

Realization dawning. "Oh," she said.

"Bridget doesn't like that, either."

Alice said nothing, unsure where to go with any of it. According to what Panacea reps had said at Monday's press conference, all designer formulations were being discontinued effective immediately. Base Necrophage would still be free, but now it would be government money, not profits, keeping the company afloat. Little room in the budget for salaries like the one that had kept the Keys family so comfortable.

"Are there going to be layoffs?"

"We're not sure, but do the math. We're only here to churn out Necrophage. Even the other drugs are being released from their patents, and our competitors are getting subsidies to make generics. The people Panacea put in to replace everyone who died are temps, so they lift right out. I'm not sure why half these people would want to stay anyway."

"It's a government job."

Ian laughed, again without humor.

"Are *you* leaving?" Alice asked.

"Not sure yet. I don't have prospects lined up, and certainly nothing that pays anywhere near what I made before the readjustments. But it's like a morgue in here. Almost literally. Kate, Gary … I think Smyth is still around, and nobody's blown his cover just yet. Oh, and I'm pretty sure my buddy and sometimes home invader, Danny must've bitten it, too. I didn't see his name on the list for the big funeral, but they're still … you know … sorting parts."

Alice felt her eyes close.

"But hey. Every cloud has a silver lining, right?" Ian said, falsely bright.

For Alice, maybe. She had her nightmares, and her dream. She hadn't been paranoid about Hemisphere; they really had been hiding something worth keeping secret. But was the world better off? Maybe and maybe not. Now it had no real champion to rally behind, no true savior. Hemisphere was now the nation's merciful captor, who'd slit its throat then rolled its eyes and handed over a rag to staunch the bleeding.

"If you say so," Alice said.

"Seriously. Look what we learned that could have been learned in much worse ways. I mean, what if some feral had decided to bite a necrotic in an area that wasn't so neatly contained?"

"Ian … "

"But now, in the new formulation, the PhageY component has been greatly increased. I guess they can be pretty aggressive with it, seeing as the disease-killing half of Necrophage can't hurt someone who, really, is kind of already dead. I hear that now, if a jerky feral decides to bite someone who's on Necrophage, all that new Sherman Pope flooding their system won't make a dent."

Alice wasn't sure what to say. It wasn't just Ian's wallet and home life (and maybe marriage) that had taken a hit. His identity was in the gutter. Two weeks ago, he'd been working for the world's favorite shining star of a company, near its top, proud of all he'd accomplished. Now he was a gear in a machine. Burgess was gone. Without him and with Panacea in charge, Hemisphere was just turning a crank. Government allocations went in one end, and a single, boring product was spit out of the other.

"What will happen with people like Holly?"

"You mean psychics who saw this coming but didn't bother to warn any of us?"

Holly *had* warned someone. She warned Bridget, who'd used the warning without causing damage. Bobby had heard of it after the fact and established exactly why telling him before would have been a bad idea. He'd returned to Yosemite and resumed the search for his white whale, sure that Holly's information had somehow crossed the entire continental US to reach her. Sure that modified BioFuse had succeeded after all, creating an upgraded mind amid the mindless horde.

"People on designer formulations."

"They'll live," Ian said bitterly.

"August said that if you're on a designer drug for too

long and then go back to base Phage, there can be side effects."

"Yes. Sometimes, people get depressed. Sometimes, they get despondent. Sometimes, they get bummed out. Oh! And I forgot one. Sometimes, they get sad."

"I thought maybe — "

"Believe me — we'd still be making Truth and Beauty and all the other designers if going off them is harmful. But Phage is Phage. I've learned a lot about it, now that every channel on my TV and every fucking website I visit is discussing what used to be my company's secrets. The base is what matters. The mix-ins that come with the designers add more life-extension sorts of benefits, nothing vital. Ask Bobby. August has been giving him gene therapy manicures for years. Or ask Holly. *Use your psychic mind* to ask her, maybe. Because I kind of doubt August will stop making custom formulations for her, given the way he talks about Holly and her progress." He laughed. "Shit. It's the same exact way Bobby talks about his Golem. Like they're superzombies."

Alice sighed, waiting this out. She didn't like to hear Ian so bitter, but it was hard to imagine what he was going through. She'd lost nobody and nothing. If anything, more people knew Alice Frank today and wanted to talk to her than they had before. Ian and Bridget's changes hadn't been as pretty.

"I'm sorry," was all she could think to say.

"I'll be okay. We both will. But it's a bummer. And I lost some friends."

"You still have me."

"Yeah. Well, do you drink beer?"

"I drink wine."

"Not good enough. You're no Danny."

"And it's *Danny* you're missing. The guy who was in your bushes, scaring your wife and daughter."

"Danny was a good guy. Just ... maybe a bit too ambitious."

"What do you mean?"

"When Panacea took over, they did an inventory audit. They asked me about a whole shitload of designer Necrophage I'd requisitioned. I asked a buddy here to pull security footage, and it turns out Danny must've been using my codes. Emptying the stores, practically. But I played it off. Spouted some Hemisphere jargon and made them go away. Because fuck it. If I'd known how things would turn out, I'd've sold designer shit on the sly, too."

Alice wasn't sure, from Ian's tone, if she should laugh or act shocked. "He was stealing drugs and selling them?"

"Good for him."

"If you say so," Alice said.

"Crafty kid. Smart. A total hustler. I miss him; really, I do, as dumb as it sounds. But a stupid kid sometimes, too. Because he took way too much — I guess sure it'd never catch up with him. The best lines. Must've made millions. Good for him. And even components, though I have no idea why he'd have done that unless he was planning to sell Hemisphere's secrets, which I kind of doubt."

Alice felt her mouth form a frown. "What are 'components'?"

Ian laughed. "Just goes to show what a lovable fuckup Danny is. Or maybe was. We've got these superexpensive designer formulations — like Stardom, which costs the price of a luxury car each month. But what did Danny take the most of? Go on, guess."

"How the hell could I possibly know that?"

"PhageX. That's what he took most. What was he even

doing with it?" Now Ian was laughing. It felt nice to hear, but Alice was still confused.

"What's PhageX?"

"Come on. I thought you were an expert?"

"Just tell me, Ian."

"It's the stasis half of base Necrophage. It's not even available for order. I guess my code could requisition it, but it's only meant to go up our own chain so the labs can make Necrophage. But seriously, Danny: What the hell? And he kept going back for more, week after week." He was laughing harder now, maybe too hard. Maybe a bit manic.

"What would anyone do with it?"

"That's my question. PhageX plus PhageY is Necrophage. PhageX plus one of the designer mix-ins — which contain PhageY, of course, but also all that fancy stuff too — is high-end Necrophage. But PhageX is … just PhageX, I guess."

Alice gave him a little fake laugh, but something was bothering her. Something she couldn't articulate.

"I've gotta go, Ian. Nice talking to you."

"All right, Alice. Don't be a stranger." And he hung up.

# Chapter Eighty

## EVOLUTION

AFTER SHE HUNG UP WITH Ian, Alice called August Maughan. Something was troubling her. Something she couldn't articulate, and that Ian would no doubt find worth mockery.

"What would happen," she asked, "if someone took PhageX and nothing else?"

"Just PhageX?"

"Right."

August's voice became inquisitive. "Why would anyone do that? It's not even available."

"Just intellectual curiosity, August. For an article I'm writing."

She could imagine August thoughtfully tapping his goatee-covered chin. Finally, he said, "Well, I guess *nothing* would happen."

"Nothing?"

"See, back when Sherman Pope used to be BioFuse, Archibald's intent was to 'upgrade nature'— to make a better body and brain, one molecule at a time. BioFuse was a gene therapy virus, and it gained access to nerve cells by bonding to a receptor on their surfaces. It worked because BioFuse had more affinity for those receptors than the natural, flagging compounds had for the same receptors. So BioFuse essentially shoved the natural process out of the way, bonded *better* to the cell receptors, and took over. The effect was supposed to be an *upgrade* of the system, kind of like putting performance tires on a race car rather than the tires the car came with. Make sense?"

"I guess."

"Sherman Pope works the same way, but does so in *many* types of cells, not just neurons. Unlike with BioFuse, vascular decay in the infected actually lets Sherman Pope cross what's known as the blood/brain barrier, which viruses can't typically do, and work on both sides: brain *and* body. It's also self-replicating — another thing BioFuse couldn't do — so it can spread efficiently throughout the body to do its work. And here's the funny thing: Sherman Pope actually seems to upgrade the body's cells fairly well. The only downside is that it's killing you at the same time."

"Sounds like a deal breaker," Alice said.

"It seems that when BioFuse fell flat, Archibald increased its reactivity and did a few other things I'm just figuring out and won't bore you with. Doing so made a better BioFuse, but that better BioFuse became one of the worst plagues mankind's ever seen."

"But what about PhageX?"

"There are two components to all Necrophage formulations. PhageX is what's known as stasis. Like BioFuse, PhageX is an engineered, non-replicating, *safe* virus. It basically does to Sherman Pope what Sherman Pope originally did to the body's natural systems: PhageX has *even more* affinity for those cell receptors than Sherman, so the body preferentially uses it instead of SP, even though both are floating around in the same place."

"So far, so good," Alice said.

"But all Necrophage also contains PhageY, which is the eradication component. PhageY is an artificial cell receptor that looks just like the natural cell receptors Sherman Pope bonds with in order to do its damage."

"An artificial cell receptor?" Alice asked. "Are you telling me that PhageY is a *fake body part?*"

"A very small one, yes, and there are millions in every injection. When PhageY is in the system, free-floating Sherman Pope bonds to it just like it would the real cell receptors. Once that's happened, all that free-floating Sherman Pope — which is constantly created because the virus never stops replicating — becomes inert. It can no longer do damage, like putting a sheath on a knife. It can then be flushed from a person's system by the body's natural defenses."

"Okay."

"But you need both, see. If someone were only to take PhageY, they'd be flushing out all the newly-produced Sherman Pope, but then their bodies would fall apart and die because there'd be no stasis component to keep the body propped up. Do you understand?"

Alice nodded for no one to see. "Right. I get it. Take PhageY and you cure the disease but kill the patient. But what if you only took PhageX?"

August seemed to think. Then he said, "Well, I guess you'd get a sort of below-the-surface crumbling. The body would be superficially propped up, but they'd still be flooded with active Sherman Pope."

"Is that bad?"

"Well, they'd be contagious, for one. But if they were *propped up* by PhageX, they'd still have all their marbles and so I guess they wouldn't think to bite anyone."

Something felt like it was crawling up Alice's backbone.

Something unwanted, unknowable, but somehow terrifying.

"But even if they did bite someone," Alice said, realizing she was asking more for assurance than for an answer, "it wouldn't matter because the person they bit could just take Necrophage, same as normal. Right?"

August's pause was too long. Alice felt the creeping feeling on her spine tighten its grip.

"Hmm. Maybe."

*"Maybe?"*

"Viruses evolve quickly in the presence of selective pressures. The body's natural defenses might make for an excellent training ground. Like an *in-vivo* gauntlet."

"What does that mean?"

August must have heard her fear, so he laughed and went on, giving a security-blanket answer: "Relax, Alice. Sherman Pope takes over the entire body in three or four weeks. That's not enough time fighting for survival that the virus is required to adapt, so it's not a problem."

"Oh," Alice said, unsure if she should feel better.

"Of course, if someone really *could* survive for an extended period on just PhageX, the virus might be forced to adapt plenty, creating something newer, heartier, and much more evolved."

Alice swallowed, unsure why she felt naked, like a thousand eyes were on her, assessing.

"In fact," August said, "in someone like that, PhageY might not even work anymore. Dosing with PhageY at that point might just cause an inflammation response that would upset the PhageX equilibrium and do … well, who knows? … in the patient or in anyone bitten."

Alice looked out the window. Toward the horizon. Toward the edge of Dead City. It was such a beautiful day. She wanted it to last forever. To make flowers bloom and the present moment continue, frozen, unchanging, unaffected by evolution's subtle forces.

On the phone, August said, "Alice? Are you there?"

Then he said, "Alice?"

Such a nice day. Such a fine new dawn.

*"Alice?"*

# Chapter Eighty-One

## DO YOU LOVE ME?

THE SUNLIGHT MADE A JESUS beam that sliced through the trailer's gloaming like a solid pillar. Jordache watched motes of dust dance in it, making lazy circles. She'd stood to open the blinds a moment earlier, and the day's beauty had struck her. It only made sense to share what struck you as beautiful.

"It's nice, isn't it?"

Danny watched her, not answering.

Jordache breathed slowly, stopping to wonder why she was breathing at all. She'd had a lot of time to think over the past few days. She was pretty sure she was dead. But then again, she couldn't stop breathing if she tried — and it was uncomfortable when she did. She'd even tried to drown herself in the sink, just to see what would happen. She'd chickened out after nearly losing consciousness then had staggered back and practically fallen into the shower. When she'd drained the sink, the water had been pink, specked with floating bits of matter. Not her own. And she'd needed a bath anyway. Or at least a face bath.

If she'd managed to drown, would she die? Because

again, Jordache was already dead. It wasn't just an intellectual concept. She could feel the life within her. She could practically *see* it, and knew its shape — not the way scientists saw shapes. This was experiential. The way a person can know a cube without looking at it, simply because she can sense it in her hands.

With her deep, possibly habitual (and possibly not strictly necessary) breaths, Jordache became newly aware that the trailer smelled bad. Or rather, it would smell bad to most people. To Jordache's old nose, maybe — or, really, to her new nose, given that her sense of smell had been lackluster since she'd first been infected. Now it was better. Almost like that shape she sensed — the life scientists might call disease — had infiltrated her olfactory cells. Made them better and fresher, like the rest of her.

She hadn't tried to run for a while. She should try it again. She'd probably be better now. Faster. Stronger.

"Does it smell bad to *you*, Danny?"

Danny had no opinion.

Jordache stood. Began making slow, pacing lengths of the trailer. Cool air kissed her bare skin. She could feel every inch of it. Forget asking Danny about the smell; she should ask him about sex again. It felt better each time, given all that she'd changed with that odd, old sense of limitation out of the way. She wondered if it was better for Danny now, too, but she didn't want to ask. He seemed so tired. It had been a hell of a week for them both.

So much to see, do, and hear.

She went to the bathroom. She turned on the light. She saw more or less the same face as always, except that her eyes had changed a little. It wasn't a big difference. They were lighter now, still mostly dark around the edges. It was like eyeliner for her eye itself, for the iris. The look was ghostly, but her skin seemed to have most of its usual glow. She wasn't sure if she was warm to the touch because she could only touch herself.

"Danny, am I hot?"

Jordache laughed and told him to never mind because she knew how he'd answer *that.* Danny was so immature.

She put her palms on the sink's edge. Leaned into the mirror. Bared her teeth. They were covered in red, black, and brown. She also badly needed to floss.

*It's almost time,* said the tall blond inside her head.

"Okay," Jordache answered.

*You're the harbinger. You're the reaper.*

"I'm just a girl."

*You're the crucible. The one I've been waiting for. The one who brings the change.*

She almost wanted to blush. But she wasn't positive that she could still do that, either.

"Are there others?" she asked.

From the front room, Jordache heard Danny ask who she was talking to. She told him to mind his own business.

*Some like me, and more as the days pass. None like you.*

"None like me."

*None like you.*

"Should I stay? Should I go?"

*Soon,* he said.

She thought of pressing him, but she'd been hearing the man for over a week now. She knew when he was done, when he'd said all he wanted to say. She knew the time was imminent. And that she'd know opportunity when it knocked.

Jordache strolled out of the bathroom, nearly tripping on the dead mailman's arm. It was no longer attached to the rest of him. She'd been hungry, and there was very little to eat in here.

She looked at Danny's turned back, suddenly sure he

was giving her the silent treatment, and pushed down a wave of melancholy with no clear source. This happened lately, probably because she wasn't getting outside enough. Wasn't getting that vitamin D to make her happy. But looking at Danny brought it back. Often. Because they'd been together before, for a while, and they'd come close to a normal life. Her future was bright — epic, even. But sometimes she wondered what might have been, if they'd stayed as they were.

Pancakes in the mornings.

Donuts in the midmornings.

And both of them somehow staying rail thin, like immortals in unchanging bodies. Except that was truer now than before, and really she was being silly.

"Danny?" she said, moving around to his front. "Do you love me?"

He didn't have to say it. He never had to say it.

Jordache sat beside him on the couch. She kissed him. He seemed cold. He'd also lost a lot of blood where she'd impaled his brain with the ice pick. So she wiped at his upper lip to clear it, draped the afghan across his body, and leaned against his side. Or at least what was *left* of his side. There'd only been so much mailman meat to go around.

Her head slipped down into Danny's lap, into the partially congealed puddle. She closed her eyes and sighed. A tear squeezed out and ran down her shaped nose: penance for a wrong she felt sure she'd somehow committed, a right that another part of her seemed to have betrayed.

"Promise you'll never leave me," she said.

Danny, always solid and sure, seemed to promise.

After a while, Jordache sat up and wiped at her eyes, feeling both melancholy and ridiculous. There was no point in worrying at the past. The past was over. The future — for Jordache, for the blond man, and for the revolution she carried inside her maybe-flowing blood — was at its tipping point.

There had been a change before, and humanity had adapted.

They wouldn't adapt to this.

There was a knock at Jordache's door.

"Miss Dale?" came the park manager's voice. "Open up, please. I've gotten some complaints."

Jordache stood. The manager's name was Todd, but Jordache could only hear it as *Opportunity*.

The knock came again.

"Miss Dale?"

Jordache turned the lock.

Turned the knob.

Opened the door.

And greeted Todd with her new hello.

## The story continues...

Want to find out what happens next? You're in luck! You can get your copy of *Dead Nation* now.

Read Dead Nation Next

# A Quick Favor...

If you enjoyed this book, please take a moment to write a short review on your favorite online bookstore so other readers can enjoy it, too.

Thanks so much!
Johnny and Sean

# Acknowledgments

I just typed out the title of this page as "Acknowledgement" because I really only have one to make, but then I saw how stupid it looked singular like that and added an S to the end. I guess in books, you have to acknowledge at least two people if you acknowledge anyone. Such bullshit.

(So, okay, I guess Sean and I should acknowledge our wives to make it official. But hell, we acknowledge them ALL THE TIME for putting up with our crap. It's totally implied.)

My single *real* acknowledgement for this book — the first acknowledgement I've ever put in a novel, in fact — goes to my friend and college roommate Eric Alexander, who helped me figure out all the science in this book.

That's right, Dave: *SEAN AND I DID RESEARCH FOR A BOOK.* So there!

I fondly remember the moment when I realized this would be necessary. I was about halfway through the first Ian Keys chapter when I got the distinct impression that I might just be talking out my ass. I have a background in biological science; I actually got a year into a PhD in molecular genetics before deciding I hated working in a lab. It was my major in college and a nerdy hobby before that. And so I figured, "Hey, a book where zombies make a semblance of biological sense? I can do that!"

Anyway, it was during this chapter that I realized that maybe I couldn't. I was tossing out some good jargon ("enzymatic digest," "nuclear magnetic resonance imaging," "electrophoresis") but was 1) maybe using out-of-date terms (college was a while back) and 2) was, again, talking out my ass as far as how an actual zombie plague might work, and how a cure might arrest it. This brought to mind paranoid fantasies of scientists pelting us with tomatoes at book signings, and I couldn't sleep. Something had to be done.

You can hear this full tale of my research and our idea of how zombies might actually work in the *Backstory* that goes with this book (http://sterlingandstone.net/go/dead-city-backstory), but the short version is that I just took a shortcut by calling Eric, who does shit like this for a living.

(Not making zombies. Doing biological work. Unless he *does* make zombies? It's possible. He's an odd dude and I wouldn't put it past him.)

Eric is the one responsible for steering me away from prions (misfolded, self-replicating proteins) as a disease agent and toward a host of possibilities, including stem cells and, ultimately, simple viruses. I didn't give him an easy task beyond that (figuring out how a drug could stop zombieism where it happened to stand, then how the whole PhageX/PhageY debacle with Jordache might be feasible), but he helped me work it out. I owe Eric a big thanks for hopefully keeping Sean and me from embarrassing ourselves.

Eric endured phone calls, emails, and a 15-minute voice memo of me blathering on and contradicting myself. He also read the draft for us.

So: BioFuse mutates into Sherman Pope? Cleared by a real scientist, folks.

The idea of Necrophage competitively inhibiting against natural receptor-binding agents and then being usurped, in turn, by PhageX? Also cleared.

Ditto less-central concepts like whole-genome sequencing as an at-birth procedure in the near future and the ability (again, in the near future) to "proofread" epigenic changes in stem cells against that "original" genetic code.

(My favorite is the synthetic cell receptor component of Necrophage. I never would have thought of that. To me, that one conjures images of blood that's polluted by extension cords with exposed prongs. So what do you do? Shit, you flood your system with electrical outlets for those things to plug into, of course.)

Oh, and as it turns out, viruses can shuffle their DNA with other viruses and the host cell in a phenomenon called "genetic shift" — another thing that made them perfect for the disease agent over a prion like mad cow disease. That will be important later, so that means he'll have to read the sequels, too. (Sorry.)

Big thanks, Eric. Oh, and some day, your wife will actually meet me and believe I exist.

## About the Authors

**Sean Platt** is an entrepreneur and founder of Sterling & Stone, where he makes stories with his partners, Johnny B. Truant, and David W. Wright, and a family of storytellers.

Sean is the bestselling author of over 10 million words' worth of books, including the Yesterday's Gone and Invasion series. Sean is also co-author of the indie publishing cornerstone, Write. Publish. Repeat. and co-host of the Story Studio Podcast.

Originally from Long Beach, California, Sean now lives in Austin, Texas with his wife and two children. He has more than his share of nose.

**Johnny B. Truant** is the bestselling author of *Fat Vampire*, adapted by SyFy as "Reginald the Vampire" starring Spider-Man's Jacob Batalon. His other books include *Pretty Killer, Pattern Black, Invasion, The Beam, Dead City,* and over 100 other titles across many genres.

Originally from Ohio, Johnny and his family now live in Austin, Texas, where he's finally surrounded by creative types as weird as he is. His website at JohnnyBTruant.com features his Creator Diary, additional works, fan extras, behind-the-scenes peeks, early access, and a whole lot more.

## Also By Sean Platt

**The Dead World Series**

Dead Zero

Dead City

Dead Nation

Dead Planet

Empty Nest

**The Beam Series**

The Beam Season One

The Beam Season Two

The Beam Season Three

**Robot Proletariat Series**

En3my

Robot Proletariat

The Infinite Loop

The Hard Reset

Cascade Failure

Reboot

**The Tomorrow Gene Series**

Null Identity

The Tomorrow Gene

The Tomorrow Clone

The Eden Experiment

**Karma Police Series**

Jumper

Karma Police

The Collectors

Deviant

The Fall

Homecoming

**Yesterday's Gone**

October's Gone

Yesterday's Gone Season One

Yesterday's Gone Season Two

Yesterday's Gone Season Three

Yesterday's Gone Season Four

Yesterday's Gone Season Five

Yesterday's Gone Season Six

**Tomorrow's Gone**

Tomorrow's Gone Season One

Tomorrow's Gone Season Two

Tomorrow's Gone Season Three

**Available Darkness**

Darkness Itself

Available Darkness Book One

Available Darkness Book Two

Available Darkness Book Three

**WhiteSpace**

WhiteSpace Season One

WhiteSpace Season Two

WhiteSpace Season Three

**Stand Alone Novels**

Burnout

The Island

Crash

Emily's List

Pattern Black

Devil May Care

## Also By Johnny B. Truant

**The Dead World Series**

Dead Zero

Dead City

Dead Nation

Dead Planet

Empty Nest

**The Fat Vampire Series**

Fat Vampire

Fat Vampire 2: Tastes Like Chicken

Fat Vampire 3: All You Can Eat

Fat Vampire 4: Harder, Better, Fatter, Stronger

Fat Vampire 5: Fatpocaplypse

Fat Vampire 6: Survival of the Fattest

**The Fat Vampire Chronicles**

The Vampire Maurice

Anarchy and Blood

Vampires in the White City

**The Beam Series**

The Beam Season One

The Beam Season Two

The Beam Season Three

**Robot Proletariat Series**

En3my

Robot Proletariat

The Infinite Loop

The Hard Reset

Cascade Failure

Reboot

**The Invasion Series**

Longshot

Invasion

Contact

Colonization

Annihilation

Judgment

Extinction

Resurrection

**The Tomorrow Gene Series**

Null Identity

The Tomorrow Gene

The Tomorrow Clone

The Eden Experiment

**Stand Alone Novels**

Pretty Killer

Pattern Black

Burnout

The Target

The Island

Devil May Care

CPSIA information can be obtained
at www.ICGtesting.com
Printed in the USA
BVHW080822180623
666010BV00025B/1611

9 781629 552095